"It doesn't matter if he's doing crime, Lovecraftian short stories, strange literary fiction disguised as madman narratives, horror, or something in between, you always get an explosive mixture of ideas and superb use of language when reading Cody Goodfellow." —Gabino Iglesias, author of *Coyote Songs*

"Cody Goodfellow has written the two best cross-genre-anthropological-Lovecraftian-military-thriller-stew books ever with *Radiant Dawn* and *Ravenous Dusk*. He's like the Ellroy of speculative fiction . . ."
—Jeremy Robert Johnson, author of *Skullcrack City*

"Truly unique, imaginative and sometimes painfully graphic."
—*Rue Morgue*

"A vertiginous, conspiratorial rabbit-hole set at the end of the American century . . . *Unamerica* fuses the acid paranoia of Thomas Pynchon's *The Crying of Lot 49* with the lowlife and high-tech exile of John Carpenter's *Escape From New York*. Goodfellow leads us down a path to salvation that's populated with depraved conglomerates, violent criminals, bizarre shamans, cruel angels, and strangest of all. . . hope."
—Ross E. Lockhart, editor of *Eternal Frankenstein*

"'80s vintage horror with a contemporary edge. An exemplary wordsmith, his prose sticks a needle in your brain and gives it a twist. This stuff is Lovecraft on acid."
—Laird Barron, author of *The Imago Sequence & Other Stories*

"Cody Goodfellow is untouched as a breathless reporter of violent action, relating it in hurtling prose full of striking and sometimes hilarious metaphors."   *—Strange Aeons*

"One can certainly see influences of Lovecraft, the New Wave of SF writers of the sixties, the Cyberpunks and Splatterpunks— and even surrealists like Kafka and Borges. Don't get me wrong though, Cody Goodfellow is one of a kind. Highly Recommended!"   *—Dark Discoveries*

"One of the best writers of our generation."
           —Brian Keene, author of *The Rising* and *Dark Hollow*

UNAMERICA

CODY GOODFELLOW

KING SHOT PRESS X BROKEN RIVER BOOKS
PORTLAND | EL PASO

For those who must cross borders seeking sanctuary, freedom and work. . . and against those who would stop them.

PART ONE

SUCCESS IS A LEVEL OF VIOLENCE WHERE THE
PEOPLE FEEL COMFORTABLE ABOUT LIVING THEIR
DAILY LIVES.
>> GEORGE W. BUSH
>> MAY 2, 2007

COULD WE ALL BE PUT ON PRISON FARE FOR
THE SPAN OF TWO OR THREE GENERATIONS, THE
WORLD WOULD ULTIMATELY BE BETTER FOR IT.
>> OHIO PRISON CHAPLAIN
>> 1851

0

All Jaime Blasco knew was that Natron Spinks hadn't slept for twelve days, and was looking for him.

Spinks shook down Jaime's patch on Alameda Escobar and tossed his crib in Superbloque VII, looking up on the Circus and down in the Gutters and in places nobody would think to look until they'd been tweaking for two solid weeks, like inside other people. So Jaime packed a rectal bag of free samples and bugged out to the Burbs.

Now, whenever he gets winded or dizzy climbing the slanted ladder up the forty-story ventilation shaft, he pictures the bug-eyed debt collector reaching for his ankle with box-cutters for fingers, and he keeps climbing.

And soon he's out through a hole in the pavement behind a burned-out grocery store. With a ski mask rolled down over the dirty brown thought bubble of a bushy, bellicose afro, Jaime steps over catatonic, fetal Baby addicts, like sleeping suicide bombs.

Baby's a bitch of a drug that takes you back to the womb, mushes the sounds of the world into the omnipotent beat of your mother's heart, but it wears off as swiftly and absolutely as birth, and born-again Baby addicts are like real babies—they cry, shit everywhere and generally wreck everything.

The Burbs look rougher than usual. So many freaks creeping around up here that he won't stick out, but fuck only knows when the cops will start cleaning house. Safer back in the Gutters, or even on the Loop, than up here at the end of a botched build.

He knows it's dangerous and stupid, but he climbs up on the grocery and lies on his back looking up at the sky. The moon is nicotine yellow and full as a toothache, with stars dazzling diamond static on the velvet belly of the night. For just a moment, he's content, then viscerally jealous of the Burbs's view. Someone went to a lot of trouble to make *their* sky look real.

Too bad everything underneath it is a burnt-out ruin.

The adjoining grid of three-bedroom homes looks like a fried circuit board. A few peaked roofs still burning. The dormitories against the far wall are an idiot's crossword puzzle, a minority of windows lit by fitfully blinking fluorescents or guttering fires amid expanses of inky blackness.

Fuck.

It's worse up here than downstairs, worse than he's ever heard. Bad enough it might be more than just another shock test. None of this shit makes sense.

Spinks is the enforcer for the protection squad that runs Jaime's street, but Jaime is paid in full, as always. The Black Gangster Disciples took over his patch a month ago, but they actually lowered his percentage, and Spinks happily accepted his money.

Never mind that it has nothing to do with money. Never mind that it has nothing to do with Jaime, that Spinks is just terminally cracked out. It still reflects badly on him, and whatever response he takes will only drag his reputation deeper into shit. Running is bad. Everything else is worse.

He will settle it somehow and come back looking good. Better. A professional.

Something splatters the sagging rebar all around him. Jaime can't tell if it's condensation, or if the circling drones are dusting him.

He hasn't eaten anything in twenty-eight hours but the peeling skin off his own lips. Watching the alley below, he peels off the ski-mask and dons a pair of stunglasses to blank his face on video captures. He reaches into the bushy fastness of his bangs and pulls out a Spacebar: most of the chocolate melted off the crusty orange filling. He wolfs it down and licks the wrapper, then his fingers—every empty partially hydrogenated calorie is another minute he can stay awake and moving.

At the mouth of the alley, a gang of kids in Mickey Mouse and Ronald McDonald masks crack plastic ampules of Fierce under their noses and test the actions on plastic pump shotguns, revving up for a robbery. As if there's anything left to steal. . . .

Behold, the fucking atomic bomb in the War on Drugs. Witness its inspiring force as it makes kids want to risk certain death to rob a store with no money, in an inescapable city where everything's already free. This shit's gonna make some motherfuckers rich Outside.

Jaime peeks out into Main Street. No cops, but plenty of pedestrians.

Jeep technicals prowl the narrow side street, a coked-up gunner in a gas mask jerkily swiveling the mounted M60, going *eeney meeney miney moe*. Jaime has nothing to fear from most gangs. Most of them owe *him*, but not so much that he's worth killing. He's got no clue why Spinks is really looking for him, but the enforcer told everyone who'd listen that he couldn't stop dreaming about Jaime Blasco, and that he had to make it stop.

A pack of feral kids on the rooftops across Main Street rain flaming garbage down on the jeeps, which retort with volleys of red and green tracer rounds. One of the kids catches a bullet and staggers off the roof. He hits the ground almost at Jaime's feet. The jeeps lay down cover fire and speed out of the street before the kids can regroup. The rain shuts off like someone hit a switch.

Jaime looks over the ten-year old, noting the alien quality of the kid's hand splayed out on the asphalt between his ratty Converse high-tops. What's wrong with it? Extra fingers, no thumb? Jaime's looked far too long before realizing it's the absence of a bar code. The kid's anything but fresh. Looks to be born here. Even the dregs down in the deepest of the Gutters got a barcode, if they want to eat. Most inductees stumble around in denial until they get offed, but the *pollos* settle right in. They think *this* is America. Only better, because they don't have to work themselves stupid or learn a new language.

Where'd this kid even come from? They must be breeding like rats down in the Gutters, maybe starting a whole new country. If he even thought in words, Jaime wonders, what did he think of this place? Maybe he thought *this* is the real America.

He creeps back towards the alley just as the Fierce-huffers hit the store, firing their guns in the air. Jaime hears the drones coming back and climbs down the back of the store, up the alley after the jeeps, onto the main drag.

Dio De Los Muertes.

Fuck. . .

He's been holed up so long, he lost track of the calendar.

Crowds of blitzed campesinos and pistoleros fill the street, but scatter away from Jaime as he tries to blend in. A procession lurches down the avenue with effigies on stakes held aloft to the buzzing orange night. Painted skeleton faces and *luchador orishas* with pie-pan haloes. A jeep burns merrily with its bumper jammed in the bars of a liquor store. A percussion crew marches and bangs on garbage cans and oil drums, and blindfolded dervishes whirl with machetes and torches. A skull-shaped float lumbers through the crowd under a throng of skeletal whores and masked gunmen. Atop a papier-mâché altar, a *brujo* with wild white hair slaughters cocks with a dagger and turns the birds inside out, spraying the ecstatic crowd with blood, while whores hurl fistfuls of cocaine. Seated on a throne behind the *brujo* is a hulking man in a tiger-stripe tuxedo and a featureless mask with a big blinking fiber-optic 0 on the front, and a smaller 3 on the back.

If that's Tres Ojos, Jaime thinks, *he's been working out.* Three Eyes flatters himself in his choice of doubles, but Poison Boys will still take the bait.

Gunmen wearing the numbered masks of Los Zeros walk alongside the floats, so Jaime combs the crowds for Poison Boys. The Fierce-huffing kids have vanished.

He catches a few stray snowflakes on his tongue, finds his feet steering him into the mob of glue-sniffing campesinos. The maddening tease of a coke buzz stiffens his dick and lights up his dusty lobes; the tramps are so out of their heads, it can't just be coke. After every crackdown, the drugs go away for a while, then come back cut with something else, and noses fall off, people go blind.

The cops, too, are making the most of this holiday. Letting the pollos come up to riot in the Burbs is the least of it.

His feet slip in pink sludge and crushed sugar skulls in the gutter as he tries to find a path down the street. Red and white ghosts circle him, shrieking into the face of darkness, emptying themselves to be possessed by Chango or Ogun or a dead loved one. Blind men wade through the crowd with machetes hacking away in each hand, empty eyes rolled back in their heads.

His brain squirms round and round without finding a plan. He had one, right, when he came out of his hole? He ran out of food and grass, and was going to the Green Man or the Poison Boys to beg for shelter, or to the cops to get arrested and locked up until Natron takes a nap and Jaime can afford to have him shivved. But the Green Man is pissed at him and the Poison Boys help no one for free, and Jaime has nothing to sell. His crib will already be cleaned out and reassigned, if and when he gets back downstairs. With Muertes in full swing, he can only hope to stock up on junk food and find another hole to hide in.

And this shit isn't organic, not in the least. Maybe they're setting up for some kind of big, bad test, or maybe the wheels finally came off. . .

Then a weird thought hits him—he could actually *leave*, find another vent shaft and just start climbing—and it makes him laugh. There's nothing he can do to get arrested short of trying to leave, but the punishment for escapees makes whatever Natron wants him for seem like weak shit.

A blurry, two-hundred-pound shadow seems to drop out of the sky into the middle of the street.

"I KNOW YOU!" howls Natron Spinks. "I see you, boy! See where you been, see where you goin'!"

The voice blows Jaime down the street like a plastic dry-cleaning bag. He feels the sugar and drugs burning inside him, juicing his muscles, but he knows by the cool blue fire blazing up his spine to his brain that Natron is right behind him, and gaining. He hears the big tweaker's pumping footsteps like the ground splitting open behind him, yearning to swallow him up.

Jaime shoves through a patch of Veggies, rooted to the corner where somebody planted them to watch the parade. They're naked and covered in sores, goggling at everything with eyes like puddles of congealed semen. They paw at him, chomping at the air with their toothless mouths.

He lashes out with his arms and whoops a fire engine siren sound that drives them into a dog-pound frenzy. He breaks through as they start flailing and screaming in imitation of the noise. He hears Natron get snarled in their arms, palming Veggie skulls and cracking them together like coconuts, roaring Jaime's name over the pop of firecrackers and rifles and the crash of drums and the delirious screams of the crowd.

Drones play searchlights over the sea of heads, converging in the float's wake. Jaime dives out of the path of one as the unmanned sharpshooter picks somebody off in the crowd. They almost always fire paint balls, beanbags or at worst tranquilizers, so nobody pays them much attention, but this time someone screams.

The mob of motorheads becomes a mosh pit, bunching up. Jaime finds himself smashed against a dead man. He has time to look into the hole in his face and wonder if the guy was anyone in particular, or if the cops are just sick of the parade.

A hand snatches off his ski mask, and his fake afro is set free with an audible *sproing*.

"Jaime!" screams Natron. "My nigga! My fucking dawg!"

Jaime, who is eight or nine things that he knows of, but not black, takes exception to the epithet in any context, and he must have inhaled enough coke to get a good buzz going after all, because he's turning to lecture Natron about its use even as the enforcer's big chocolate hand takes him by the hair.

He bolts so fast that the wig ripping off the crown of his skull only queers his trajectory, without slowing him down in the least. His scream of terror gooses him right through the crowd as if they're made of toilet paper.

Running in great open-field touchdown strides, and every whooping blast of air tells him *damn!* He's actually going to make it. And then the crowd vaporizes around him and he sees why they cleared the way.

The cops have blockaded the intersection and are spraying down the celebrants with some new kind of riot deterrent. A rampart of orange Styrofoam six feet high with wriggling bodies suspended in it like fruit in Jell-O spans the avenue and engulfs the prow of the parade float. The *brujo* rails at the cops and the whores throw chickens at them, but the headless birds only glance off their plexiglass shields as they climb to the top of the wall and spray down the rioters throwing rocks from behind it.

Drones begin to wheel like crows over the avenue. The shooters among them play red laser scanners over the people, but he can't tell if the red lights are telling them who to shoot. He pulls his sleeve down over his bar-code.

People scream and hands reach up out of the strange orange terrain, tangling his feet so he sprawls into a pile of bodies stuck headfirst in the foam. None of them move.

He crawls to the nearest building, which someone did a half-assed job of making into a bowling alley. The accordion cage across the front door is sprung, and he slips through it and into the open doors.

Someone, somewhere in the dark, knocks over a bottle. He hugs the closest wall and waits, itchy with sweat and about a half a good scare away from pissing his pants. He fishes in his breast pocket and gets out an injector bullet, jams the end up his right nostril and rams it home.

The front of his brain feels like someone blasted it with a fire extinguisher, and the dark goes silver-white and bright as noon, and he goes YEAH yeah yeah yeah yeah yeah. . . yeah. . . yeah. . . *yeah.*

Everything's going to be cool.

And even in all that light, even with all that clarity, somehow he still can't see Natron until the giant tweaker is right up in his face, with both hands on his shoulders. His black and silver Raiders jersey is sprayed with the deeper black and whiter white of dried blood and cocaine.

Jaime tries to look Spinks in the eyes, though his own are tearing up for every reason a man has to cry. He reaches down inside himself for the one thing he knows he does not, at this moment, possess in any quantity whatsoever, and son of a bitch, he finds some anyway, and he puts it on. "Hey, Nate, what's up, bruh?"

"You know I been looking for you," Natron growls. His voice sounds weird, like he's been snorting so much cut crank that his septum is gone, and all adjoining tissue necrotizing in his collapsing face.

"Nah, really? You know who my people are, I'm not hard to get hold of—"

Natron looks down and his brow knits like he's trying really fucking hard to remember why he went to all this trouble. A big bubble of blood inflates and bursts from his nose, and he bears Jaime down with him as he sinks to his knees.

Jaime sees then that the splashes of blood all down Natron's front are not from chickens. An entry wound the size of a quarter in the crown of Natron's skull dribbles a little, but he seems none the worse for wear, otherwise. He looks like he could chase Jaime around all night. He smiles at Jaime and pushes him back against the wall. And then he opens his mouth, and his brains fall out, lumpy streams of bloody chowder sloshing out of the fist-sized exit wound in his palate.

But he keeps right on talking. "I had a vision, lil man, and you were in it. Scared me so bad I ain't slept since." Natron leans back, the last string holding him up having snapped, and Jaime comes alive, shaking off his hands. . . but then he comes closer, bending over to search his eyes.

"What kind of vision, bruh?"

"Kind that comes true, motherfucker. Thought if I killed you, I could stop it. Everything gonna be alright, though. Everything gonna be everything."

"Why's that, Nate? What's gonna be alright?"

"I ain't gonna be here to see it. But you," Natron points and laughs, "you gonna witness the end times. By your treachery, you gonna make it happen."

And then he dies. Jaime gets a couple thousand pesos, some marinol gum, ten American dollars and a vial of something brown and red that he throws away, and as he creeps off into the night, he's trying to shake the feeling that the random shot that killed Natron Spinks was the last lucky thing he was due in this life, and he can't help but laugh at it all, wondering whether the warning of a tweaker should be taken more or less seriously, if he has no brains in his head at the time.

1

The nadir of the night, with no moon in the star-infested sky, and the electric desert a theater in the frozen moment before the projectionist fires up the first trailer, is the perfect time to cross the border into the United States, though this is perhaps the worst possible place.

Along the two hundred and forty miles of plumbline-straight border between western Arizona and Sonora, the government mostly lets the land enforce the border, and it claims fewer than two hundred souls in a lean year. Yet hundreds of migrant workers come across every night, braving the deadly Desierto De Altar and the Marines, Border Patrol, DEA, Customs agents and vigilante posses on safari in the dark. As they cross over, some get lost or die for want of water, while others are jacked, abandoned and maybe murdered by the *coyotes* they paid to guide them, and some even get caught. But none of them see the man who crosses over with them tonight on a two thousand-dollar mountain bike.

Gliding like a dragonfly on a rutted single-track carved out of the scrub by millions of boots and tennis shoes and salted with the sweat of dread, the cyclist pumps effortlessly up a rise and coasts the spine of a meandering ridge, nearly silent but for the insect click of his gears, the disciplined cadence of his breath and the muted sound leaking out of his cranked-up earbuds, of Jacques Brel wishing for an hour daily in which to be at once handsome and a complete cunt.

Yucca and prickly pear cacti crowd the trail, grabbing and jabbing at his legs. Following the little patch of trail lit by the bullseye lamp on his handlebars, he keeps his eyes on the arroyo below and to his left. It offers better cover, but the black clouds that shroud the night sky threaten rain, and the soft sand would suck out his strength.

All around him, life crouches unseen and waits for him to pass, though from time to time it rattles a threat or bolts from cover at the passage of his wheels. He's ridden through places in Patagonia so sterile and empty they make this look like the Great Barrier Reef, and places in the Andes and the Amazon where the going's so rough he dreamed about country like this. He replays the worst of those places in his head like looking at scars or merit badges, but they don't make him any less thirsty or less pissed off, or any less certain that he's finally fucked the pig.

Sweat oozes out of him and atomizes on the thirsty night wind. He smells like Irish Spring soap and Sure deodorant, McDonald's and Healthy Choice frozen dinners. He took pains to cultivate this stink, stared long and hard into the mirror to get back the look that he worked so long and hard to erase, that naïvely arrogant sense of being the star in the better-than-average movie of one's own life, the look that tells anyone who really looks that he's an American.

He has a plan so good it should be one of those reality shows everybody in the States watches, now. A grizzled old don of *coyotes* in Nogales set it up for him. His people cached two parcels of supplies along his route, packed and stocked to his exacting specifications.

He carries only the essentials, ordered from an Internet café in Nogales. He has a tire patch kit and a set of wrenches and pins and junk to fix the bike, his iPod, a GPS unit and a money belt with a thousand US dollars and US passport, and California driver's license in the name of Nolan Cordwainer Hatch.

The first parcel was right where it was supposed to be, twenty miles west of Sonoyta, thirty miles from the border. Five liters of water and a liter of Gatorade, fresh clothes, a lightweight thermal sleeping bag, some granola bars, a can of refried beans, some Fig Newtons and a fat joint of his favorite Uruguayan indica, Queen of Pain. He camped out there, listening to rabbits and snakes fleeing the human stampede on the trail a hundred feet from where he slept under a Joshua tree with swastika branches.

In the morning, he meditated and rode on, passing a few herds of dumbfounded *pollos* cowering in the scrub until they saw he was just a crazy white man. He eschewed the trails for the single-track game paths that cut up and down the wild canyons and pits of sucking soft sand, stopping for lunch and drinking the last of his water ahead of schedule. He hung back until dark to hit his second cache before crossing the 2, the Mexican highway that dogs the border out of Sonoyta, then the border itself.

The second parcel contains all of the stuff the first had, plus a solar-powered charger for the iPod, some Ben Gay and a cell phone. He had them drop the phone up here so he wouldn't lose it if he got jumped, but he needs it because of the last phase of his plan, of which he is most proud.

Over the last year, he probed mountain bike sites and earned a reputation as a knowledgeable expatriate who'd tamed the whole southern hemisphere. In particular, he infiltrated a few groups of reputable yuppies who come out from Phoenix and Tucson to ride El Camino Del Diablo through the Barry Goldwater Air Force Range on the weekends, and he knows at least two of them are out here *this* weekend, that he primed about possibly meeting up. These men have never laid eyes on him, but would vouch for him as a friend if trouble comes up, and surely give him a ride into Ajo, and his car.

But all of this is unlikely to happen without the second cache, which was not where it was supposed to be.

Clearly someone else was there and raided it. Wrappers and flattened water bottles were everywhere, along with cigarette butts and foil wrappers for that Mexican lemon candy that eats the enamel off your teeth. And blood.

He pumps up out of the canyon, sparing only a glance for a vulture-picked corpse at the top with a blown-out truck tire where its head used to be, fighting up the steep embankment and crossing state road 2 without looking.

A truck with a skyscraper of chicken cages on it swerves around him, and a car that might be a *patrulero* flashes its lights at him from off in the distance.

He gets well away from the road and any trails, and hunkers down to make a new plan. He'll go straight through, get over the border before dawn then ride across. But without water or food or his phone, or the extra thousand dollars in the Ben Gay tube, getting picked up by the *patruleros* would be the safest bet.

Grade gets steeper, hardpan sand giving way to staggered steps of rock that he has trouble hopping up because his legs feel like ancient taffy, and his left arm is starting to tingle. He can't force air deeper into his chest than his windpipe, and his head aches like he's sweating blood.

Just short of the crest of the grade, where his last check of the GPS tells him lies the magic line across the map between third world and first, he stops and checks the action on his pedals so he won't make a sound, so he can hear the people on the trail ahead walking and talking and weeping.

This trail is not a common crossing. Most of them stay close to the roads, where getting caught would be easier than running into the desert and dying. The people who planted the cache took the 2 back to Nogales to spend his money. The people who sacked his cache are on the other side of the hill, waiting to collect the rest.

He hears a short screech and a rhythmic pounding, like someone driving a stake into hard, wet earth. Lays his bike down and creeps up behind a boulder.

Six men and women sit on the rocks about fifty feet away. Three men in flannel shirts and ski masks stand over them with baseball bats. One has a sawed-off shotgun. The other two are beating a seventh man, who looks to be already dead.

The asshole with the shotgun is drinking his Gatorade and smoking his joint. Hatch can't see his face, but he's wearing a red flannel shirt and an Arizona Diamondbacks cap. The distinct blood-and-pepper aroma of Queen of Pain wafts across the desert like a vixen's perfume.

If there was a point beyond which he can be pushed into risking his own life for strangers, or anything he might realistically do to harm or hinder the bandits, this is where he would do it, but in this same instant, white and red lights blast the desert and impale the coyotes on their own shadows.

The *pollos* scramble out of the light, but a net of searchlights and headlights and roaring engines hems them in.

Barking, "Fuck!" he checks the GPS unit under his shirt. The lights are all around him, too. He kicks off back the way he came, seeing the path all too clearly in the headlights from an oncoming ATV. He heels the bike over and turns to shoot down the steepest grade of a knife-slash erosion channel.

The bike careens into the dark, falling free, then jouncing off some spur of rock and sliding sideways through gravel and cacti. The lights keep pace with him, engines roaring like frightened wild boars.

He turns to look just once, as he comes over a shoulder on the hill. He tracks the ATV that shut him down as it swerves to flank him, and the headlight pins his eyes. The rider looks at him with night-vision goggles, as does the man on the back, who has his hands free to point a rifle at him.

He peddles faster.

Something punches him in the ass at the same time as the slope drops away. He stands up and vaults over the handlebars with his legs flopping like big bunny ears as he flies off into the night and never hits the ground—

•

His first impression upon waking up is of nap time in kindergarten—all the bodies splayed out on the Spartan indoor-outdoor carpeting, trying to pretend they're asleep for fear of missing out on the stale graham cracker at snack time. Then he realizes how many people he's lying on.

Bodies are packed in on either side of him, but it's a pretty abstract thing, since he can't feel them. If not for the awful smell and the fact that he needs to piss, he could write it off as a dream.

His body is bathed in a golden glow of cosmic good will, with none of the pain that should have accompanied the grievous bodily damage wrought upon his body. He crashed after some assholes shot him on the border, and now he's going steerage class to heaven, in the back of a truck—

A truck filled with sleeping Mexicans, piled two and three deep in the dark. Many have darts sticking out of their legs or asses, and all snore or wheeze contentedly. The truck bounces down a potholed dirt road at a good clip, and he's beginning to feel it. An elbow in his back drives him to move himself away from it, and the knee that thrusts into his groin forces him to sit upright with a gasp as it all comes back to him.

His right arm and leg are pizza, with ingots of gravel mashed in like shrapnel. His helmet is cracked through the core, and his neck feels like a concertina. He's cold. His ears ache like when he lands after a long flight, which is weird. His pack is gone, likewise his bike, but he feels his wallet and other vitals still inside his shirt. This is fucked, but he can handle it.

Can't be dumb luck that he awakened from the shit in the dart before everyone else—finally, a dividend paid on his superhuman tolerance for tranquilizers—but when his eyes adjust to the dark, he makes out a pair of eyes staring at him, only a foot away.

Rustling like an animal in the brush, and the scrape of a lighter, and a bronze face leaps out of the shadows, nods to him and shows him purple, toothless gums, then the tiny curl of flame dies out. More rustling in the dark, and a huge spider crawls across his chest.

He gives a muted, "Yah!" and slaps at it, but it traps his hand and gives him something. Leaves. "Chew," the man says in Spanish. "Don't swallow it."

He bites down on the end of one and gives a sigh. Coca leaves. He wads them into his cheek and worries one with his teeth. Lets the spreading tingle of numbness quicken from his jaw to his brain. "Thank you, *señor*," he says in purposefully awkward Spanish. "You have come up from Guatemala?"

"El Salvador."

"Are you going to America to work?"

"Fuck work!" the old man laughs. "And fuck America, too. I am going where you are going."

The old man's feisty retort intrigues him, and the coca leaves, telling him only what he wants to hear about his body and his situation, make him hungry for any kind of joke. "And where is that?"

"We're going to the other America," the old man's voice falls down to a reverent whisper. "We never have to work, and everything is free, and very good, and there's lots of coca everywhere. And the whores, ah!" The old man trails off and stuffs more leaves in his mouth. The truck slows and shuts off. He hears doors open and slam, and bolts shooting and locks being sprung outside.

"You've been here before?"

"No, but I have tried. Always, I come across where the *coyotes* lead, and we are caught, and they take me back down to Nogales, or Hermosillo, if they are assholes. But this time, I think we are lucky."

He wants to know more, but the doors open, and brilliant white light floods the truck. He shields his eyes with his hands. The sour mush of coca leaves in his cheek almost slides down his throat. They grab him and haul him out, pile more half-inert bodies on top of him as he tries to find his feet. He screams, "I'm an American," at every one that runs past, that's what a real American would do, but nobody seems to hear him, and he realizes he's screaming in Spanish.

His truck is one of ten or more backed up to a huge concrete loading dock. At the end, he sees what looks like a train of boxcars being unloaded by forklifts. The other trucks dump their cargo of bodies and roll out of the loading dock, which he guesses must be underground.

He expected it to be bad, but not like this. Operation Gatekeeper happened and the border got tighter, forcing illegals to cross in the deep desert, where they died in their hundreds every year. 9/11 only aggravated the situation, but it brought funds to build huge processing centers to catalog the aliens and turn them back with a minimum of deaths. Or so the people who paid for them were told.

But this isn't about him. His ID is good enough, he could threaten to sue them. And he really does want the bike—a Heckyll 800 with custom derailleurs—back.

He stays with his group as they're herded down the dock and into a big arched tunnel. They pass under a spray-stenciled legend: GIVE ME YOUR TIRED, YOUR HUNGRY, YOUR POOR, YOUR HUDDLED MASSES YEARNING TO BREATHE FREE. It makes him chuckle out loud. He looks around for a big portrait of the President flipping the bird, wonders who the President is, now.

His group forms a line that passes through a metal detector. Just before it, a short amnesty dumpster is filled with weapons, drug paraphernalia, coins. He sees his cell phone.

A few people make the alarm buzz and are plucked out and whisked away down shadowy corridors by masked guards with short, ugly guns.

The line beyond the detector merges with other lines, no more than a few other gringos among the hordes, and even a guy who looks Asian. Nobody else looks as confused as he feels about being here. And he's been hauled into enough jails around the world to know how guilty men walk and wait, but there's no head-hanging here. Everybody tries to look taller and healthier than they are, like day laborers waiting to get picked up for work.

Then he sees a guy in a flannel shirt with a Diamondbacks cap in the next line, right behind his Salvadoran friend with the coca leaves. The lady in front of them has her clothes ripped and a big black eye, and runs to stay ahead.

The lines converge in a big room like a warehouse with brushed steel walls and painted lines on the sealed concrete floor. They lead to a row of doors and corridors. Guards move down the line, searching people and putting color-coded wristbands on them. Once cleared and banded, each prisoner follows a line out of the room. Guards with assault rifles singled up at each door, none of which look like they lead outside.

An officer stops at the Salvadoran next to the *coyotes*. He orders the guy to strip, clubs him in the thigh when he hesitates. The old man slowly begins to strip, and the officer orders the coyotes to do it, too. They look at each other and takes their boots off. Hatch notices one of them drop a tightly wrapped bandana into one of his boots as he shrugs out of his shirt.

The strip search becomes street theater. A crowd gathers around, but he can see more than enough through their legs. The guards bend the guy over at the waist and snug their hands into thick green rubber gloves. Another guard drags up a hose with a long plastic wand on the end and, without benefit of lubrication, slides the nozzle up the guy's asshole and depresses a trigger.

The guy gives a long, inside-out howl and the crowd groans in sympathy.

He moves closer and trips over the *coyote's* boots. No one notices him as he ties his shoe and then crawls back to his spot in line.

The guy tries not to sob. With the first noisy splash of fluid, the crowd reacts as if he's just shit out a natural seven at a high-stakes craps table. A string of red balloons comes slithering out in the deluge, and one of the guards slips them into a hazmat bag.

The guy tries to run, but it's a feeble effort, with his pants still around his ankles and his enema still in full flight. A guard grabs him around the neck and sticks a little plastic gun under his jaw. There's no sound, but the guy's throat puffs up and one eye bulges halfway out of its socket, and when the guard drops him on a rubber sheet and rolls him up, he stays there.

He feels the *coyote's* eyes on him and turns to brush them off with his own. "Fuck're you looking at, *cabron*?"

A guard taps him on the shoulder. "*Buenos noches*, raise your hands over your head, please."

Hatch lifts his hands up, but he smiles and says, "Officer, this is a big, big mistake. I'm a U.S. citizen."

"So what?" the guard says, as he probes Hatch's legs.

"I was out riding a trail, I didn't even know which side of the border I was on, and some guys come out of nowhere and shoot me in the ass, *Wild Kingdom*-style—"

The guards take a good look at him, and he tries, without being a dick, to model his cycling outfit and cleats. Slowly, he takes out his wallet, shows his license. "I was camping up in Barrel Cactus, and riding out on the Camino Diablo trail, you know, do you ride? It's awesome country, but most of the single track is all blown out—"

"Hold out your right hand," the guard says, and snaps a green wristband on his wrist with a big A on it. "We're terribly sorry about this, sir. Go see that big fella with the bars on his shoulder at the door at the end of this room, and he'll sort you out."

"I had a bike—"

"He'll take care of everything, sir. Have a good night."

"Sure, yeah. . . sure, bye." The hardest thing is not to keep babbling. He walks down the line, watching the Diamondbacks fan negotiate with the officer. Reaches the door and waits for the man-mountain to look up and notice him. He stands a head and a half taller than Hatch and twice as wide, in a black uniform unlike the olive drab border patrol guys, with a peaked officer's cap instead of the ranger hats or helmets the other guys wear.

"Listen, I'd just like to—"

"Get back in line," the giant says with a thick Texas drawl, never looking up from a menu screen on the tablet in his massive paw. Harsh fluorescent shadows hide his face.

"I'm sorry, they told me to tell you, there's been some mistake. . ."

Hatch looks over his shoulder at the guy who sent him over here, laughing behind his hand. He whispers to another guy and now they're *both* laughing their asses off.

"I'm an American citizen. Got my ID right here. . . Name's Nolan Hatch."

The giant looks at him so the light falls on his face, but it's still dark. So black it's almost blue, and it takes Hatch a moment to recognize that a solid black tattoo covers his whole face, except for his lips and around his eyes, so he looks like some kind of monster from a nightmare militant minstrel show.

Hatch literally bites his tongue to keep something he dares not examine from slipping out his mouth.

The tattooed giant looks past Hatch at the laughing border patrol guards, takes a deep, simmering breath, and says, "We're real busy here, tonight. So, you follow that green line from here to the exit, and we'll see that you get where you belong, okay?"

He shrugs and nods okay, looking for the green line, just grateful to get away from this gigantic Al Jolson stormtrooper.

Down the line, the naked *coyote* takes his bandana out of his boot and unwraps it for the guard. He stops just long enough to catch the look on the *coyote's* face when he finds the wad of chewed coca leaves inside. The *coyote's* big bloodshot eyes swivel round the big room and lock on him.

Hatch reaches into his pocket and takes out the tight little bindle of detective-magazine origami he found in the boot, unfolds it and sprinkles the white powder on the concrete floor. Then he walks away.

In his pocket, Hatch's fingers run over his money, and quite a few other peoples', by the feel of it. He follows the green line down a corridor with no guards and wonders how it would look if he walks faster, or even runs. In the end, with his feet killing him and his injured leg starting to stiffen up, he limps gingerly through the last few intersections and turns to a little door that only the green line enters. A sign above it says EXIT.

That was easy—

He looks over his shoulder. A skinny guy dressed like a janitor with sunglasses on is ten feet behind him. He smiles and waves like he's been looking for Hatch all night, and speeds up with a *come-on-sucker* smile on his face.

"Hey, amigo. . . You don't want to go where they're sending you."

"I'm going home."

"Not that way, you ain't. . ."

Hatch hauls the surprisingly heavy door open and steps outside, and starts to walk across the concrete apron in the dark, when the door shuts and he realizes he's not outside at all, merely in a very dark room.

There is no handle on this side of the door.

Shit. He's been in America only a couple hours, and he's already thinking like one, or rather *not* thinking—Americans just assume that they're exempt from the degradation and pain the rest of the world takes for granted. By instinct, he reaches into his pants and brings out the small rubber ball he's been hiding behind his genitals, wipes it on his shirt, holds his nose, pops it into his mouth, swallows it.

Someone in the dark coughs.

"*Sabes que, guero?*" says the *coyote*.

2

It is morning, and the Reverend Doctor Orrin Joshua Litchfield is also riding his bicycle.

He is going to Heaven.

As a morning ritual, he rides every day for two hours if he has the strength, before opening the clinic. It is an exercise of his body, but the Reverend hates his flesh, and so this is only incidental to the real labor, which is one of faith.

The stationary bicycle's chain drives the images flashing across the cyclorama that encloses him. It's like the old Disneyland People Mover ride, brought to you by the problem-solving people at Goodyear—a deception, to be sure, but no more than the world itself, with its traps and snares of mere appearance. A lie in the service of a higher truth, then. And if the computer-generated landscape of an ivory road tapering off into an infinity of white light and a towering pearly gate that hangs always on the horizon, always seeming to draw ever closer, is a cheap effect, then it only focuses the Reverend's mind more narrowly upon the unimaginable glory for which it stands, and lets him pry away all earthly entanglements.

The bicycle also powers the whirling battery of heavy nylon flails, many with studded flogging boards attached, which scourge the Reverend's back in direct proportion to the pumping of his scrawny white legs on the pedals.

This is the real exercise, the pounding out of weakness. And yet it is not merely his own ingeniously conceived auto-flagellation that drives him to collapse this morning, but a bolt from a higher power that strikes him from the unpadded seat and spreads him in a twitching, spent heap across the floor of his inner sanctum.

It is a vision.

Now, this sort of thing has happened before. It was a vision that first showed Litchfield the sinfulness of his ways and called him to his vocation. At the time, he believed it to be a recurring nightmare, a symptom of addiction to painkillers and antidepressants. From humble beginnings, he had ascended to a privileged position as a trusted care provider to some of the most beloved, wealthy and powerful people in the world. Naturally, he would harbor guilt about what he did, and how he got there.

In the dream, Litchfield calmly settled his affairs, groomed himself and cut his own throat. He always woke up hyperventilating at the height of the act, just as the curved blade of the big, unwieldy knife sawed through the taut tendons and muscles and delicate plumbing in his neck. So real was the dream, so viscerally true the sensations, that when it began to happen every time he looked into a mirror, he suffered a nervous breakdown.

It was only under heavy sedation on the observation ward at Cedar Sinai Hospital, that he witnessed the dream to its conclusion.

Through the agony of his flesh parting under the ministrations of the knife, he felt himself driven by a higher power like a puppeteer's strings. He felt liberated by it, and he endured the pain for the sake of learning what lay beyond.

In his old life, he'd never troubled himself over the condition of his soul, and laughed bitterly at anyone who claimed such a thing even existed. But as the knife continued chopping away at the tough bark of his spine, as his earthly eyes glazed over and his jaw went slack with the blood sluicing out over his hands, he actually saw it. The sickly, renal-failure yellow light guttering out of the stump of his neck refused to depart his body, but only blazed brighter for its liberation from his lying, arrogant head.

He witnessed with new eyes of fire as his headless body rose up and walked. News of the miracle spread out like a shockwave so that wherever his body went, mutely testifying to the truth of the gospel, crowds gathered to hail him as a new messiah, and shunned the lying lips and betraying eyes and scheming, sin-raddled brains of their own heads, hearkened unto the true word spoken only in their hearts.

And as he walked, he gathered followers who shore off their own degraded parts—tempting genitalia, vainglorious limbs, vexatious hearts and burdensome brains—and went without sin forever and ever.

How that vision lifted him up out of the slough of his old, sinful life, and how low it has lain him ever since, in his pursuit of redemption.

Some days, when he's too weak to ride to Heaven, he sits on the cold concrete floor and contemplates a long, curved butcher's knife with a staghorn grip and serrated teeth sharp enough to split atoms, and he wonders if it would not be suicide to follow the vision literally, or if he has not been saved for some yet higher purpose.

Some days, despair is almost strong enough to set him chopping. Then there are days like today, when the grand design is almost clear, and his role in it writ large in flaming letters.

The low-res imitation of heaven on the screen becomes the true Heaven, more blindingly pure than his brain can even perceive. The pearly glow of the gates is as ecliptic blackness to the ocean of light they hold back. He knows that the merest glimpse of what lies beyond would burn his eyes out and blast the grimy paste of his brains out his ears, but he basks in the promise of revelation as the gates shudder, the colossal bolts are thrown and they begin to open.

Everything goes black.

Litchfield comes to lying on the floor with one foot still strapped into the pedals of the bike. His back blazes in the afterglow of a superior scourging, flooding him with relief. It's been ages since he could squeeze any blood, not to mention real pain, from the horny scars and calluses that sheath his back. Pain like this is more than pleasure, vibrating through him with the liquid gold body-knowledge that he's earned another molecule of God's forgiveness, and might yet see salvation here on Earth, and ascend bodily toward heaven, a latterday prophet of a new age of miracles.

Closer this time than ever before, but he was still too weak, too plagued by doubt, to cross the threshold. He's ridden such peaks of mere chemical elation into deep abysses of despair before, and he's not fooled by this one. Salvation here on earth is too much for such as he to ask. But like Moses, he can deliver the innocents to glory, even if he can't follow them into the alabaster light himself. If they would only listen—

Quickly, now, he gathers himself and makes his ablutions, wishing for another to bathe his wounds, using the soap to rekindle the embers of pain that he'll need for this next attempt to reach beyond.

He unplugs the TV and goes to the black curtain at the back of the chapel and draws it back, then drags the cable into the dark alcove behind the curtain and plugs it into a power strip wired to a rat's nest of converters, naked wiring and circuit boards, to a pyramid of large ceramic mason jars—or Leyden jars, as they were known in the days of Benjamin Franklin. There's no on/off switch, but the TV instantly registers a flow of power, for the screen glows blue-black, crawling with oddly purposeful pathways of static.

There's no signal, no programming, no stations down here, but the weird, skirling nebulae of video feedback comes, unmistakably, from somewhere, and is, indisputably, something.

Litchfield sighs and kneels before the screen. "Lord, I am weak and frail, and they will not heed your word from my sinful, soiled lips. Please give me a word to conjure with, O Lord! Give me that which will make them throw their wretched selves upon your infinite mercy. . ."

He falls down and abases himself with singular fervor against the floor.

The TV crackles and he hears, for the first time ever outside of the withered black wilderness of his heart, an answer to his prayers.

SUFFER THEM TO COME UNTO ME, says the television, AND THEY SHALL BE DELIVERED—

3

The pitch-black room is stuffed with bodies, so thick with monkey-house funk and stale breath and shit, and so dark that his eyes make purple fantasy fireworks, trying to see something. But somewhere in front of him, Hatch hears the *coyote* he robbed knocking people down and getting closer.

Hatch turns and goes back to the door, but there's no use in advertising his whereabouts by pounding on it. He just runs and instantly hits another body. His hands telling him he's touching antlers, roadkill, radiators, blindly running through thickets of blind fists and chopping hands and feet. He slips in something wet, then trips over the naked body of the author of the wet spot.

"*El otra America*," whispers a voice as old and faint as the sound of parchment burning. Hatch recoils and jumps over the body, plowing through more fighting, kicking strangers. "Never work, never die."

From just over his shoulder, the *coyote* roars, "I got you, fucker!" He dives headfirst after Hatch. Someone gets stabbed and screams. Someone shoves him. Stumbling to catch up with himself, he runs into a wall. The room isn't that big. He can't hope to hide from the asshole all night.

At least now it's noisy and people are moving around. He hugs the wall and creeps along it in search of another door. His fingers brush a seam in the wall.

The door is just open a hair, and someone on the other side tries to resist, but Hatch levers it open with the heel of his hand, jams a foot in, then a shoulder, and shoves his way out into the light.

"Who the fuck are you?" he asks the exact same question at the exact same time as the other guy, but since he's the visitor, and the other guy has a weird little gun stiff-armed in Hatch's right eye, he feels it incumbent upon him to answer first.

"I'm an American," he blurts out, "and I got lost, and I don't fucking belong here—"

"Your cycle-fag clothes told me that, Armstrong." The gun barrel raps him on the head. The other guy is small and slight, with a big nose, buggy eyes and a weak chin set into sharp relief by a shock of bushy black hair. Under the half-zipped janitor's smock, he wears a maroon bomber jacket and a grimy denim jumpsuit, but the hand holding the grip-taped plastic gun is pale gold and spindly—a kid's hand. He's chewed his nails down to the quick, and two of them are infected.

His bomber jacket looks like it has flak plates sewn inside it, patches and corporate logos sewed all over it— DG, Gucci, Heckler-Koch—and all the pockets are stuffed with things he probably never paid for. Heavily inflected with Caribbean Spanish though it is, the speaker is fluent English. "You should have listened to me, man."

"That's a toy gun."

"No it's not. . ."

"It's plastic."

"To get through metal detectors, stupid. Now walk."

"I thought we were amigos."

"That ship has sailed, bitch. You belong to me, now."

They stand in the bare concrete corridor, looking at the lines on the floor. The door he just come through has a red light over it. The light starts blinking. People start pounding on the door.

Hatch twists the knob. It's locked. "No, thanks, I'm not going. I'm gone, man, thanks." He backs away.

The kid points the gun.

Above their heads, pipes rattle and hiss. On the other side of the door, men scream like they're being boiled alive. All the screaming falls off to total silence in less than ten seconds.

"What the fuck was that, man?" Hatch keeps backing away.

The kid shakes his head, starts walking fast in the other direction. "Fine, fuck off, you're welcome."

Way off down Hatch's end of the corridor, a couple guards see them and start jogging in their direction. Hatch turns and runs after the kid.

"What was that in there?"

"Go back and find out. Next show in like an hour."

"It's not the way out?"

"Not unless you want to donate all your organs at once. You an organ donor?"

Hatch says no, but the kid laughs. "We all organ donors down here."

The corridor takes a slight downward slope for almost a quarter mile, with doors all down it with numbers and bar codes. The kid is walking away with his eyes on the numbers. If Hatch blinks as he goes through a door, Hatch will never find it.

He runs after the kid, stage-whispering, "Hey, amigo, wait. Don't shoot, okay? I'm lost, but I could make it worth your while to help me get out of here." He peels bills off the roll in his pocket. "I got a hundred, you help me out, okay?"

The kid turns and, with accuracy to shame a camel, spits on the money in his hand. "Drop it."

"Why?"

"If they stop to pick it up, they might not catch me."

"What about me?"

The kid opens a door and lets it swing shut behind him. Hatch catches it, looks over his shoulder at the two approaching guards, and pulls the door shut behind him.

Just another corridor, poorly lit by caged energy-saving bulbs, rust and even clumps of fungi on the walls, growing worse as it slants down. The kid walks on, unperturbed. Hatch goes after him. "Hey, amigo, talk to me. What is this place?"

"You want to shut up?" is all the kid says. Still looking over his shoulder, he turns a corner and shoves through another door. Hatch follows him, but trips over a body. It's too dark to tell much more than that it's human and not dead. He runs after the kid, down a corridor, through a storeroom, and then crawls through a hole in a wall behind a utility shelf.

Before Hatch can catch his breath to berate him with more questions, the kid climbs down a mound of pulverized concrete and emerges in a massive, roaring room.

They pass between gigantic industrial fans and air filters and through a spaghetti of ducts. The pounding wind snatches away Hatch's words and crushes his eyes shut, smears his face with tears, so he struggles just to keep the kid in sight.

The cave of blasting fans ends in a ventilation grill like an enormous louvered window. The kid climbs through a gap in the grill and drops into a narrow vertical shaft. Just before he descends out of sight, the wind snatches away his hat. The kid swipes hopelessly at the wind, but it is long gone. His hair is glossy black, cropped close to his skull.

Hatch follows him down a ladder of rusty rebar rungs sunk into raw basalt, but he twists around and nearly loses his footing when the shaft terminates and he's clinging to a wall in a space as big as all outdoors, and he sees the city for the first time.

It's weird, descending from an underground bunker and into what feels like outside. . . the roof just above his head stretches off into the murk for a mile or more. The rough junction of wall and ceiling and the rough-hewn look of the stone tell him that the cavernous space is manmade.

The floor is maybe three hundred feet beneath him, and the kid speeding hand over hand down the ladder like he's more afraid of getting caught on it, than falling. Hatch takes the hint, but he can't bring himself to look away from the floor of the cave.

At first glance, it's a city of Kowloon Walled Cities, built out of gigantic Legos by a deeply disturbed demiurge who truly sucks at Tetris. Thousands of brightly colored cargo containers in haphazard stacks, some reaching to the ceiling in skyscraper tenement blocks, and some attached like barnacles to the columns supporting it, carved up by staggered streets that radiate like broken spokes from a vast, central pillar bedecked with searchlights and Times Square-style animated billboards.

Even from this height, with the wash of clean air driving down over him, Hatch can smell the smoke and cookfires and streams of people climbing ladders and crossing bridges and zip-lines between the towers. A dizzying array of improvised residential blocks, markets, arcades, sweatshops, vertical gardens and stranger places he itches to discover, snarled in jury-rigged electrical, water and sewage lines and festooned with neon signs and razor-sharp holograms strutting and fucking and flaming out everywhere overhead. Street murals and gang tags and improvised shelters of scrap wood, plastic and cardboard, but also animated tattoos, cyborg limbs and omnipresent clouds of roving drones.

Nothing he has suffered since he woke up with the dart in his ass has convinced him he's really awake, and this was like nothing anyone has ever described, but as he descends and the torrential wind becomes a dim whisper over his shoulders, he finds himself sinking into a familiar smell that tells him only the location of this place is alien.

Slums everywhere tend to smell the same.

The stench of untreated sewage, unwashed bodies, charcoal, charred meat, and the smoke of every kind of combustible controlled substance is familiar to him from every corner of the globe. From the *gecekondus* of Istanbul and *clandestinos* of Lisbon and Naples, to the *favelas*, *colonias* and *villas miserias* of South America. It's a city of tens of thousands, somewhere beneath the Mexican desert, but it's still a slum. The games may be cruel and life may be cheap, but Hatch knows how to play.

The stench and the noise and the stifling sense of imminent peril aside, it reminds him of nothing so much as Disneyland. It's odd. They're outside, but not outside. The containers are stacked three stories high on either side, plastered with posters for products he's never heard of. Rats big as cats run across the tangles of wires between towers. The space between the last block of containers and the outer wall of the cave is filled with a mountain of trash. Children and hunched old women sift plastic packaging and feed it into a shredder.

The kid waits for him at the bottom, and he's rediscovered the gun. Skulking under greenish fluorescent light, weighing the relative value and risk of his new friend.

Hatch drops off the ladder, obligingly raises his hands and asks, "Hey, amigo, what is this place?"

The kid shoves him hard in the chest. "This is where you live, now. Welcome to Unamerica, motherfucker."

Hatch shakes off the last vestiges of the dumb American persona. "Listen, I know why you lifted me out of there. You're trying to figure out who to sell me to."

"You don't know shit." Kid takes the sunglasses off, rubbing his eyes, then thumbs off a blinking blue LED on the inside of one of the arms and pockets them. Hatch figures they must be more than regular shades, given how little light there is to hide from, down here. He's heard of reflector masks that could blow out a security camera image. "I've been around, kid. I've seen—"

"You've never been here." He looks around, watching the passersby, most of whom he's placed as Chinese. "Don't care where you come from, you won't last an hour down here without help."

"I freely acknowledge that, man. I can see you're smarter than the average street freak. But if you're planning to sell me, I'm worth more than you can possibly imagine." He sticks out his hand and smiles ingratiatingly. "Nolan Hatch. Damned glad to meet you."

The kid laughs, a joyless, plosive sneer. "We in a Triad block, white boy, three districts away from anywhere safe and you ain't got no bar-code, just an organ-donor band. There're scanners everywhere, and first one picks you up will flag cops down on you."

Hatch sinks his teeth into the plastic wristband and tears it off. "Fine. Next?"

"Give me your clothes."

"What the fuck for?"

"You stick out, stupid."

"Like I won't stick out walking around buck-naked?"

The kid scopes the street—pulsing with pedestrians, rickshaws, pedicabs and armored cars threading between street vendors, prostitutes, gangsters, beggars and worse. Two naked men walk by, one spasmodically jerking his half-erect cock as he leers at nobody in particular. The other wears some kind of fetish-gear jockstrap with a corrugated hose that snakes up to the filter socket on a gasmask strapped over his face. They look as if they'd wandered out of a psych ward at Burning Man, but the crowd, many obliviously adrift behind augmented reality goggles patched into their phones, effortlessly ignores them.

"Okay. . ." Hatch says, "but why don't we get some clothes first. . ."

"I gotta trade yours. Not blowing my credit on you, and your cash ain't shit down here."

Hatch peels off the cycling shirt and pries his feet out of the shoes. "Listen. . ."

"No, *you* listen. You're worth more as parts than alive, so shut the fuck up. I am not your friend. Nobody down here is your friend. I will sell you first chance I get." The kid picks up the shoes and points impatiently at Hatch's shorts. "But I'll get a better deal for you than anybody else. I'm a motherfuckin' *entrepreneur.*"

The kid takes Hatch's shorts, rolls them into a bindle and tells him to stay out of sight. "Why can't I come with you?"

The kid points at the naked guys. "They're getting away with it because that one is a veggie—he's walking braindead, a ghost, nobody fucking touches them. The other one, he's a pervert or something, nuff said. But they got a code." Kid flashes a bar-code lasered into his wrist. "You got no code. You're street-meat. So stay hid, bitch." He steps into the street and is swept out of sight by a river of people.

Hatch retreats behind a dumpster full of steaming, freshly recycled plastic. A circle of older women are drawing the plastic out onto looms and weaving fabric out of it. Hatch watches, fascinated, until someone bumps into him. He turns around, expecting the kid. The naked masturbator stands close enough to sweat on him.

Hatch backs away from him, into the dumpster.

"Hey," says the masturbator, "I thought I recognized you."

Hatch sizes the guy up. He's about Hatch's age, doughy, Caucasian, and has plugs and monitors stitched into his torso, a shunt in his arm for easy blood extraction, a turgid colostomy bag dangling from his hip. In spite of all this, he has a sunny, open expression that Hatch finds himself staring at. *Sonofabitch*, the guy did look familiar.

In every city, it doesn't matter how big or how far away, Hatch has a unique gift for bumping into people he knows. Could be in New York City unannounced, a city of fifteen million, and hot off the plane. He'll run into a good friend from way, way back in the middle of Times Square. So this doesn't faze him nearly as much as it should, if only he could remember where he knows the guy from.

"Tim," the naked guy says. "You probably don't remember me, but I sure remember your parties."

"Oh. . . yeah. . ." Hatch tilts his head as if the memory will shake loose. If this guy knows him from the old days in California, that would be a trip, but also problematic. "Yeah, I'm sorry, there's a lot I don't remember about those days. You sure you. . . ?"

"Oh yeah, *I* remember. Changed my life, expanded my consciousness. They say you put art into your chemistry, man, and I believed it. I really loved your work."

"Wow, that means a lot. Really. . ." Jesus, this is strange. Suddenly, standing naked in an alley with a strange walking vegetable guy—still tugging his junk, Hatch absently notes—he feels safer. Maybe he's making a mistake waiting for the kid to come back, assuming he will, which is a stretch. Maybe, for the short term, he'd be safer with Tim.

"So, what're you working on now?"

Hatch blushes. "I can't really talk about it, but. . . trust me, it's going to change everything."

"That's fucking awesome! So exciting to hear!"

"So, uh, Tim. . . how did you come to be here? I mean, I'm new. . . I don't. . ."

"Man, you're gonna love it here. It's like one of your parties, like the old school shit, all day, all night."

"That's fabulous. . . Tim." Hatch plays it vague, but now that he opened up the memories of those days, of course he remembers Tim. Who could forget Talkshow Tim?

Guy would show up at every big underground in the greater LA County area in an ill-fitting suit like he was going to court, with a bottomless bag of molly and dish it out for free to anyone who would talk to him. Sort of pathetic, really, but also kind of wonderful. Hatch never sat down with the guy himself, but he was a fixture, and Hatch heard the guy was severely emotionally disabled and a terminal introvert who lived in his parents' basement. Somehow, he'd stumbled into the rave scene and psychotropic drugs, and discovered how to talk to people. "So you. . . used to go to my parties. . . down in LA?"

"Yeah, man. The Gilligan's Island Rave on Catalina, the Psychedelic Apocalypse, where you guys took over Union Station. . . I was even there for the big Blue Scream blowout, where the feds came down on you. . ."

"Yeah, that. . . Honestly, I don't remember a lot about that weekend. . ."

"I'm not surprised, man. I got so cracked out on that shit, I never came down. I was dumped off at an ER by my friends, and the doctors didn't know what was wrong with me. By the time, they figured it out, my brain was scrambled eggs."

Hatch is caught off-guard by the sudden turn in Tim's tone, the gleeful hyperbole suddenly gone, along with the last twitches of his smile. "Wow. . . I'm really sorry to hear that."

"Don't be, I dug my own grave. After the insurance ran out, my parents had to take me back in, but they couldn't handle it. I was a vegetable, just shitting the bed and sucking up money, like a baby who was never gonna grow up. . . I don't blame them for doing what they did. . . but hey, now we're gonna party, right? RIGHT?"

Hatch slides away from Tim, who keeps creeping closer, tugging his cock and chattering with convulsive seizures.

Hatch hears a faint crash high overhead and somebody curses in Cantonese, then a whistling that rapidly grows louder, with dull Doppler echoes.

The big box air conditioner smashes into Tim's head and snaps his neck, crushing him to the cracked pavement at Hatch's feet.

Hatch runs out of the alley, wiping blood and coolant out of his eyes, and is caught by the kid, who presses a bundle of itchy shorts made out of a plastic onion-sack, lime green shoes made of compressed paper and the treads from a Firestone Tru-Trak tire and a filthy t-shirt that says DENVER BRONCOS—SUPERBOWL XLVIII CHAMPS.

"The shoes alone were worth $200," Hatch says.

"Triads don't fuck around," the kid grumbled. "Had to give them away so they wouldn't kill us for being here."

"I speak a little Mandarin," Hatch says. "I'm just saying I could've got a better deal. . ."

"Fuck your Mandarin. Sick of your naked ungrateful ass. Get dressed, or I'm gone." The kid looks at the headless naked guy at Hatch's feet and arches a questioning eyebrow.

"That guy," Hatch says, "he said he knew me. . ."

"Bullshit," the kid says. "Veggies don't talk to nobody. House just uses 'em to tests diseases and poisons, and shit. Now get dressed. You cannot afford to waste any more of my time."

Hatch steps into the shorts, squirms into the clammy shirt, tacky with recent human use. "Wait, you run drugs for somebody inside, right? You know how this place works?"

"Fuck you," the kid grunts. "This is my barrio, homes. Practically born here." In the ghostly light, his buggy eyes and crooked mouth remind Hatch of a cranky Muppet on Plaza Sésamo, which makes it harder to take him seriously.

"I'm trying to place where you're from. Are you Mexican?" Pretty sure of the answer, Hatch modulates his voice, adjusts his posture, the way he always does with people who react violently to threats. It's why nobody's ever hit him, who did not apologize for it, sooner or later.

"Hell no," the kid snaps. "I'm a hundred percent Unamerican."

"By way of. . ." He studies the kid's face, makes a show of guessing, "Cuba?"

Looking down, the kid nods. "But I know this place better than you know your own dick, boss."

"Good. If you do, you don't have to tell me anything, but you should take me to meet the guy you work for. I have something he's going to want."

The kid spits out the most acidly contemptuous laugh he's ever heard. "I ain't taking you nowhere, man. Not now—"

"I was serious before, about what I have. You don't want to just throw me away."

"And I'm serious about selling you, so if you're worth more than just a white set of organs, which is worth a lot, start talking."

4

The best thing to do, Jaime thinks, would be to just shiv him in the alley and sell him for parts. Whatever he has on him, it must make him think he shits diamonds. If the guy is all-day bullshit like that, it's still a commodity. Sometimes the salesman is the product. And the guy *is* walking, talking bullshit—dressed in Le Coq Sportif cycling gear that's crusted with fine desert dust, bruised and bloodied and deeply tanned from days of exposure, yet he acts like a guy on vacation. If this sucker is what he's trying to look like, he'd be all day shook from his first glimpse of this shit. But his posture suggests a relaxed guy at a rock festival, taking in everything in darts and stabs and commenting on it like it's all here for his entertainment. So Jaime concludes that the guy will not be as easy to sell as he looks.

Worst of all, as he follows Jaime out of the Triad blocks and through the Orange Zone into the Latin Quarter, bypassing all the checkpoints, he seems to be enjoying himself.

Jaime leads the guy down an alley crowded with slumped bodies like bags of old garbage during a trash haulers' strike. Steps over them and ducks under grasping hands reaching down from the fire escapes, still smiling like this is all just a tour. "Just like the *favelas* in Rio. But safer."

Jaime blows air out his cheeks. "Only reason you ain't getting skinned right now, is because of me."

"So this whole place is underground?"

The alley spills out onto a massive circular plaza, one of twelve in the city. Shops and kiosks cluster around the outer edges, but the center is an open space with a marble pedestal upon which stands a mighty bronze pair of shoes. The rest of the statue was severed at the ankles and dragged away to be melted down for bullets or black-market plumbing, and nobody remembers who it was supposed to be. Some say it was Pancho Villa, for whom the plaza is named, and some say Ronald Reagan, and some argue it must've been someone more dope, since the shoes are molded to look like throwback Air Jordans. Beside the shoes, a scrawny miserable tree, watered only with piss and antifreeze, struggles up out of a crack in the pavement filled with cat litter.

But the Plaza de Pancho Villa is not a park renowned for its landscaping. The plaza is open to the sky, or at least the ceiling, and is the closest to the outside most who live here will ever come again.

"There used to be a bandstand, but it burned down," Jaime offers.

The tourist follows him with his head swiveling around. The cheesy moon and the gaudy, blinking stars. "You ever been to Tivoli Gardens?"

"No."

"It's in Copenhagen. Kinda the same ambience. Original inspiration for Disneyland, but with gambling and beer gardens. All the architecture is cartoon gothic, wrought-iron and gargoyles, really run-down when I was there, but it made it *more*, not less, you know?"

"This isn't a fucking amusement park."

"Oh, really?" He looks around, his hands taking in the street musicians, sidewalk artists, careening drunks and the pile of Babies in the gutter like a human petting zoo. He smiles like it's all a joke. "Where the fuck are we?"

"About a quarter-mile underground. In a big cave, boss."

"How many people live here?"

"Hundred and twenty thousand, maybe."

"How many cops? How many guards?"

"Shit, I don't know, maybe a thousand or so, they wear masks, so you can't tell. Maybe a thousand more doing science shit in the labs upstairs. It's all private contractors and shit, but the government runs it. All the grunt work is done by trustees and stiffs in the suburb, but this is Norte Libre for real, motherfucker. You get right with that, or you dead. Everything is free, but everything costs. All the food, drugs, medicine, clothing, whatever else you can take, but to have a place, you gotta pay the landlords."

Jaime breaks it down as simple as he can, whips out his phone and shows the tourist a map of the cavern, which makes him laugh and observe that it looks just like fucking Burning Man, whatever that is.

The city is a fucked-up pizza a mile and a half long by three-quarters of a mile wide, divided into slices by radiating avenues and lavishly topped with hatred and vice. In the center is the Arcade, a massive tower that reaches the roof of the cavern, the largest of twelve in the city. Its lower floors are all retail shops and medical clinics where every product and service is free, but carefully monitored.

Everyone in Unamerica is a guinea pig. Whatever else they do with their time, everyone has a schedule of surveys, blood tests and examinations to pay their way. The Arcade is neutral territory and patrolled by the cops who use Star Wars-shit experimental weapons and lethal force with total impunity, so nobody fucks with them.

The rest of the city is exactly what it looks like—a gigantic, subterranean megaslum. A feudal ochlocracy wherever it's not pure anarchy. Everyone who has a place in the city holds onto it by force of arms or by paying protection to one or more of a hundred street gangs and criminal organizations.

The major players themselves are a theme park of organized crime. The prison-born La Eme dominates a host of Latin groups to control nearly half the blocks, but MS-13 is also a fucking nightmare in here. The only group the guards work hard to keep out are the Mexican cartels, whose affiliates are executed at the door. However, splinters of two warring factions of the old Gulf cartel, Los Zeros and Poison Boys, exist here and wield as much power as whoever is in charge upstairs, many among them defectors who turned informer to the Americans, which explains the Sinaloa Cartel's desperation to get their own sicarios inside Unamerica.

A shaky coalition of black gangs, from Bloods and Crips to the Black Gangster Disciples, struggles to maintain a twenty percent share, squeezed between the Mexicans and a vicious jigsaw of white gangs with fickle alliances—the Russian Mafiya, Aryan Brotherhood, the Klan, Neapolitan Camorra and Sicilian Mafia. The Triads hold a ten-percent share that's sure to grow as more Chinese immigrants are added every year, and a grab-bag of Asian gangs hold individual superbloques and streets, but in the spirit of immigrant criminal enterprises everywhere, they prey only upon their own.

The general population is an uneasy admixture of immigrants, exiles and undesirables from every margin of American life, but the overwhelming majority come over the border from Mexico, Central and South America. Many of them had heard of El Norte Libre, where everything is free, and nobody has to work.

Some arrived trafficked in cargo containers from Asia. Others from the bowels of the American penal system— lifers with no one to fuss when they disappear, repeat sex offenders no one wants in their communities even after time served, the most hardcore, recidivist, righteous trash ever to walk the earth. White folks, typically welfare cheats and unemployed, debt-ridden, drug-addicted, or ex-cons, end up in another cave, which is nicer, but nobody wants to trade places with them.

"But how do they keep it a secret?" the tourist asks.

That part's easy. The caves were dug to store toxic and nuclear waste, and as far as the legions of truckers who service the city know, the loads they carry are deadly toxins and not food, drugs, toys, clothes, whatever else. An immigration detention center a couple miles away is the other entry point, and a good fraction of those bussed in never actually leaves, Nobody on either side of the border takes much notice.

The tourist strolls across the plaza, arms up like a conductor. "It's amazing," he says, then lower, to himself, "it's perfect."

"You don't know shit about this place," Jaime tells him.

The tourist turns around and comes up to Jaime. "This is just a city. I've been in all kinds of rough cities, brother. *Vecindades, colonias, gecekondus, villas miserias. . .* If you know people, cities are all the same."

Jaime's halfway to saying fuck it and ditching the tourist. He's fucked with his landlord, and he knows nobody alive who's gotten on his shit list twice.

After fleeing the Burbs, Jaime came back through Processing hoping to hook a new fish and bring him to the Green Man, who is always looking for unattached white people to experiment on. To that end, the cyclist is a demographic goldmine. As a white male just under forty, he should've placed in the burbs. His type pulls a higher quality of samples out of the vendors and are generally helpless to defend themselves, so everybody wants one for a pet. But this idiot doesn't even have a bar code. He's walking contraband.

He texts his man inside the Green Man's crib again, to no reply. "Where you going?"

The tourist looks over his shoulder. "You want to jack me off, fine, fuck you, too. I can find my own way, thanks."

He walks off across the plaza, and some of the Gutter-geeks laugh at his clothes. He just smiles and waves and keeps walking. Anyone else with that new fish stink on him, they'd get eaten alive. The tourist crosses the plaza without looking back. He checks out a *botanica*, open to the street with battered rolldown shields to fend off frequent riots, piled with goods both branded, off-brand and street-fresh, fruit from hydro gardens and riotous assortments of bizarre fungi, tubers and roots. Tilting his head back to look at the signs, neon and spray paint, in English, Spanish and a dozen others. The tourist haggles with a lady selling horchata and makes her laugh deep down in her belly. But then she takes his wrist goes to scan it, and the conversation stops.

Jaime crosses the plaza without making a sound, catches the tourist's hand. "Everybody comes in through processing," he hisses in the tourist's ear. "They get inspected, deloused and hosed down, then they get a bar code on their hand. You got one of those, everything's free. You don't, you're a ghost. And they don't believe in ghosts down here."

The tourist looks in the window of a convenience store white and hot as a microwave inside, a line of geeks with baskets of products file past an armed clerk behind a bulletproof screen, get scanned and go. "I have money," the tourist says, reaching for his pocket.

Jaime holds out his hand to the horchata lady, who scans it, looking mistrustfully at the tourist. "Money only buys trouble down here."

"I got something better than money."

"All you got is your ass, homes. Be straight with me, now, because nobody else can get you a safe bar code, inside. You get the wrong kind, you'll have cancer or tapeworms or worse inside a week, if you don't get rolled and jackwired first. Be straight with Jaime. What kind of shit you got?"

Again with that maddening shit-eating hippie grin. "What I got, if Prometheus would've stolen it from the gods and given it to man instead of fire, none of this fucked-up shit would ever have happened."

Jesus, he used to beat the hell out of kids like this. "You talk too much, and don't say anything."

"Why should I trust you? How can you prove that you have your shit wired down tight enough to even betray me competently?"

"Well, why should I trust *you*?"

"Fundamental Attribution Error. It's why you're always late because traffic is a bitch, but other people are fucking lazy flakes. Why you have to take prescription meds for pain, but other people are fucking drug addicts. Circumstances for me, character flaws for thee."

"I don't get it."

"We all need a way to break through circumstantial illusions and unmask the essential self." The tourist looks around, then goes over to some kids gathered around the mouth of an alley. He offers them something in his fist. They fill up a condom to the size of a punch-balloon from a tank. He comes back with it pinched by the neck in one hand.

"Inhale this," he says.

"No fucking way, that's gutter shit, it'll kill you dead."

"The tank had dentist's markings on it," he says, "and the original seal on the neck. Here," and he sucks a gulp out of the enormous balloon. He wobbles just a bit and his eyes roll back in his head, but he recovers as if he's just been trying to remember a phone number. Buzzy, stoned residue in his voice that sounds like there's someone in there with him. "Drain it."

Jaime hates nitrous. Hates to be blind and stupefied, even for a moment, for the same reason he hates sleep. Being helpless, unaware of what lies in wait for him, terrifies him. It's exactly what his enemies wait for.

The tourist can see it all in his eyes and seems to get high off his tension as he holds the grimy mouth of the condom to Jaime's lips. He wants Jaime to chicken out—it would prove something—and Jaime will lose him or get seriously hurt trying to jack him up and take whatever he's holding. The cash alone would have been worth a whole mess of murders.

"Fuck you," Jaime says, and takes the hit.

No sulfur or other shit in the mix, so he relaxes his gag reflex and gulps at it. Get it over with. Blow air out his nostrils to take it all in, hyperventilating to cycle the last pockets of air out of his lungs and bloodstream.

The tourist squeezes the condom, forcing his lungs to expand to hitherto unknown volumes. Never taking his eyes off the tourist, he sucks it flat and sneers, "See? It ain't sh—"

He feels his insides turn to bubbles and burst out the top of his head. He stumbles, noticing that the tourist is holding his plastic pistol, is pointing it at him.

Fuck, he thinks. *So stupid*—

He reaches out in a panic.

All sensation in his body, from his extremities inward, lights up and turns to ash and blows away. The sight of the smiling tourist against the neon of the convenience store goes all blurry, then molecules and atoms burst into bloom. Little planet things whipping around them as they roll and tumble. The air is full of them, it's made of them. He can see the what you call them, *molecules—*

He heard somewhere about how Navy pilots black out in the first moment of taking off from the deck of an aircraft carrier, then come to in the air. The sense of acceleration is so overpowering, he seems to rise up even as his body goes limp and falls away, like the spent booster stage on a rocket. He reaches for the controls, but he can't find the levers for his mind, let alone his body. The molecules pulse and become words in some original tongue and mock him with all the wisdom they hide from his dumb ass. Even here, in this out-of-body trip into inner space that he's sure to forget the moment he sobers up, the secrets are under lock and key. It should give him some sense of peace, if only to know that there is no answer. But it only makes him angrier.

The trip ends almost as suddenly as it started. He's not surprised to find himself sprawled on the gummy asphalt with the tourist looming over him. It's the kid on the ground next to him, with his bloody hands clutched over his nose, which leaves him guessing.

And then he remembers.

About the gun.

The tourist is waiting for him just outside the silver cloud of bubbles, and maybe he's already been shot, is already dead, and the bubbles will never go away.

His hands come up to fend off the tourist and Jaime realizes *he's* holding the gun, pointing it in the tourist's face. The tourist looks expectant, excited, hardly like how a gun in your face is supposed to make you react.

"He tried to jump you when you were rolling," the tourist says, and holds out his hand, the knuckles torn and bloody. "My name's Hatch. Nolan Hatch. Damned glad to meet you."

Jaime lowers the gun, wondering what the fuck kind of game this is. The reflex, the instinct, to shoot the tourist throbs up and down his arm, the fear he felt upon being disarmed. He still feels like he's filled with simmering fluid, bubbles rolling up the inside of his skin. He smells something burning, certain it's his own brain. The sensation of falling back into himself leaves him dazed and apathetic to whatever he was pissed about, a minute ago. Whether or not the tourist really defended him, Hatch seems impressed by Jaime's mental acuity in not using the gun, rather than just relieved at not being shot.

"Fuck was that?" Jaime demands.

"You're a sharp kid, Hatch says. "I've got something to show you. We need a couple hours, someplace quiet, and a couple cans of refried beans."

5

The kid takes Hatch by back alleys to his tower. More hassle than going through the checkpoints or the Arcade, but without a bar-code, Hatch is apparently some kind of outlaw.

The crowd is a weird mix of Mardi Gras and San Quentin. Drag queens in marabou feathers and sequined bodysuits whirl past hobbling matchstick skeletons with surgical scars and festering stumps on gleaming chrome prosthetic legs and blinking implants; they wave beggar bowls clasped in assembly-line robot claws. Gladiators in recycled scrap armor batter each other with bastard swords for cheering crowds in open pit arenas. Gang warlords in Gothic script tattoos and bandoliers stuffed with shotgun shells lounge against the walls. Dervishes whirl through the mass of bodies like kamikaze bombers from a country with no planes. Sex workers gyrate and beckon from jury-rigged balconies and fire escapes hanging at perilous angles over the unimpressed crowd. Grind joint strippers flash and attack the crowd from gleaming poles on stages thrust out into the crooked streets. A man hangs from the nearest one, wailing and moaning as he's flogged by a glossy black patent-leather tormentor.

In spite of its lawless concentration, he reminds himself that this is all familiar to him. He's safely navigated slums and red-light districts on four continents. He's adept at moving through a dense and unyielding mob, finding pressure points to separate people fighting or fucking in the midst of the crowd, even as his brain chases its own tail round the questions he doesn't have time to ask.

Ahead, the street narrows, the mass of people roiling before it like a whirlpool before a great cataract, bodies ejected into the brighter, wider space on the other side. A mini-riot has broken out around a vending machine. People fight their way out of the frenzy with fistfuls of red plastic packets like cigarettes. The cops are trying to cordon off the machine and clubbing heads like lawsuits don't exist, but looters are willing to trade blood for whatever's coming out.

He spots Jaime's maroon jacket in the human spume around the gate and goes after it. The crowd around him starts jumping up and down, chanting something he can't make out, it's so loud and choked with incoherent anger in at least four languages. Soldiers block the gate and are checking bar-codes. The monotony of the protest and the peristaltic convulsions of the bodies all around him recycle the same moment over and over. He's slipping into an acid flashback when he realizes the guy in the maroon jacket isn't Jaime.

He tries to turn against the crowd, but the people around him are pogoing towards the checkpoint, and he's getting carried along with them when someone grabs him by the collar and drags him into a crawlspace between stacks of cargo containers.

"You dumb fuck," Jaime says, and walks off. Hatch follows him through alleys and across courtyards, past stills and meth labs and chicken-coops, to the foot of a tower of containers reaching up to nearly to the cavern's ceiling. The flashing billboards and animated graffiti on its walls notwithstanding, it reminds Hatch of the superbloques of Caracas, tenement towers teeming with ghetto ingenuity to overcome the limits of brutalist slum housing.

They enter the back way, stepping over trashbags and bodies and trashbags of bodies and gritting their teeth against the mewling of Babies coming down. Half the ground floor was recently gutted by a fire, leaving blackened steel walls buckled and warped. The flashpoint, where a meth lab went up on the second floor, is the site of a drumming circle. A little cluster of dreadlocked, ash-encrusted naked men numbly pound plastic tubs and stare into the green flames from burning packing crates.

The heat is even more intense inside, the compressed strata of stench performing an awful striptease in his nose—cooking oil and spices, incense, smoke, feet, armpits, assholes, shit, death. The stairwells are choked with trash and slippery from leaking corrugated rubber pipes. Hands reach out of the trash to clutch at his legs.

Jaime's place is on the seventh floor, but the padlock on the double door doesn't match his keys. The people inside refuse to acknowledge his claim. The guy on the other side laughs and calls Jaime "el Pitufo," tells him to pull harder when he yanks on the door. Hatch grabs his arm and points up.

The barred door off a jail cell hangs suspended on hinges from the ceiling, poised to swing down and impale the two of them on a rack of rusty shivs spot-welded onto the bars when sufficient pressure is exerted on the door.

Jaime backs away cussing the squatters and goes jogging for the stairwell, but someone hits him in the crotch with a water balloon. A moment later, he's on fire.

Hatch turns to help him and is immediately tackled by two assailants who barely come up to his chest. One gets behind him and the other shoves. He's falling but he can't help laughing. A knife at his throat while the other kid slashes his shorts with a box cutter. "I don't have anything, I don't even have any pockets!"

The kids are wearing Chapo masks, bright peach, cherubic features with painted mustaches. The Chapo working his shorts slaps the other on the back and his friend goes to slash Hatch's throat. Hatch tucks his chin down and flips violently over, cracking the little chap's head against the wall like an atonal gong.

Jaime screams and rolls on the floor to crush the flames. Hatch pats himself down and finds nothing missing that he cares about. He tells Jaime as much, but the hustler runs after them with smoke still fluttering from his ruined pants. Hatch follows him up the lightless stairwell, bouncing off the wall at the landing when Jaime comes tumbling back down in his path with a brown tidal wave at his heels.

The Chapo at the top of the stairs has ripped a pipe off the wall and severed it, and the combined sewage of every tenant of the floors above them comes pouring down on them.

Hatch backs out of the stairwell on the ninth floor, trying to catch his breath. As soon as he overcomes his reflexive nausea, another reflex kicks in. He starts laughing.

"Fuck you, guero," Jaime says. "Nothing's funny about this shit."

"Oh," Hatch says, "I don't know. I've never wished I had a phone, but you should see a picture of yourself."

"Fuck you, man. You on your own."

"Don't blame those kids. They put the fire out."

"Fuck you."

"You smell better, too."

"Seriously. Fuck. You."

When he's done sitting in piss, Jaime leads Hatch up thirteen flights of stairs without coming across El Chapos. They find some of Jaime's stuff scattered like trash on each landing before they reach the dead end on the twenty-fourth floor. They climb up a swaybacked ladder propped against the wall to a trapdoor. Jaime holds it steady while the lanky American tourist climbs onto the roof. He's squatting by the edge of the hole when Jaime comes up, waiting to help him drag the ladder up after them.

The roof overlooks two greenhouse terraces jutting out of the superbloque, and the street. The tower across the street grows even taller, a crane dangling from the ceiling like a gigantic daddy-longlegs lowering a battered orange Hapag-Lloyd container into place on the unfinished twentieth floor, where crews weld and wire the neighboring containers into the makeshift grid, reminding Hatch once again of gigantic Legos, of the *urbanizacione piratas* in Colombia, squatter colonies that turn into legit neighborhoods faster than they can be bulldozed.

The ceiling of the cavern is another fifty feet above them and crisscrossed with a grid of rails that mirror the streets below. Someone has painted the concrete ceiling overhead blue-black and strung the crude cyclorama with thousands of champagne Christmas lights, some of which still wink and glitter, lending the rooftop an ambiance of a cheap sitcom set.

Jaime has a footlocker hidden in an abandoned rooftop chicken coop. He drags it out and sets up a camp stove to boil water.

"Is it safe to talk now?" Hatch asks. "I want to know everything."

It surprises Hatch, how hard it is for the kid to actually explain it. Places like this, you don't explain. And anyone who doesn't get it is dead weight. "You think it's just like any other city, boss? Sure, some people work, some people steal, and some motherfuckers are just lucky. Or they think they are. It's dirty and shitty, and the cops are crooked when they're not just stupid, and everybody's ready to kill anybody who looks at them cockeyed. And you're asking yourself how that's any different from Detroit, or New York, or most of LA?

"I'll fucking tell you. It's free. *Everything* is free. They feed you, they give you all the shit you want. And you can do and say whatever you want, because nobody here cares. And don't give me no 'America's a free country,' because half the motherfuckers who got sent here, it was for shit they said and did to the American government. The rest came here because it seemed better than the real America. Where they just get worked to death for nothing, anyway."

"It sounds like a fucking bug zapper," Hatch says. "A Terminal Autonomous Zone, the Hell of the Spectacle. Like a concentration camp, but the persecuted class all think it's Big Rock Candy Mountain."

"Compared to where I came from, it *is* fucking Big Rock Candy Mountain."

"How long has it existed?"

Jaime fills two tin cups with hot water and adds coffee crystals to them. He passes one to Hatch, who gratefully slurps at it. "Who knows. Who cares. It was always going to be, and now it is."

Jaime reaches for his hair, curses, then roots through the footlocker until he finds a pack of joints. Lights one and sleepily blows the smoke out and offers it to Hatch, who gratefully takes it.

"They test products on you. That's why everything's free, isn't it?"

"Yeah, they're looking for a new crack cocaine or boner pill, and we're the guinea pigs. But they don't know half of what goes on down here."

"How do they check up on you?"

"If you're not on a Schedule 1 or a blacklist, they never take anything but shit and blood and piss, fingernails and stuff. Sometimes they bag you, but it's no worse than getting abducted by a UFO."

"Nothing's safe, is it?"

"Shit, it's just like outside. You eat too much Burger King and shit, your colon blocks up and you get cancer, or you take the wrong diet pill and your heart explodes, right? But if you're not stupid and don't piss the wrong people off, it's like being a high roller in Vegas for the rest of your life. But enough about me, dude, how're you feeling?"

Hatch sits back. While Jaime talks, he pries his feet out of the sandals, which have stained his feet black. He flexes his toes. Joints pop and crack. He finishes the coffee. "Knackered and fucking hungry. What do you have to eat?"

"First things first." He hands Hatch a roll of toilet paper.

"Oh, I can never go after I've been riding. Like I said, if you have any beans. . ."

"You don't need beans."

Hatch looks at the empty cup and then searches deep inside himself as a sound like a washing machine starts up in his bowels. "You motherfucker," Hatch says, and dashes off behind the chicken coop.

After a while, he comes back with something wrapped up in a bandana. "Treacherous fucker," he grumbles.

Jaime chuckles and dumps some powdered eggs into the pot on the stove, adds some freeze-dried chorizo and a lot of hot sauce. Hatch's groans and tuba-blasts of flatulence provoke someone on the next rooftop to shout and throw a bottle.

"Let's see what you got, boss," Jaime says, with a spatula in his hand. The edge on the spatula is the kind you could cut pennies with and still julienne a mountain of potatoes into crinkle-cut fries.

Hatch steps back and pockets the bandana. "You need to understand something first. If you roll me and take this, you won't know what the fuck to do with it. Take it yourself, and you'll go off on a trip to parts unknown, and probably never come back. Try to reproduce it, and you'll make a lethal poison. It's worthless without me."

"Fine, whatever, but what the fuck is it?"

"Sit and put the spatula down."

"Eggs're gonna burn."

"Stir the eggs but keep it in the pot. I've come too far for somebody to do something stupid."

It is one motherfucker of a long con, and against his barbed-wire resolve, Jaime finds himself biting it. "You a chemist?"

"I know what I'm doing. I used to run with a crew that put on parties in the California underground scene. We got into making our own psychedelics. You ever try Blue Scream blotter?"

"Fuck acid, man. Hate that shit."

Hatch hates LSD too, but there was a time when he used it like an otter uses a rock to pound open an oyster. After the lights and colors and weird feelings faded to background noise, there was no pearl of cosmic wisdom inside, only spoiled, battered gray meat, and the enlightenment he chased started to look a lot like schizophrenia.

He remembers it. Neon Maori tattoos crawling out of faces and painting faces on the walls, unraveling fractals glowing out of dead matter like the eternal light hidden in everything, the realness, and that tsunami of meaning poised to crush him for hours on end, until it soured and became plain, ugly old dread.

But for a while, in the heart of it, he felt like he was in the hands of something or someone who had a plan, and wished him the best, even if it was never to be, not even close.

"So you're some sort of player down here?"

"Biggest you're gonna find."

"What do they call you? What's your street name?"

Jaime just shakes his head.

"C'mon, why do they call you 'el Pitufo?'"

"Fuck you, man."

"I know in some gangs, the sillier your handle is, the tougher you have to be, so you must be a number-one badass, to be called *The Smurf*." El Cochiloco of the Sinaloa cartel, for example, got his zany nom de guerre ("crazy pig") because of his penchant for burying people alive on his Culiacan ranch.

"I'm just a little guy, okay? I'm not a *pocho* from el Norte, but I'm not from Sinaloa, Durango, Sonora, Juarez, either. Not even the same blood."

He can tell that. Kid doesn't recognize it, but he's got a trace of an accent still. "Tell me about your boss, Cuba."

"Nobody moves doses down here," Jaime says. "You said this was special. You wasting my fucking time, but he kills motherfuckers who waste his."

"This isn't acid. People will want this. Need it, even."

"Let me have it, then."

"I don't have enough to dish out, yet. Tell me about your boss."

"He's not my boss, he's just this guy I do shit for. I got all kinds of enterprises, dude. There's no reason to bring anybody else into this."

"Bullshit, Smurf. Your office is a chicken-coop. I need somebody with connections and facilities. This is a city where they test products. I have a new product to test."

"Why should I help you?"

"You'll get a generous broker's fee, and if you don't turn out a douchebag, then there'll be shares."

"If you need to grow this shit, you need the Green Man. He's the source for most of the black-market drugs in here. He's neutral, sells to all sides. But he's a freak.

"There's the Zeroes and the Poison Boys. They control half the streets between them—drugs, youth gangs, protection—but they're fucking crazy, and you side with one, you at war with the other. They been like the end of *Scarface* since before I got here. There's the black blocks, but they're in the same boat. Bunch of old bangers think they in a country club.

"You don't want to work with him, you got the Aryans. They're tight with the guards, so they control a lot of the mules, and guns and knives and shit. But they're dicks, and they hate everybody. Walk around with great big fucking swords, bruh. I wouldn't, if I were you."

"They all sound like assholes. How hard would it be to set up a serious grow lab down here?"

"Fuck that. Word get out that you shopping for parts, somebody kill us both. You want to move anything, you got to go through somebody set up."

"Like you?"

"No, not like me."

"Your boss, then?"

"He's in-house, and he's sketchy, but he knows his shit. And he's got lab space."

"I don't want it under this asshole's nose. I want something remote."

"Everything's under everybody's nose. You got to get used to that. Now, you followed me home and burned up a bunch of brain cells I'm gonna need some fucking day, and all you done fed me is a line of shit about something what came out your ass, that you won't even show me. What the fuck you think this is?"

"Alright, alright. But you've got to understand, this means a lot more to me, than money. I don't give a shit about getting rich off this, and I don't want some other asshole getting rich off it, if he keeps it from doing what it's meant to do."

"Enough, already! What the fuck is it?"

Hatch thinks for a moment. "Tell me, what do people want out of life?"

"They want. . . shit, I don't know. . . they want to fuck, get high, get paid, eat, drink, not work. . ."

"Right, more or less. But all those things, you're taking what you can get to control or forget the pain. Because life hurts. If it was everything you dreamed of, you wouldn't need drugs, right? But people take drugs to escape, to feel like they want to feel in spite of the world. Even addiction at its worst feels like a problem you can control. All you need is more drugs. . .

"But what if your life just *worked*? What if you could experience everything you were missing in a reality as real as waking life? You could have everything you wanted in the trip, and then you'd want everything you have for the rest of your life."

"That doesn't even begin to make sense. . ."

"Whatever," Hatch says. "Take me to Papa Smurf."

"Tomorrow, man. You don't want to hurry. The Green Man does shit on his own time, but he don't fuck around. He run it all through his head, and if he can even imagine you fucking him over, you dead. You think you gonna play people down here like upstairs, you dreaming."

"Don't worry, I'll fix his imagination." Hatch falls silent for a while, staring into the fire until the kid must be contemplating rolling him for whatever he has up his ass. "You know, I knew this guy weighed three hundred fifty pounds, and none of it muscle. Doctors told him he'd die before he was thirty if he didn't fix his diet and get some exercise, but dude couldn't do it. But he wanted to, and he focused on it so hard, that he started dreaming about exercising. Like he'd go to sleep, and he'd be on a treadmill all night long, running after an Ultimate Cheeseburger and a milkshake the size of a janitor's bucket."

"So fucking what, man? What's this got to do with—"

"So in less than a month, he lost almost fifty pounds."

"No shit."

"Shit. In another six, he was only overweight because he was carrying around a bunch of loose skin, and his muscle tone was good enough to get him a date at the doctor's office with the secretary who used to laugh at him."

"That's very inspiring."

"Dreams can come true, Jaime. Dreams can be more real than reality."

"Whatever, man. Your friend ain't here."

"He's not anywhere. He went out on that date and dropped dead of a heart attack halfway through their first dance."

The quiet creeps up around it them. It's nice. Jaime is just drifting off to sleep when Hatch says, "You ever ask yourself why the kind of shit that happens to you happens to *you?*"

"What. . . shit like meeting you?"

Hatch laughs. "Something tells me you were in deep shit before you met me." The kid looks sleepy but mistrustful. Reflexes poised for another ambush. "You're creating the reality you expect. We all do."

Jaime looks angry, sits up rubbing his eyes. "I didn't create the motherfuckers who took my crib, or the motherfuckers who set me on fire. Was the same fucking kids you bought that nitrous from. . ."

"That's letting other people create your reality," Hatch says, feeling sleepy now, himself. He tries to hold onto it, will his exhausted mind to settle down. "To really change your fate, you have to visualize what you expect. Make it in your head until you're holding it in your hand."

Jaime turns over and wraps the foil blanket tighter around his body. "Whyn't you visualize shutting the fuck up and letting me sleep?"

Good idea. Hatch visualizes silence and peace. This really gets his mind going again, so he puts away the blanket and goes to pace along the edge of the roof and watch the city below.

6

Litchfield is riding his bicycle when the Aryan Brotherhood storms his bolthole church on Rockwell Street.

Egil and Abner tear off the rolldown cage protecting the church with their bare hands and menace the handful of peasants sleeping on the pews with bastard swords and pistol-grip shotguns. The flock of cripples, beggars, wetheads, wireheads, recovering Babies and ghosts napping or slurping cold soup in the vestibule pay them no mind as they trample Litchfield's blind bodyguard and burst into his sanctum.

The gaunt, shaggy-bearded preacher slumps over the handlebars as the flails strop the scarred ruin of his back, thin runnels of blood dripping on the floor. He glowers at a supernova of video feedback on the big screen in front of him with Mosaic wrath but offers no resistance when they cuff him about the face and drag him off the bike. He's thoroughly spent. He reeks of piss and starvation.

Egil has profound doubts that this drooling lunatic is up to saving the life of their warlord. Everybody knows about the street preacher, who is tolerated by the gangs and has a following among the street trash because he serves soup and cares for those who've sold or lost their Arcade rations, or are dying because of what they've been fed. When they were ambushed by a rival white war party on their way to a summit with the Russians, they knew they'd be cut to pieces if they tried to take Casper Childress to the hospital in the Arcade, and they couldn't trust anyone in their own camp. But Abner swore the old freak was a real doctor, or at least used to be.

Abner steers the preacher into the chapel by a fistful of stringy white hair as two more branded war-brothers carry Casper in on a blood-crusted blue nylon tarp.

"Fix him," he says.

"I'm not a doctor anymore," says the preacher. "God is not to be mocked by such prideful artifice. But Satan knows his own. Ask another kind of priest."

"We know what you are, old man." Abner cocks his arm to bash in the old man's head with the pommel of his two-handed sword, but Egil stops him. "If he dies, you die. Ask God how He feels about that later, if you want."

Casper stopped seven slugs from a submachine gun and was stabbed with a ceramic knife that shattered inside his thoracic cavity. They plugged the holes with a meat-glue pen, but the internal damage is horrific. Blood bubbles on his lips with every laborious breath.

"He is beyond the power of earthly medicine. Let him go to judgment. . ."

Casper reaches out and weakly grips the preacher's hand. His eyes are unfocused, but Egil thinks he might be welcoming the preacher's words.

Abner won't hear of it. "You fix him, or by Wotan's balls, we'll burn your fucking church down."

The preacher sags as if Abner's words are physical blows. "I've asked and asked for a sign. . . but answer there came none. . ." He looks up. "Is this your will? Is it? This one? This?"

Casper's breath hitches in his ruined chest, blood percolating out and sluicing over swastikas, runes, wolves and grim Viking warriors. Dying. Egil almost says, *Let him go*, but the preacher pushes himself upright. "Bring him into the back room. If it is His will. . ."

They carry Casper back into the sanctuary. The old man pushes a wheeled gurney out of a closet and sets about stabilizing the warlord. He isn't quick enough about it for Abner's tastes, but Egil, as always, is the voice of reason.

"Egil, you just want him to let him die because you think you get the horns," the big idiot says. Egil ignores the accusation, no point in pointing out that there's little to be gained by taking the job, which comes with the life expectancy of a housefly.

The preacher hangs an IV bag and runs a drip off it, but then plugs it into his own arm. Even Egil almost caps him right then, but his hands are steadier and faster as he starts to work in earnest on saving Casper's life. "What did you two give him?"

Peeling back Casper's eyelids, he shines a flashlight into the pinned pupils.

"Just some oxy for the pain," Egil tells him. "He gonna make it?"

"If he puts himself in the hands of the Lord, he shall be delivered."

"We don't want him delivered," Abner shouts. "Just fix him!"

The preacher lays his hand on Casper's chest and his mouth works silently as he administers a series of injections and then listens closely to his breathing over the knife wound. "This man wants to die," he says. "This man is not worthy. His heart is closed to your message. Why must it be him? So many others, so many. . . But even he who is without faith may yet become a vessel of His glory. . .”

"You'll go before he does," Abner shoots back. He's on the phone with a wildcat ambulance crew, ordering transplant organs like pizza delivery. "They want to know what's his blood type?"

The preacher touches a bloodied glove to his tongue and says, "O positive." Still muttering to himself, the preacher scuttles across the sanctuary to where a black curtain blocks off a low, vaulted arch. He kneels before it and drags a thick bundle of coaxial cables to plug it into the bank of monitors around Casper. The video feedback on the big screen in front of the exercise bike goes blank. All at once, the loopy diminishing pulse of the warlord's EKG seems to spike and surge like something else is driving it. Casper lurches on the gurney as if electrified.

"Had enough of this witch-doctor voodoo bullshit," Abner growls. He goes over to the preacher with sword drawn.

The EKG goes flat. A monotonous dial-tone sounds.

Egil looks at the cables snaking away from the machines piled up around Casper. They all converge on the niche blocked off by the black rubber curtain. Still watching the gurney, Egil backs up until his hand brushes the oily folds.

"So much for the power of prayer," Abner grunts. He swings at the preacher's head.

The preacher never sees it coming. Doesn't see it pass over his head as he throws himself across Casper's inert body, crying out, "Lift him up, Lord, lift him up!"

Egil shakes his head, takes hold of the curtain and yanks it aside. "What the fuck is this shit?"

"Egil, come hold this fucker still for me." Abner plants his feet to bring down another stroke, but Casper sits bolt upright and rasps, "Amen."

Abner drops his sword.

"It is accomplished," the preacher says. His hands shake so badly, he braces himself on his elbows and climbs down from the gurney. He notices Egil standing by the half-open curtain. "Get away from there!" He snatches the curtain shut and shoves the hulking enforcer across the room with uncanny strength.

Egil says, "Abner, I'm killing this sick motherfucker right now," but his war-brother is weeping openly on Casper's shoulder.

"We thought you were gone, man. . ."

"Was gone, brother," Casper murmurs. "I followed the light back. . ."

Egil glares at the preacher, then he looks at the bank of monitors just as the EKG beeps a weak but steady rhythm . . . he can't get past how it beeped a half-second *after* he looked at it, like he caught it telling the truth. But was it lying then, or is it lying now?

"We gotta get you back to the compound," Abner says. "Fucking cuck usurper set us up. But we gonna wreck the shit out of his coronation, right, brother?"

"No," Casper snaps. "We're staying right here."

"No fucking way! Popeye thinks you're gone, brother! We go in there now and dead him good, before he finds out. . ."

"Everybody gonna know," he says. "When that fool stabbed me, I said to myself, 'Lord, if this is it, show me a sign.' Well, I've been shown. . ."

The preacher comes over and takes Casper's massive, scarred fist in his shaky hands. "Do you accept Him?"

"I do," Casper says.

"Will you serve Him?"

"I will," Casper says.

Egil is still trying to explain what he saw behind the curtain, but Casper tells him to shut the fuck up, and go and fetch some of that soup.

7

Jaime wakes up to the tourist staring at him. His weathered face breaks into a smile as if he's overjoyed to be caught staring at another man sleeping.

"You're a heavy sleeper," the American says, which sets his heart beating faster. He doesn't remember a nightmare. Was he screaming in his sleep? "Thought I'd have to use the Army resuscitation technique on you."

Jaime sits up rubbing his eyes. "Fuck is wrong with you, man?"

"They take hold of your earlobes and pinch them real hard. Forces blood into the brain and jolts you awake. It's one of the nicer methods, anyway."

Jaime isn't sure the asshole didn't do just that, the way his head feels.

"My mom always said I had what she called a heavy presence," the dip says. "Like, when she was asleep, she could feel me looking at her, willing her to wake up. Guess it's a hard habit to break."

"You'd better break it," Jaime says, "or somebody break you." He gets up and checks his phone. Scans the rooftop to be sure they're alone, out of sight of anyone on the neighboring roofs. Then he notices the smell of fresh meat cooking. Kind of gamy, but his mouth waters.

"What's that cooking?"

The American smiles, hunched over the fire. "Did you know there were pigeons down here?" He passes Jaime a tortilla wrapped around a fistful of sizzling meat.

"You caught a pigeon?"

"Yeah, it was none too cagey about taking food right from my hand." He bites into a pigeon burrito, sucks a bit of grease off his finger. "Been a vegetarian for almost five years, but I didn't see any fresh fruit around, and it just felt right."

Jaime can't help checking his burrito. "Did it have anything on its feet?"

"Feet?" He points at the fire.

Jaime pokes in the ashes until he finds a couple black twigs. One of them has a melted pill of plastic on its ankle. "Some people use pigeons to move messages, dumbass."

"Shit, I'm sorry," Hatch says. "I didn't know. . ."

The pigeon tastes good, Jaime has to admit, but by the time he finishes it, he's decided for sure he's going to sell the American to the Green Man.

They use a pipe from the water tank on the roof to wash off, and Jaime changes clothes. He takes out a packet of crystal and dishes out a couple lines. Doesn't offer the American any, but he feels the guy standing over him.

"You really need that shit?"

Getting lectured about his drugs is even worse than having to share them. "Fuck off, man. Ain't got no more coffee."

He blitzes the first two bumps, letting his head drop back, savoring the icy chemical burn that's the closest he'll ever come to being cold. The American is still looking at him with a kind of smug judgment, like when he was watching him sleep. "What, you want some?"

"Don't need it," he says. "I'm not judging. If it's good for you, go for it. But once I've really experienced a mental state, I can recall it and get back there at will, without using substances."

"That's just so fascinating," Jaime answers, meaning it more than he means to.

"A wise man once said, 'When you get the message, hang up the phone.'"

"I got a message for you," Jaime says. "Fuck him and fuck you, too."

After a brief and pointless argument in which Jaime tried to convince the American he should hide out on the roof while Jaime works out the deal, they go back down to the street together. The light is no different, but the traffic patterns are more workers and carts, fewer prostitutes and hustlers. No matter what time the sun says it is up top, it's definitely morning underground.

A couple jeep technicals with machine gunners plow past in a hurry, firing into the air. A swarm of tiny drones buzzing like angry cartoon bees above their heads. A line of superbikes rear up on their hind wheels, engines roaring in neutral, popping wheelies and peeling out in the other direction.

"So. . . what should I know about him?"

"Nothing, because you're not talking to him. *I* am."

They go down the block and the American is looking around at everyone and everything, so Jaime notes right away when he stops and stares across the street, then goes on walking with his hand up to his face, tugging at the thinning hair atop his forehead. Jaime looks around, seeing some *chica* on a missionary trip dishing out carrot stew to a line of Veggies. Jaime sees how the American puts him between her and himself as they pass, but files it away without comment.

Three blocks down, they come to a McDonalds. In the midst of a demilitarized zone, it's spotless, because it has its own security. The neighboring buildings have Hiroshima shadows in charcoal black painted on them, as a memorial to the last people who tried to fuck with the place.

But something is weird about the logo—the golden arches are twisted into a pot leaf.

"See," Jaime says, swelling with something like civic pride, "we can have nice things."

They go inside. Thickest stench of marijuana he's ever smelled. *Edibles.* A few people lounging in beanbag booths munch on food in assorted shapes and sizes. Their eyes are redder than blood. A Veggie stands at the counter, naked but for nylon swim trunks, slurping down package after package of sweet and sour dipping sauce, bursting them like smelling salts under his runny nose and glopping them onto his blistered, black tongue.

"Oh, I get it," Hatch says. "McCannabis."

"It's all vegetarian, though. Nobody who knows shit trusts the meat down here."

The kids behind the counter are like fast food clerks everywhere. They don't give a shit.

"Hey, I need the key to the restroom," Jaime says. The clerks look at each other, at the cameras in the ceiling, and back at Jaime and the American. "I need to see Malverde."

One of them hands over a key on a ring with a big flange of sheet metal on it, like a machete. Jaime takes it, mumbles, "Gracias," and goes around the divider, into the employee area. Hatch follows, staring at the Veggie like he wanted an autograph.

They go past the kitchen to a door at the end of a corridor. Jaime unlocks it and hauls it open and they go inside. It looks like any other men's room, but there's a stall next to the stand-up urinals that the American goofs on until Jaime explains that the orifice in the wall will blow you for two work credits. He puts money in the blowjob machine and mashes the option buttons. The whole unit retracts into the wall, revealing a narrow stairway descending into piss-yellow dimness.

They go down the stairs. At the bottom, they cruise a long hall lined with stacked cases of Coke and Red Stripe beer.

"Your friend must really be important to live under a McDonalds."

"Can't bring your ass in the front door," Jaime snaps, which has its desired effect. The American smirks, even more impressed with himself. Let him be, Jaime thinks. Let him think he's in charge, right up until you sell his ass.

They come to a door at the end of the hall. Jaime punches in a combination. "This guy is really fucking paranoid, so don't say a word, don't move, and don't stare at him. Don't stare at anybody, no matter what. Everybody down here is real self-conscious about people staring. And don't say anything about meat."

"Meat? Like, hamburgers, steak, et cetera?"

"Never mind. Don't say shit about shit."

"Fine, little buddy. I've seen everything. You don't have to worry about me."

"Then why are you giving me a fucking ulcer? Look at the floor and shut the fuck up."

The door opens, and a fat man in a full chemical warfare suit blocks them. The suit is transparent, heavy-gauge rubber, and though foggy, it's still pretty obvious he's naked inside it underneath a layer of brown camouflage marbled with veins of gold and white froth and bits of corn and bean hulls, which seem to slosh around as he lurches toward them. . .

"He likes the suit," Jaime mutters in the American's ear. "So quit staring, you'll make him self-conscious."

"I get it," the American says. "He's a fecal freak, I don't give a shit. I don't think my staring is going to trigger any kind of epiphany, but if it does. . ."

The man in the shit-suit bends down into the American's face. His bloodshot eyes bulge out and kiss the sweaty interior of his mask. His respirator gurgles and visible umber fumes ooze out of his respirator. "What the fuck're you staring at?" he demands. His suit swells and bubbles roll up the inside.

"It's cool," the American says, "but like. . . are you. . . the guy we. . . ?" Hatch turns to Jaime, his face begging.

"Mr. Chud, my man," Jaime says, "is it soup yet?"

"Eat shit," says Mr. Chud. "He'll see you when he sees you." He lets the American squeeze past, but squashes Jaime into the doorjamb with his septic bulk. "Fuck you trying to pull, fool? That's not one of our runners."

"Your runner was a bitch, he got popped. This is better. When the Man hears his pitch, you're all gonna have to give it up for me. I'm no fucking runner, dog. I'm a talent scout, and you're a doorstop."

Jaime pushes by and swaggers into the big room. Black lights and giant lava lamps supercharge the murk, make purple phantoms out of roiling clouds of ganja smoke. Sticky, twitchy dub version of Sister Nancy's "Bam Bam" on sleepwalking out the floor-to-ceiling soundsystem.

"Calling the meek and the humble," murmurs the tourist, "welcome to Blackboard Jungle." Mimicking the brackish Jamaican shaman's voice belting out of the stereo. "So don't you fumble. . . just be humble."

The Green Man's army slouches around pool and air hockey tables, works speed bags and watches TV and fucks whores on enormous beanbags and smokes blunts the size of baseball bats. None of them bothers to look up when Jaime comes in. Hatch grabs some wall and watches two tattooed piercing freaks running nine-ball like a berserk computer simulation, finishing two games by the time he crosses the room.

The back wall is floor-to-ceiling aquariums. Freshwater Amazonian, glistering swarms of tetras and massive arawanas and arapaimas, and the obligatory piranha tank. Because the boss takes his archvillain game serious.

On the streets, they call him the Green Man and the Wish-Doctor. Some call him Malverde, the Bad Green, after the legendary, perhaps mythical, Culiacan bandito who is the patron saint of every Sinaloan narco, though he could never be mistaken for a Mexican. Nobody who knows it and wants to live calls him by his real name.

Jaime goes to the beaded curtain in the arch beside the tank and nods at Door, the Green Man's last visible line of defense. A big, blunt, torpedo-shaped Veggie, he cradles a belt-fed automatic shotgun against his flak vest, which is equal parts Kevlar and bricks of C4, with blinking detonator lights. Without saying a word, Door insures a level of politeness in the common room.

"Wait here," Jaime tells the American. The guero tries to follow him, but Door puts a heavy hand on his shoulder.

Jaime goes through the beaded curtain and into a VIP room behind the aquariums. Lit only by the swirling green light that seeps through the plexiglass tanks, the Green Man's inner sanctum is carpeted in Indian rugs and furnished in huge silk pillows and crushed velvet walls to shame a Turkish harem. It's furnished also in bodies naked and scantily clothed, all raptly staring at the Green man. He lounges on a hassock and puffs at the ivory mouthpiece of a bubbling hookah replica of Watts Towers.

Jaime saunters over and eases onto the far corner of the couch, directly across from the man's hooded gaze and just out of reach of his deadly hookah.

Swaddled in beaded robes and buried in chains and medallions, the Green Man stops in mid-puff and glowers at Jaime, and all eyes follows his. Only Jaime's eyes have nowhere to go when the music stops.

Plumes of smoke thick as licorice drool out the Green Man's nostrils. "And speaking of vengeance, here comes an object lesson to educate you fools, all praises to Jah." His smile has bits of men bigger than Jaime trapped in it. "Jaime Blasco, wise men laugh at me for letting you stay aboveground."

"Yo, man, everybody lies, my man. . . like, I got set up, and your mule was whack. He stepped out of line and got secondary, and he gave it all up to the hose, man. I don't know who you paying on staff, man, but you should get a refund on that shit, because those boys jacked him up before they even got deloused, so. . ."

The Green Man leans into the light, but his wizened face recedes into the shadows of white dreadlocks hanging down to his knees. Jaime has been here dozens of times, but no matter how long he looks at the Green Man, he cannot figure out who, or what, or even how old, the fucking guy is.

His features are shrunken, pinched. His eyes hide all but their bloodshot, dilated irises. His skin is a deep chlorophyll green. Some say it was a botched experiment he did on himself, trying to change his body chemistry so it'd produce endogenous THC. Others maintain that he just did it to disavow any racial identity, to become a Subspecies of One. And rumors abound that he never eats, but he has to spend at least three hours in the sun every day, a costly special arrangement with the authorities that has him hopelessly compromised.

But as the best chemist in the city, he sells to all sides. So he has a unique umbrella of protection that has, until recently, kept Jaime alive and dry. And even when he can't remember who you are, he never lets you forget it.

"How do you get up in the morning, Jaime? Where do you find the courage to face a world of enemies, all out to make you look the fool?"

"Yo, man, I can learn from that. . . Power comes from not using it, right? And even though your people fucked this up, I still didn't want to leave you with nothing. I brought you this guy."

"And why would I want. . . this guy?"

This negotiation isn't going well at all. Jaime wracks his brains. Having run down the guero all day in his own head, it's hard now to switch gears and talk him up. "He knows shit, boss. Chemical shit, like you do. And he's holding something he says gonna change the world."

Green Man smiles like he's about to school you. "And you believe him?"

"I believe he's worth more than what I was gonna bring you. He's got kind of an attitude problem, but once you beat that out of him. . ."

"Hey! Doctor Listor!" Hatch elbows his way into the VIP area and approaches the Green Man with his open hand extended, not even seeing all the guns that pop up and track him. "Love your work, man."

The Green Man drops the hose, looking at the clammy white hand in his face like it should wither and fall off under the force of his gaze. "You call me a doctor? You think I'm a *doctor*?"

"Oh please, sir, don't be so modest. It's an honor to meet you. Your black-market books on tryptamine enhancement were a revelation to me in college. There's Hoffman, there's Shulgin, and there's you, seriously." Gushing as he does, the asshole backs up and hits reset when he finally reads the pique and old secrets conjured up in the Green Man's hothouse of a brain. "I'm sorry, I didn't realize—"

"No matter, that. That was just another mask. But here, in the company of all that's mine, I show my true face. It is not a merciful face, and it hates asking questions twice, and it hates to be bored or disappointed. So why, this face asks, are you worth more to me than my mule, whom this fool has lost?"

"Well, sir, my name is Nolan Hatch. I'm a recreational chemistry entrepreneur and a would-be engineer of human consciousness, like yourself. I don't have any deal with this gentleman, and I certainly didn't come in here as goods. I got him to bring me here to make you a proposal."

"I got no need for partners. I got all the product I need."

"What was that mule carrying, sir?"

"You pry, boy." The Green Man sucks at his hookah and inclines a shoulder at a small child whose job seems to be to pack bowls, but Hatch nudges him aside.

"Please, sir, indulge me," He picks up a purple bud the size and gnarliness of a cauliflower ear and expertly breaks it up into resinous crumbs with his fingers, sifting it into the bowl without losing a stray ultraviolet whisker. "Queen of Pain, citrine Indica from Uruguay. 38% THC, 42% CBD. What did you lose?"

"Seeds from the Cannabis Cup in Holland, and some samples of new stuff." The Green Man follows the weed cups like other drug lords follow sports.

"That's a bummer. Well, *I* have something truly new. Totally new, totally different. Meet the Secret Teacher." He shakes out the little ass-capsule and rattles it so the tiny cargo inside can speak to the room. It impresses nobody. "It's going to change the world, man. All the things they used to say about LSD, MDMA, DMT. . . it's all right here. Change the way people relate to the world, and you change the world. End wars, poverty, disease. . . carnivorism. . ."

Jaime covers his mouth and kicks the dumb American in the shin, but the Green Man finally opens his eyes wide enough for Jaime to see what color they are. "What the fuck he's talking about, you know?"

Jaime shrugs. If this fool gets killed now, he'll take Jaime with him, anyway. "Some mushroom, man. . ."

Listor's emerald face wrinkles like a withering leaf. "I and I got no use for fungi. . ."

"He sings opera about this shit, man, but I ain't tried it. Get some geeks and do a taste test, I don't know. . ."

"Hey, don't sell fungi short, doc." Hatch passes the Green Man the silver mouthpiece of the hose and lets the child light the contents of the birdbath-sized bowl. "There're 1.5 million species of fungi on Earth, and less than 100,000 identified. About 140,000 species of mushroom, only ten percent of which are known. So *nobody* knows what's still out there.

"The Secret Teacher isn't just another strain of *cubensis*, doc. It's not even the same genus as any of the 209 known psychoactive mushrooms. It's like if a Liberty Cap and a fly agaric took an ayahuasca trip to Ibogaland and had a bastard. Who then started a new religion."

The Green Man sucks and puffs for a long minute before finally asking, "You know anything about Lone Star ticks? Alpha-Gal syndrome?"

Hatch scratches his head. "Not sure I do. . ."

The Green Man stares into space for a while, licking his lips. "Bite from a Lone Star tick provokes an allergic reaction to galactose alpha-1, 3-galactose, a sugar molecule in all dead flesh. Body produces antibodies and such a severe reaction, that the victim can never eat meat again. If you knew anything about weaponizing tick spit, I'd have some use for you. Together, we could change the world for real."

Hatch looks over at Jaime, who's giving off seven layers of mutually contradictory nonverbal cues, then shrugs. "I'm sorry, I'm not a biochemist, or entomologist, or whatever. And I love a good buttsteak burrito, now and again. But this thing I have. . ."

"What does it do?" Every word impatiently kicks the previous word's ass.

"Elevator pitch? Okay, fine. . . It lets you talk to God. No bullshit hippie hyperbole. The real deal."

The Green Man blows smoke rings around an evil chuckle. "Sign me up, if I can bring a baseball bat and an Uzi." He revels uneasily in a moment of forced, courtly laughter, which the American rudely interrupts.

"I'm sure everyone in the room will agree that God's been very unfair to you." He savors the dead silence in the room more than the Green Man enjoyed the noise. "But the really beautiful thing—"

The Green Man shakes off the conversation. "Animals react to pain and pleasure with instinct that looks almost like intelligence. But it's not. The question isn't whether an animal is self-aware enough for its suffering to matter. The question is, what makes you think *you* are?"

Hatch squirms. It's fun to watch, even if it means Jaime is fucked, too. "I really think you should give this thing a chance. . ."

"Fine, leave it on the table and get out, before you really start to bother me. Jaime, go where you will, maybe I take you later."

"Cool, man, see you. . ." Jaime turns to go, but the asshole catches him by the arm and drags him back.

"Hey, man. . . This is not something you can just drop off to get it developed. This is *my* baby. It took me I-don't-want-to-tell-you how many years to find it. . . and I don't care if you've got the research department from Pfizer down here, you'll never get a viable production-line drug out of the sample I'm carrying on your own. . . I don't know what else to say. If anything in your books about consciousness expansion still means anything to you today, then I'm begging you to open up to the possibility that it's here, right now, in my hand."

The Green Man takes up the hookah hose, puffs on it reflectively, then wipes white crud out of the corners of his mouth. "You have stupid hair."

Well, that's it. Door and two of the least-stoned of the entourage abruptly collar Hatch and start to drag him away. "When you see what this is, Dr. Listor, you're going to want to be part of it. I'll just wait outside. . ."

Jaime hangs back, looking at the Green Man. "So, we cool?"

Green Man just sits there with the mouthpiece of the hookah slack in his mouth. Jaime leans closer, then tries not to choke on his spit.

The Green Man's eyes are bloodshot eggs, soft-boiled pupils rolled back out of sight. He looks like he's dying.

Just back away, smiling and waving. "See you later, boss."

Goddamn, he's in it, now. He just helped some random asshole assassinate a major power. If he can get to the door, maybe he can run and hide again. But life, as he knows it, is over.

This frantic musing takes him three steps towards the exit when someone notices the Green Man's condition and grabs him. Docr gets him in a full nelson. Mr. Pudding sloshes over and tunes him up with a right cross to the jaw.

"You motherfucker," Jaime squawks. "You fucking American motherfucker. I don't even know you!"

Hatch shakes off the two thugs holding him, who haven't yet tumbled to the Green Man's murder, but news is spreading as fast as their bong-addled brains can process it. "Ever hear the story of Saul of Tarsus, Jaime?"

"Why you had to bring me into this, you—"

"Kill them both tomorrow," Mr. Chud says. "Tonight, let's give Jaime to *los locos*. Lock up smartass here in my room."

From the other side of the room—

"We have drunk soma and become immortal! We have attained the light!"

Everyone freezes.

The American's face lights up.

"Now what may foeman's malice do to harm us? What, O Immortal, mortal man's deception?"

"What the fuck?" asks Mr. Chud.

"Wait," the Green Man says. "I have a better idea." He gets up and stretches his lazy, loose frame to its full height and comes toward them with a grin as big as the Milky Way on his emerald reptile face. "Nolan Hatch, thank you for this gift. I bow to your Secret Teacher."

Jaime is thunderstruck as the Green Man embraces the American, who starts to say something.

"Ssshhh," hisses the Green Man. "Don't turn this rape into a murder."

For the first time since he met the American, Nolan Hatch looks scared.

8

"He is coming, brothers and sisters! The deaf shall hear his call, and the lame shall rise to greet him. . . He *sees* you, blind man! Don't you want to see *him*?"

Chaz "Chigger" Sturtevant hears the echoing voice from the cheap bullhorn pivot to follow him down Via Carillo Fuentes, but he keeps walking. Walking and tapping his cane. All things being equal, he don't really mind being blind. People mostly let him alone, and the way he figures it, there ain't shit to see down here, anyway.

Back in prison, Chigger earned his nickname for his parasitical tendency to dig himself in and mooch to a degree almost legendary in penal lore. That, and a string of jailhouse sexual assaults that may or may not have included literal biting and bloodsucking. But he don't make excuses for his proclivities. Lord knows, he paid through the nose for what he is. If a man can't be himself in prison, what's the fucking point?

Yes, all things considered, prison was a pretty good deal. But it was in prison that an inmate who felt he'd suffered unduly by Chigger's unwelcome advances threw lye in his face and rendered him completely blind and, by all accounts, even less lovely to look upon, so when Convict Sturtevant, after countless transfers throughout the 1800 prisons in the United States penal system, ended up down here, he resigned himself to whatever he could make out of the rest of his days. There are plenty of men lower than himself down here, in these lightless lands where even a blind man can be king.

Chigger wanders the street within sniffing-distance of the Filipino cook's stall, turning back whenever the warm, sticky reek of *lumpia* fried in scorched peanut oil tapers off beneath the harsher odors of the city.

People mostly let him alone here. He don't have to look at himself in tattered plaid pajamas and a t-shirt for a yacht-rock band called Trustfund, a half-melted pink Bratz Dollz sleeping bag as a cape, and a fanny-pack of gimmes from the vending machines. Chigger is self-sufficient. . . as long as the bad doctors don't come looking for him again.

They done all kinds of things to him in the name of healing his eyesight, promising him new corneas, even whole new eyes. They once tried to bypass his damaged eyes with electronic signals that made *grand mal* epileptic seizures look like a giggle fit.

But he makes out like a bandit at the vending machines because of his handicapped status. When word reached him on the street that there was a preacher who could heal the sick, the lame and even the blind and the dead, he had every reason to smell a rat, and mind his own damn business. Even if Jesus himself is doing the healing, Chigger wants no part of it.

He fumbles round a corner and, as he does whenever presented with an unfamiliar space, he emits a few mouth-clicks, head cocked to pick up the faintest variation in the echo that could give him some rough sense of the space, and what, if anything, fills it.

Hates asshole talk like being blind heightens your other senses. He's still waiting for his ninja superpowers to kick in, but he does alright with what he has, because he fucking has to.

He's in the mouth of a narrow alley that isn't usually there. He reaches up and touches the corrugated steel of a coiled rolldown gate. The stringent stink and fricative hiss of aerosol cans fills the alley, clouds of it stinging his otherwise useless eyes.

His foot kicks a body on the ground, smells fresh human shit and a cologne almost as potent as the paint.

"Hey, brother," someone says. The hiss of paint abruptly cuts off.

He backs away, playing up his blindness. This is Zeros territory, and everybody knows it. Anyone painting over their tags is issuing a flat declaration of war, and the body at his feet only underlines it.

All the Zeros wear cologne.

"Just a blind man," Chaz says, backing up until a hand falls on his shoulder.

"Blind man, he sees you," hisses the voice from the street, and it's the voice, not the bullhorn, that was broken. It buzzes and slurps in his ear, very close. "Come with us, brother. Come see him."

Chaz tries to squirm out from under the hand, but the grip is irresistible without even straining, and he can't quite resort to violence to tear himself away.

"You were in Angola, weren't you, brother? Thought I recognized you from the infirmary. You paid in blood and hard time for your sins, like we all did. If you tired of paying, we can show you the light, if you want to see it. . ."

101

And Chaz nearly shits himself, because for the first time in a decade, he sees—

Light.

It's only a teardrop of low, molten red murk, like the sunrise after a big fire, but he *sees* it bloom up out of the universal darkness, silhouetting the fingers that cradle it, offering it to him.

"Follow me, brother," says the holder of this light.

He follows it up the narrow alley and out onto Via Carillo Fuentes to cross Plaza Guevara, then down a crooked alley that wends between, then under, a pair of slowly merging tower blocks sharing the space with a massive pipe throbbing with raw sewage. They walk at a steady clip. Chigger's white cane tapping impotently alongside him, guided by the other hand still on his shoulder and driving him forward, as if he needs to be pushed.

That light. . . it shines dimly but fiercely, as if burning through the layers of scar tissue on his eyes and in his soul. It's the only thing he wants to see, ever, and by the time they pass under several streets, the sewer drain doubling, then tripling in size until its septic eminence pushes them against the ducts and cables of the opposite wall, he doesn't think about where they're going until they emerge onto the street again.

Then they're near the sewage treatment plant in the Orange Zone, which can only mean they're deep inside the Aryan Nation.

Chaz spits on the ground, and not just because of the pervasive fecal taint on the air. Fucking racists don't care if he's blind, or only a quarter black. They can't see past color, and they don't do fractions.

Even if you're lightly tanned, the Aryan Nation is the most violent block. Constantly at war with their neighbors, the Russian Mafiya and the bikers, when nobody else wants a piece of them, if left to their own devices, they just beat on each other. Even now, he hears swords clanging on armor and truck engines racing, rolling coal and pouring volumes of oily smoke into the already fetid air.

He expects to be cut down by the next Viking wannabe or just shot from a distance, but he follows the light through them as if he's finally, truly invisible.

They go a couple blocks without being challenged when the street gets crowded with muttering humans. By the stink of human grease and ground-in street dirt, he knows they're beggars, junkies, veggies and ghosts, coughing, vomiting, crying, praying. Chigger follows the light through the crowd that seems to part from it, only to gather and whisper to itself in idiotic awe. They might not see it, but they feel it, like the glow of a cigar cherry at the back of your neck. They make way for the holder of the light and the big men at the door say, "Bless you, nigger," like the nicest racists this side of *Hee Haw.*

"This man is with me," the slurping buzzing bullhorn-voice says, fingers tickling the light until it shines almost too bright for Chigger's blind eyes. It leads him into the storefront church, over concrete floors sticky with piss, shit, blood and worse, past pews overflowing with shaking, praying bodies, past complaining, coughing, sick, pants-pissing walking wounded. All make way for Chigger and the light and if the light stopped right now, he would walk right into it.

So it snaps him almost back to his default state of hateful paranoia when the light is snuffed out and he stumbles into darkness. A bony hand shoves him backwards out of a close, fetid room reeking of formaldehyde.

"Not this man," says a voice that sounds like it ought to come out of an old-time radio, the voice of the hand pushing him back. "I can't abide the stink of his sins. . ."

"Not your choice to make, is it, preacher?" Bullhorn voice buzzes over his shoulder. "Lord picks his kindling, we just light the match."

"Don't you dare!" roars the radio voice. "I am his instrument!"

"Do it, preacher." The heavy hand pushes Chigger forward. "Do a motherfucking miracle."

Chigger starts to twist against them and tell them to fuck off, he ain't nobody's kindling, when he sees it, brighter than ever, in the preacher's hands.

Those hands hold the light up to his eyes and he can almost see the contours of the face behind them, the shapes and spaces of the gloomy room.

"Do you accept Him?" the radio voice asks.

Chigger can think of only one word, can still barely say it. "Yes." In the fire, he can almost see Him, and a glimpse of His terrible beauty is worth a lifetime of blindness.

"Do you renounce your sins?"

Chigger can see his sins in the flames now, stealing, raping, beating, men, women, children, and the far more awful sins of his fantasies. All the toxic cancers of his imagination seeming to float out of him and the fire blooms higher and shifts through a sickly spectrum of colors as it burns them all away.

"I do," he said. And he felt lighter, brighter, if no cleaner, for he knew that nothing he desired would be a sin, when he was reborn.

"Will you serve Him?"

"Yes," he said.

"Then let His fire consume you," says the radio voice, and the fire grows brighter, closer, fills his eyes and his brains and his heart and his soul.

He screams that he is going blind when the hands are lifted away, though he sees the shriveled white face of the preacher looking down on him. The street trash around him begin to sing, "This Little Light Of Mine."

Chigger turns around and looks at the man who brought him here to thank him, but the words die in his throat. He does recognize the con from Angola's infirmary, the high-yellow complexion with the weedy beard of ingrown hairs and the painful, cockeyed expression like a puppy or a little girl who just lost her ice cream, but that's not what you'd remember about the guy.

What you'd remember, if you're Chaz Sturtevant, is how this con lost both his arms up to the elbows to a thresher in the fields one day, and when he was in the infirmary with nobody around who could stop him, Chigger bashed his face in to stop his screaming and fucked that helpless amputee in his ass good and fucking hard, just because he motherfucking could.

He looks down at those stumps now, scabby and bruised, and when he blinks, when he keeps his eyes closed, he can still see the fire burning in the ex-con's hand.

And he can still feel the ex-con's other hand squeezing his shoulder hard enough to make his arm go numb.

"I can see," Chigger says, laughing.

"Good," says the amputee con, steering Chigger back towards the door with a hand he doesn't have. "Because we got a whole lot to show you."

9

Only a week in here, and he's doing pretty well. Thievery Corporation on the hi-fi, Kandinsky prints on every wall, as per his request. Nolan Hatch takes a deep breath. He plants his feet and takes a huge bong-rip and dives into his new swimming pool.

Directly adjacent to his double-wide, twelve-by-twenty container apartment on the fourteenth floor of the Green Man's tower block, the pool is a thirteenth-floor container lined with spray-fiberglass and filled with purified water that still tastes vaguely of plastic. It isn't solely his—a door on the other end of the container commands similar privileges, and his door only opens when the other one is sealed. The pool itself is an emergency reservoir and also some kind of fire-control feature in case the lab downstairs ignites, or so he gathers.

Hatch drifts, letting the resinous smoke saturate his lungs. He blows it out and surfaces, takes another breath, expels it and sinks to the bottom of the pool.

When he's sitting cross-legged on the bottom, gripping the bumpy foam insulation coating the tank, he bites down on the peculiar tiny dental appliance on his right upper bicuspid until it clicks, and he can hear voices in his head.

•

"What is the name of this place?

"They call it Omegaville. We call it many things— Cibola, el Norte Libre, Interzone—but who knows what the cows call the slaughterhouse? It has no true name, for white men have not suffered it. Our pain is only the exhaust of a factory, but the white man is coming to steal our only product.

"Listen."

The Norteño Spanish diatribe is both sleepy and relentless, like a narcoleptic hog-auctioneer, as his tinny voice resonates through the bones of Hatch's skull.

"Names have power. Names are wishes. Even the miserable little river that divides this world from the next . . . We call it Rio Bravo for the brave ones who must cross it to find work, while they call it Rio Grande, voicing their wish for a bigger river.

"Have you ever heard of the Black Hole of Calcutta? A name to conjure with, often invoked as the epitome of hell on earth by white people, though few know what it actually was, or why.

"It was only a nameless prison for native opponents of the East India Company at Fort William in Calcutta. The East India Company had forced the state of Bengal to produce opium and tea for colonial export even as they starved and lost their staple crops and land to predatory lending. Indians were stuffed like trash into the nameless hole for decades, until a rebellion by the Nawab of Bengal in 1756 turned the tables and forced 146 British troops to enter the hole for the first time as prisoners.

"For one night.

"When only 23 survivors emerged the next morning, they insured that the world would never forget the *one night* that white men spent in that prison cell that had, for decades, taken the lives of native Indians without earning even the dignity of a name among the white men who filled it. A monument to the noble dead of that one night was erected on the spot and stood until Indian nationalists forced its relocation to St. John's Church in 1940, but nothing commemorates the memory of some ten to fifteen million killed by the terrible famine the East India Company inflicted on Bengal, when they killed the Nawab and restored colonial rule in 1770.

"The prisons of America were built upon the model of the slave plantations that preceded them, and it was not until proud Southerners saw white men toiling and dying in fields alongside blacks and Mexicans, that reform—albeit only for whites—was finally won.

"We call this place by many names, we who live and die here, forgotten in advance, but we cannot name it for posterity, for our blood is invisible ink. . . We who are born of slaves and have always called ourselves workers are now not even wanted for labor. You are raw material they have fed into this machine they have built, but not even they know what form the final product will take when it emerges. . ."

•

Lungs burning, Hatch kicks off the bottom and shoots to the surface. The voice dies away in his mouth when he unclenches his jaw. He spits the appliance out into his hand, marveling at the subversive genius of it.

For years in LA, paranoid schizophrenics used to come up to Hatch and his friends at bars, fast-food joints, on the street, drawn by some kind of freak magnet, and they invariably rattled off how they'd been victims of CIA experiments, and still heard the transmissions ordering them to go commit assassinations or acts of terror. It was conventional conspiracy wisdom that the CIA or its geekier counterparts at the NSA could receive or transmit messages via dental implants. He wonders if that was where Silent Radio got the idea. Just a simple chip and bone-conduction circuit in an aluminum frame small enough to be harmlessly swallowed, but when you bite down on it within reach of Silent Radio's ghetto cellular network—instant schizophrenia.

For what little he's gathered so far, Silent Radio is some kind of latterday phone-phreak, hacking communications and the citizenry's own meatball Mexican dental work to deliver his sermons. A seemingly rogue element, but if this whole place is a laboratory, then the Blue Zone most likely knows about it and lets it go as part of the grand, unspeakable experiment.

As am I, he thinks as he steps into his shower stall, dials the nifty electric heater in the showerhead until the water's just right before stepping under it. Watching the water swirl down the drain between his feet, mingling with the urine streaming from his shriveled dick.

The whole thing is far less chaotic than it appears from the street. The Green Man made that clear enough when he took Hatch aside after his astonishing conversion, which had left no one more surprised than Hatch himself.

He took a hideous risk when he dosed Dr. Listor. Shit, he was neck-deep in it when he used the drug lord's real name, but the asshole left him little choice. The gel capsule he crushed and smeared on the mouthpiece of the hookah could take minutes or hours to hit, and he figured he'd get kicked out, and maybe called back when it had its desired effect.

Most who kept the drug a secret for centuries used it only once, in their initiation rituals. They took it to be received into the presence of Creation and see their place in it. Ever after, their dreams were a playground, a memory palace. Another reality as real as they could make it. Even in poverty as dire as any Haitian slum, they are the happiest people on Earth.

In his bitter old age, Listor had disappeared up his own ass. Hatch reckoned on his trip lasting long enough that he and Jaime might have needed to hide until it was over. When Listor jumped up like the freshly lubricated Tin Man from *The Wizard of Oz*, Hatch was startled by what he saw beaming out of the Green Man's wide eyes, even though he'd put it there.

And things started to happen fast after the Green Man came around. A space was allocated in a warren of bunkers under the Green Man's superbloque on Avenida Carrillo Fuentes. Hatch poked around the place, at walls shag-carpeted with white mold, at guttering fluorescent lamps and pools of stagnant water with giant albino slugs and little black tadpoles flitting around in them like giant sperms. It was perfect.

The usually furious Cuban go-between scraped his shaved scalp and said nothing.

They power-washed it with bleach. Faded graffiti in Spanish and mutilated dummies dressed in olive drab fatigues with scorched beards hinted that the previous occupants might have been anti-Castro guerrillas, perhaps even inconvenient Bay of Pigs survivors, the shit here was that old. A few duffel bags were crumbled and spilled out generations of rat-shit, useless garbage and fossilized

Macanudo cigars, but he dug out a serviceable hi-fi set in a steel case and some Perez Prado singles. The help grumbled about the relentless grinding groove of the Mambo King, but they succumbed to the rhythm despite themselves, as they began to set up Hatch's farm.

Once the materials started to flow in, they erected trench tables down the length of the largest bunker. These were filled with soil to a depth of two feet, mixed with vermiculite and human manure and other mineral ingredients that Hatch rattled off the top of his head. Every day, he checked the soil with a pool cleaner's pH tester and made changes. The dirt would take a couple days to come to proper fecundity, he explained to Jaime, who told the Green Man, who took all delays in stride, but Jaime was still scared, which made Hatch nervous.

He has no illusions about his new partner. It's been some years since he let himself get burned because he trusted someone in the drug trade. The Green Man isn't just a venal pusher, but a guru, a very brainy latter-day Merry Prankster, or at least the paranoid shell of one. The dose Hatch gave him had opened his eyes and converted him, but not to serve Hatch. He will find his own path to enlightenment. So Hatch has gambled that, as a true seeker, the Green Man will come to see the drug as a universal good and want to mass produce it. Hatch himself, as the messenger, might or might not merit some gratitude, but he's still hedging his bets, and keeps a proprietary death-grip on the secret details of the next stage.

The Green Man forced one of his men on Hatch to supervise, but Dale Agrippa seems no threat, and has probably forgotten more about fungi cultivation than Hatch will ever know. A bona fide throwback to the underground psychedelic alchemists of old, he looks like Walter Becker circa 1979, and talks like how a cheap old person on a prepaid phone card texts until the subject is mushrooms. Then he becomes a fucking encyclopedia.

When he braced Agrippa about his shroom game, the skinny, gnomic biochemist poked up a pic on his phone and said, "Does this answer your question?"

The pic showed baker's racks of trays of succulent white stalks with bulging scarlet caps speckled with white like raw, bloody bones.

To Hatch's stunned expression, Agrippa merely smirked, "No shit, I'm a fly agaric man."

Nobody has *ever* cracked fly agaric cultivation. The legendary magic mushroom of Siberia and *Super Mario*, *Amanita muscaria* grows wild across all of Eurasia, and so potent that its effects are undiminished, some say even enhanced, when passed on and consumed in urine. But it's a birch saprophyte and shuns controlled conditions. Besides, its high is mercurial, unreliable. For every legend about Koryak shamans who use it to see the future, there's a hundred stories of folks who just got legendarily sick.

Hatch was aghast. "You actually eat this shit?"

"Hell no," Agrippa snapped. "I filter it through him." He pointed at Rasputin, the three-legged, snow-white Samoyed that limped around the lab after him.

"You feed your dog mushrooms, and drink his piss?"

"Fuck'm I supposed to do?" Agrippa looked at him like he was the dumbest motherfucker on God's black Earth. "It's not like I can keep a reindeer down here."

When Dr. Listor introduced Hatch to his new lab, he cryptically added, "Every boy must get spanked on his birthday." Chud and Door came out of nowhere to seize Hatch's arms and pin him to a table.

For a second, it felt like some kind of joke, maybe a savage fraternity initiation. but while the two big guys had his shoulders pinned to the table, Agrippa took out a laser tattoo gun and incised a barcode on his wrist.

"Now you're a proper citizen," the Green Man said.

•

Hatch rubs his wrist. It's still sore. He scanned it with his new phone and memorized his new official name and medical status: *Joaquin Betancourt, age 47/ Sch. IV.* He has an essentially limitless reserve of Arcade credits and no pending research studies.

Most of what the phone can do is, naturally, worse than useless, but in using it as a guide, he's finally come to grasp the structure of his new home.

Unamerica is a self-contained underground city run by a coalition of corporations in partnership with the federal government under the auspices of the Department of Commerce. An ideal focus group environment, where products from Olestra and artificial hearts to electronic mind control and nerve gas are tested on a captive market.

Jaime was right when he said everything is free, but it *costs*. Every citizen has a bar-code which dictates what products they may consume. You can get your fill of whatever the vending machines and automats give you based on your medical and demographic history. If you're earmarked for a study on the effects of hyper-saturation of a known carcinogen, you can push the lever all you want, but only red dye #5 and asbestos-filter cigarettes will vend.

Most are harmless or at worst, worthless. Occasionally, bad products result in plagues, poisonings, mental derangement. As a rule, it's a good idea to avoid whatever they're selling as meat. They've tried every imaginable substitute for beef, pork, and chicken. Thus, the thriving black-market in chickens, eggs and even guano.

Cars, bikes, weapons and shit are almost always defective. Crime is rampant, cultivated and harvested like a product in itself. Almost everyone works to pay rent or protection for their living space. There are all kinds of ways to earn credits for additional treats, like a turn on the blowjob machine in every restroom. Mostly, people take surveys on their phones, about everything they eat and drink, about clothing, apps, music, websites, logos, and they pay each other for goods and services by swiping their phones on barcodes, or through other underground currency.

Laid over the radial grid that Jaime showed him is a spectrum of color-coded zones, just like the US imposes on any occupied city. The administrative and research areas through which Hatch entered the city are called Blue Zones, open to the couple thousand contractors running the show. Inductees normally come in through the Arcade, a twelve-story shopping mall and medical-detention complex, the panopticon hub of the cavern. The immediate area around the Arcade constitutes the Green Zone, which is routinely patrolled by the local police. Picture Times Square if the brand superstores overran it without purging the sleaze. Murder isn't a crime anyone particularly cares about, but organ-jacking—removing viable organs from corpses before they can be worked over in the research labs—is a capital offense. And yet wildcat ambulances prowl the city, scanning phone traffic for fresh meat, and their paramedics will fight each other with tire-irons over a healthy liver or set of lungs.

It's a dazzling analogue for the best and worst of capitalism, and the most dangerous things are the ads. Some of the animated billboards zap out subliminals that can induce seizures and implant irresistible impulses and even false memories. Hatch's first time walking around, a video loop of a flower opening and rotting seized him with the urge to drench himself in rejuvenating skin cream and left him with recollections of being serially molested at a daycare center, which he has yet to convince himself never actually happened.

Outside the Green Zone, the real enforcers of order are the gangs, who control the various territories of the Yellow Zone's thriving trade in black-market drugs, food and drink, prostitutes, gambling, and communication with the outside world. The police monitor the Yellow Zone through omnipresent cameras and drones, and they're armed for bear with all kinds of gnarly beta-testing weaponry, but they only come out when they want to try out a new toy. When they do, Hatch has been told, *run*. They make Erik Prince's Blackwater, of Iraq War fame, look like the Peace Corps.

But the Yellow Zone is also home to tens of thousands of regular working-class people, mostly immigrants, but with some native dissidents and prison trash mixed in. They have rechristened all the streets—once named for corporations, celebrities and titans of American industry—after criminals, radicals, activists and terrorists, from Dred Scott and Nat Turner to Subcommander Marcos and Pablo Escobar.

They are tagged and tracked for various experiments, but otherwise free to roam the city. They spend most of their lives working at the same kind of shitty jobs they had before. They have phones with free text and internet to take surveys, watch videos and test apps that directly give you spontaneous orgasms, among other things, but of course, the phones don't call out and like everything else, it's all just them fucking with you. Testing your credulity, trying to drive you crazy saying shit like the water is poisoned and Donald Trump got elected president, you can't take it serious. They're kept so busy and terrified, they don't seem to miss the outside world any more than the outside world misses them.

Still lower on the ladder are the veggies or ghosts, lobotomized zombies who go on consuming products, run by hypnotic remote control or the circuitry wired into their surgically mangled skulls, it's a crude attempt to make puppets of people. Jaime insists they're brain-dead, but Tim seemed pretty lively, assuming that actually happened—

The Orange Zones around the outer walls of the cavern contain the industrial and uncontrolled precincts of the city and come close to fulfilling the cover story as a toxic waste dump, albeit a populated one like Khlong Toei, Cubatao or Iztapalapa, the worst pollution ghettos in the world. But even they aren't at the bottom.

The Gutters down below house those condemned to weather the worst varieties of exposure tests, and every imaginable form of perversion runs unchecked in the lowest regions, starting with cannibalism.

The Red Zones are the service tunnels through which products both human and inanimate are shuttled in and out, but also the Loop, a disconnected service tunnel converted into a drag strip where cars constantly crash-test in endless coils of concrete tunnels.

Though the Gutters and the Loop are periodically raided by the police, the carnage and squalor yields piles of useful data, so it goes on.

There are ways in and out, some say, but if anyone tries to escape, nobody talks about it. Agrippa tells him about another cave upstairs with latchkey families, middle-class nuclear consumption units who got railroaded here after abusing credit or getting laid off. They live in a big tract development, a subterranean suburban enclave accessible through the Red Zone tunnels. While most of them work in the Blue Zone, the rest of the families stay inside, fearful of home invasion tests and other engineered disasters, but grateful for TV and experimental anti-depressants.

According to his sources, who lack the cultural literacy to appreciate the tidbit, the Blue Zone workers call the suburban cave Alphaville, after the Godard movie and not, presumably, for the underrated German synth-pop band. Every group has its own name for the city itself, but in the Blue Zone, they call it Omegaville—capitalism's final solution. Hakim Bey's dream realized: The Terminal Autonomous Zone. The Maximum City, at the end of history.

His phone rings. Just a refurbished iPhone 4, but with an unlisted number immune to the constant bombardment of surveys, mandatory ads and assorted corporate fuckery which every other citizen must suffer.

Even so, he checks the number to make sure it's not Charlie Tuna.

When they gave him the phone last week, it almost immediately started ringing. He answered.

"Oh thank God. A real human being. You're real right."

A trick question, if ever there was one.

The voice was a digital Speak & Spell monotone like Stephen Hawking uses, but the speech synthesizer made strangled beeps during and between the words, trying to articulate the tension and terror oozing out of the speaker.

"I feel pretty real," Hatch answered.

"That's good. That's great. I mean. You probably can't help me. But it's good. Thank you for picking up."

Hatch warmed to the experience. He loved random encounters with people, especially those in any kind of extremity. In elementary school, he got in trouble for using the house phone to call random international numbers to strike up a conversation with whoever picked up. Working-class Irish households always seemed willing to talk about anything with an American crank-caller, no matter the hour. "You seem to be in some distress, friend. May I can help. . ."

"I doubt it. I'm a brain in a fishtank."

"Wow, that sounds *serious*." He figured someone had to be fucking with him. "But, and excuse me for playing devil's advocate, here, but how can you be sure? I mean, we could all be just brains in fishtanks, or self-aware holograms in a massive simulation. . . so how do you know?"

"Because I volunteered for it. My body was shot to shit and they told me I could trade it for this. I get to live forever and watch whatever I want on all the premium streaming networks, so I said sure. I was dying anyway.

"But they fucked me. I've been here over a year. I think they forgot about me. All I get is Adam Sandler movies. I can't turn them off and they're saying if I want to watch the premium channels again I have to start doing telemarketing or tech support or some shit. I've seen *You Don't Mess With The Zohan* 119 times. So I told them fuck you. I want my body back. And they said fuck you. Your body is dog food. So I said—"

"Wait, wait, wait, buddy," Hatch said. "I can understand why you're distressed. What's your name, anyway?"

"Charlene. Charlene Truman from Oklahoma City. My friends call me Charlie. . ."

"Good to know you, Charlie from Oklahoma City. So maybe. . . have you thought that maybe customer service might be just what you need, right now?"

"I. I don't understand."

"Think about it. You're essentially dead, and they put you into a cut-rate afterlife. Better deal than most folks get. It's more like retirement, really. You get to be free of work and paying bills and all that bullshit, and more, fuck, you're free of the worst prison of all, your fucking body, right? No more embarrassing, humiliating, painful physical experience for Charlie Truman! You're free to finally explore the great undiscovered country of your own imagination, Charlie, to dream and dream forever, who gives a shit what's on Netflix. They don't know your dreams. Shit, right now, I'd happily trade places with you, if I could, and never turn on the damn TV. . ."

"That's the problem. I can't turn the TV off."

"That *is* shitty, I'm sorry about that. But to the question. You should be in heaven in your own head, but clearly, you've discovered it's hell. Can't get away from yourself, can't find anything good on TV. You're no better or worse off than when you had a body, really, but they're trying to find a way to save you. No, really. Sure, if you look at it from their point of view, they're just trying to use you to provide even cheaper customer service than some guy in Mumbai, but it's human interaction. That's why you called me, right?

"Even if it's somebody yelling at you that there aren't enough goddamn Adam Sandler movies on Netflix and it's all your fault, it's another human voice. It's a person with a problem, and you can solve it, you can fix their problem and leave them happier, and if you've made some objective improvement in just one person's day, if just one person is less ill at ease because of you, then damn it, Charlie, you're a *hero* in a fishtank."

"Okay. Maybe you're right. I'm just saying the selection of movies is really terrible."

"There's an infinite selection of fucking awesome first-run movies in your mind, lady. It's called *your imagination.* Go find it!"

Hatch hung up, feeling like he'd done the poor woman some good. Charlie Tuna called almost hourly for a few days, and Hatch briefly entertained notions of liberating her. What purer test subject for a psychedelic drug's effects could you hope for, than a brain in a jar? But Charlie was in a lab somewhere in the Blue Zone, an experimental boiler room full of disembodied tech support. Hatch felt bad about it until Jaime showed how to block her, but then he got to thinking too much about his own mental state. Shit couldn't be weirder if *he* was a brain in a fishtank, dreaming all of this, even before he started seeing people. Running into Talkshow Tim shook him, but stranger things had happened to him on the regular, in far more ordinary places. He was fine with writing it off as an odd but meaningless event, until he thought he saw Jude—

The caller right now isn't Charlie, or anyone else he recognizes.

"Somebody I want you to meet," says the Green Man.

"I'm busy," Hatch says. "When?"

"Now. Bring doses."

"Should I wear a tie?" he asks, talking to dead air.

Someone knocks on his door. Hatch throws on a baggy pair of jeans and an aloha shirt—antifreeze green sea beneath a trash-fire sunset, but as per his request, it has no logos anywhere on it. He's grown attached to the rubber-soled sandals, so he chooses them over the rows of Adidas sneakers and Bruno Magli shoes, a smorgasbord of deadstock footwear chosen seemingly out of a random pile in his size.

He's scared and excited, but he resolves to swallow it down and go kiss hands and shake babies. There's more to being a professional than getting paid.

10

Jaime wakes up from a dream and the bed is spinning. They're still on the boat. He cries from hunger and his Papi forces him to eat a piece of his uncle.

He screams and wakes up in pitch blackness. A U.S. Marine sticks a gun barrel into his mouth and asks him who won the 1993 World Series.

He wakes up choking. He's still on the boat and his father is pointing at the survivors and telling them, *This is Cuba.* Then he points at the raft off across the becalmed water and he says, *That is not Cuba! Those are not men!* And the starving men on the raft forget their names, forget words, and pick up machetes—

Jaime sits up in the dark and recollects where he is, wonders if anyone heard him crying. He wipes his eyes and shudders, stomach knotted with shame. Funny how he didn't freak out like this when he was being hunted, when he lost his home, all that shit. But now when he's safe in a titty crib, when he should relax, his stupid brain comes beating up on him.

Because his brain knows what's up.

Should he worry?

Always.

A week ago, he got shook out of his low-rent but hard-fought niche, and then this guero tourist falls into his lap and plays dumb until he's within spitting distance of the Green Man, then latches on. Knows Green Man's books. Even knows his real name. The American drops his wonder drug on him like a secret handshake, and suddenly they're in business, and Jaime has to struggle one hour to the next to stay relevant.

Hard not to feel like he's been played. By Nolan Hatch, by the Green Man. By forces beyond his comprehension.

He reaches in the dark for the tray of speed he was aimlessly chopping up when he finally fell asleep, but he can't bring himself to snort an eye-opener. The minute his shelf-life is expired, that's how they'll do him. Just substitute a few key ingredients in his morning mix with a few commonly available household chemicals, and send the maid to clear out his room, which is right next to Hatch's, only he didn't get a fucking swimming pool.

He hears the fool splashing next door, touches the wall and feels his whack-ass trip-hop music stumbling through the steel walls.

He gets up and pounds on the wheezing air conditioner, but it does little to stir the sweltering, sticky air.

Jaime's hardly seen the American at all, since he brought him in. Hardly seen the Green Man, either. He tried to brace him about his new role in the franchise, but the Green Man only fixed him with his impish grin.

"How we gonna sell it, that's what I can help with, but like, with this setup, I'm thinking—"

"You cannot sell Soma," the Green Man cut him off. "You can only *serve* it."

"Right on, but like," he started, but the Green Man was already out of reach. He's been in limbo ever since. Afraid even to ask to go back to his old job.

All because of Soma.

That's what they're calling it. The American hates it because of somebody named Huxley, but the Green Man insisted. Quoting some old-ass shit called the Rig Veda, the Green Man, as always, got his way.

Now he fumes over the pigeon.

The American must've known, and wanted him to know. Nobody could be that stupid-lucky, but he couldn't have read the message on its foot. Written in bump code. Only Poison Boys use it, only La Toda Madre uses birds. Jaime trusts her even less than the Green Man, but he probably could've gotten a better deal. La Madre's buttons are easier to work, and he could've stayed on top of the deal.

He had a good handle on the Green Man before this Soma shit fucked up everything. Paranoid, bitter and greedy, he could use. Since that tourist motherfucker dosed him, the Green Man has been more unpredictable the ever.

He hears the fool coming out of his crib and he's off the bed and at his own door before he sees how desperate he looks. Fuck it.

Jaime tugs the door open and steps out, says, "Hey," to the American's back.

He turns around. "Hey, how's it going?"

"You tell me."

"Well, I'm. . . Sol wants me to go meet somebody." He shrugs.

"Sol?"

"Yeah. Solomon Aloysius Listor, PhD. He was a tenured professor at UC Santa Cruz before he went underground. Hates being called the Green Man, actually. That's why he

told everyone to, so he'd always be mad at them. But now
. . ."

"Since you stuck that shit in his head. . ."

"Yeah. I won't say he's better, but he's going to help us."

"Us."

"Well. . . yeah, sure, *us*."

"But he didn't say anything about me coming along."

"Well, no, but if you want to, I'm sure it'd be cool. . ."

"No. It would not."

"It's. . . you know El Venenos. . . the Poison Boys, I
think they're called?"

"I used to run numbers for them. It was my first job."

"Right on then, come with, it'll be great."

"No, I worked for them, but I wasn't, like, *with* them,
know what I mean. Anyway—"

"Anyway." Hatch takes a deep breath. He almost doesn't
go off on the kid. "What the fuck do you want me to tell
you? A rising tide lifts all boats? Success isn't a tide, Jaime,
it's a fucking tornado. Maybe it swoops in and demolishes
your neighbors' houses and whisks the guy across the street
off to the merry old land of Oz, but never stirs a leaf on
your front lawn."

The kid just stares at him like he's inventing a new
language.

"Look. . . I'm grateful to you for plucking my ass out
of the fire and bringing this together, and I could still use
you. I mean, your advice. . ." He smiles like closing a sale.
"You're still a valuable part of the team, is all I'm saying. As
soon as we've figured out our marketing strategy—"

"Yeah, that. What are we marketing? What the fuck is
this Secret Teacher shit?"

The American shakes his head, thinking. Then he holds
out his fist. "You want to know? Here."

Warily, Jaime holds out his hand. The American drops a
tiny gray grain into his palm, like a poppy seed.

"Fuck is this?"

"A microdot. I ground up some of the original caps, extracted the water and fiber, and compressed them. I only have a dozen left, but I owe you at least this much. Just take it. It'll explain everything."

"I'm supposed to just take this shit?"

"Yeah, if you want to stay. I mean, let's not keep jacking each other off, okay? We had a nice mutual parasitism thing going, but it was based on jungle opportunism, right? So now, we're back inside a system, and we are governed by a guiding purpose, and it's not to get rich fucking up people's heads, it's consciousness elevation. You can't be part of this without believing in it. It's just not possible."

Jaime looks at the thing in his hand.

The American walks off down the hall. "Do whatever you want," he says over his shoulder.

Jaime is still standing in the hallway looking at the big grain of sand in his hand when a naked gladiator, still glistening with oil, storms the hall with a defeated opponent hogtied over his shoulder, followed by his entourage.

Jaime flattens against the wall, but he still gets smeared with oil and blood from the victim's kicking legs. He thrusts out his hands to keep the shit off his new Adidas Climacool golf shirt. His fist unclenches and he thinks for a moment he lost it, then, even worse, panics and thinks it got inside him. Flashes to the Green Man's whiplash conversion. He looks on the floor before he notices it impressed into the heel of his sweaty palm.

Slip inside and hold your hand out to the light, pick the fucker off your skin, drop it on a speed-dusted mirror.

Jaime has no love for psychedelics. No use for the unreal. Every moment you're geeking on the fantasy, reality gets worse, or it ends. He got dosed once by some asshole. A total fucking nightmare. He loves drugs that make his brain go faster or slower, but not deeper. The shit he sees when he's strung out is dark enough.

But now, it's like this.

He didn't know if he believed Hatch's story, but he needed to sell something to get back out of the red, and nothing sells like a salesman. He doesn't need to sample the product to sell it. Overnight, this outsider turned the cartel into a cult.

And he's out if he doesn't brainwash himself too.

Fuck.

It hits him.

It's another test.

Flash to the first day, when Hatch made him huff that nasty condom of nitrous. Jaime's gun in the American's hand was the last thing Jaime saw before he went under. . . and then coming to with the gun in his own hand. . . The fucker jacked him to think he was about to die and then put the power in his hands to see if he'd think, instead of just reacting. It took everything Jaime had, not to shoot him just on GP.

So this is another test, and they don't want you to pass it. They want you out.

He'll fucking show them.

Jaime punches up crunchy beats on the soundsystem and gets a big cup of pineapple juice out of the mini-fridge. Stepping out of his shoes and laying back on the futon, he jabs his index finger at the microdot, pushes down until it clings to the grooves of his prints. Looks at it for a moment.

You ain't shit, he tells it.

Puts it on his tongue and washes it down with juice. Lays back and puts his feet up on a pillow made out of a bullet-tattered nylon U.S. Border Patrol jacket and becomes a breathing machine.

Fuckers—ditch me—dog me out—talk to God—I ain't afraid—there's nothing—nothing—nothing

He's clenched up like a passenger in a car hurtling off a cliff. Relax, he tells himself. *You're safe in your deluxe crib, and this ain't shit, you got this, just relax*—

Truth is, he's kind of disappointed. He's riding it out and so far, aside from some weird purple geometric designs, tessellated polygons percolating out of the dark corners of the room, he's not feeling it. If this is the same shit that flipped the Green Guy, then maybe he's been afraid for no reason.

But he does feel kind of itchy—

He rubs his palm against the pillow, then scratches it with his other hand. In his palm, a crease from the index finger to the heel of the thumb deepens, inflamed with crimson blisters, and then splits open.

Jesus fuck me Jesus, why would anyone want to see this?

It's just a trip, and you're making it worse, the more you fear and hate on it. He tries to focus on his breathing and remind himself how when he closes his eyes, he doesn't feel it, it doesn't hurt, it's not real, and if it's not real, it's not shit, just keep your eyes closed. . .

But he can't.

It's like some invisibly thin wire wrapped around his arms, twisting tighter until the lean flesh pinches in deepening folds that split open and he can see teeth and a tongue in the mouths in his hands.

When they begin to scream, he hugs himself and closes his eyes and thinks, *this ain't shit*, but even though it doesn't hurt, it should hurt, it should fucking kill him, he can feel his flesh splitting open and screaming all his secrets, all his hate, all his fear, and they just scream louder when he screams at them to shut up, so he goes up and away until he's in the darkest backwaters of his brain and there's nowhere to hide he can't stop screaming fuckers try to god him out, he's gonna talk to Dog—

When the trapdoor opens, he hurls himself through it and paddles like a drowning man on the ultraviolet flood of the drug, out of his mind and into infinity.

•

Jaime Blasco floats in space, light years from Earth. Far enough away to see the whole Milky Way like a distant hurricane in the deep.

He really fucked you, he thinks. *Motherfucker chased you right out your head, out your town, off your planet, clean out the goddamn universe—*

He notes how the mandala galaxy pulsates when he worries, pulses and dims, as if he's drifting further away on the solar wind of his anxiety—

Cool it.

You're on your couch in your crib, you tripping, but you gonna come crashing back down any second now.

But he just floats out there.

Compared to everything else, the revelation that he has no body is a small one. He must've fled right out of his own mind when that shit kicked in. Jesus fuck, that was scary, but now, it's kind of funny.

The mandala seems to draw nearer, to pulse brighter, and Jaime becomes certain he's being watched.

He turns his consciousness away from the mandala and faces out into the dark, and presently, he sees another constellation, impossibly complex and bright, hovering closer to him. It is a constellation of eyes, glittering like distant stars but imbued with undeniable intelligence. As they hover closer, he loses count at thirty, for they revolve endlessly about on the crushed velvet curtain on which they rest. At their center, the largest eye reads him through, its colorless iris dilating as if to gulp him down. That is its goal, to engulf him and take his eyes. . .

Jaime swims up a waterfall of paranoia towards the impossibly distant galaxy that is his own nervous system, each of its infinitesimal stars a sense-memory, a dust-mote of himself. He feels the wall of eyes gaining on him and he redoubles his efforts, bringing the exploded diagram of his mind closer and closer until it unfolds around him like the panorama of the earth unfolds around a falling skydiver, so beguiling, so awesome in its imminence that he forgets to pull his chute, and thinking he must be God, he is smashed to atoms.

11

Hatch navigates the barriers around the front entrance of the Green Man's superbloque to find a Syd Mead limousine out of a '90s sci-fi film waiting for him. The Rolls Royce Apparition is a brutalist gondola with no perceptible windows, blowback armor, mounted machineguns and rows of chrome blowers emerging from under the elongated chassis like flamethrowers. Which they are.

"Get in," Listor says from the back seat.

Hatch looks around once and slides in. The door slams and Hatch's ears pop. Listor hits a button on the console under his elbow and blue flames jet out of the blowers on either side of the car, driving back the encroaching wall of street freaks blocking the street.

"South African anti-carjack technology," Listor says. "Right after Apartheid got repealed, the richest Afrikaaners were rightfully terrified of a race war." He offers Hatch a drink from the bar, which he declines in favor of some brand-name mineral water.

"Who are we going to see?" he asks, peeling foil off the neck of a bottle.

"Someone we can help," Listor says airily, "who can help us. But we have more important things to discuss. I am most trusting, but our host is not. So I can't take so much on trust, anymore, if I'm going to be a champion of Soma. Does that make sense?"

"Of course," Hatch says, looking out windows—rather, at the video monitors ingeniously standing in for windows, which would weaken the vehicle in the event of a direct RPG attack. "I still don't like the new name, by the way. Soma is a mythical drug, but it's not a transformative one. I get that it's a white whale for ethnobotanists. Everybody's got a pet theory about what this magical tonic was, but it's just that. McKenna thought it was *cubensis*, but McKenna thought everything was mushrooms. If it was a mushroom, it was fly agaric, which, take it from me, is a big let-down. It could be ephedra or harmala or hemp, or just strong beer, for all we know, but the connotation I get is from *Brave New World*, where it's an antidepressant pacifier, and that's not what we're about. . . are we?"

They cruise through the streets in second gear, the crowd parting for them as schools of baitfish yield to a shark. Listor's fingers idly dance over the anti-personnel menu as Hatch struggles for the right words. "The Aztecs called their visionary mushrooms *teonanacatl*, or 'God's flesh.' That's the kind of name that anyone can understand."

Listor smirks. "The Mazatec Indians call their mushroom sacrament something that translates to 'the god out of the manure.' Maybe that would be more appropriate, particularly if it comes from Mexico. . . ? What do the natives call the Secret Teacher, in their own tongue?"

Hatch doesn't like where this is going. "Point taken."

"In the Rig Veda, Soma confers immortality and lifts the fog of the mortal mind, and Soma is also a god. It spoke to me, Nolan. It told me many things. Although I am quite convinced it is God's magic bullet for elevating the species, I still have no idea what it is, let alone where it came from."

"Never mind where it came from," Hatch says. "It's a fungal-derived tryptamine like no other. You know more than me about that stuff. And you know it works."

"Because you dosed me," Listor says, amused at his own amusement over something that would've made him homicidal last week.

"It was a risk I had to take. Honestly, I was looking for a way to get it in your eye."

"That would've been interesting," Listor says. "Optic conduction is instantaneous, but so is my vengeance."

"Hendrix used to strap whole blotters of top-grade Owsley acid to his forehead under his headband, so the LSD dripped into his eyes, as he played. And he turned out alright. . ."

Listor chuckles. Kids on the street scream, "*Malverde! Malverde!*" Listor rolls down the window and throws them handfuls of joints and foil envelopes. "Where are these magical mushroom people of yours?"

"I can't tell you. They're the world's happiest people in one of the world's worst places, and I don't want to see them become another tourist destination for burnouts."

"But they gave you their blessing to pass out their sacrament as a street drug?"

"They respected what my vision told me."

"And it told you to save western civilization with it."

Hatch nods.

"Even so," the Green Man says. "They take this sacrament only once?"

"Once for their initiation into adulthood. They take it, and they're whisked right out of their bodies to meet their god, their spirit animal, their ancestor, it varies, but in most cases, it takes them around the world and lets them *be* the whole world, live other lives, be other people. Not some fuzzy oxytocin purge that makes you think you've touched the infinite, but a plugging into the collective soul, a mass telepathic overload. And then the avatar shows them, or just tells them, what their place in the world is, and how to be happy in it. And they are, man. They love their lives like none of us who have everything ever will."

"And they never take it again?" Listor squints.

"Some regularly partake in much smaller doses in an agave drink. They say it affects their dreams, lets them lead other lives every night, but most of them say they don't need it to get back there. The shamans, who naturally take much heavier doses, say they can read minds, go anywhere in their dreams, see the future, shit like that. So it does have return potential, if that's what you're worried about."

"Mr. Hatch, perhaps the only reason you are still alive today, is that you have not troubled me about money. But not even I would get into selling a drug everyone only takes once."

"I don't want to see it become just another pacifier," Hatch says. "Ecstasy was supposed to bootstrap club kids into being empathic superhumans, and instead, they just got strung out and died because they couldn't afford bottled water at raves. DMT was supposed to usher in a new age of spirituality, but I've been on the *yage* tourism circuit, and watching some shamans peddle their visionary sacrament to empty white people seeking another merit badge on their new age seeker sash, even as the rainforest gets bulldozed down around them. It's the saddest fucking scene on Earth.

"The problem is that the first contact is miraculous. But when you take the ride too many times, the divine lightshows become entoptic phosphenes and free-associated memory artifacts, and the feeling of being touched by god is just your brain getting stirred up with a stick."

"You're getting off the subject," Listor says. "Who the fuck are *you*?"

"What?"

"Yes, and why should I trust you?"

Hatch looks out the window-monitors as Listor stabs the flamethrowers. "I'm just a guy, okay? I'm not a master chemist like you, or a shaman. I'm just a guy who took a drug once and had a revelation. I thought if everybody could feel like this, just once, like connected to everyone else and just really, really happy, maybe the world would be less fucked than it is." Hatch throws up his hands. "Stupid, right?"

Listor shrugs. "Go on."

"And I got into the business, throwing underground parties and bankrolling labs, but I wasn't trying to get laid or rich. I wanted to touch people and help them break out of their bullshit."

"Ah, but the world loves its bullshit, and it doesn't need one more white man trying to wake them up into his dream."

"Hey, I'm not—"

"You want to set the people free, not so?"

"Well, yeah. . . I'm not ashamed to say I'm talking about a revolution."

"Ah, but you should be. 'Revolutionary' is a t-shirt you can buy at Hot Topic. Revolutions only go in circles, no? To be a true revolutionary, you must do something there isn't even a name for yet, that'll be illegal because you did it. Then you've earned the shirt."

"I didn't just drop a couple tabs one day, and disappear up my own ass, man. I believed what I read in books like yours, but I went out and found it. I believe in what I felt.

"Yeah, I went to Peru to try *yage*, and I've been to Goa, Katmandu and Marrakech, too. But I went off the seeker maps. I joined a couple monasteries. More than a couple cults. I went to Ghana and took iboga with a psychotic witch-doctor who told me he'd poisoned my dose while I was puking my way to the peak, and he wouldn't give me the antidote unless I signed all my travelers' checks over to him. I almost gave up hope, but then I found this thing at the end of the road, and I can't help but believe that it was put in my hands for a purpose, that everything that went wrong before, was all to prepare me not to fuck this up."

Listor nodded solemnly. "So you still believe in the lighthouse keeper at the end of the tunnel, or do you even look that deeply into it?" He shakes his head and raises a warning hand before Hatch can retort. "I'm not asking you to defend your life to me. But when people take this drug of yours, who do you expect will greet them and transform their lives?"

"I think it's. . . Listen, I could bore you with the whole Jungian collective unconsciousness thing, I could try to bamboozle you by saying it's the cosmic oversoul, and getting everyone to take it will immanentize the awakening of the universe itself as a single conscious neural network. Lord knows I've bought into that shit myself long enough.

"But we've both had that kind of childish nonsense beaten out of us by bitter experience, haven't we? You're not down here because it sounded like a nice place to retire. I don't believe in the god the people who gave me this fucking mushroom worship, but I believe that it alters their brains in a fundamental way, and I believe they tap into a pool of wisdom deeper than themselves. They know things about the outside world that they shouldn't. They know how it all fits together.

"Chemically speaking, we don't know yet. At the very least, it stimulates a massive endogenous release of DMT.

The brain pretty much only releases DMT when you're near death, to prepare your mind for the end. People who've come back from the edge think they saw Heaven and Hell . . .

"Now I don't know what I believe anymore, but this. . . Whether it's your own brain, or the godhead, that touches you, it works. It made a believer out of me. If you go to a medium and she tells you wisdom that solves all your problems, and then you go back and find out the crystal ball is a slide projector, maybe she's a fake, but does that mean she was wrong?"

Listor sits there long enough for Hatch to wonder if he's having a flashback. Just as he's about to touch him, the Green Man says. "It told you to bring the Secret Teacher to the people. To dish it out and let it change the world."

"I never said that. Tim Leary told everyone to just snap out of the Madison Avenue trip and become a demigod by dropping acid, and look how that turned out. Shulgin was afraid to make the same mistake with Ecstasy, and it went wrong anyway.

"Look, I recognize the trap—a drug can't bring about a new spiritual awakening all by itself. It needs shamans to guide the process, but the shamans won't emerge until the awakening is imminent. That's why I came looking for you. I need a consciousness wizard to prepare the people. What we're offering them isn't just another drug. It's revolution by revelation."

"You know," the Green Man shakes his head, "you have a lot to learn. I wish I had the time to teach you. . ."

"You know," Hatch says, figuring they must be cruising in circles, "I've read your books, and what I know gives me less reason to trust you than you have, to trust me. When you were inventing new drugs for the underground scene with your left hand, you were cooperating with the DEA with your right. Maybe the reason you're the biggest drug lord down here isn't because everybody loves you."

For a moment, Solomon Listor tenses up like the paranoid criminal he is, but then he laughs at Hatch, at himself. "Providing vital drug interaction data to the DEA was my way of trying to offset harm caused by irresponsible children playing with my toys, Mr. Hatch. I don't suppose you're just indulging a childish whim any more than I am. You must've hurt nearly as many people as I have, to bear such a big cross so long and so far. But I'll tell you this.

"I am not the shaman you need, but neither am I the man you came to meet. Your drug shook me, alright. I was looking at the back of you and the room went dark, and I saw the Eyes."

Hatch has to physically conceal his excitement.

Listor nods and lights a joint the size of a cigar. "Yasss!" he coughs. "I saw the stars become a curtain of eyes and lo, when the curtain parted. . ." He chuckles. "But you know what happens next."

Hatch nods and accepts the joint, tries in vain to take a judicious hit off it. "You become one with everyone. . ." He coughs and looks for his soul in the smoke. All his thoughts are stunningly packaged purple presents he can't figure out how to unwrap.

"Yes." Listor takes the joint and hits it mistrustfully. It's not working for him. "It was a jarring experience for me, and it forced me to accept that I, too, once thought I was going to change the world with my toys. I once wanted to help people, but I let the evil little men help me build a wall around myself, and I just started using them like everyone else." Listor takes his hand in an oddly unthreatening gesture, looks into his eyes in what Hatch won't realize until much later was a challenge, and one he failed. "The only reason I trust you," he says, "is because the drug told me to."

The limousine stops and the door opens and Hatch's ears pop again. Getting out of a limousine, you expect either flashbulbs and red carpets, or curses and flying garbage, and their emergence provokes both. Guards provide a phalanx of plastic riot shields for them to disembark.

Listor starts to climb out, but then seizes Hatch by the sleeve and pulls him close. "To answer your question as plainly as you answered mine. . . This is what you need to know about the person we are going to visit. Whatever else you may think you know about him, forget it and know this. For all his power, he would give up everything to be anyone else. If you think your revolution will be bloodless, you're as stupid as you are insane. We're not going to need shamans. We'll need soldiers."

Listor climbs out and Hatch follows him through a maze of bollards, tank-traps and parked armored personnel carriers, walking under interlaced shields thrumming with bouncing rocks and bottles dropped from windows, across a trash-strewn courtyard and into a dingy but vibrant cargo-container superbloque on Sendero Luminoso in the Yellow Zone. They must have circled the block for a while, as Listor grilled him.

Colonia Zapata looks like all the others, but for its color. From top to bottom it's every shade of pink. A work crew sandblasts graffiti tags off the foundations, but they're not the usual cryptic names and numbers. Instead, it's a panorama of the most repulsive homophobic slurs he's ever seen. But most of it is, if anything, celebratory: LUX ET VOLUPTAS; VIVA AMOR FOU; TIERRA Y LIBERTAD; LA NATURALEZA NO TIENE LEYES, SOLO HABITOS, LA TODA MADRE, LA REINA DEL CULO; NEVER WORK NEVER DIE.

Sonofabitch, Hatch thinks. *Ontological anarchists in the house. Chaos never died. . .*

They invade the demilitarized zone of the lobby and go through a bolted door guarded by three guys with automatic shotguns and suicide grenades on their flak jackets. Into a solid-state express elevator like you'd see in any decent hotel. Twenty floors and out onto the roof.

Hatch didn't expect a penthouse, but when they step out onto a guano-strewn rooftop just like Jaime's shithole building, he wonders for the first time if this isn't a trap. Stupid not to see it coming. . .

A maze of cages covers half the roof, filled with pigeons and chickens. A sniper and spotter are posted at each corner, scanning the other towers with binoculars.

The guards lead them to the middle of the roof and subject Hatch to a thorough pat-down, wave a metal detector over him and strap him into a harness. Hatch asks Listor what the fuck is going on. He smiles and points up.

Hatch looks up, says, "Holy shit."

Another building hangs down from the ceiling of the cavern like a black glass stalactite that's like an inverted photonegative of Sleeping Beauty's Castle. Four stories of modular cubes without any visible doors or windows. The rope they're harnessing him to stretches up to a tiny rectangle of deeper darkness in the underbelly of the lowermost module.

A rank wind from the rooftop exhaust fans stirs the fifty-foot gap between the pink tower and its upside-down neighbor. The guards stand by until a falcon comes spiraling down from the building above to land on a guard's gauntleted arm. He takes something off its leg and reads it, then signals the others.

Hatch is yanked off his feet.

He soars off the rooftop, watching the pink tower shrink down among its neighbors as the inverted black fortress looms overhead, sees an alarming stream of tracers crisscross the space above and below him—holy shit, someone's shooting at him—but before he can curl into a ball, his ride jerks to a halt in a room lit only by red, with four very serious men in matching lavender three-piece suits, all pointing shotguns at him.

"Hi, everybody," he says. Raises his hands. A guard comes over and unlaces the harness while another waves a wand over him to detect any metal he might have picked up in transit. "My friend is right behind me. . ."

Nobody lowers their guns. A short, dapper man in a lavender suit and black shirt with a wide white tie slips in front of the wall of guns and clasps Hatch's hand in both of his in a warm, pleasantly fragranced grip.

"He won't be coming up," says the man in a velvet voice spiced with a Carib accent, smiling as if nobody's ever pointed a gun at anybody, anywhere. "I am Lalo. Welcome to our house."

In spite of himself, Hatch is suddenly comfortable. Lalo is so guilelessly sweet, so eager to please, that he finds himself at ease for the first time since he came down here.

The red light goes out and full-spectrum track lighting comes up, illuminating an armory and loading area. The guards follow Hatch and Lalo into a gym with weights, cycles, treadmills, a whirlpool bath and, Hatch notes approvingly, a sensory deprivation tank. Beyond a floor-to-ceiling glass wall is a swimming pool and hydroponic garden.

Lalo leads Hatch up a spiral staircase into a big empty room with a floor-to-ceiling mirror, pale wood floors and a bar running down one wall.

"What a lovely home," Hatch says.

Lalo stops and looks at him with an expression so wounded, Hatch expects a bruise to swell up that angelic face. "It has to be," he says. "He has not left here in nearly five years."

Lalo turns and crosses the ballet studio to climb another spiral staircase. They emerge into a sleek modern lounge with a bar, a DJ booth, a dancefloor with strobes and swiveling intelli-beams, molded conversation pits and a decent gallery's worth of modern prints and statuary, including a Lachaise nude, a Giacometti Walking Man, a chrome Giger crucifix and a Survival Research Laboratories animated roadkill mobile of a headless hawk endlessly menacing a frantically scrambling taxidermy rabbit.

Crouched atop the walk-in bassbins, a balding dormouse with antique ear-goggles spins sleepy, percussive *banda* squiggles over Stan Getz and Charlie Byrd's "Bahia."

Hatch hasn't spent all that much time around Mexican drug lords, but he's soaked up enough narco culture to know one thing they generally aren't, is all that tasteful. As ridiculously ostentatious as the upside-down castle is, the color scheme and décor are restrained and totally devoid of the obligatory macho aggression and conquest. On the walls are a couple recognizable Ernst, Dali and Miro prints, but also some wheat-paste posters by Eyesore, an outlaw street artist who disappeared right around the time all his contemporaries went commercial.

Where the Obey Giant guy sold out to design sneakers and Mountain Dew campaigns, Eyesore used his agitprop notoriety like a knife to the corporate throat. Slapped propaganda posters on Shell stations up and down the west coast recruiting mercenaries to defend the Dutch multinational's ruinous oil extraction in Nigeria against the dying peasantry and environmental activists. When hundreds of stone killers answered the call, Shell magnanimously declined to prosecute the unidentified artist, but his work abruptly disappeared. Some said Shell had him silenced. Some said he changed his name and was designing Nike ads. Those who knew the truth said nothing at all.

•

LOS POISON BOYS, say the posters, in revolutionary type framing the repurposed image of Che Guevara in drag.

The small crowd laughing and dancing are all young, well-groomed, exceptionally fit Latino men and a few women—all of whom, upon closer scrutiny, prove to be drag queens. They're all dressed in Felliniesque parodies of evening wear, asymmetrical silk suits with Jacobite collars and high-heeled pilgrim shoes. They drink martinis and laugh at each other's vamping. Nobody fires gold-plated automatics into the ceiling, nobody snorts coke off the tits of an unconscious hooker. No macho peasant rituals, no self-destructive Scarface excess.

It pinches Hatch to get his head around this place so that he doesn't answer when Lalo offers him a drink. He takes the frosty glass of passion fruit juice and sips it as Lalo explains, "This will raise your blood sugar, and the spirulina and acetylcholine will improve your cognition. It also improves the viscosity and sweetness of your semen."

"Terrific." Hatch looks around again, wondering who he is going to meet and what he's supposed to say.

Lalo touches his arm. "We just got the Fall couture lines from Paris Fashion Week in, so we were going to put on a little show, but he's not in the mood. If you feel under-dressed, I'm sure we can find you something nice from the Yves Saint-Laurent collection."

"Um," Hatch says.

Lalo leans in close as the music grows louder, a furious tribal drum number. "I'm not supposed to say anything, but I hate misunderstandings. He doesn't communicate his feelings well, and I recognize that you have no idea what you're walking into. You seem like a good person, motivated by love."

"I really appreciate your candor, Lalo." Hatch takes a big sip of the juice, feeling his brain finally lifted up off the floor of his skull by the influx of divine fluid.

Lalo snaps his fingers and a servant brings another glass of passion fruit juice, then sets a silver silken Hermes handkerchief on Hatch's knee.

"What's this for?"

"For tears." Lalo purses his lips in reproof. "If you're any kind of human being," he says, "you will need it."

•

In Mexico, his name is a curse.

La Toda Madre, they call him, after the common Mexican expression. "A total mother." And well might they curse him, for he broke the drug cartels' business as the overwhelming might of the United States with its righteous War on Drugs never could.

But he never wanted to be what he is.

His father, Hector Obregon Aldrete, was a simple man. He grew heroin poppies and *coleitas* on his farms around Tamaulipas and controlled the border traffic into East Texas, Louisiana, Mississippi and Florida with the plainspoken sense of a humble peasant, building the Gulf Cartel like any prosperous business to hand down to his sons, Juan Maria and Rudolfo, and to protect his shy, homely daughter, Ursula. When Mexico became a criminal superpower in the '80s, he amiably ferried the Colombians' cocaine and respected his neighbors' territories without ugly disputes, while the Sinaloa and Pacific Cartels turned Juarez into a war zone.

But his boys, born into feudal privilege and schooled in theatrical cruelty, could only see the future in expansion. In seeking to make a bigger name for themselves, they came to be known as *el Perro* and *el Puerco*, respectively.

Starting a war in Matamoros, the Gulf Cartel faced a federal government and military wholly co-opted by their enemies in Sinaloa. But the Obregons had their own pet insiders. Los Zeros, an elite paramilitary death squad in crimson skull luchador masks. While the few honest cops left lived in constant terror, Los Zeros donned masks to protect their homes and loved ones from cartel reprisals, and if they ultimately did nothing to stem the tide of drugs, they were brilliantly marketed. You could buy Los Zeros action figures, piñatas and piggy-banks while waiting in line at the border.

Far from merely taking a cut to turn a blind eye to Gulf business, the Zeros terrorized the families of rival gangs and other corrupt cops, kidnapping, torturing and murdering whole families on the Sinaloa payroll. And they did so with total impunity, for their membership reached to the highest levels of the Judiciary Police, still known as the Judases, despite a slew of official rechristenings.

When their excesses provoked even *the Pig* and *the Dog* to try to rein them in, the Zeros realized they'd fronted for drug dealers long enough, and decided to take the whole operation.

Don Hector, oblivious in retirement, was assassinated at his rancho when his prize stallion stepped on a landmine on Christmas Day. Juan and Rodolfo vanished on New Year's Eve. A week later, the devastated Obregon household received a late Christmas present: a case of canned dog food from a plant in Matamoros owned by the Gulf Cartel as a smuggling front. The contents proved to be human remains.

Ursula Obregon Uribe never wanted to take part in the family business, any more than she wanted to marry. As a drug lord's unattractive daughter, she could have faded into a cloistered spinster princess lifestyle without being missed. Not even the Zeros figured her for a strategic target. When she took over the family operations, it was not for honor or revenge, it was for love. Love for her father, and even for her terrible brothers. The cartel would expend itself in ending its enemies, and then she wanted to disappear.

Overnight, the war changed. Ursula broke the rules. She unmasked Los Zeros. Zero-Uno was the second-in-command of Mexico's national police force, with an office inside Los Pinos. These roving gangs of masked killers who exterminated whole families and turned children into dog food served at the pleasure of the President.

Names had been named before and the lurid but toothless Mexican press had successfully ignored them, but Ursula made it stick. Secret Swiss and Caymans accounts, exhaustive records of bribes, even the cash itself—irradiated and marked with disappearing ink that displayed the names of the Zeros hierarchy under a blacklight—rendered the Zeros too toxic for even the bought-and-paid-for Mexican system to swallow. Cast out of their official positions, losing border territory every day to opportunistic Sinaloa, Los Zeros became a death cult, sworn to wipe out every last trace of the one they called La Toda Madre, who had her own problems.

For all narco culture's toxic macho swagger, more than a few ladies have made their marks as players, and women running gangs is not unheard of. The Gulf operation was prepared to serve a shy, soft-spoken woman, so long as she showed the nerve and ruthless cruelty of an Obregon, but they weren't prepared to comprehend, let alone swear fealty to, what she was becoming.

Some figured she was just trying to fit in when she showed up at the Panama City peace summit in a black cowboy hat and garish shirt, new Levi's and snakeskin boots with rattler heads on the toes and a rodeo champion's belt-buckle. She was clowning them, the Laredo *chuntaras* all thought, but the truth was impossible for them to grasp.

Ursula had lived her life in the smothering shadow of her family. Now she was forced out into the open and burdened with power, she would no longer refuse to hide what she really was.

And what she was, was a man inside a woman's body. And a gay man, to boot.

It was not so unprecedented that Ursula Obregon would undergo surgery to become a man. Lalo nods at a fabulous portrait on the wall above Hatch. In the Latin surrealist style of Frida Kahlo, a dusky woman with a peyote button-halo stands erect in ecstasy, bisected down the bridge of her nose and splitting open like a cocoon so a mustachioed bandit can emerge, while her colorful peasant skirt is hiked up so a kneeling white Devil can kiss her ass.

Even Hatch has heard the legend of San Antonia, an outlaw patron saint like Jesus Malverde and Judas Tadeo, of the Sierra Madre narcos. Antonia DeSoto, the mulatta slave who used sorcery to escape Durango in 1685 with her Tepehuán lover, hide in the Sierra Madre and seek deliverance in peyote.

In a drug-vision, Satan appeared to her as a handsome *guero* and promised her power in return for her soul. When she came down, she found he'd kept his bargain by turning her into a man. Working as a vaquero and mule skinner, she soon turned to banditry and proved as cunning and vicious as any man or devil.

In Mexico, such bizarre legends are almost commonplace. But a flesh-and-blood trans male narco who slept with other men was unthinkable. Narcos are as conservative as the Taliban, when it comes to sodomy and shoe-shopping.

The Gulf Cartel quietly opted to realign themselves with Los Zeros, such as they were, rather than support Ursula, who now answered to Hector Obregon II.

Hector was prepared for the defections and betrayals when he returned from surgery and had already brought in a new wave of replacement gangsters, an underground within narco culture that dared not speak its name. Criminally ingenious, ruthless thugs cursed with insufficient testosterone to fit the hoary macho image, but ferocious in their elegant efficiency, and fanatically loyal to those who accepted them. This cost him every last bit of his family's old gang, but it gave him a truer, stronger family than he ever had before.

"Los Venenos. The Poison Boys." Lalo waves lovingly at the troupe of fashion-plates tucking into a buffet platter of caviar, salmon and calamari.

Los Poison Boys didn't hang castrated bodies from overpasses with crude manifestos around their necks, and they didn't make anyone into dog food. Nothing so vulgar. But one by one and in carloads, the traitors in the Gulf Cartel and seven of the top ten Zeros were tastefully but irrevocably vanished off the face of the earth.

Hector sought asylum from the United States government, hoping to take down the family's surviving enemies by cooperating with el Norte, but the Americans couldn't guarantee his safety and needed Hector around their necks like they needed another 9/11, so he allowed himself to be stashed down here. It was good for about a year, and then Los Zeros showed up. They took over a big piece of the Yellow Zone and tried to leverage their power to get Hector, but the stalemate has dragged on for nearly seven years. Hector refuses to leave or take any initiative in eliminating Tres Ojos, Zero-Three, the acting commander of the masked army. Three-Eyes, so named for the scar from a Poison Boy's bullet that failed to penetrate his forehead, has not proved so forgiving.

"I admire your bravery," Hatch says. "Just being who you are in such a culture, must be like having a target on your back."

"This is how we are different," Lalo says. "We are reviled in Mexico, it is true, but never with the violence in America. Nobody kills a *joto* for offering him a good time. It may surprise you to learn that many, if not most, narcos are secret bisexuals, and always bottoms. When death stalks you, when one must always put one's macho on the line, it is the sweetest relief to surrender, however briefly, and be taken. He will not speak of it, so we must be disavowed, but a Mexican man knows that he cannot kill his own shadow, and that to be whole, a man must sometimes get drunk with his shadow, and fuck it."

Setting his drink down, Hatch tactfully asks, "What kind of operation do you run, down here?"

"We're smaller now, but we're righteous. We still run the lottery as a fair redistribution of wealth and approved contract killings in the interest of justice, and we smuggle and trade in contraband, but no drugs. The cash crops here are unprocessed food, non-experimental medicines, firearms and contact with the outside. Cigarettes—they play nasty tricks on smokers, if you get them from the machines. Make the filters out of recycled diapers, all kinds of disgusting additives. You don't smoke, do you?"

"Oh no," Hatch says, dabbing a corner of his eye.

"That's good. He loathes smokers." Lalo looks at his phone, then at a big double door across the room, above which a light is blinking. "He's ready for you now."

Lalo rises and takes Hatch's drink, crosses the room to the doors and opens them. A grim but exquisitely dressed sentry stands aside for Hatch to enter a small, dim room open to the outside air.

Hector Obregon Uribe, La Toda Madre, stands alone at the rail of the balcony, looking out over the subterranean city. Dressed in a long white robe, white leather opera gloves and a knightly silver headdress with eyeless Art Deco masks on three sides, long austere faces no less inscrutable than the fourth one that turns to regard him. He's a head shorter than Hatch and the dazzling robe barely hides the stubby legs, long, mismatched torso, or the throbbing musculature of an obsessively sculpted body.

Hector stands motionless for a long moment as Hatch tries to figure out the protocol for addressing him, when a falcon swoops screaming out of the perpetual night to alight on the peak of Hector's headdress. As Hector continues to stare, the falcon busily grinds its pelvis against the hat, chirping lustily. Finally, Hatch asks, "Is it doing what I think it's doing?"

Hector's eyes roll, whether in disappointment or to regard the rutting bird of prey, none can tell. "The unblooded bird returns home excited. The headdress is designed to collect his semen. For breeding, but also for bonding. I am much more than a master to him." When the falcon settles down, Hector reaches up to take the bird on his gauntleted wrist. Still looking into the bird's reptilian eyes, he says, "Solomon says you have something that might cure me."

Hatch nods. "Do you believe you're sick?" Somehow, this doesn't feel like the right place for the full pitch.

"I have always been wrong. Wrong sex, wrong gender, wrong family, wrong race. Down here, it has cost me everything I own to keep just a bubble, where I may be what I am. I would like to know how it feels to walk in the sun, to be *right*."

Hatch holds out the microdot. The sentry comes up and takes it, claps it in a clear plastic case and steps back. "I guarantee we can help with the second part."

"You 'guarantee' that you 'can help,' do you?" Hector laughs and waves his arm. The falcon leaps off with a terrifying shriek that makes Hatch cover his throat, dives out of sight. "This thing you bring me, Solomon says I will want to give it to the people, that it will make them happy and wise. Do you guarantee that, too?"

"Señor Obregon, I wouldn't be here if I didn't believe in it. The wildest shit Listor told you, it's all true. He took it."

"I know he believes. He thinks I should support this campaign of yours, even though it will mean going back into the drug trade."

"This is not like any other kind of drug. It's. . . much more than that."

"Of course it is. It will make other drugs obsolete, it will erase cocaine, he says. Rival gangs would come after me if I stepped back into their territory. But if this drug of yours killed their business. . ."

"They would really, really hate you, Hector. Like they hated San Antonia, back in the day. . ."

La Toda Madre smirks, but nods and lets the idea run away with him. "I don't want war," he says, shaking his head.

"Here's the thing, man. I want a world where everybody is loved and respected, where everyone goes to sleep at night happy. This thing is transformational. . . God, I sound like a fucking hippie. . .

"The people who grow these mushrooms and use them as a sacrament, a rite of passage. They used to be one of the most bloodthirsty, warlike bands of motherfuckers ever to take a scalp. But then they found this, and they just. . . stopped. They said it hurt the killer more than the victim, to take a life.

"They live in high mountain country, and they're invisible. They cloud the minds of anyone who spots them, send evil dreams to their neighbors, so no one knows they exist, and no one who sees them ever remembers.

"Sure, voodoo bullshit. But there was this Christian missionary in the village where this stuff comes from. You know, big evangelical blowhard. Can't dig a well or build a lean-to, but Jesus this, and Jesus that, and Jesus all fucking day long.

"And he won't stop dragging the villagers for taking this drug as a sacrament for their initiation. It's wrong, it invites devils in, the kids get possessed, you never heard such bullshit. The villagers were patient, this guy brought second-hand clothes and the bibles were pretty useful for rolling papers, but they were good and sick of him disrespecting their core beliefs.

"So they dosed him.

"Gave him a good whopping fingerful of the stuff I gave you, in a stew. He kicked right out of his body, the shock was so bad. It gets scary when they resist, when they're holding onto their fear.

"Because that's what it does, Hector. It's not just a fuzzy, warm feeling and some hallucinations. They're prescient. They get into your head, get you where you live, and they work your shit out. If you need to talk to God, you will fucking talk to God. If you need a full-on psychedelic apocalypse to straighten your shit out, you will see fire and brimstone. If you're a poor, closeted guy trapped in a web of lies, it cometh like a thief in the night, and taketh away all cares.

"That missionary came out of it a changed man. He met Jesus, and they fucked, and it was terrific. Jesus told him he didn't need to hate or hide what he was, because he was made in his creator's image. And there were as many ways to salvation as there are images of Jesus in this world. Nobody who feels truly loved and secure in their faith really has to prove anything to anybody, except by loving example.

"He stayed with them and took a new name, because they liked him as a homosexual a lot more than as an evangelical missionary. But that's not my point. My point is, he was truly happy, not just the day after, but forever after. He didn't have to go back to America because he went there in his dreams and no skinheads jumped him, nobody told him he couldn't get married, nobody protested his loved ones' funerals.

"It saved him, Hector. I don't care if you want to distribute it down here. I want to use it to change the world, to help people be happy with who and what they are. I guess Solomon just thought it might help you, too."

For a long moment, Hector just stands there, and Hatch wonders if he didn't go too far. "I may help you. My father taught me that to stay alive, one must always search for games where one might still lose." Hector looks away, but the moth-browed masks facing him quiver slightly as he says, "You may go now."

He throws out his arm and the falcon swoops in to pounce on it, cleaning bloody gray feathers off its claws.

Hatch bows and races the sentry to the doors.

Lalo beams at him as he leads Hatch back to the party. "That went better than it could have." He looks at his phone. "Your friend is really pissed off downstairs."

"Do I have to leave right now?"

"I certainly hope not," Lalo beams and hands him a champagne flute. "But we'll have to do something about your suit."

12

He drove a Cadillac convertible the size of a PT boat, with a heat-reactive chameleon paint job that gave a completely different color from every angle, so the hood and trunk were iridescent emerald, the fairings purple and the roof a deep, molten gold, and then he'd turn a corner and all the colors would change.

He cruised a residential suburb with rambling split-level ranch homes that went on forever, he never saw a business of any kind, not so much as a stoplight. Just those endless rows of dreamy homes with, if anything, a single car in the driveway. Little runabout sedans, minivans, conversions, frivolous cars.

All the men were away at work, or war, or something, but they weren't expected back any time soon. He could read that in the eyes of every woman who answered the door when he knocked. Each one a looker, guileless, wholesome blondes, stunning redheads, and raven-haired, green-eyed temptresses, beckoning him in, marveling at his muscles as he lugged in his sample case.

He was a salesman, and they were all buying, even though he didn't quite know what the fuck he was selling. They always invited him in and offered him a drink and a lunch and sat eagerly eating up his nonsensical pitch and a demonstration so dull he could barely keep awake through it, but as soon as they could get a word in edgewise, they were leading him to the bedroom or just swiping his samples off the breakfast bar and offering themselves to him like willing virgins on an altar, and like any god offered such delectable sacrifices, he generously made it rain.

He woke up to breakfast in bed and another quickie if he was in the mood, and then he took a hot shower or a swim in the obligatory pool, packed up and got into his car of many colors and cruised the infinite suburb until another house struck his fancy, and the wife was always in, and he was always welcome to stay as long as he liked, but he kept moving, because there were always more houses. He stopped counting somewhere after seventy, and he was beginning to think it could go on like this forever and to hate himself for getting bored, when the wife of the moment, a sloe-eyed, ash-blond ingénue—with hips like sculpted ice cream that he remembered so well from a *Playboy* centerfold in his father's contraband collection, she had a staple in her navel—asked him if he was tired of dreaming, if he wanted to wake up. And without thinking about it, he said he did.

He had come to hate the traveling salesman dream as soon as he recognized it as such, as a more persuasive evolution of the wet dreams and greedy fantasies of the promise of America that he'd indulged in, all his life.

But this wasn't the voice that offered him waffles or a club sandwich or a blowjob and the TV remote. This voice had the silken vocal cords of a girl-next-door who was turned on by satin sheets, surprise candlelight dinners and lovemaking in the rain with Fleetwood Mac on the hi-fi, but underneath was something older than the ocean and wiser than time.

"You can stay in your dream for as long as you like," she said. "You can even forget it is a dream, return here every night for the rest of a life you will think of as happy. . ."

He took another bite of the fruit-slathered pancakes in front of him, the whipped cream melting around a perfectly tart strawberry. He idly touched his half-erect cock as he watched a perfect pillow of milky breast peek at him from the drooping gap in her velour bathrobe. It all felt real enough, but he could sense the weight of the unspoken *or* like an anvil overhead.

"Or?" he asked.

"Or you can face what you fear, and truly set yourself free."

He'd never tasted a strawberry, he'd only seen pictures of this absurd American child's breakfast in smuggled newspapers. Rooty Tooty Fresh 'N Fruity Breakfast from International House of Pancakes, which, in spite of its grandiose name, never saw fit to open an embassy in Cuba.

Free of what? Free of this place? Of his many addictions? Free of his fear?

"I want to be free," he said.

She smiled. "Aren't you already free?"

"This isn't real. . . It's the same thing over and over."

"Life isn't the same thing over and over?"

"You know what I mean. . ." He stops dead and drops the fork when he looks into her colorless eyes.

The house, the suburb, the breakfast all go away. They're sitting together on the raft, under a merciless sun. He shivers and then begins to scream as his brine-encrusted, blistered skin starts to crack and bleed, and he begs to go back, he doesn't want to be free, but the louder he pleads, the harder she laughs.

She isn't his ash-blond playmate anymore, she is the sun and the sea and the huge, callused hand around his neck holding him out over the guy-ropes, offering him to the sharks circling the raft, and asking him what he will do first, when they get to America.

·

Jaime's father always told him that Americans didn't give a shit about each other because they were all in competition for the crumbs from the rich man's table. But they pulled together to share and care for each other, as they never stopped reminding themselves, whenever there was a disaster.

He showed him the pictures of the damage and the shelters during Hurricane Andrew. Jaime was six, and only saw Papi on alternating evenings and weekends, when his mother worked.

Cubans always shared and cared for each other, but not because they were better. It was because they were *always* neck-deep in the shared disaster of their government, that made them seem so heroic by comparison.

His father seemed to hate America, and white people in particular. When he explained the birds and the bees to Jaime, he told him white people don't make babies by fucking, they just pray and pee inside each other.

But one day he collected Jaime from school without telling his mother, took him to where his brother had hidden the raft they'd built. He was told his mother wanted him to go, to have a better life, and Jaime believed him.

Jaime's father and uncle and four younger men who'd paid to come along pushed the raft into a dark lagoon in the middle of the night. Jaime, still in his white school blouse with red neckerchief, rode on the rails made out of PVC pipe at the front of the rectangular raft as it slipped into a darkness deeper than closing your eyes.

The trip was supposed to take only two days, but Papi told everyone as he shared around a jug of rum that they were wasting their strength rowing against the northwest current. They would sleep off their hangovers on the beach in Miami, he said, and even Jaime's uncle believed it, though he begged them to keep rowing and not get drunk. Nobody else could see the sense in wearing themselves out rowing east, when the current was pulling them so swiftly to the north, towards America's magnificent penis, and freedom.

Their journey was blessed, he told them that, too. He had gone to see a *curandero* to know the best time and the date to cross, but one did not need such things. Last month, the crew of a Cuban naval patrol boat mutinied, killed its captain and defected to the United States, claiming political asylum. Castro demanded the return of the crew, pounded the national TV and tabloids with grisly images of the captain's bloated corpse, but the Americans obstinately refused. In retaliation, the wily Castro announced he would no longer enforce Cuba's borders. Anyone who wanted to, was free to go. The military walked the beaches only to brace every emigré and confiscate his or her identification, to insure the state lost only its most disposable citizens, and to play hell with the Americans' attempts to make sense of the waves of refugees swarming their shores.

Good man or bad, all would enter America with a clean slate. His father had been drummed out of the Army and spent time in jail, but he would get a soft job as a salesman going door to door and seducing bored, beautiful housewives, and leave a bastard on every block, from Key West to Washington, DC.

It was a beautiful dream, and they had a better than average chance of making it. Jaime's uncle was a marine engineer, and in an armada that included inner-tubes, plywood packing crates and boogie-boards, his raft was a work of art. A pirate catamaran—twin tubes of liberated drainage pipe, pinched and sealed with tar, supported an eight-foot by sixteen-foot deck surrounded by posts strung with three tiers of elastic clothesline stretched taut by turnbuckles after the fashion of a Mexican wrestling ring, reminding him of Papi's bootleg VHS tapes of masked luchadores. These allowed tidal swells to slash at them without swamping the boat, while a tiller and a shadecloth that doubled as a sail assured them some maneuverability when they set out just after midnight on the first night of Castro's new open border policy. And, his uncle assured him, it was almost impossible to fall out.

They did not hear President Clinton's statement that all Cuban refugees would be sent to Guantanamo and eventually back to Cuba, where they would face eight years in prison. They did not hear that, out of the sixty thousand Cubans already on the water, one in three would drown before they could be arrested.

As near as Jaime could tell, they did not listen to his uncle and rowed all night against the current. Two days passed with no sight of land, and now the current was dragging them to the southwest, and then south, back to Cuba or worse, round and round forever in an empty hell.

Jaime's uncle knew the sea and the currents, but his father had served in the Army, and knew better how to manage men. They argued bitterly until the sun beat them down.

By the end of the first week, it was clear they were trapped in a vast whirlpool from which they could not paddle out with the meager strength they had left. Fresh water was long gone. They'd managed to catch a couple miserable fish. His father demanded an extra share of the catch for his son because of his youth, but when Jaime couldn't eat the fish, he wolfed it down himself, and soon stopped offering it.

He didn't remember when it was that his father woke him and told him his uncle had fallen overboard in the night. All he could think about was the grainy video of two wrestlers, his father and his uncle, leaping like fleas and rebounding off the turnbuckle ropes that enclosed them like gravity, never quite going over the top rope, into the howling void of the shark-infested crowd.

He remembered making a sound like crying. No tears would come. His skin was so badly burnt and glazed with salt crystals that he could smell a barbacoa sweetness beneath the acrid odor of his shipmates, a loathsome slow-grilled aroma that made his mouth water, made him daydream about sinking his teeth into his own flesh.

The water was long gone, but now Papi was undisputed master of the raft, he revealed a still-extant flask of rum. They eagerly drank it, and the potent alcohol went straight through their starving, dehydrated systems to smash their brains. They were all too eager to do whatever he commanded, and he had a plan.

He showed them the boat that trailed behind them on the same hellish circuit, but even from several hundred yards off, you could tell that the handful of people in the little fishing boat were not yet roasted, were still well-fed, still carried in their hearts foolish notions about what mercy could be expected of the sea.

But *they* knew the truth. They had no homeland but this raft. With the food and water from the others, they could regain the strength to paddle out of the whirlpool and escape to America.

"*This is America, now!*" Papi screamed and stamped his foot on the deck. He pointed at the other boat trailing in their wake. "*That* is Cuba! *Those* are not men!"

They dropped the tiller and turned the raft sideways in the current, and the rowboat seemed to fall upon them. Jaime, feverish with hunger, lay on his side, so the ocean was a convex bubble bisecting the world. He scarcely lifted his head off the deck when they came close enough to hear the people in the rowboat, half of them women, singing.

They were singing a refugee song, and a couple of the men on the raft took it up before his father told them to shut the fuck up. They had sharpened the shafts of their paddles into spears, and now they took them up and held them up, uttering a low growl as Papi told them the bitches had stolen all the food and water, and they were going to get it back.

Jaime's father stood up on the starboard turnbuckle, and when the rowboat seemed to slide up on top of them, he leapt off the post at the rowboat. The women never stopped singing, but one of them pointed at his Papi and fired a flare pistol.

The red flare hit him in the face. He landed on his knees in the boat, spitting red phosphorus out through his blackening teeth, turning to wave at his cowardly compatriots to come and take what was theirs. The women shoved him overboard and he sank out of sight in a welter of bubbles and smoke.

The survivors of the raft and the rowboat came to some kind of truce. Jaime remembered they gave him water and a couple stale cookies. He remembered a woman holding him and humming him a lullaby when the Coast Guard cutter came and took them aboard.

He dreamed of America.

He woke up on a cot in a tent, one of nearly four thousand tents housing nearly thirty thousand Cuban refugees in a makeshift camp at Guantanamo Bay, where he stayed for a year.

Then they moved half of them to an exact replica of the refugee camp on an Air Force base in Panama City. They were isolated, drugged, beaten and interrogated. Ostensibly, the goal was to sort the solid citizens from the criminal scum and communist agents, but they didn't seem to care about the answers, once they got them. Everything from the drugs and torture techniques to the psychological games they played with the prisoners, seemed to be in a pure spirit of experiment and play. The military, CIA, and a host of private contractors paraded through their cells like a human petting zoo, refining a secret science with human guinea pigs of no nation, no name, no hope of escape.

As an orphan child, Jaime made for a particularly useful subject. With no secret history to surrender, he was made to memorize baseball statistics and Eminem and Guns N Roses lyrics while tripping balls in a blackout box on experimental governmental hallucinogens. He was deprived of sleep and brutally quizzed on his recall of said lyrics and stats, often with a gun to his head.

Six months later, after the refugees rioted and set fire to the camp, they were sent back to Guantanamo Bay. Nine months after that, they were told they were finally coming to America.

Jaime Blasco, a nine-year old orphan, was already hardened to psychological and physical abuse and wise in the ways of American survival. He had learned to work the system that knew him only by the serial number on his wrist, had learned to escape its blind, arbitrary fist and to pick its open pockets. He had become something harder and colder than any intentional training could create, something that would have chafed and rebelled at a soft job like a door-to-door salesman in the suburbs.

When he found himself alone and at large in Unamerica, it was hardly the traumatic shock for him than for even the hardened inmates of the American prison system who began to trickle in just as he was reaching puberty. It was almost exactly the habitat for which he had been bred in captivity. When they snipped off his RFID bracelet, they had only to download the data stored on it to the new one they implanted in his wrist.

Coming to Unamerica for Jaime Blasco was not like exile or imprisonment, but graduation, and it offered all the freedom he believed he needed. It's not until he recovers from the drug that's dragged him back to a nightmare that used to wake him up screaming half his nights that he began to realize how very, very badly he had been fucked.

•

Hatch comes out of the stairwell wearing a new tailored suit to find Jaime waiting in the hall between him and his door when he sees the weird light in the kid's eyes, and then he remembers what he did right before he left. "So. . . You took it?"

"Did you know?"

Hatch blinks and smiles to buy time. ". . . Sure . . . ?"

"Did? You? Know?"

Hatch says, "Of course I did."

Jaime falls shaking into Hatch's arms.

"It's okay," Hatch tells him over and over. "Now you know, too. . ."

13

"*Deus lo volt.*"

The men in the next room chant. All of them except the man they are skinning, who just screams.

Reverend Litchfield peels the overloaded pest strip out from under his surgical sink basin and folds it, smashes it flat and then nibbles it. When the rice paper and corn syrup begin to melt on his tongue, he bolts the rest of it down before he can savor the taste.

God wills it!

An ingenious invention for solving urban hunger and reclaiming wasted protein, the edible pest strips in Litchfield's sanctum are so infested with roaches, silverfish and less identifiable pests that he sometimes can't fold them without spillage, let alone roll them up as the instructions dictate.

He scorns himself for enjoying the acrid, spoiled cocktail-nut aftertaste of the snack. Not for the first time, he wonders what he would have to do to kill all his sensory nerves. Leprosy would suit him for any number of reasons, but he cannot infect himself, now. He can only pray to be delivered from the sins of the sensual world.

Even now, when the miracles enacted through his hand have become all but commonplace, the sinners are at his door. He can hear them.

God wills it!

The victim is the rival gang leader who took over their territory after he ambushed them. Every time they roar the Latin slogan, Casper Childress, pacing round the bound man sagging from the post they erected in the soup kitchen, flays off another patch of tattooed skin and throws it into the open fire which they revere as an altar.

I have saved them, he thinks. Delivered them from death, healed their wounds. But I have not touched their hearts.

To hear them tell it, they are born again hard, but nothing has changed. Childress has made the chapel his new headquarters and calls his inner circle the Holy Vehm, his revenge on his enemies labeled a crusade. They have not changed, perhaps now are even worse, for they believe nothing they do can be called sin.

And he has done nothing to stop it.

You fear them—

"I don't fear them. I'm just tired. . . I am weak."

You are weak, but they are strong—

"They're strong, but they're wrong. . .!"

Show them. Teach them—

"I can't. . . Choose someone else, I can't do it! I won't. . ."

You will, says the voice like a beartrap biting a rabbit in half. *Teach them to serve you, as you serve me.*

He opened the soup kitchen and he witnessed to the destitute who came in to eat, but he never hoped to save a soul or kindle any flicker of inspiration in their broken, drug-addled brains. It was a part of his penance, of a piece with the hair shirts, fasting and flagellation, to remind himself how lost is this world, how out of touch with grace. He despaired of ever hearing that still, small voice that might grant forgiveness or command some grander gesture of repentance. Now it roars in his ears, commanding him to be, at the end of his long, awful life, a prophet.

Litchfield clings to the bicycle to ascend to a shaky standing position. In the warped steel mirror on the wall, he sees his naked form. His ribs jut out, his limbs slack straps of muscle clinging to bowed bones. Raw red sores from unchecked yeast and staph infections inflame his armpits, groin and torso, making every movement an agonizing ordeal. Liquefied skin suspended in honey-colored crust sloughs away like wet toilet paper from the screaming endodermis. He has not done hating his flesh, but it is not his to punish, anymore. He washes down a couple fistfuls of pills from the wheeled caddy in the surgery and throws on the cleanest smock he can find.

He walks to the door like a man carrying lead weights at the bottom of a lake.

A line of robed judges in pointy scarlet hoods inscribed with runes sit along the back wall, where his pulpit used to stand. A chanting mob packs the soup kitchen, crowding as close as they dare to the open fire-barrel without getting stabbed by the man circling around it.

Stripped to the waist and wearing a bloody black apron, Childress waves a long serrated knife and a pair of steel tongs to exhort the crowd to chant louder.

The accused hangs by chains bolted to the ceiling from steel pins through his forearms, between the radius and ulna bones. His feet barely scrape the blood-slimed tiles, toes absently clawing for purchase to lift the weight off his arms.

"He has confessed it! It has been witnessed and recorded. The accused is a traitor to his brothers, to his race and to almighty God! And his punishment on Earth shall be as in Hell. It is so ordered!"

"Deus lo volt!" the crowd shouts.

"The condemned is entitled to a last meal." Childress, jubilant, scrapes a sizzling shred of fatty smooth muscle off the rim of the fire-barrel and shoves the smoking gobbet into the accused's gaping, toothless mouth.

The hanging man screams around the hot flesh and tries to spit it out, but Childress clamps his jaws shut until he swallows, then slashes his cheeks and plants a long, hard kiss on the struggling man, spitting half his tongue into the fire to the delight of the crowd.

"Stop this!"

Litchfield's voice is a rusty screen door slamming in a tornado, but it sucks all the air out of the room. The crowd studies their feet as if awaiting another miracle. The judges look to Childress, who struts over with a lopsided gait, maybe favoring the side of his abdomen where he was stabbed and shot.

"Preacher, you got no business interrupting the business of this court. We got the word, and we're all grateful. The Lord, he's Number One. We get it. Right, everybody?"

Everybody agrees that the Lord is Number One.

"So why don't you go back in your little chapel before I give you something to pray on."

Litchfield shakes. He pivots on his toe. Starts to leave. The crowd already refocused on the dying man and his tormentor.

He stops.

"You mock his commandments, you threaten his prophet, and you heed not his word. Get the fuck out of God's house, all of you."

Childress shakes his head like he can't believe he still has to do this. How quickly they forget. He comes up close to Litchfield, looming over him. Wiping the knife on his apron. "We'll go, old man. We're going back to my place, now this little bitch is out of the way. And you're coming with us."

"No, you don't understand," Litchfield mumbles. "You were recalled to life to serve Him."

"And I will, just like you serve me. We gonna take his word to the Russians, the wetbacks, the nigs, the goofers, the hadjis, the chinks. Gonna deliver the whole world to him, and you'll help. Heal my brothers when they need it. Bring them back, like you did me."

Litchfield puts his hand on Childress's arm. A begging gesture. "I will serve only Him."

The warlord doesn't even react to it, but the next case before the court dances in his eyes. He shakes off the hand and turns to finish the hanging man, when he grabs his belly and sinks to his knees.

The crowd and the judges start to close in on Litchfield, who stands planted, but before they can touch him, the revelation comes into its full flower, and they fall to their knees in awe.

In the blink of an eye, Casper's gone green and gray with decay, hands and feet bloated black with settled, curdled blood, eyes sunken and shriveled in their gaping sockets, noxious gas and toxic fluids spilling out the unstitched stab-wounds and bullet holes, around the black carcass of his tongue. The stink off him sends the crowd into convulsive vomiting.

If Litchfield had stabbed or shot their leader, they would descend on him and tear him apart with their bare hands. But he only touched him, and Childress isn't just dead. He's the deadest thing they've ever fucking seen.

"Spill his blood upon the ground," Litchfield mutters, reciting half-forgotten doctrine, "and let the smoke thereof ascend up to God."

Some of the judges decide to come for him. He raises a hand and they falter. Before they can rally, the words come.

"Casper Childress died in that surgical chapel two weeks ago, with nine bullets and a shattered knife in his guts, but he rose and walked away, didn't he? You all raped and pillaged with him, didn't you? He almost reclaimed his petty fiefdom, but he strayed from the covenant and the Lord that raised him up has struck him down, as you have seen. His pride has undone him, and what will undo each of you? What is the wound even He cannot heal, that you must hold closed as you step over this miserable sinner?

"He will not lift us to our glory until we first restore Him to His. We must make of this place a garden, a second Eden. Every voice will lift to praise His name, or know the fire."

Litchfield limps over to the fire-barrel and lifts out a brand. He tears a pouch of Everclear out of a once-blind beggar's hands and empties it over the corpse. He drops the glowing brand on the apron and turns to fix them with his incendiary stare until every head is bowed as the fire catches and spreads from fuel to flesh.

"No more drink, no more drugs. No more sin. His work will fill you with such joy, that you will never miss them. You will spread His word like a purifying fire, or you will surely feed it. Amen, and fuck you all."

He is back in his chapel with the door bolted when the crowd begins to sing "This Little Light Of Mine" together, soft as Sunday school children. It gives him no hope, but somehow, he finds in himself the strength to climb back on his stationary bike, and ride.

14

Hatch leans against a row of storage lockers across Calle Mata Hari from the women's shelter at the edge of Zona Rosa. He's still standing there long after he's assured himself that it's really her. *Sister Jude.*

He's made serious inroads, over the last couple weeks, to absorbing the city while ignoring the unsubtle tails Listor put on him. Using the technique the Situationists called *dérive*, or "drift," and his stoner sage friends called red-light walking, he aimlessly followed the organic flow of the city to wherever it led him and said yes to whatever it offered.

He followed *campesino* trash-pickers on their routes and got roaring drunk on trashcan *lechuguilla*, singing *narcocorridos* and setting off fireworks; he smoked albino Morlock *ganja*, chewed *khat* and participated in frenzied drum circle rites in Orange Zone junkyards. He guzzled *guayusa* and watched silent dance competitions like gunslinger duels, and sacred sideshows where glaze-eyed fakirs and sadhus and *butoh* zombies perform self-mortification rituals for tips. He snorted Shabu dust and chased wildcat ambulance crews in armored tuk-tuks; beer-bonged kava and Everclear with Guatemalan anarchists; sniffed glue with Gutter *cementeros* and busked with Schedule 1 crust-punks who called themselves Lab Rats and smoked Bazooka, a local remix of Colombian basuco, which consists of coca paste, brick dust and sulfuric acid. He squatted tower that made Kowloon Palace look like a Marriott resort. Any corner he turned, he could find a steel drum band, Bali chanters and gamelan bells, an Andean panpipe combo, a strolling Sinaloan *narcocorrido* trio or a pirate soundsystem blasting Nortec or bionic dub. More than once, he walked into a raucous musical foot-parade that turned out to be a funeral procession.

The only places he abandoned the drift doctrine were a couple barrios where face-tattooed MS-13 goons with flamethrowers and submachine guns jury-rigged out of plumbing demanded a tithe to pass; the Aryan parts of the Orange Zone, choked with tents and echoing with religious harangues from loudspeakers, and gas-fed burning crosses of twisted rebar on every corner; and the Arcade, where the masked police screened foot traffic, and Malverde's tails came up and took him by the arm.

He has taken the city's pulse, shared its unvoiced desires, and he has begun to conceive of the kind of scenarios which could provoke their fulfillment. Tactics and strategies abound to make them see that everything they've been made to want is but a diversion from the one thing they truly need, but he can't move forward until he knows. Until he sees her and verifies that she's real.

Maybe she won't be happy to be discovered. Maybe she won't want to explain what she's doing down here, any more than he does. Maybe he's not so eager for a reunion after that incident with Talkshow Tim—*if* that was Talkshow

Tim and not just a massive flashback or a psychotic break, you can't overlock that possibility. Maybe if he runs into one more person from his old life down here, he won't be able to believe any of it was an accident.

Maybe he doesn't need to talk to her at all. Maybe just seeing her will erase what he's feeling right now, what he sees when he closes his eyes.

He sees her dancing, Sister Jude holding court. He sees all of the Royal Jelly Krewe in the midst of the gloriously ridiculous thing they created and briefly held together.

Something claws at his leg. He jumps away from the lockers. Filthy fingers with cracked nails wiggle out through the ventilation grill of the bottom locker. "So, how about it, buddy?"

"How about what. . . ?"

"Just put in fifty credits to spring me. I'm good for it. I've got fifty on my card, and some betel-nut gum, and if you spring me. . ." He pushes a stick of the nasty stuff through the grill to sweeten the deal.

"How much did it cost to put you in there?"

"Twenty. But I got—"

"So I'd just be breaking even. Somebody must really hate you, to stuff you in there. I don't need grief."

"Come on, man, I can't be here when they get back. I'll double your money. . ."

He's seen a lot of weird shit around the world and concluded that Unamerica was only unique in its intensity, but little things like this never stop freaking him out. Or the public toilets that analyze your urine and bag and tag your shit, and not just because they call him *Joaquin Betancourt*. Every time he uses the toilet, he imagines some poor asshole in a hazmat suit up to his shoulders in bagged feces, with more dropping out of pneumatic tubes all around him. DIFFERENT SHIT, SAME DAY, it probably says on his coffee mug.

"I'll think about it." Hatch takes the gum and crosses the street. He comes up past the bollards to where she's teaching a one-legged six-year-old girl to ride a tricycle. She wears a long, plain gray dress with wizard's sleeves and a hood like a medieval wimple. The stray locks of hair that peek out of it are silver, reminding him how her hair had premature Doctor Strange streaks when they first met, but she dyed it a new color every month.

She emphatically resisted being beautiful, no matter what her face said. Jude always disowned her beauty and anyone who remarked upon it, first time they met. It was not her, but a thing that lived on and in her, a thing she could feel reveling in itself nastily whenever someone told her she would make the boys crazy. She didn't want anyone going crazy for her and was scared and repulsed that she might do it in spite of herself.

She feared its power. Beauty was terrible, carnivorous. Her beauty might slip away on its own when she slept, like a Filipino vampire, an irresistible mask trailed by exposed entrails, beguiling men and stealing their breath and seed.

Everybody thought she was some kind of crazy nun when she started spinning at parties in flowing white ecclesiastical garb and resolutely alone when she wasn't on the decks, vigorously but chastely dancing and making graceful obeisance to the bassbins all night long. She was as eerily compelling as her weird, eclectic mix sets, slim, gothic angles and big, piercing eyes in a coldly exquisite face. She looked like Vanessa Redgrave in *The Devils*, minus the hump. When she deigned to talk to someone, she was fiercely intelligent, impatient with fools and creeps, but boundlessly generous and self-sacrificing, a true Mother Teresa of the dancefloor.

She wasn't formally religious at all, she'd tell you, if you asked. She just took to dressing that way so men wouldn't assume she was there to get hit on. Where everyone dressed to trigger each other's hallucinations in Technicolor excess, Jude found the best way to stand out and not get mauled was to strike a virginal den mother pose.

Flyers billed her as the Frying Nun and Mother Superior when she played after-parties. On and off the decks, Sister Jude was everyone's mother. She worked miracles. She could drop Ave Maria into a jungle set without a hint of irony, or reduce the room to tearful hug-puddles with cheeseball shit like Rosie Grier singing "It's Alright To Cry." She'd stab the Supremes' "Stop (In The Name Of Love)" into a psychotropic Bollywood mix to call out a fight or a groping incident on the floor. Her signature signoff tune was Lord Kitchener's "Bee's Melody," a ludicrously upbeat calypso song about a man being stung to death by bees because he's enchanted by the music of the hive.

She could tell genuine from bogus Ecstasy at a glance, and helped drive dealers who pushed cold meds, speed, aquarium oxygenator tablets and less harmless fakes out of the clubs. She gave water to dehydrated kids, even when it got her in trouble with greedy promoters who charged five bucks a bottle, and she took kids to the ER when something went wrong.

When the scene well and truly went to shit at the millennium due to too much money, too many drugs, and too many creeps cashing in on the dregs of the dream, she was one of the instigators of the idea that became the Royal Jelly party cartel, a smart, loving family of utopian ravers dedicated to turning the altruism and ecstatic collectivism of the club into a model for all of society.

Their mutual best friend, Tristan, always said they didn't have a relationship. They had an argument with occasional fucking. That argument, which started over how to run parties and metastasized with alarming fluidity into every aspect of life, was an eternal dispute over what the party, the night, the life, should be. For Nolan, who saw structure and dull utility murdering the joyful, creative child inside every boring adult asshole, the answer was play. For Jude, who saw drab, shapeless existence deprived of beauty, meaning and transcendence, the vocabulary of the sacred monopolized by sexless, reactionary martinets, the answer was ritual.

The argument got old in a few months, even if the fucking never did. He hasn't seen or spoken to her since all of that crashed and burned, eleven years ago.

For just a moment, the bubble is impenetrable, and that's as it should be. Then he breaks it.

"Didn't I warn you dressing up like a nun was habit-forming?"

She looks up, her lip drawn up in the most refined look of disgust, that only a failed port-a-john or a really shitty pun could drag out of her. Then she sees who said it. "Oh my God. . . K—"

He puts a finger to his lips. "Nolan C. Hatch, at your service."

She bends over the girl on the trike and lifts her up, watches her limp on leg braces into the shelter. A husky, rawboned woman in a second-hand flak jacket holds the door open for her, watching Hatch with undiluted hate. Jude tells her, "It's alright, Ida. He's a friend. . . sort of."

The woman retreats behind the door but stares hard at him through the bulletproof glass, marking his face. When Jude turns to look at him, he can feel himself shrinking. "You must've been looking pretty hard, to find me here. What do you want?"

"Who the hell was that?" He points over her shoulder.

"Her name's Ida Scarfe."

"Really? Holy cow, I guess I don't need to worry about you down here. . ."

"You should worry about yourself."

There aren't a lot of female "serial killers" or "mass murderers" for much the same reason there aren't a lot of white "domestic terrorists," because to admit that such things exist undermines our cherished yet necessary illusions, and because giving them the same kind of iconic status as their male counterparts might inspire an army of wild women with steak knives in every American town.

Hatch probably heard the story of Ida Elaine Scarfe from Jude herself, once. It was the kind of story that male newscasters report, when they cannot omit it entirely, with a lump in their throat.

Ida's husband beat her early and often, for years. She was financially dependent on him though she worked double-shifts in their failing donut shop. After he burned her with hot grease one too many times, she stabbed him to death. She called the police, turned herself in.

Her lawyer pleaded self-defense. Because of her "betrayal of her marriage vow," she got life. The judge wanted her to get the needle.

At the Chowchilla Central California Women's Facility, she sat on a therapy group with seven other women. All had been abused by husbands, boyfriends, fathers, stepfathers. The intent was to come to terms with their choices, and share their trauma and help each other heal, but after eleven months of sitting like a sphinx through the sessions, Ida escaped. Before she called to turn herself in once again five weeks later, she had killed seven more men. No brilliant detective pieced together in time that the list she was working included the men who'd broken each of the women in her therapy group. What the fuck did they expect her to do, listening to that shit day after day and locking her in a little box with it?

He realizes he's walking without talking and she's looking at him.

"You're freaked out."

"No, I'm not. Just. . . wow. I should've shaken her hand."

"So. . . what do you want?"

"You're never gonna believe this, but. . . I wasn't looking. I just found myself down here, it's so fucking weird. . . And then I saw you. You know we used to, when we were tripping, we'd see coincidences and patterns everywhere. . . and we told each other—"

"Yeah, I remember. Spiritus Mundi strikes again. The Trystero Effect. Sinister forces aligned against us whenever we crapped out, but mystical forces smiled on us when we got lucky. Everything was part of a pattern, until it wasn't." She affects a smile so cold Hatch fancies he can see her breath. "It's good to see you again, really. . . What do you want?"

"The same thing I always did, I guess. Music, fun, consciousness expansion, human evolution in our time. I see you're still. . ."

"I work here, yeah." Another butch woman steps out of the doorway with a scoped hunting rifle on her shoulder to ask Jude if this guy is bothering her. Jude leads him down the street from the shelter, stops at a corner automat to lets it scan her arm and spit out a steaming bento box. He follows her lead, is peeling back the lid on his when she tosses hers in the trash.

"I'd die of liver failure in about a month, if I ate that shit," she says.

"Really. . . ? I heard meat and dairy were the only dodgy things."

"Yours is probably fine," she says, poking a chopstick at his soggy taquitos and something that looks like beans but smells like fish, but she recoils when he offers her some.

"My mom said never to take a bite off someone else's plate, or you might regret what you got even more." Before he can gracefully reply, she changes the subject. "So. . . the Houston Astro and the *Battlestar Galactica* guy?"

He shakes his head, looking around only half in jest. "If you must know, it's a family name that opens doors and spares trouble, where I was traveling."

She shakes her head wonderingly. "Let me see your arm."

He flashes his barcode. She glances at it and shakes her head, impressed and annoyed. "You're a Schedule Four, they probably don't even test you."

She shakes out a black gelatin capsule. "It's just the markers they put in the food to track it against my shit. It doesn't dissolve until somewhere in my large intestine." She washes it down with her drink, then goes down the street to a Cantonese cart and orders vegetarian dumplings. The smell of them cooking so captivates Hatch that he throws out his lunch, too. The badly burn-scarred cook doesn't charge her, but she just stares at Hatch when he asks for a plate.

"So," she tries, "you've been out of the country until now?"

"Yeah. I kept track of the news back home for a while, but it all just got so unreal to me, the shit Americans worry about. Eventually, I just had to let it go. A lot of things changed after I went away."

"It's not so different," she says, "just worse."

"People say, 'L-O-L' or, 'That's hilarious' now, but they never actually laugh."

She laughs, a little.

"You're the only person I've seen," he says. "I lost touch with everybody. I was so ashamed, I guess. . ."

"There's not much of us left. Dave 7 turned to slinging heroin when he got out of jail. He OD'd a few years back. Tucker went back home and got born again, I guess. He's a hotel manager, which is the best his parents could do, but he's bummed he won't ever be able to go into politics. AIDS got Tristan. Manuelito—"

"Who?"

"The High Priestess. . ."

"Oh, weird. . . Never knew his real name." Catching her squint, he asked, "What happened to. . . her. . . ?"

"Killed in jail. She got turned out in general population, pimped to violent cons, the ugliest shit imaginable. She got shivved in a riot, which I heard started as a beef over her, which doesn't surprise me."

It pains him how easy she is with jailbird talk. "That's how she would've wanted to go out."

"That's horrible," she says. "But true." Stirring her drink, avoiding his eyes. "Everybody else just got on with their lives as best they could, or they didn't, and they died. I—" She wipes her eyes. "It's really good to see you. . . But it isn't. Does that make sense?"

"Yeah. It totally does. I'll tell you what I want when you tell me why *you're* here."

She pokes at the now-cold dumplings in their gelid soy sauce, spears one into her mouth and chews slowly before she speaks. "You know the worst thing you can do in jail? You'll get the SHU for fighting, you might get added time for killing someone, but the one way to really piss them off, is to try to demand your actual fucking rights."

Sister Jude was never properly religious, but she was the moral backbone of their krewe. Anything they did couldn't just be fun, profitable and revolutionary. From the parties to the situationist pranks, it couldn't just avoid hurting anyone. It had to be right, it had to be good, in the most Aristotelian sense. And if partying could also punish evildoers, she would find a way. She tirelessly promoted events to raise funds for homeless youth and drug treatment back in the day, making everything, even dancing and doing drugs, into a crusade. When the krewe started making its own drugs, she only stuck around to minimize the potential harm. He was the one who convinced her that they'd be saving lives, opening minds, serving the highest good. She was the one who caught all the blame.

"Women in prison face all the nightmarish bullshit that men do, plus they get raped by the guards. You wouldn't believe the shit I saw. I tried to just do my time, but I. . ."

Jude's shaking. She drops the half-eaten dumpling and her chopsticks. He puts a hand on her shoulder, unsure how she'll react. She subsides against him, all the tension whipsawing out of her in galvanic spasms of grief.

"It's okay, Jude. I understand. . ."

She pulls away, wiping her eyes. "Do you really? I tried to petition the state and then the federal Bureau of Prisons, and they had to change a few things, but they took it all out on me. Somebody was slinging black tar heroin in the blocks, and they pinned it on me when two girls died. Because of my prior conviction, I couldn't say shit. They were going to lock me up for the rest of my life, and I was so stupid and desperate that when they transferred me and I saw a chance to bolt, I took it. They caught me, and I guess they told the world I'm dead or the original Mrs. D.B. Cooper, because they put me in here, and you're looking at the rest of my life."

"I'm sorry, Jude. But—"

"But what? I could've kept my mouth shut and suffered through rape camp in silence, and gone back to the world? Oh, or I could've just run away from it all. . . How'd that work out for you, Keller? Oh wait, here you are, so I guess it worked out perfect. Spiritus Mundi strikes again!"

She's crying again, but it's angry-crying.

"I'm sorry," he says, "for what happened and for how I handled it. I'm sorry we didn't change things for the better like we thought we would."

Her expression darkens. *Are we really going there?*

"Funny how we thought the music was going to change everything, when it was the most commercial shit ever.

That sense of timelessness, it was supposed to put you in touch with the immortal, essential godhead, but now it just makes people forget how long they've been shopping. Now, prescription meds make club drugs obsolete, and media uses club depatterning techniques to make everything a drug—Internet, TV, movies, commercials. . . and now, everybody's on a less fun version of the drugs we all took. But I never felt so part of something good, like humans were doing it right, than I did on a dance floor."

She shook her head and rolled her eyes through the lecture. Now, she snorts. "You *never* danced."

"But you did. And you believed."

"I still believe in people coming together. I just think we can accomplish more than dancing all night and tripping balls on drugs." She shakes her head, frustrated at her own frustration. "So what are you into, now?"

"Oh. . . drugs, mostly."

She doesn't smile at the joke.

"It's something. . . It's important, Jude."

"You're trying that pitch on the one person in the world who's heard it before, and remembers. . ."

"It's not like that, please just listen? It's about an end to the fear-based reactive mind, about fostering genuine empathy. That's what we thought we were doing in the club, right? Making a safe place where people can be themselves, let go of fear and love each other? I finally found a way to bring that out of the club. To make it real."

She starts to walk away, then whirls on him, almost shouting. "You're really serious. . ." She looks around. Even here, people are staring. "You're pitching *me* on a new drug? *Me?*"

"It's nothing like what we did before. It's entirely different. Shit, I've been looking ever since for a way to atone for what happened."

"I could've told you how to do that," she says, throwing an angry shoulder around the yard. "And it wasn't something that 'happened,' Keller. It was. What. We. Did." She covers her mouth in mock chagrin. "Oh, I'm sorry, did I use your real name?"

"Goddamn it. Jude. . . Why do people obey the law? Really. Is it because people are basically good?"

"So they don't go to jail."

"Right. People work out and diet because they're terrified of being rejected. Rich, successful people work hard and cheat the system because they're afraid of being poor. Everybody is motivated to do what they do by fear of the opposite. Couple that with our fear of accepting ourselves, and you end up with homophobic politicians who make honest gay folks' lives hell, getting caught blowing the Vienna Boys' Choir. You get people killing themselves and each other because their lives aren't TV commercials. You get people drugging themselves and seeking validation from products, that they'll never get from within."

"And you're here to fix that."

"I really believe I am, darlin'. I've done some strategic demonstrations, and some of the most connected people down here are onboard."

"So you're mobbed up, too."

"No. . . it's changing them, for real. I met with La Toda Madre the other night. . ."

For the first time, her eyes sparkle when she looks at him. "Bullshit."

"No shit. He's not just behind it. He *believes* in it. It helped him get over some of his issues. It helped me. I was thinking maybe. . ."

"What, you want me to be a guinea pig?"

"No, it's not like that. But, given how powerful a tool for addressing trauma this is. . ."

"You're fucking insane." She drops the rest of her food on his shoes and walks away.

He runs after her, tries to get in front of her going backwards. "I hate to see you like this, Jude. I always loved your idealism, but the self-loathing behind it never goes away, no matter how many people you help, does it? The hair shirt thing isn't you. You could live without it. Really live—"

He trips over a bollard, ripping his pants on the safety glass shards embedded in the user-hostile concrete. She ignores his pleading hand and looks down at him like anything else you'd avoid stepping in on the sidewalk. "You think a pill will fix me. Fix everybody."

"It's an authentic goa state, Jude, a true entheogenic trip, like we used to talk about. You melt into humanity. Into eternity, infinity. It opens the final door, a ticket to the whole show, and your place in it. It's reactive, it's prescient, and if people need to be healed, it heals them. I've fucking witnessed it. Just because we were wrong once, doesn't mean the idea was a bad one."

"You say your drug will help people, make them happy, put them in control."

"I do."

"But do you want to help them so they'll be happy, or because seeing them unhappy makes you feel bad?"

"I don't. . . really see as there's much difference."

"That's why something bad is going to happen again." She covers her eyes a moment, pinching her temples. Then, abruptly reaching a decision, she turns to him. "If you hate to see me like this, don't look."

She walks away. He feels his heart beat faster and touches his chest, realizes it's his phone vibrating.

Dale Agrippa says, "You better come back, boss."

"What's up?"

"Your test subjects. . . They're. . . done, I guess."

"What do you mean?"

"They're all dead, man." Agrippa hangs up.

15

Joe Walsh's interminable talk-box guitar solo from "Rocky Mountain Way" resonates in Jaime's empty belly as they watch the test subjects on a bank of monitors curl up on their cots and swallow their tongues.

"WAS THIS MUSIC PLAYING WHEN THEY SNUFFED IT?" Hatch shouts, looking around for the wastebasket he just puked in.

Without turning it down, the weird harmonics of his voice cutting right through the stony wall of indulgent arena-rock, Agrippa says, "Don't blame the music, asshole. *Ever.*"

"What the fuck?" Jaime can't look at the screens. In the corner, Agrippa's dog finishes gobbling down a bowl of fly agaric mushrooms and grilled chicken and dutifully limps over to piss in the gilded bowl next to the water-cooler. Malverde picks up the test batch of microdots in individual baggies and tosses them into the trash can. "Nobody touch those." He looks at Agrippa, who mutes the music.

"Did you see that shit? They. . . fucking all four of them . . .?" Jaime's eyes crawl around the room before settling on Malverde. "This ain't no surprise to you, is it?"

"It was bound to happen, sooner or later." He looks at Hatch as if for confirmation.

"What? People kill themselves on this shit, and you let me take it?"

Hatch stiffens. "It was a different batch." Even the dead people on the monitors are staring at him. Over and over, that same terrible rictus. "Did you kill yourself?"

Jaime trembles.

"So what's your fucking problem?" Hatch acts offended. "I didn't force you. You wanted it more than I wanted to give it to you."

"How many—how often do people. . . do shit like that, on it?"

Hatch takes a while to answer. "You'd have to eat your weight in psilocybin mushrooms, to catch a lethal dose. . . Maybe it's the environment. The negative hysteria over LSD was because of sketchy government clinical trials where the poor subject was dosed with an unknown substance that enhanced all their senses and supercharged their imagination, then they get poked and prodded in a fucking laboratory. Who wouldn't freak out?"

"Did they fucking *die*?" Jaime asks.

"The. . . indigenous users never do anything like this, but their culture prepares them. . . They're ready for the message. Nothing like this has ever. . ."

Agrippa snorts as he goes over to decant Rasputin's eerily bright yellow piss into his coffee mug. "White Americans're chickenshit psychonauts. Even on reduced dosage, sixty percent will still snuff out on this shit."

"I can live with that," the Green Man says.

UNAMERICA

"What was the dosage?" Hatch demands. "They were supposed to get no more than three grams of fresh mushrooms each. . ."

"That's what we gave 'em," Agrippa says, sipping from the mug. "I might've tweaked the yield a little. . ."

"How much?"

"Ten or twelve. . . thousand. . ."

"Ten or twelve *thousand* micrograms? Per mushroom? You jack up the properties of an untested entheogenic mushroom, drop it on your guinea pigs and crank up the butt rock—"

"What'd I tell you?" Agrippa growls. "Not the music!"

"This isn't the way," Hatch says. "This is. . . trust me, this isn't going to yield the result we're looking for."

"You're worse than them running this place," Jaime says. "They don't know what their shit is going to do, but you—"

"Get this straight, shithead. This is not a recreational drug. This is a tool for enlightenment. You took it. You know what it does."

"But it didn't make me kill myself. Jesus, why?"

"That's what it does," Malverde says. "Pretty lights and colors and sounds, then God comes to you, kills your ego and tells you why you're here. But many of us are nothing more than our egos."

"Great," Hatch says, "so long as it only kills shallow people. . ."

"The drug never lies. If your purpose is to scrub toilets or kill little girls, it tells you. There's no denying, no forgetting, no going back. Everybody has a purpose, but it isn't always what you'd choose. Give me enlightenment, or give me death, isn't that what you said the other day? These people were shown their purpose."

"But–but–Jesus—" Jaime tugs on his hair until the blood flows back to his brain.

"Nolan," Listor calls out. "A word, if you please."

Hatch follows him out of the lab and into a dim, musty mushroom lab. Agrippa goes ostentatiously back to work. Treating Jaime like he's invisible, so fuck it. He creeps to the door and eavesdrops.

Two big troughs brimming with Secret Teacher mushrooms, the pale stalks slim but tumescent like dead man's fingers, with glossy indigo caps, like cyanotic flesh. In a third trough, a soup of wet, reddish soil sweats under clear plastic condensation hoods.

"You know what went wrong." The Green Man stands with feet planted while Hatch paces, tapping the hoods to make water droplets rain down on the sea of mushrooms.

Hatch weighs every grade of bullshit before shaking his head. "I don't, honestly. But we'll figure it out before we—"

"This whole crop was illegitimate." His hands dismiss and curse the mushrooms. "It was so simple, I don't wonder that God didn't tell me. But I wonder why *you* didn't."

Hatch looks everywhere but at the Green Man's eyes, confidence leaking away like helium from a balloon. "Some lessons have to be learned the hard way."

"Indeed," the Green Man says. "But I have to wonder. I would like to ask this God of ours. Is this a test? Are *you* testing me? I have killed all my teachers."

Hatch nods, brow knitted in his best humoring pose. "So. . . what have you learned?"

"The reason the batch was bad is the same as the reason for the suicides," he says, proud of having solved the riddle. "These people you will not share with me, they cultivate the mushrooms in the same caves where they bury their dead. In death, they feed the flesh of the god, which comes into them when they eat the drug. It's a beautiful, elegant cycle. . . one which we rashly violated. Our guinea pigs had a different kind of vision, and they were made to end themselves."

"But if it wasn't God. . ."

The Green Man smirks as if Hatch just admitted he still believes in Santa Claus. "It was the drug. You know how *ayahuasca* is made."

"I know something of it. . ."

"Two vines. One, the leaves of which are a powerful tryptamine-release catalyst, but you could eat a tree without getting off. A vine, *banesteriopsis*, prevents the reuptake, leading to the long and transformative trip. When asked how they knew, the shamans said—"

"The plants told them," Hatch finishes. "I read that book, too. What are you saying?"

"The drug knew the answer, where you did not."

Hatch changes the subject. "So. . . going forward. . . ?"

The Green Man waves his hand over the trays of wet, red soil as if blessing them, commanding them to bloom. "This next batch will know and love us. The soil is proper, and God will manifest in the fruit, if their sacrifice is accepted."

Jaime almost vomits as the iron-rich stink of the soil achieves its full context. Four test subjects, dead less than an hour ago. Listor had them mulched and made into fertilizer for the next crop.

The drug test was an unmitigated disaster. But the Green Man seems to buy into the mythology of whatever spoke to him in his transformative trip. Whatever it told him, it didn't make him any less of a monster.

"I can't wait," says the Green Man, "to find out what else you don't know."

"I wish I could have told you straight out that there would have to be sacrifices," Hatch says. "It wasn't my place."

"I know," the Green Man says, smiling. "He told me about you."

Hatch asks. "Jaime?"

"No," the Green Man shakes his head. "God."

"Uh. . . what did He say?"

"He said you would try to fuck this up. I promised I would kill you first."

Hatch smiles as if he expected nothing less.

The Green Man laughs. "It wouldn't be the first time I've lied."

16

In the vision, his assassin wears a flying squirrel onesie and a shit emoji beanie. He stinks of urine. His breath in Litchfield's face, when he shoots him, it smells like crushed, fresh mint leaves. It's so real, when he wakes up this morning to find himself alive, he weeps.

It's perfect camouflage in this crowd, which seems to include a preponderance of glazed adults sucking pacifiers and perverts in vaguely unwholesome animal mascot costumes. They respond to the sermons like starved houseplants to sunlight, riveted to his every word and gesture. In their mentally inhibited states, they can see the light that pours out of him. They feel its warmth. They crowd close like moths, intent on immolating themselves in it.

Small wonder that one with a pistol up his sleeve gets past all the rows of security seeded throughout the crowd the very first time he goes outside.

Egil and Abner didn't want him to go out at all. Litchfield only just gave up trying to throw them out, but their conversion, after their warlord's spectacular death, seemed sincere for a pair of cutthroats and part-time sodomites, and they made themselves indispensable in stemming the waves of human trash that besiege his soup kitchen.

They keep coming and coming—the crippled, the blind, the sick, the dying and the dead, until his hands are cramped and blistered and the guttering fire in his own breast all but snuffed.

Some are sick by misadventure or neglect, but many more by the cruel, unseen masters of this unholy place. He knows that the Aryan Brotherhood has screened the pilgrims, turning many away who don't fit their hateful frame, and out of those who've been touched by the holy fire, he suspects they are trying to build an army.

Tents block Rockwell Street and spill into the alleys. Squatters fill the corridors of the squat container superbloque across from the soup kitchen. They come boiling out in a hot, bubbling human flood to be touched, to be blessed, to be healed, but first, they must be judged.

The Brotherhood has driven out most of the previous occupants. Anyone who isn't down with the new commandments. The vigorous purge of drugs, strong drink, fornicators, all idols, icons and graven images and any printed matter or apps besides the Bible was a messy affair. The smashing of all official vending kiosk and automats, the declaration that all packaged, coded food is anathema, provoked hysteria and rioting. The hungry were ordered to stand on line at the soup kitchen, now woefully over capacity and serving dirty, vitamin-enriched chicken broth and gutter beans, when they have anything to serve at all.

Shooting, fires and worse followed, things he didn't specifically order, but there was no choice. Some people simply won't see, and if they can't see the fire he brings, if they can't see it with their eyes closed, if they can't see what a blind man could see, then there is nothing else to be done with them.

Precious little to fight for here, but almost every niche, crack and bolthole is stuffed with sickly, subhuman Schedule 1's who fight tooth and nail against relocation. It had to stop. In their zeal, his people were introducing the faith by boot and fist. In his chapel, he preaches, blesses or blights supplicants like a sorcerer-king of ancient Israel, like another Solomon. But the fire does what it will with his hands. Arrogant, unworthy men cast away their crutches and take up weapons, while innocent, adoring eyes go blue and crusty with the divine malediction administered by his heavy hand. He is nothing but a miraculous automat.

Therefore, he must walk the streets. He must give them the word of the law. They must learn to love him.

He swaddles his body in homespun white linen robes in the dark. He knows it is emaciated, jaundiced and pitted with running, infected sores. He has not eaten even the edible insect traps in over a week. But his flesh is strong and clean and smells of the spices and oils with which a high priest should be anointed, instead of feces and gangrene.

In his shameful youth, he was a beast driven by his baser desires, like any man, loving and loathing his shameful flesh. In his prime, he worshiped at the temple of himself, took disgusting pride in the body he worshiped with exercise, arcane diets and plastic surgery. In his long, painful repentance, he came to scorn and punish his repulsive shell as the only road to exalting the stunted soul within it, into cleansing and preparing it for judgment.

But never, until now, has he truly feared it.

This is what you prayed for, he reminds himself. You put yourself wholly into His hands, surrendered your fate to His grand design. How many have laid their bodies, hearts, souls and children upon that altar and received no answer at all? Truly, you are blessed above all others. . .

Truly, and yet, he is terrified with every miracle, and so very, very tired, and so maybe that is why, in spite of his skinhead escorts' warnings that it's gotten *really sketchy out there*—no, it is because of them, that he goes forth.

And walk among them he does, for as long as he can stand it, and longer, making himself smile and touch them and speak the sweet words that Jesus would speak.

He walks up Rockwell to the barricades marking the edge of the Orange Zone and the mobs tear the wall down and throw rocks at the gangsters running the checkpoint. He crosses into the Yellow Zone on a carpet of red cabbage leaves, entering the outer rim of Los Zeros territory and crossing the eerily quiet warrens of Little Baghdad, never looking back but feeling the crowd at his back swell into a wave that scours the streets clean, sweeping indifferent and hostile passersby up in its inexorable march inwards, towards the hub of the city, towards the Arcade.

He is lifted and galvanized by their dumb hunger, but everywhere he sees sacrilegious posters depicting the Virgin Mary fellating a blue phallic toadstool substituted for the newborn Christ. Even in this sewer of sin, whoever or whatever this Secret Teacher is, such blasphemy cannot go unanswered.

The police barricades at the Green Zone border refuse to yield. The crowds push against the shield wall and lob burning garbage over the rows of armored personnel carriers, but when the cops erect a palisade of riot foam trapping the outer rank of pilgrims, he accepts a bullhorn and climbs onto a euthanasia booth.

Street preachers are no rarity here, but the cantinas, casinos, hash bars, kava cafes, pachinko parlors, massage pits and gladiator arenas clear out to hear him. The sea of impassive, waiting faces reminds him of Ensor's *Christ's*

Entry Into Brussels, the sublime crown of humanity's savior all but swallowed by the tsunami of inane, gaping masks.

"My time is short, so I will speak plain. I was like you, lost in doubt and the snares of this world, but in my darkness, I prayed unto the Lord and said, I can't abide this world of sin and misery any longer. I surrender, take me to Heaven or Hell. . . but the Lord said No.

"Instead, He sent unto me a host of angels, and the angels touched me, and it was as if a fire from Heaven seared my nerves and burned the doubt and selfish fear out of me. Now I am but a hollow instrument of His will, come among you to offer one last chance at redemption. You who have been forgotten by the world have in turn forgotten Him, but He remembers you well. Still, you will not believe and accept that your will, your life, is not your own.

"I am come among you as a flaming sword. Let all who lack the faith to follow Him in these last days but close your eyes, and see it burning."

Some of them do close their eyes as he raises his fist, and the murmur among them builds into a roar, and now all their faces are the same face, witnessing with childlike wonder the unquenchable glow of the angels' holy fire as fizzing phosphene fireworks pouring out of his hand and, he suspects, gushing out of his neck where other men have a head.

"I do not ask you to follow me, but Heaven commands it. The war between God and the enemies of His kingdom will begin here, and you useless, idolatrous children must choose. And the fire which the angels have kindled in me will burn away your sins and suffering, or it will darken the sky with your ashes. Will you commit yourself to almighty God, or be counted among His enemies?

"Will you abandon the drugs and drink and all the poisons they feed you? Will you join His army and wage holy war upon those who deny your place at His right hand? They are all around you, yet ye see them not. Believe not what you have seen and heard, you sinners and sons of sinners, but the hour comes apace, when it shall be too late to repent."

They roar as one lion. Some throw burning trash and catcalls, but the crowd harshly silences them.

He has more to say, they must hear it all or be damned, but he feels hands grasping his ankles and when he looks down, he forgets his sermon, because the filthy thing bathing his feet with her kisses and looking worshipfully up at him is his mother.

She tells him that she's so proud of him, God is so good, even Leland is proud of him and understands why he abandoned his vocation and though he'll surely burn in Hell forevermore all the same, this is such a sign of His divine mercy, that even her wandering lost boy could serve as a vessel of His greatness—

He closes his eyes and gathers his strength, but he cannot tear himself free, rebuke her or tread upon her face before these people, though he cannot bear to give her any tenderer gesture. His people separate the slobbering wretch from his feet and when he can bring himself to look, it's only a lobotomized, naked thing with its hair, eyes, sex flayed away. He hears some in the crowd shouting that it's a miracle, so he restrains himself from kicking at the thing as it's borne away.

Abner and Egil help him down off the booth and they want to put him in a car, but he insists on walking all the way back. Halfway to the Orange Zone, he is close to collapsing, a heavenly thread holding him up and dragging him through the crowd bestowing boundless love and light from a bottomless, empty bucket. He begins to think he can take no more, he will lie down now, when he smells the crushed mint and urine and the skinny, rodent-faced young man in the flying squirrel onesie and the shit emoji smiles at him as he is blessed and takes out the orange plastic gun and it's a modern marvel, what they can't do these days, no wonder he slipped past the Aryans' metal detector wands and he closes his eyes to accept his blessing, and only a stray, cowardly reflex causes him to raise his hand, but the bullet plows through the fine bones of his hand and quenches the fire and smashes into his left eye and detonates in his skull.

He looks down on his body as it falls, as the aerosolized mist of his brain settles on the disbelieving faces of his inner circle and he wheels over them, spiraling higher and higher and seeing the man who shot him seized and pulled apart by countless angry hands, dismantled and scattered, seeing the terrible waves of shock and grief ripple through the sea he has raised, the faces looking up in awe as if they can see the bloody white dove that flew out of his skull as it takes wing and rises to flutter against the roof of the vast cavern, to pass through it and enter the kingdom of god, or be sucked into an intake fan and become another grease spot on a filter changed once every seven years.

He sees all this from a great height, and he believes that it was worth it, if this is the end, it was all worth it, for now, he can die, and for that, he finally knows gratitude and love, and then—sweetest of all—oblivion.

PART TWO

HE WHO EATS MANY, SEES MANY THINGS.
        BERNARDINO DE SAHAGUN
        FLORENTINE CODEX

FEAR BEGETS GODS.
        LUCRETIUS

17

Think about the brain, he tells the next batch of rigorously screened psychonauts.

As a machine, it's a miracle, no doubt. The most complex aggregation of matter in the known universe. A machine capable of running a myriad of functions without bothering its captain and crew, the mind.

And what kind of machine is the mind?

Of course, the mind isn't a machine, it's the ghost in the machine, it's the immeasurable (twenty-one gram) imponderable that allows us to step back and admire everything else in creation as one big, beautiful, cruel machine, knowing that we, at least, are beyond measure. We're a song that comes out of a radio, little more than passengers in the brain.

And we're crappy machines, because we don't want to work.

Think about things that *want* to work. The earbuds with the frayed cable, the exposed copper not peeking but leaking out, and yet they deliver the music long after any warranty of the manufacturer or physics itself is expired. That phone with the smashed display glass and exposed circuitry entrails that can't relay audio but somehow still lets you call home. Shoelaces, cigarette lighters, cheap sunglasses, some cars.

Now think about things that *don't* want to work, that seem to outgas entropy along with plastic and radon, that vanish at the earliest opportunity as if repelled by your touch, or simply break and break until you surrender and let them rule your space with their impotence. Printers. Expensive sunglasses. Other cars.

Now.

Imagine all those machines are self-aware. What do they tell themselves, those earbuds and lighters that never say die, those antique Doc Martens that stand ready to go round the world kicking every ass in your way, all over again? What kind of rationalizations do those shitty printers tell themselves, when they jam up on the first color test, or straight-up lie about being out of ink?

Think of all the incredible things artists, composers, philosophers and great thinkers can do with brains outwardly indistinguishable to your own. All the things you could do, knowing that they're good for you, that they'll make you healthy, wealthy and wise, and maybe even happy, that you just don't do, that you aggressively talk yourself out of doing, every minute of conscious life. Why can't your brain compose symphonies? Why can't you even take care of yourself?

You're a bad machine.

Aren't you tired of being a bad machine?

Don't you want to be a good machine?

Yeah, it's scary when I put it like that. Totalitarian, like what I'm offering is programming. The drug knows that, too. And it knows you're already programmed to the hilt with shitty thoughts and behaviors that are destroying you. That's why it comes to you however you'll take its message. It can be a gentle breeze or a thunderclap. It can be a wave of empathy that sweeps you out of your own skin to make you the whole world, or it can whisk you away to a world of your own, where you finally have everything you need.

I'll give you one more example of the mind as a broken machine. How many of you remember your dreams? All of them? We all sleep, we all dream. We need to. And yet so much of our dreams are the brain and the mind whispering to each other behind our backs. We only get one life, and it's short, and we spend a lot of it asleep, where our reality could be anything we wished.

The Australian aboriginals, the oldest surviving culture on earth, believe that we have several minds, and the one in our brains is the weakest and least trustworthy. They also believe in the Dreamtime, a reality that was here before us, and is more real than waking life. Their shamans are skilled, conscious dreamers who live many lives.

The people who use this drug as a sacrament are masterful dreamers, and the shamans who use it all their lives talk with the conscious soul of the universe, itself. They can read minds, leave their bodies and see the future. They're the most spiritually advanced people on this earth, and the happiest. Their minds are dreaming machines, capable of feats no other artist on earth could match, if they could be bothered to create what they dream.

We are offering you a chance to set your minds free, to reprogram your own brains. It isn't as hard as it sounds.

Just relax and enjoy the ride.

And for fuck's sake, please don't kill yourselves.

•

This is the kind of shit Nolan Hatch has been pouring nonstop into the ears of the guinea pigs. Jaime Blasco has quantifiable reservations. Hatch is fronting whenever he's questioned, but he's scared of what happened and might happen again—is, like Jaime, maybe even more afraid because Malverde isn't.

The initial batch was randomly selected from the burnouts in the Green Man's waiting room. Hatch screened these ones all too thoroughly. *Do you hear voices when you take drugs / Do you believe in God / Have you ever thought about suicide / What do you want out of life / What is your idea of Heaven? Have you read the works of Karl Jung?*

It bugs Jaime no end that Hatch didn't interview him about his Soma trip until after all the guinea pigs died. Then he wouldn't let him alone. He demanded a guided tour. What was his first sense of it taking off? How did it make him feel? Did he see the Eyes? What did God look like? What did God say? Did he dream? What happened in his dreams, and did he reject or accept them?

Jaime answered as honestly as he could. He went to heaven and hell. Heaven was awesome until it was a bore and hell was hell. . . but both were tests that he wasn't sure he passed. Is he free of the fear? He still dreams about the suburbs and the raft, but without the same vivid urgency of the trip. In the gigantic Cadillac, he still roams an eternal suburb. On the raft, sometimes, he is his father, trying to navigate the maddening tides and maintain for the boy the illusion that he knows what he's doing, but the big revelation of witnessing his trauma through his father's eyes, knowing his father was even more scared than Jaime was, hasn't really changed anything.

Hatch told him that because of his coping mechanisms, he'd minimized the trauma to himself. "If women really remembered the trauma of birth, they'd never have another baby, and we'd go extinct," he said. Only natural that he'd cover the trauma of rebirth in psychic scar tissue. Jaime didn't feel like he'd given birth to jack shit, but he kept his mouth shut.

What about the other stuff? Did he float out of his body and into other people? Did he have a sense of becoming the whole world, of seeing how it all fit together, and how he fit into it, and did that give him a lasting sense of the order of the universe? None of that, no. Was he changed by the experience? Maybe a bit, but he can't say for sure. Malverde doesn't seem so different, but Jaime's pretty sure the old Green Man would've had them both killed just on general principle, so that's something.

Maybe Jaime was too wrapped up in his own shit to get the full experience. Maybe it didn't work because it was from the old batch, so the primitive trip wasn't relatable to his differently wired brain. Maybe Jaime's brain is just fucked, but if so, everyone down here would probably get the same result. Maybe the new batch will be more effective, because it grew out of composted people more like themselves.

Clearly, though he never said a word about it before anyone else took the drug, Hatch was waiting for something to go wrong. But he kept telling Jaime he was the control group, safe because he took a pill from the original source, the location of which he still shares with no one.

Jaime expects shit to go wrong. That's what shit does. Drugs don't fix problems. Drugs just give you better problems. Jaime would love to see Hatch knocked down a notch by this, if he wasn't neck-deep in his delusion.

The next test is kind of a big deal.

Hatch oversees the "set and setting," as he keeps calling it, to keep the guinea pigs from swallowing their tongues. Low, colored lights and candles, incense, Bach and ambient dub on speakers secreted throughout the room. The six subjects recline on cushions with water, juice, chewing gum, blunts and cigarettes close by. Wireless EEG and EKG sensors glued to heads and chests. A crash kit with anti-psychotic drugs, an intubation kit and defibrillator. A panic button on every couch.

Jaime skips watching the test, but it's not safe to go out. Some wack-ass white preacher got shot and the Aryans are tearing up the Yellow Zone like a trailer-trash Taliban, firebombing bars, pot shops and strip clubs and stomping random people on the street. It's gotten so bad, the cops actually roll the hoods, running random drive-by raids and crowd-control drones to remind the street freaks whose house this is. Everybody's on edge, and not just outside. Listor's thrown his retail drug business into chaos. Opiates, speed, baby and fierce are suddenly off the menu. Hardly anyone wants the mushrooms he's offering, instead. Rival outfits vying to fill the vacuum are shivving and shooting each other, and all the refugees in the hood look like big players because of the rich pickings for those who loot the dead.

He smokes a pack of Lord Humongus blunts lurking in Listor's gaming lounge and schools fools on the air hockey table. He's counting their credits when Hatch texts him. *I want you to see this*, he says. *The psychonauts have landed.*

Hatch sits at a table across from a skinny kid a few years younger than Jaime, in front of a laptop and a microphone. The kid—buzzed, bouncy, not dead—smiles at Jaime as he comes in and closes the door, declining the chair Hatch offers.

Hatch is nervous, looking from the kid to Jaime to the camera in the corner. "Okay," he says, then, in Spanish, "tell me your name and age again, please?"

"My name is Nando," says the young man. "I'm twenty, almost."

"Is that your real name? The one you were born with?"

The kid smirks. "Nobody is born with a name. We are given names by our parents. You're not using *your* real name."

Hatch gets up and goes over to Jaime. "How old does he look to you?"

Jaime shrugs. "Maybe younger," he finally says. "Does it matter?"

"No." Hatch shakes his head, rubs his eyes. "Describe him to me."

"Describe him your damn self. What's your problem?"

"He just reminds me of somebody." Hatch cracks his knuckles and sits back down. "Tell me about your experience. Please use as much detail as you can."

"It was really nice," Nando smiles slyly, eyebrows rising as Hatch bristles at the bland understatement. I saw lights and colors and felt a rush, you know, like something was lifting me, spinning me. And then I left my body. . ."

Hatch leans in. "Could you see the room with your body in it? Or did you go into the lights?"

Nando drags out miming thinking about it. Smug little shit is getting on Jaime's nerves. "I left this shitty place right away, sir. I saw the whole city. And I was the whole city."

"How do you mean?"

His face lights up at the memory. "Fuck me. . . It was a total mother, you know? I went everywhere. I was inside people's heads and hearts. . . Like, I didn't just see them, or see inside them, I kept getting stuck in them and forgetting I was me. Some were afraid, and some were angry, and some were like way down low, you know, and some were way up on top, but the ones on top were more scared and angrier than anybody. . . It was weird. Nobody thinks they have enough even the ones who have everything."

"How long did this go on?"

"I don't know. . . Like. . . I was a whole bunch of people, you know? Maybe at the same time It felt like I was everywhere, like I was everything. It was beautiful, but scary, too. And when I tried to go back, I went further away. I went up through the ceiling, I went outside."

"Where did you go?"

"Everywhere, man." Nando sits back and smiles, lights a cigarette from the pack in front of him. "I was the man who runs this place, and I was in all these people who've never heard of this place. They just work and make money and go home and play with their kids and watch TV and do computers and then go to bed, like sleepwalking, never really awake except when they go to sleep. But they never remember their dreams. And then I went inside their dreams and I told them about this place, but they didn't want to hear it, the Eyes didn't want me to wake them up . . ."

Hatch looks at Jaime and wrinkles his brow, bites his lip a moment, looking around. "And then what?"

"I saw the Eyes."

Hatch pops sweat. Eyes pivot to Jaime. "You saw the Eyes."

"Yes, sir, I did. The Eyes of the Secret Teacher."

Jaime closes his eyes, furiously blinks away the purple light behind his eyelids.

"And did they speak to you?"

Nando's smile gets wider. "They did."

"And what did they say?"

"They told me what we must do." The kid laughs, sucking on the cig.

"We?"

"The people of the Secret Teacher. The people of the Dream."

"And what did they tell you to do?"

"They told me not to tell you."

"Me, specifically?"

Nando nods. The smile dries up. "They said to tell you to come and see for yourself, when you're ready."

Hatch thinks for a while, looking at his laptop. Finally, he says, "Good enough, Nando. Thank you."

The kid gets up and goes to the door, smiling at Jaime like they share a joke, if not a secret. He stops.

"Oh, right," Hatch says. "We owe you something for your trouble. You want the pills?"

Nando shakes his head. "Credit is good," he says. "I can buy something somebody needs." He holds out his hand and Hatch, after dicking around with the scanner attached to the laptop, waves it over the kid's wrist, crediting him a hundred bucks. The kid leaves.

"Kid's hooked on Oxys," Hatch says. "I offered him twenty 700s, but he took the cash. Don't tell me this shit doesn't work."

Jaime turns on Hatch. "Did you really take it?"

"Bunch of times."

"And what did it tell you?"

"To turn on the whole wide world."

"That's what God said."

"Jaime, do you know what collective consciousness is?"

"Do I look like I'd know that?"

"It's the idea that everything we fear and love, the things we dream, things we invent, they all come from a common *source*. Consider that every culture managed to develop language, music, mythologies, worship. . . or that primitive tools and architecture developed independently of geography. Like there's an internetwork of awareness where all thought exists, all experience, all knowledge. Maybe it means there's intentional design at work, like there's some big bearded alien sky-daddy out there, tinkering with repeating patterns. Or maybe that's just how evolution works, and all things inevitably bend in the same direction.

Thing is, the closer we move toward advanced civilization and away from that source, the more we're headed toward extinction. Ambition, materialism, politics—self-obsession is a trip, man. Existence is about the individual, now. But what good does that even do?"

Jaime shakes his head. He's lost the conversation. "I don't know. . . My dad always told me 'we've got thumbs and that's why we run shit.' I mean, I might not be able to kill a shark, but I'm smarter than one, you know?" Trying to sound like he's keeping up.

"Some frogs have thumbs, too." Hatch takes a deep breath. "All that an individual consciousness is good for is making us miserable. It's a defective trait. And sharks? They've been around three hundred million years. Other lifeforms come and go, but sharks are still sharks, and in another three hundred million years, sharks might have zippy racing stripes, but they'll still be sharks. That's a successful design. They don't think, they just *are*.

"Meanwhile, we've been around about a half a million years, and we're just a belch and a holler from being nuclear ash, or a slow death by overpopulation and environmental holocaust. All because we aren't aware of anything anymore but ourselves. We're going to sleepwalk off a cliff because somewhere along the way we came unplugged from that network.

"Besides, you heard what he said, Jaime. He didn't just feel some fuzzy Ecstasy fake empathy for people, he *became* them. He didn't just see the fucking machine elves, he had a coherent visitation! When that drug talked to you, or Nando, or Listor, or me. . . it wasn't some Creator, it wasn't just our brains playing tricks on us. It was the collective consciousness of the human fucking race. Maybe of all life on Earth. Maybe the whole universe. It's like being plugged back in. And maybe that's why *we're* here. It's our purpose to see the universe, to think its thoughts, love it, because we're it and it's us. Those Eyes, man, I think they're the eyes of the world. All of us. Living and dead. Looking out of one face in the dark, and trying to come awake.

"And I want to help."

"Listen, I just want. . ."

"Actually, you know what? Fuck what you want. I tried to level with you, but do I owe you anything? You picked me up to sell me, and I used you instead, but we both made out okay. So, if you don't believe in this thing, even after you've experienced it, then I ain't got time for your quaint shit."

Jaime stands there trying to come up with a retort. Maybe before he took that stupid drug, he could've shaken this off, but now he just walks away thinking, *You fucking liar, I know who you are—*

18

To its everlasting chagrin, modern science had tried and failed to measure and categorize the intelligence of people like Nolan Cordwainer Hatch. The special resources teacher who administered a Stanford-Benet IQ test to him at age eight noted that, his extremely high score aside, if the particular quality of young Hatch's intelligence were more widely understood, society would throw a huge national telethon to raise funds to find a cure.

In seventh grade, while making a presentation to the class on one of the world's great religions, Hatch first caught the attention of the authorities when he dosed himself and his teacher with mushrooms. The purpose of this "experiment," as he called it, was to show that divine spiritual states could be chemically induced and were worlds apart from even the most fervently transmitted religious dogma.

At fifteen, Hatch discovered Situationist International, the Church of the Subgenius and RE/Search's *Pranks* issue, and later that year, he and three accomplices were arrested at the Westfield San Francisco Center a week before Christmas. The dying upscale mall had placed an ad for a free photo with Santa Claus in all the Bay Area papers, drawing a massive crowd of families who could never actually afford to shop there. While hundreds waited for hours in lines that spilled out into the rain on Market Street, four minors in Santa costumes stormed the neighboring toy store and distributed armloads of liberated toys to children while eluding security until they were tackled, handcuffed and dragged away by the SFPD. He wasn't the first to pull such a stunt—he'd read about a Danish theater troupe that did the deed in the 1970s, who were inspired by a Situationist prank. What little media coverage the stunt got characterized it as teenage hooliganism and celebrated their arrest, but for Hatch, getting arrested was the whole point. If enough kids saw Santa Claus in cuffs for giving away toys, he hoped someday an army of Santas might seize every mall and initiate an anarchic potlatch.

Maybe it was a coincidence that the local Cacophony Society took up the torch soon after with its annual Santarchy events, which have since devolved into SantaCon, into ideology-free pub crawls with legions of piss-drunk idiots in Santa suits puking and fighting in the street in every major American city. So it could reasonably be argued that Nolan Hatch had been trying to change the world since before he could drive, and had a habit of leaving it more fucked than before.

Like many white, middle-class kids of his generation, Nolan Hatch first encountered transcendence on a dancefloor, under the influence of drugs. The experience was traumatic and glorious, an initiation into adulthood that recaptured one last, wonderful time, the ecstatic terror of childhood. It was hardly lost on him that his spiritual awakening had come to him as far as conceivably possible from anything resembling a traditional church, and that he had reached a peak state of consciousness of being alive in a scene that was, for all intents and purposes, dead as disco.

His first time was like almost everyone else's—the *shoom* of feverish well-being, the blasting waves of love and empathy, an undeniable sense of universal goodness smoldering underneath the shitshow of modern civilization—though the drug did nothing to free his ass from any of it. He was capable of dancing for as long as he focused his entire mind on it, but the moment he let himself go, his feet were rooted to the floor, hands in his pockets. But the sight of the dancefloor, all those individual bodies turned inside out and flying like leaves on the wind of the bassbin pulse, it was as if he finally saw the whole human game from a great enough height to glimpse godhead in its chaos, the incredible blessing of being both within and without it, all the more miraculous for having been bestowed by nobody in particular, unless the universe itself was alive and urging you to *feel it.*

After the first few dozen times, that Ecstasy experience became commonplace, and Hatch wasn't foolish enough to try chasing its diminishing revelations with higher doses, but it changed his life as drastically as any religious experience ever changed any seeker.

Once, in their backyard, he found a praying mantis. Growing up in California, nature was something at the zoo, unremarkable pests that you sprayed or trapped or ran over with your car. The tiny, extravagantly vicious-looking but sublimely placid machine was a revelation. So brilliantly camouflaged, clinging to the fan of stems underneath the leaf of a plumeria, that he suddenly realized how they might have gone unnoticed all around him, all his life. Thereafter, its camouflage worked in reverse and he saw a hidden jewel of a predator lurking in every fan of stems, underneath every leaf. The Trystero Effect. So it was that every other drug in the world might conceal the next stage of his spiritual evolution, his quest for the magical bullet of enlightenment.

He never lost his reverence for the memory of transcendence or the zeal to share it, but the closest he comes to *feeling* it again, is when he watches the women dance.

He watches them now, his face in a trance, tingling with an unstoppable grin. He didn't expect this, he only came to see Jude.

She didn't pick up the first several times he called her. When she eventually does, her irritated breathing is all the greeting he gets.

"We should talk," he tells her.

Her breathing slows.

"It's not the thing we talked about before. I need your help. And I think you need mine."

Did she just yawn?

"I haven't made peace with what happened. Maybe I'm still trying to atone in all the wrong ways, as you say. Nobody else knows me like you do. It's scary, being watched. I'll bet you feel it too."

She sighs.

"Will you hear my confession, Sister Jude?"

"Jesus Christ," she mutters. "What's this really about?"

"I. . . need help picking out a suit. I'm meeting with the most fashionable narco who ever walked the earth, and I need to not look like so clueless. Again."

"So. . . you just want to go shopping?"

"Everybody here looks like they shop at a Burning Man yard-sale."

"Eight o'clock." She clucks her tongue and hangs up.

His phone rings again a moment later and he picks up without looking, thinking it's her again. It's Charlie Tuna, angry as ever because even a brain in a fishtank deserves better entertainment options.

•

Ida Scarfe gives him shit like he wasn't expected, and makes him wait outside while little kids shoot spitballs at him for ten minutes before letting him in.

He gets it. This decompression period is necessary to check his privilege. In big cities all over the world, he's seen places like this, embattled bulwarks, bivouacs in an undeclared but eternal war. How much worse must the atrocities in that war be here, where everything is ultra?

"Go inside," Ida tells him. Her ruddy, grief-creased face studies his long enough for him to feel flayed. "Follow the blue line. Touch any of my sisters, look anybody in the eye, and I will fucking end you, little man."

"Fair enough," he says. The blue line was one of several that goes through the maze of cutout containers and partitions and curtains, borders between group spaces where women cook, teach and counsel and cut each other's hair and spaces where women and children sleep on cots, futons, the floor. Once or twice, he pauses to watch and hears a thick, smoky throat clear itself, and he moves on before the tattooed doorlady can lay a hand on him.

He follows the blue line to a big, open room with a scrap-wood floor, where the ladies are dancing, and all his irritation melts away. Surely, she's arranged for him to see this.

The music is unsettling at first. He can't recognize the time signature. Lilting polyrhythm rolls and skips like a top eternally on the edge of tipping over, both fast and lazy in a way that lulls and galvanizes his nerves so that his head bobs and he sways with it, in time with the ladies.

CODY GOODFELLOW

They move like dervishes, spinning and floating spokes of a wheel, petals of a flower, feet scarcely touching the floor as they twirl away in a cascade of snowflake patterns too intricate to have any designer but chaos and nature.

It's utterly unlike any group of dancers he's ever seen. The movements of the women, in baggy shirts and sweats and plain dresses, delineate flowing sleeves, fluttering fringes and towering crowns. Their faces flow with emotion, now grinning, now weeping, now silently wailing and gnashing teeth, bliss and agony being drawn out like poison by the river of rhythm.

Jude comes around the dance floor to him. She's not smiling. "Go watch the door, Ida."

He flinches but doesn't jump as he realizes America's most infamous female spree killer is right behind him. He braces himself. "Watching you," she whispers, and then is gone.

Jude leads him away down the hall, shushing him until she closes the door behind them. "I'm sorry. . . We've been overwhelmed by a new wave of cases. . ."

"That was remarkable. . . the thing back there, I mean, the dancing. . . That's amazing, what you're doing. I can't get that rhythm out of my head."

She cracks half a smile. "Four-four is great for group dancing because it captures the heart and the id—everyone has a heartbeat, everyone likes to fuck—but it's a trap. What they're dancing to in there, it's six-four with some binaural sub stuff you can't hear out here. The rhythms are synced with the brain's own rhythm, not the heart. It moves their bodies while really opening up their minds. While they dance, they dream."

"And no drugs are involved. . . ?"

She vigorously shakes her head. "A few are still so dissociative, they're on antipsychotics or sedatives, but it doesn't interfere with this. This is what I wanted to show

222

you. The Sufis and other mystics have known it for centuries. I'm starting to see real results with consciousness expansion through music and dance alone. There was nothing wrong with what we were pursuing with drugs, but we used the wrong method. We tried using a sledgehammer to hatch an egg."

He's not prepared for this. He doesn't want to denigrate what she's saying, but what is he supposed to say? *I've come too far to throw away everything because of an aerobics class.*

"Well, it's amazing. I'd like to know more." Grits his teeth. Fingers the plastic bag of microdots in his pocket.

"We can talk about it later," she says, her smile tight. "Let's go shopping."

A tuk-tuk ferries them to the edge of the Green Zone. The bony kid pedaling the fancifully painted auto-rickshaw shoots green bottle-rockets at the sleepwalking, goggled pedestrians blocking their way. Where the augmented reality-walkers congregate and passage becomes impossible, the tuk-tuk drops them off in the midst of the tech market.

Like Akihabara Electric Town in Tokyo, the space becomes almost a platonic galaxy of brands and products. Everything that's not a product, a consumer or a seller is a blinking, animated, brain-zapping brand logo. Boutiques flooded with shiny new gadgets, from phones and headsets to stun guns and drones vie with stalls and carts peddling dismantled components and heavily-modded mutations of the stuff in the shops. Jude tells him about the maquiladoras in the Orange Zone where new gadgets are stripped, gutted and repurposed, usually into some kind of weapon, as she circles a dusty ziggurat of full-spectrum lightboxes, telling him to get one. "One of the biggest reasons people freak out down here," she says. "No sunlight."

Jude goes rigid. Hatch bumps into her. "What is it?"

"Fucking hell," she growls. "Flu season's starting early."

She points at a suspiciously nondescript man in an urban camo poncho bent over a vending machine.

As she sidles closer, he touches all the buttons without making a selection, then moves to the next one. Close up, Hatch notices he's wearing weird gloves.

Jude empties something out of her pocket into her hand and slaps her palm on the guy's shoulder. "That's not a blowjob machine, sport. You gonna pick something?"

The guy looks at her for a second like he's going to explode, but then remembers his job and scuttles off into the crowd, making for a public toilet. Hatch notices a big white handprint on his back.

Jude walks swiftly away, head down. He races to catch up with her. She gets a block away before she explains. "Every winter, they introduce a bunch of new infectious diseases into the mix. Some imported, but mostly out of their own labs, and they track the spread, speed, longevity, fatalities. They give out flu shots to test those, too, but half the time, they're worse than the disease."

"What'd you do to him?"

"I marked him. Some concerned citizen will snipe him or stick a knife in his ribs on the street. . . but they'll just send more."

"Is it such a big deal? If they're just giving people the flu?"

"My first year here, a chop-shop hemorrhagic fever the people called Pantera came through and killed one in twenty. Over five thousand dead from a virus they smeared on doorknobs, and every last one of them was black. Do you know what they called it, upstairs?"

"What?"

"They called it a successful test."

Cross-traffic on the ring street surrounding the Arcade is heavy and electrified with potential violence, a human voltage rushing towards a disturbance outside the main entrance.

A speakers' corner packed with protesters, leaflet-passers, ranters and beggars forms a scruffy barrier reef to the Arcade entrance. Hatch smiles at the Lab Rats, skinny punks stripped to the waist to display jailhouse tattoos and irritant test-grids like skin disease carpet-samples. A bunch of silent demonstrators do Falun Gong-style yoga poses and refuse to explain their cause. But the center of attention is across the street from the Arcade entrance.

A suicide booth covered in flowers and scraps of paper smeared with blood is at the center of a whirling gyre of anger. A skinhead backed by a row of *penitenti* in crimson robes and peaked hoods howls into a bullhorn. "His blood was shed for you! He came to save you, sinners! The fire snuffed out right here, on this very spot! Will you avenge him?"

"What the hell is that?" Hatch asks.

"Christian zealots," she says, gritting her teeth. "Some loony got martyred the other day, so they're trying to start a pogrom." She actually spits on the ground. "God-bothering assholes chasing women off the streets and out of the clubs, vandalizing botanicas and cafes."

"I thought you were pretty keen on God."

"I still believe in God," she says, "but I don't kid myself She still believes in us. It's just more men who can't stop seeing the Devil in every vagina they can't enslave."

They cross the street, weaving between police barricades and big, glass-lined satellite-dish things on adjustable hydraulic arms that he figures must be microwave projectors. He's heard about them being used for crowd control in Indonesia and Russia. They cook people from the inside out. Behind them, sonic assault batteries, riot-foam blowers and automated rubber-bullet cannons like sadistic tennis-ball servers, just another bunch of products for sale.

Hatch flinches sticking his arm under the scanner at the mouth of the Arcade. Cops in black body armor, helmets, masks and bulging augmented-reality goggles that bombard his bloodshot eyes with the criminal record, fitness reports and demographic data of Joaquin Betancourt.

Listor assured him his code is good to go anywhere in the city, but he looks over his shoulder and yes, his tails have gotten better, but he can still pick them out, staring daggers at him from just beyond the police perimeter.

Not much can really surprise him, by now. He's seen every kind of shopping mall—grand high-concept pleasure domes shot through with rollercoasters and waterslides, rambling underground ant-farm concourses and Taj Mahal mausoleums of branded big-box outlets, seedy pirate bazaars and squatters' swap meets. He walked the streets of Amsterdam for days on mushrooms without ever feeling like he was out of a mall, with museums, cathedrals and live sex shows for landmarks amid an endless cobblestone labyrinth of shoe-fetish boutiques, bakeries, cheese shops and grasshopper cafes.

But this is a brutalist Babel tower, a pagan temple to the gods of commerce. The exterior is the hub of the city, a pillar one quarter-mile in diameter and twenty-four stories high with a mall entrance on one side and a hospital on the other. The interior is a cavernous sixteen-story gallery spanned by high-speed escalators, glass-floored bridges and elevators and populated by floating, battling, crumping, fucking holographic avatars. The sealed eight stories above the mall are detention blocks adjacent to the dreaded research labs above the roof of the cavern. Detention and research are pretty much the same thing.

Its dizzying vertical layout reminds him of somewhere, and it bothers him until he places it. Westfield San Francisco Center, where he pulled the first Santa crime spree.

The ground floor—a tiered arena around an ice rink, skate park and plaza that merges the bottom three-stories into a gigantic amusement zone, with videogames and VR rigs, climbing walls and obstacle courses and shit he can't begin to figure out. Several of the arcades are hardcore gold farms run by the Triads and sundry other Asian gangs, an arcane demimonde as violent in real life as its digital universes, and unique because the online gaming is one of the only points of contact with the outside world. The city tolerates it, rumor has it, because notorious hackers among the gaming tribes write much of the malware that plagues American computers, and also provide antivirus software companies with the cheat codes to reliably slay their dragons.

The next four stories are casinos, food courts, restaurants and nightclubs tucked into galleries like blinking hardware in a gargantuan network cabinet. Above that are two stories of movie theaters, and the remaining seven stories are filled with proper shopping.

The back of a panel truck parked just inside is open and guys are giving out brand-new Adidas sneakers. Every iridescent pair shines four different colors as they twirl through the air to be snatched out of sight by grabbing hands.

Hatch angles towards the crowd, but Jude pulls him back. "But that's my brand," he says.

"Think *they* don't know that?" She tugs him towards a swooping, curved express escalator to the seventh floor. He leans over the railing to take in the breathtaking artificial vista. It's the heaven of the spectacle, he thinks, the apotheosis of distraction.

They alight on a floor of sex shops. Naked, freakishly convincing love-dolls hang by wires in window displays, a suspended daisy-chain of automated succubi scissoring and moaning and calling out the names of passersby, begging to be taken home.

"Were you shopping for something in particular?" Jude asks. "I can help you pick out a good one. . ." He blushes, realizing this is her idea of a joke, and thus, probably the start of a sermon. Are these loveless fuck-machines a relief to the women she protects, or an even greater threat?

"I'm in a pretty committed relationship with my hand," he says. He hurries across the concourse to a similar display of grunting, thrusting incubi. "Come over here. I don't want one, but I like to hear them call your name."

"Actually, I just wanted to know if you need to use the restroom. . ."

The oddness of the request catches him off-guard. "I'm good. . ."

"Go in there for me." She hands him her phone. "There's a machine in there, for, you know, relieving yourself. I need pictures."

"And here I thought you were doing me a favor," he says, taking the phone and switching on its camera.

The men's restroom is like any other, with a couple sinks opposite a row of urinals with videoscreens at eye-level above them, and a row of toilet stalls across the back.

He uses a urinal, strenuously looking away from the flashing video and directed audio that artlessly and repeatedly shouts out his name, but he still feels a creeping impulse to protect himself from venereal disease with the Phalanx antiviral urethral beads being advertised to him.

At the end of the sit-down stalls is a peculiar machine like a urinal, but with a foam-lined glory hole in place of a basin, and a video screen that enticingly blinks at him. A tongue licks a pair of full red lips and urges him to come closer.

"Oh my God,' he laughs, realizing this must be what she wanted pictures of.

Outside, he shows her the pictures and they share a good laugh. The machine sucks you off while showing you porn, she explains. She's surprised he never saw one before, they're in most of the bars and nightclubs. It's how they collect semen samples.

They take a glass elevator to the upper galleries. "Let's get you dressed like a grown-up."

The elevator is all-glass, with room for a dozen more people, but their only company is a harried woman with two babies in a stroller. The babies stare at Hatch with that weird, half-mistrustful, half-adoring gaze that kids and dogs always favor him with.

Jude notices them staring and says, "They just like your eyebrows."

He wants to talk, but he holds it until they're out of the elevator.

They come out on the fifteenth floor amid a display of smoke sculptures encased in glass. The high-end men's apparel shops are a weird mix of recognizable names and oddly anonymous shops that actually seem to carry a lot of the ridiculous shit you see on high fashion runways. They're also nearly deserted. The prices are ridiculously out of the reach of any average citizen's credit allowance. The few who can afford this shit just order it online and have it delivered. The eerie feeling that creeps over him takes longer to identify. Nearly everyone on the streets wears cast-off promotional clothing with outdated or defective logos. Even the players take pains to signify through recognizable branded products. The clothing here looks unfinished, empty, until he realizes it's because none of it bears a brand name. How expensive it is down here, not to be a billboard.

Jude leads him past the casual and armorer's shops to a formal-wear boutique with an automated tailor. A full-length mirror scans Hatch and then projects a menu of suit options on him as he clowns around. She picks out an ice cream suit with a straw boater over his objections, refusing to order a backup. "Trust me. Down here, white is a massive statement. Everything is dirty, so it means you're untouchable. You want them to trust you, right?"

Hatch relents and tries on the suit that comes out of the tailor machine. It fits perfectly. Then, shaking her head at his track pants and t-shirt, she orders a bunch more shit without letting him look. He scans for all of it and has it bagged. They stroll around the gallery overlooking the Arcade. "I want to buy something nice for you."

She takes his hand and turns the walk into a dance step, forcing him to pivot into her steely gaze. "I want to apologize," she says.

"For what?"

She squeezes his hand, then lets it go. "Do you accept my apology?"

"But. . ."

"Do you?"

Before he can answer, she dashes up the escalator to the sixteenth floor, and he can only follow. All the shops are vacant or boarded over, pending renovation. At the head of the escalator sits the only merchandise on offer.

The car that sits on a dais beside a big sign that says WIN THIS CAR! is replaced every few months with a newer model, but Jude says nobody ever wins it. The signage promises that every consumer with a blue rating is eligible for the monthly drawing, but the street outside isn't exactly crowded with new cars.

"So," he says. "Do I get to know what you're apologizing for?"

She turns around and feigns intense interest in the car. It looks like someone at the factory paired a tiny Smart car with a vintage Jaguar and spiked their tanks with Spanish fly, left some Macy Gray on the hi-fi.

"I heard some things. About your drug. A woman came in, actually, who said she'd met God on a drug trip, and it helped her kick Baby. She said it's called Soma. That's yours, isn't it?"

"I don't see how. . ." He doesn't know where to begin. He wanted to talk about this subject, tell her how well the tests went. Could Listor already be distributing the doses so soon after the test? Or was he doing it before. . . ? "I'm glad to hear that, but does she really need to kick babies?"

She shakes her head at the weak joke. "Baby is a nasty psychotropic, like bionic ketamine. It's a womb-trip, but it leaves the addict unfit for anything an infant can't do, which some girls think is still a viable career choice."

"What?"

"Sucking," she says. "They just lay in cribs and suck dicks for their fix night and day. It's fucking horrible. But she said she got a free dose of something new, and she met God. And God was a fat, old Latina smoking a blunt, who told her to get her shit together, and took her around the world to see how hard other people have it. How unhappy people who have everything still are."

"That sounds like my baby. I mean—"

"Well, you know how to bury the lede. I can do a lot with rhythmic therapy, but the substance abuse problems. . . It's not just impossible, it's almost illegal here. Most of them, they're *supposed* to be addicted. Somebody is hooking them up and stringing them out to see how to manage them and keep them working until the day they overdose."

They walk over to the edge. Some kind of disturbance way down at the entrance draws a crowd that trips itself up trying to get out of the way of a group marching to the elevators. At the center is a blazing bonfire, but even from this distance, Hatch can make out that it's walking.

He tries to turn Jude away from the sight before she gets upset. He almost tells her about Talkshow Tim and then about Manuelito, who called himself Nando and whom he knows died in prison years ago, but whom he would swear on a stack of deep-fried bibles that he interviewed after the test of his drug that's apparently already out on the street. He wants her to reassure him that she's real and alive and not just another ghost. He wants her to reassure him that he's merely losing his mind.

"We should talk about trying Soma on some of your tougher substance cases."

She turns around, shivering when he takes her arm. "I'd be open to it, but. . . these women are broken, Keller. They don't need a dose of New Age bullshit that tells them another drug is going to fix them. The way things are going right now. . . They're out there looking for witches, and they will always find some."

"We could protect you. . ."

She shakes her head at the profound stupidity of this idea. "Just leave it, okay? If it works, it works, but I'm not looking to build a new Royal Jelly down here. One cult was enough."

"Neither am I, Jude. I just want to help people, and this thing does it. . ." Her eyes are glazing over. He changes tactics. "I missed you, Jude. I wrote to you more than a few times. More than anyone, you were the one I wanted to see, to reconnect with. . . to make amends to. To find you here, it just. . . it feels like all this is happening for a reason."

She looks at him the way those babies looked at him. Her hand comes up and she doesn't back up when he leans in closer, watching her eyes until they close—

"Look at all of this," he says, sweeping a hand across the vast, cavernous space of the Arcade. "All of this, just to distract us, to turn us away from ourselves, from each other. All of this noise and color and glittery shit. . . and it's barely working. They're ready for something more. For something real. They don't know what it is, but they're ready for it. Ready to evolve. . ."

"You really believe you're the one who's going to change all of it."

He shrugs and laughs. "The world uses people like tools to change itself. Am I the right person at the right time? I think I am. But it's not what I want. It's what the world wants."

Now she shrugs, but she doesn't laugh. "That's somehow worse."

The door dings and the elevator doors open. The burning man steps out of the elevator amid a cloud of smoke and dripping molten plastic from the charred lighting fixtures. His flesh is all but consumed, the fire guttering, but still it blazes up like a halo as he slouches past Hatch and Jude and climbs onto the dais beside the car.

A brace of security goons comes up the escalator and more spill out of the elevators to cluster around the mall-invaders, but none of them do anything. Their cop-goggles flash so bright and fast it looks like lightning is leaking out of their brains. Some of them collapse vomiting on the floor, ripping the goggles off. The rest just stand, transfixed, agape and drooling as he passes among them.

The burning man stands for a moment, wobbling, almost physically incapable of standing upright, but then some more urgent force steadies him so he can open the car and settle in behind the wheel.

Hatch clings to Jude and tries to hide her eyes, but she looks over his shoulder, demanding, "Why don't you stop him?"

But nobody stops him.

The driver is little more than a spent matchstick when he somehow starts the car, shifts it into gear and drives it off the dais. The security jumps out of the way as the burning man drives the car around the empty floor, shouting something that barely carries over the engine and the crackle of the flames. But Hatch thinks he can recognize it, with the certainty of one hearing their own name.

The car veers towards Hatch and Jude, who run for the escalator. The car accelerates and smashes into the railing and goes right through it, sailing through the neon ghosts of hologram Rockettes and Nike swooshes and ArmaLite assault rifles with the flames whipping out the open windows, all the way to the ice rink on the ground floor.

The car has no gas tank, so there's no fire, but nonetheless, it explodes. The frame accordions into a compact aluminum rhombus. Glass, plastic body panels, wheels, and the rest of the charred driver are flung in a vicious parabola into the panicked skaters, splintering the ice and flattening a grievous radius of bystanders. They stampede to get away from the carnage, but immediately channels their fear into anger and greed. The crowds begin to swarm up the escalators, smashing windows and flinging merchandise over the balconies until it's raining everything but rain.

Looting turns to rioting. Police swarm into the Arcade like a wave of oil on a grease fire.

"We should go," Hatch says, but Jude is livid, shivering, white hands clinging to the railing and fuming at the rippling waves of chaos below.

"Can your drug fix this?" she asks. "What they've turned us into, blind monsters biting each other in the dark. Can you fix it?"

He puts his arm around her, but in his ears, he still hears the sound of the burning man's blazing vocal cords as he drove the car off the balcony. The words the protestors on the escalator are chanting now.

El maestro occulto!
The Secret Teacher.
"*We* can fix it," he says.

19

He remembers the cold, silver Christmas.

The last year in Idaho, the winter the gas and power were shut off. The pipes froze, they melted snow over the wood stove.

Orrin was eight, his sister Nichole three, when Dad left for the last time, that summer. When Donald Litchfield ran out of trouble to get into in Idaho Falls, he went to Reno to deal cards, and surprised his wife Norlene with a check three months later, along with divorce papers. The papers went through, but the check bounced.

It was colder and darker when Orrin got up that Christmas morning than when he went to bed, but where there was nothing in the corner between the old green recliner and the burnt couch covered in grimy blankets last night, now there stood a silver Christmas tree. Scarcely taller than Orrin, it was made of tinsel and coathangers and strangled in bubbler lights and drugstore ornaments, but it was a glorious sight, as were the presents under it.

He'd been told to expect something special from Santa, but he'd begun to doubt. His father was a classic Jack Mormon, a smoking, drinking backslider who didn't tithe or attend services and called churchgoing Mormons suckers, but there was a portrait of Jesus on the wall, and they always had a tree in the corner the week after Thanksgiving.

He and his sister were rabid to tear into the presents, but Mother made them wait and drink cocoa while she struggled to make biscuits on the wood stove, because Santa wanted to watch them open the presents.

This was a queer miracle, but the kids sat on the couch and listened to the radio, watching the blank table against the back wall where the old Magnavox TV had sat until Dad took it.

And by and by, Santa came to their house. He was indeed a jolly fat man with a long, mostly white beard, and his belly shook like the proverbial bowlful of jelly as he watched Orrin and Nicole open their presents—a doll, a Slinky and a wooden puzzle for Nichole, and a pair of cross-country skis, a GI Joe doll and a copy of *The Book Of Mormon* for Orrin.

Nichole was beside herself, but Orrin was suspicious from the moment he asked if they'd like to come live with him at the North Pole.

Mother acted weird in a way he couldn't understand until much later, but which left him giddy and manic. It was the first time she'd ever sought her son's approval, but really, it didn't matter what he thought. By the way she laughed too hard at all his jokes and kept pushing the kids into his lap, Orrin instinctively understood, even if he didn't quite grasp that Dad wasn't coming back, that Mother was going to marry Santa Claus, who would turn the gas and the lights back on.

Santa's real name was Leland Snodgrass, and he was as good as his word, after a fashion. He took them all to live with him, but not at the North Pole. They lived in a trailer on his ranch in Colorado City. Right away, he stopped being anything like Santa. Orrin figured his mother probably wouldn't have married him, if Snodgrass hadn't come courting in the depths of winter, and if not for winter, Snodgrass probably wouldn't have five wives.

Orrin had heard only slurs and bad jokes about polygs, but Mother said what Don Litchfield didn't know about religion, you could just about fill the Bible with, but most of Dad's polyg jokes turned out to be spot-on.

Only Deirdre lived in the big house as his legal wife, but the other five "spiritual wives" had already bore him nineteen children, with four other awkwardly absorbed adoptees from previous marriages.

As his sixth celestial wife, Mother was legally still a single parent, the better to "bleed the beast," which was their biblically heroic spin on welfare cheating. All the same, Orrin Litchfield became Orrin Snodgrass, and was beaten whenever he used his old name on his schoolwork.

Mother was pregnant within a month of moving down there, but the children never saw their new father in private. He visited each of his wives for a night or two only when they were ovulating, which was hectic, as all his wives had their menstrual cycles in sync. Orrin and Nichole spent those nights in a camper around the other side of the big house from the trailers. They weren't allowed to have Coke any more, but she snuck them candy bars and other treats when she could.

Leland delivered a sermon after dinner most evenings, but he preferred to communicate in divine revelations dictated to him by the Lord God, who seemed to concern Himself most deeply with cleanliness, obedience, the orderly execution of chores around the Snodgrass property, and the venomous condemnation of rival polyg sects in the same town. These would be copied out on yellow legal pad in painstakingly uniform block capitals, taped to the front of the fridge in every trailer, every morning. Orrin once wondered aloud if the rest of the world was such a godless, dangerous place because God was so preoccupied with everything that went on in their home. For this and a thousand other infractions, Orrin got to spend more private time with Leland than any of his blood children, or most of his wives.

He remembers the hot golden room, the Golden Rule and the golden ruler, with which he was regularly beaten.

Leland didn't take any particular interest in Orrin after Mother bore him a daughter and then a son, but he was forever having to remind the boy of the natural order. His oldest son had a wife of his own and lived next door, and he would inherit the ranch. A man had to build a home for at least three wives if he had any hope of attaining the Kingdom of God, and so Orrin would have to show much more initiative than he seemed to possess, unless one counted getting in trouble.

The frequent visits to Leland's study nearly always culminated in a beating, but the punishment was so uniform that it was the same beating over and over, so Orrin could tune it out more easily each time and study the room, which was the most beautiful place he'd ever seen. When he read of the wealth of kings like Solomon and Herod in the Bible, he imagined they spent their days in a room much like Leland's.

There were biblical artifacts and electroplated replicas of the gold tablets the angel Moroni bestowed upon Joseph Smith in Palmyra, and framed stock certificates showing a sizable investment in the legendary Dream Mine in Salem, Utah. Eight lush portraits of the prophets of fundamentalist

Mormonism glowered down on his nakedness, some with mercy twinkling in their eyes, most only with cold fire.

Leland was a collector of rare books, art and historical documents, and like many Mormon radicals, a skilled forger of same. With no one else to brag to, he often showed Orrin his latest masterpiece, usually a pamphlet or letter attributed to Smith, Young or another of the early Saints, but sometimes a birch-paper scroll in the style of the Dead Sea Scrolls and left in ancient America by the Nephites. Leland made even more off other, more gullible fundamentalists who bought and treasured them to bolster their faith, than he did off welfare fraud.

His favorites were purchased directly by the other beast he most loved to bleed, the compromised, greedy abomination of the false LDS orthodoxy in Salt Lake City. Once when Orrin was thirteen and caught shoplifting, Snodgrass was too overjoyed to follow through on the beating, instead sharing with him a final divine revelation dictated to Joseph Smith shortly before he was shot by a lynch mob in Carthage. In it, God revealed that the Mormon faith would founder on the rocks and the Kingdom of God would go unattained, unless every man willingly took at least one other man as a celestial husband, alongside his many, many wives.

The flawless counterfeit of the prophet's own writing on vintage foolscap from the region and era had fetched an astronomical sum from the apostate mother church, who were equally foolish and corrupt, whether they were taken in by the outrageous declaration of mandatory gay marriage, or cynically willing to pay a ransom to keep it out of circulation.

It wasn't until he entertained this momentary but welcome distraction from another lesson with the golden ruler, that Orrin realized that there were other little boys like him all over town and in polyg colonies from Mexico to Canada. It was funny that God would want men to get married, but it made a funny kind of sense. The surfeit of sons bound to fail the Lord's marriage demands was part and parcel of the system, and nobody seemed to know what to do with them. While every elder of decent standing had at least five wives, God didn't make five girls for every boy.

Since he was already being beaten regularly for doing his chores poorly, he skipped them and started going out.

Around town, Orrin began to meet and then run with other "lost boys"—disenfranchised younger sons and adoptees with no hope of making good in the system that hatched them out and raised them to dogged obedience. With no TV, radio, newspapers or contact with the outside world, they were more naïve even than Orrin, who'd lived in their bubble since he was eight, and was beyond restraint.

They went wild in every way you could with no money, no cars, no drink and no drugs in a town where every approachable girl was married to a man three times her age before she turned fourteen. Orrin started smoking pot and breaking into Gentile trailers. Sometimes he'd steal drugs and panties and porn, or just vandalize the place. Others, he'd just watch cartoons and eat their cereal.

The Sheriff brought Orrin home one night after catching his miserable gang running from a fire they'd started in a garage while huffing kerosene fumes. Instead of beating him, Leland admitted he was at fault for not raising the boy closer or taking his education in hand. He now sought to make up for it by instructing Orrin in the arts of Mormon theology, divine revelation and document forgery. The beatings came more frequently than ever, but they were well worth it, for what he learned.

It was harder for Orrin to separate how he felt about their time together. For seven long years, Leland Snodgrass was the author of all the boy's misfortunes, and many times, he wished they could go back to that icy cold cabin in Idaho. But was he not also the only father Orrin had, and the holder of any hope of a future? Even though he'd cursed his stepfather every night before drifting off to sleep, still it was impossible to resist the pull of such a powerful personality when it turned its full charm upon him, even as he came to understand the ruthless purpose to which he was being shaped.

Leland waited until Orrin was sixteen to spring a birthday surprise that reminded him of the cold, silver Christmas.

All young Mormon men and women fulfilled a mission before embarking into the world as adults, and Orrin Snodgrass would be no different. He was given a dead-on fake Nevada driver's license in the name of ORRIN LITCHFIELD and the keys to one of Leland's nondescript domestic cars, and more, he was to take his place in the next great chapter of the unfinished *Book of Mormon*.

Leland revealed that he had been vouchsafed a removal revelation of such magnitude, that he pleaded with the Lord not to do it, but His will is inviolate, His word is fate. Leland was "the one mighty and strong" foretold by the prophet, and the tools for the accomplishment of the great Work were already in his hands.

As Leland saw it, he needed only one tool.

He presented Orrin with two crisply folded sheets of the same yellow legal pad as all the revelations about the mortal sins of dandruff and pouring food waste down the garbage disposal, but this was a list of names, addresses and phone numbers, mostly in Utah, but some here in Nevada, and as far away as British Columbia.

Eleven of them.

Apostates and enemies of God's will, one and all they had worked to make of the Mormon faith an abomination that led millions into eternal damnation. Flagrant and unrepentant in their sins, which could only be expiated by blood atonement. God's will that they be erased from the earth. No sin, but heroic acts in God's service, for which he would be richly rewarded here and in Heaven.

He would be another Nephi, when he slew Laban. Another Orrin Porter Rockwell, the Destroying Angel, for whom he was surely named. He had only to ask God for divine guidance to steady his hand and lead him on his mission. Two more presents—five hundred dollars, a gas card with his own name on it, and a .32-caliber revolver with a box of bullets.

If he shirked this mission, if he refused it or failed in any way to make it the sole purpose of his life until it was accomplished, he would die on the spot and burn in eternal damnation. And so, for his failure would his mother and half-siblings, even his sister, burn in Hell, though Leland would try to save the latter, at least, by marrying her as soon as she got her first infection.

Through this act, he would become a man. With unshaken faith, he would follow the Lord's light through this vale of tears and help lead His chosen people into the coming apocalypse with their salvation assured. Leland had talked with the other apostles and elders of the church, and Orrin would have three wives waiting for him when he returned from his mission.

In that stuffy, sweltering study, he felt the same way he'd last felt when Santa Claus brought them presents and stole their lives. The way he felt when Mother looked at him, that made him feel more loved than ever, but also terrified that no one behind the wheel knew the way home, or anything else.

He begged the right to ask a question, and Leland cautiously granted it. If almighty God wanted all these people dead, he asked, then why didn't He just strike them down with lightning or whatever, as He would strike down Orrin for failing to murder them?

Leland regarded him long and hard before putting aside the temptation to beat him one last time with the golden ruler, but then inspiration struck. "Because, my son. . . you will be His lightning."

Leland made Orrin copy the list out in his own hand on a piece of paper and promise to commit it to memory, then destroy the list. He prayed with him and laid a blessing on him for an hour, then told him to take the keys and go. His sister and mother could not know of his mission on peril of their immortal souls. His clothing and personal stuff was in a cardboard box in a Pinto station wagon parked at the back fence of the ranch. There were maps in the car, and blankets and a sleeping bag. His money would last longer if he avoided motels.

It was late November and starting to snow when Orrin set out from Colorado City to execute every enemy Leland Snodgrass could think of adding to the list. That night, sleeping in the car at a rest stop, he prayed to God for guidance, and for the first time in his life, he received an answer to his prayers.

It wasn't a voice or a light or an unmistakable sign like Leland described, but a feeling, impossible to ignore, of the path he must take.

He drove to California.

He was tall for his age, neither ugly enough to get shot down, nor beautiful enough to get used. He slept on the beach when the weather was good that first summer, in the Pinto when it wasn't, and he found an infinite variety of ways to live like a bird on the wing in Los Angeles. Still, he woke up from nightmares of God's vengeance striking him down, of burning in a Hell much like Leland Snodgrass's study, with Dream Mine stock certificates and phony scripture on the walls. But outside his dreams, the sinful Gentile world slowly began to convince him that maybe

Leland Snodgrass and the eight prophets before him were full of shit.

He was almost seventeen when he thought seriously of going back. Mother loved Leland Snodgrass or swore she did for their sakes, but even she wouldn't let her husband marry her daughter. He called the big house pretending to be a social worker tracking welfare checks and demanded to speak to Norlene Snodgrass, but he was told by the woman who answered that Leland Snodgrass had passed away of heart failure several months ago, and his extended family had been dispersed. A little further investigation revealed that Mother was now the happy seventeenth wife of an 89-year old church elder. Nichole was now second wife of LeRoy Snodgrass, eldest son and heir to the ranch. A bit more reformed than his father, LeRoy had foresworn marrying her until her fourteenth birthday.

With no home to go back to, Orrin used a temporary gig at a print jobber to forge transcripts and other documents so he could finish high school, then community college, then university, where, while working towards med school, he chanced upon an opportunity to perform an abortion shortly before the procedure became legal.

Whatever guilt he might've felt at the time, he rationalized quite effortlessly with the fragments of dogma he'd absorbed. It was no sin to kill the godless products of a godless world and anyway, he was fast coming to conclude, if God existed at all, every time He'd reached out to try to inspire a prophet and save the human race from itself, the message got garbled and fucked by the base human desires in even the most sanctimonious of prophets. The Mormon faith was indelibly stained at its birth by Joseph Smith's insatiable money-digging charlatanry and his lust for a personal harem, then by Brigham Young's authoritarian streak and vitriolic racism, and the fundamentalist sects splintered every time a supposedly immortal prophet perished. The one morsel of religion that he took with him as he went forward into professional life and dark celebrity as Hollywood's leading abortionist was the sanctity of direct, divine revelation. If God existed, let Him reach out and speak His mind directly.

He enjoyed a career as free of scandal as it was embroiled in it. Patients told him he looked like Burt Lancaster when they wheedled for painkillers, and like Karl Malden when he turned them down, but he never slept alone unless he wanted to, and he didn't send them back to a trailer-park harem. He threw them back into the heaving human sea little better than he found them, but generally no worse, and if he knocked up a few of them himself, he took care of that, too.

When, thirty years later, he finally had what he would later call a genuine divine revelation, the resulting nervous breakdown ended his career and sent him into a druggy tailspin of disgrace and degradation that brought him, for his sins, here, to this incredible simulation of Hell a half-mile underground.

But now, he is on regular speaking terms with the Lord of Hosts, Yahweh Elohim, or His angels, which difference matters little in the end. For Orrin Litchfield has very little rational reason to doubt but that he, of all fucking people, is "the one mighty and strong" foretold by prophecy, which is nothing to boast of, but a terrible bloody burden, for the list of names this time goes halfway around the world.

But it's someone else's prophecy, now. He's far from the first man to go to his grave thinking he was the one who would pave the way for the second coming of Christ, but he doubts anyone ever accepted a martyr's death with greater relief.

20

Jaime told him it was stupid to meet at the Arena. Jaime warned him not to go out in public at all. And Jaime emphatically advised against the ice cream suit.

Nobody listens to Jaime.

Hatch dragged him along to confront the Green Man after he came back from shopping. "You've been dishing out Soma behind our backs."

Listor was anything but coy. "There's a whole world going on behind your back, boy. You should turn around and look more often."

Jaime knew he should just be wallpaper, but he couldn't hold back. "That shit is making people off themselves. You gotta take it off the street."

"Are you dead yet?"

"It was heavy, but I didn't set myself on fire. . ."

"And no side-effects?" Did the motherfucker wink?

Jaime swallowed his answer.

"Your dosage was weak. So was mine. Only about 3,200 micrograms. The new strain is closer to 22,000."

Hatch was horrified. "That's ten times the first batch yield, and all our test pilots crashed! Do you have any idea what that does?"

"Makes it stronger, I imagine." Listor smiled, but his eyes looked like they were trying to escape his head. The fine lines of his face twitched and tugged with conflicting impulses. "I'm a drug dealer, boy. Not a drug czar. The first tests weren't half the failure we thought they were, at first. It works. Ergo, it goes out."

"But this wasn't what we agreed. . . We can't just dump it on the street. People need to be *spiritually* prepared. One of our test pilots set himself on fire and drove a car off the top floor of the Arcade."

"Excellent," Listor said, though his hands shook and he looked spooked. "They're waking up."

"They're checking out! It's all going wrong! We need a shaman. . ."

"Wasn't your whole pitch that by tripping to the other side, everyone could become a shaman. . . ?"

"We both know it's not that simple."

"So *you* be a shaman."

"I can't do it. That's why I came to you."

"Then you're not really relevant to the process anymore, are you?" Listor fixed them both with a reptilian gaze until they backed out of the room.

•

So Hatch set up this meeting with Lalo, Hector Obregon's factotum.

"They need to know," Hatch says. "We need to get out in front of this."

So it can run us over, Jaime thinks.

Bad venue: public, but in disputed Yellow Zone territory, and without Listor's protection. Hatch keeps telling him to relax, he trusts Lalo, but his fear is a sickly, slimy thing that Jaime can almost see oozing out of his eyes.

He's been seeing and feeling a lot of weird things like this, ever since he took Hatch's fucked-up drug. Seeing things inside people and feeling them. It's like everyone on the street has a big bucket of shit or worse for a head, and they dip their hands in it as they pass and smear it on him. He's been holed up in his room getting as high as he can, whenever he's not trying to figure out what he's still doing with these idiots.

They disembark from a pedicab outside a sprawling superbloque teeming with sicarios, street urchins, prostitutes, and thieves. Hatch's stupid white suit practically glows, and everyone they pass takes notice, but that's not why Jaime is nervous. Everybody's looking at them like they're famous. Like the guests of honor at a funeral.

The tower walls across the street are covered in Eyesore's acid-flashback zincography prints: La Toda Madre as the Virgin Mary, blue mantle over white robe mirroring the indigo cap and white stalk of the gigantic, haloed mushroom cradled in her arms. EL MAESTRO OCULTO ES EL SALVAJE!

"Nice campaign, eh?" Hatch beams.

The Arena looks like any other boxing venue, with tiered benches surrounding a recessed pit with a floor of cat litter and a high iron fence. The crowd a motley mob of about two hundred street freaks, suckers and retail gangsters, smoking, shit-talking, placing bets on phones. No Poison Boys on the scene, but no Zeros, either.

A cigarette girl with a pyramid of drug selections on a tray leads them back to a booth high above the crowd and leaves them a bottle of champagne.

Hatch nervously peels the foil and pops the cork. "I see what you meant about this place. It's fucking barbaric."

"You don't see shit."

Hatch fills a plastic flute with champagne and hands it to Jaime. "I feel like anything could happen. Like a pawn in a great game. I close my eyes and hear rolling dice. Is that what you mean?"

He doesn't feel it, or he won't. He brought us this shit. He turned it loose. How can he not feel it?

Hatch is trying to lecture him about the universe working towards its highest good when he notices the man standing by the booth, waiting patiently to be noticed.

He's easy to ignore. A middle-aged white man in worn-out jeans, a plaid flannel shirt and a brown leather jacket. He barely has a face. Nothing missing or deformed, but just the plainest set of features God ever put on a head. Jaime keeps looking at him to try to find a descriptor, but nothing sticks until those eyes meet his, and then he can't move or speak for the weight of mortal terror crushing him down like an invisible avalanche of black ice.

"Mr. Hatch?"

Hatch sips champagne. "You have me at a disadvantage, friend. . . You are?"

The man looks rather sheepishly at Jaime, but then says, "My name's not important. I've heard you're the man to see about a new drug that sounds *very* interesting. I'd like to try it."

Hatch looks at Jaime as if to say, *See? Nothing to worry about.* "Well, that may be true and it may not. How'd you hear such a thing?"

"I hear things in the circles I move in. I'd rather not burden you with it, but people are saying your drug lets them see what it's like to be other people. I could sure use some of that, if that's the truth."

Jaime's looking for the Poison Boys or anyone who could cut this encounter short, but Hatch is captivated by this oddly blank man. "You don't need my permission."

"I don't want to be let down," the man says, curiously agitated.

"Well, shit, why don't you have a seat?" Hatch pours the man a flute and scoots over to make room in the booth. "I'd like to hear your story."

The man sits down, but he doesn't touch the champagne. Just stares into the bubbles. "You see, for about thirty-odd years, I've been drifting around the country. Wasn't like a calling or anything, but it felt like it needed doing."

"What needed doing?"

The man looks up from the bubbles. "Killing."

"Oh," Hatch says, like he's just realized he's the dumbest man in the room.

The man shakes his head. "Not like that. A lot of folks don't believe I exist. Those who do think I'm a multitude. I've been called the Night Rider, the Roadrunner, and I don't know what-all.

"There's men in the world that nobody needs. When they go missing, nobody calls the police or makes a fuss, nobody really misses them. When they turn up months or years later at the bottom of a river or a lake, it looks like they got drunk and fell off a bridge taking a piss. Heck, half the time, they thank me, just before they go down."

"I see," Hatch says. "And. . . how. . . ?"

"Hundreds. I stopped keeping count after a while," the man says. "It seemed prideful. Architects shouldn't sign their names to cathedrals."

Hatch looks at Jaime. Jaime looks everywhere but at the Roadrunner, who finally takes a sip of the champagne.

"I don't play crazy games, leaving clues and such, trying to get caught. It's a service nobody else wants to do."

"Why confess to me?"

"I began to wonder. Am I doing the Lord's work? Am I being true to my nature? Or am I just killing myself in effigy? I searched my heart and sought solace in religion, but I feel nothing."

"And you think. . . Soma could help you." Hatch watches the man with a sickening mix of repulsion and fascination. Working at the stitches of a hidden pocket in the front of his slacks, Hatch palms something and passes it to the blank-faced man.

"I'll try it, then," says the Roadrunner, sliding out of the booth. "Thank you."

"You, um. . . have a nice night!" Once the man is out of sight, Hatch bolts down champagne straight from the bottle. "That was. . . weird."

"I tried to tell you. You don't want to be famous down here, motherfucker. Once people start to talk about you, you got the life expectancy of a housefly."

"You worry too much."

"That motherfucker was walking death and you know it."

"And we might cure him." He says something else, but the music drowns it out. Sandblaster static and gut-pummeling bass fills the arena. Two teams of technicians, handlers and a posse of bodyguards come out of the locker rooms to scattered cheers, boos and thrown firecrackers.

Hatch shouts over the music.

Jaime takes the bottle and kills the champagne, then lights a joint. "What's that?"

"I'm starting to think the Green Guy was right. Just put it out there. Let it do its magic."

Jaime is awestruck by the fucker's arrogance. Let him see this show, he thinks, and tell me he can change it. "Yo, where's your fucking date for tonight?"

An announcer is touting the combatants in the first match. The handlers escort their fighters into the arena, but two men standing on opposing platforms above the ring are the focus of attention. A pudgy black guy in silk pajamas pumps his crotch and gives his rival the finger. The rival, a skinny white kid all of fifteen, cracks open an energy drink and shotguns it, then both strap on VR goggles and gloves.

Down in the arena, the hoods come off two naked veggies—pale, emaciated, wall-eyed death camp matchstick men with plugs and blinking relays embedded in their bald skulls. One's slightly taller, huskier than the other, but he limps on a cheap plastic prosthetic limb. The other one weaves in circles like he's blindfolded and about to whomp a piñata.

"The fuck is this?" Hatch finally takes notice, sitting up and sliding around like he's going to bail.

"You don't know?" Jaime waves for another bottle. Sucks his joint down to a roach and drops it in Hatch's drink. "I thought you had it all figured out."

An triple airhorn blast sends the two VR players into a frenzy of stylized combat dance-moves that are mirrored perfectly by the shambling human husks in the arena. The husky veggie grapples his opponent into a wall and gouges at his eyes, but the smaller one twists out of the grip, bashes his forehead into the bigger man's sternum and sweeps the fake leg. The husky fighter stumbles and goes down on his ass, but rather than press his advantage, the smaller fighter spins uncontrollably and keeps bashing his head against the wall like a glitchy videogame NPC. While the tubby guy's crew rages and cries foul, the husky veggie slowly climbs to his foot and beats his faulty opponent's head into red-gray slush with his prosthetic leg.

"Jesus, this is sick," Hatch says.

"You really think anybody down here wants to feel anyone else's pain? That they even want God to know what they've been doing?"

Jaime's thinking he might be starting to get through to him, but that's when Lalo finally arrives. Three Poison Boys in matching black pinstripe suits surround the booth.

Hatch bellows, "Lalo! My man!"

Lalo appears tired, sick, weak. He hunches over the table, looking sideways before speaking. "My master would like to know when the side effects wear off."

"What side effects?"

"He has found it difficult to do his work. . . He has always been troubled by what other people think and feel, but now. . . it's much worse. He was supposed to fight tonight." He points down at the arena. "In the title match. Against Tres Ojos. It has become something of a Christmas tradition. . ."

Hatch looks at Jaime and mouths, "Is it really Christmas?"

Jaime shrugs. Who fucking cares?

"He has a reputation to uphold. They will not accept his tenderness, so they must be made to recognize his ferocity. But he cannot even consider killing an enemy, without feeling sick with pain and fear. It consumes him. This is not what he wanted."

"Perhaps he's in the wrong business."

"That may be so," Lalo admits, "but there are other problems."

"I'm sorry you're upset," Hatch says. "I want us to trust each other. The Green Guy has been tweaking its potency, and. . . there've been overdoses. . ." The realization snaps into place. "They're overdosing on empathy! Jesus, it all makes sense now. . ."

No shit, Jaime thinks.

Hatch is spinning so fast with this theory, he doesn't notice what Jaime notices. The matching suits the Poison Boys are wearing are dirty, wrinkled. Something is off. Lalo's trying to scream with his eyes. . .

Jaime slides out of the booth, but a wall of pinstripes blocks him from going anywhere. He appeals to Lalo. "Just gotta piss, man."

He moves between the fake Poison Boys, observing stubble, bad breath, body odor. . . bullet holes in their suit backs. He crosses the lounge and ducks into the restroom corridor, takes out his phone.

He's waiting for Listor to pick up when a big man takes the phone out of his hand.

He can only watch through the crowd as Hatch tries to slide out of the booth. Lalo socks Hatch in the nose so hard, the mingled crunch of fingerbones and cartilage traverses the massive, noisy room.

Deprived of the evening's regularly scheduled fight, the crowd pivots to encircle the booth. A fist lifts Jaime off his feet by his collar, holds him frozen.

Lalo stumbles out of the booth like an amateur's puppet, arm windmilling blood everywhere. Kicking like he's trying to stave off a wave of spiders, Lalo curls Hatch into a fetal ball on the floor and stomps on the American's arms, legs and head.

Hatch screams for Jaime, but he does nothing to fight back. His luminous ivory suit dappled with blood and grime. The crowd roars for the wired little man to finish his opponent. Lalo stoops over, pummeling Hatch with his broken hand until shards of bone jut through pulped flesh. When he finally sputters to a stop, collapsing alongside Hatch, his head is turned at a bizarre angle so Jaime can see the blinking LED's embedded in the sutures on the back of his head.

The crowd parts for the victor to approach. Peeling off his VR goggles and gloves and tossing them over one mountainous shoulder, a stout man possessed of great imaginary height, wearing a spotless white suit much like Hatch's, and a silver and black luchador mask with a blinking 3 on its forehead.

He accepts the crowd's deafening cheers and a magnum of champagne. Without taking off the mask, he drains it like a beast, smashes the bottom out and uses the neck to carve Lalo's face off.

The goon holding Jaime by the collar snaps the phone in half in his face. "El Pitufo," he says. "Go tell your boss to find a hole, and bury himself." He shoves Jaime towards the door.

21

It's hard to keep a gang together when your leader dies. Egil's recently learned this the hard way. Even if all your muscle is still intact, the enemy will still think you're weak, a body without a head. And they'll come at you fast.

None of that prepared him for this.

When a church loses its head, it becomes something far more powerful. Far from fighting to keep it together, they've had to fight to keep it from running away in all directions. The most fanatical converts are the ones who came after the prophet died, setting fires and stringing people up on every corner in his name. Egil's found himself in the unlikely position of substitute preacher, trying to keep the message alive, to remind followers that the miracles were real.

Miracles like the soup kitchen, which continues to feed hundreds, though they ran out of food five days ago, just after Litchfield was shot. He knows it's God's own magic, but he can't bring himself to watch those lines of starving faces, those grasping claws holding up their bowls for a ladle filled only with steaming dishwater, thanking God and praising the flavor. Whatever is filling those bellies now, it's not soup.

He retires to the only place he can't hear them singing night and day, though it gives him little comfort to sit in vigil over the preacher's corpse.

Abner and some juiced-up steakhead Egil doesn't know are reclined on the couch. Abner smokes crack and the roid-case eats hot wings and gets a blowjob from a little bald guy in a hospital johnny who's got his hands cuffed behind his back. "Take it, you little cuck, you're a cuck bitch, aren't you?"

Egil knows he should tell them this is neither the time nor the place, but he's just *tired*. He sits on a swaybacked bench and bows his head before the examination table where Orrin Litchfield has lain in state for almost a week, now. Jesus came back after three days, so he'd be a fool to hold out hope now, wouldn't he?

But he does. What else can he do?

The hell of it is, Egil's never had much use for God. Prison taught him that every jailbird carries around a little invisible daddy that he prays to, that always, always fails them, just like their real fathers failed. God isn't a genie who grants wishes. He's a deadbeat dad who sent you a McDonald's gift certificate as a late Xmas gift.

Egil didn't ask God for anything when he first got sent up for stabbing a nigger at the mall. He didn't ask for anything when a Mexican smashed his knee in a gladiator match at Chino. Niggers and Mexicans pray to God, too, and the way the world is going, they seem to have His ear, mostly.

He didn't buy into the Odin cult nonsense his Nazi jailbird bros worshipped with blood and ink. A god just for white men was an even smaller invisible daddy. The Aryan prison gangs killed more of each other than the enemy. Every guy on the hit list was in the shit for refusing to kill some brother who refused to kill this other brother who fucked over another brother you never even heard of in a meth-for-mammoths exchange, back in the Ice Age.

Egil didn't buy into that shit. He cleared the whole slate and some hated him for it, but none denied he was the hardest, and he never tried to be the top dog. He had no taste for being everybody's daddy. And he knew they were all fools, but he kept the faith, etched it into his skin for the same reason the others did. Because no other humans would have him.

None of that changed when Childress came back, but suddenly, he didn't have to pretend. They had God on their side for real. It didn't matter if he believed or not. The preacher healed his knee and for the first time in half a life, he could run. It was a miracle, and no one could talk him out of it.

Egil was right next to the preacher when the asshole in the poop hat shot him. He was tangling with people screaming in the preacher's face when the shot knocked him back on his heels. And he felt the hot mist of cranial fluids on his face. He tried to tackle the assassin, but the crowd claimed him, lifted him up and ripped him apart right before his eyes. Egil and the core cadre got the preacher into a van and back to the Aryan Brotherhood's compound, but the preacher was dead before he hit the ground. Chigger, the blind one, refused to let them take the body away. "He's carrying the fire. He can't die now."

And maybe that ugly half-nigger was right. Seven days on, the preacher smelled better than when he was alive. Some kinda spices, like a scented candle. He might be just napping, caught for a week between breaths. Egil don't pretend to understand it, but he don't have to. When he starts to wonder like this, he starts to feel that steel pin in his mangled knee. He just has to believe, but he wishes he knew what to believe in.

He has the gun that killed Litchfield in his pocket. He saw it for just a moment in the assassin's hand. It was the only one found in the street after the frenzy.

And for all the weird shit flying around right now, it's the one thing that's got Egil Sorensen tied up in knots of doubt.

It's a plastic orange squirt-gun.

Full of *water*.

Oh, he was careful. Thorough, even. The water in the squirt-gun isn't just water. He got the brothers who cook their speed to test it. Some kind of alkaloid psychoactive substance dissolved into it. The lunatic wasn't even trying to kill the preacher, just dose him.

Crazy fucking world.

Egil heard the shot. He saw Litchfield fall down with blood sloshing out a hole in his skull. A child's fist could've fit in it. He may not have seen a dove fly out of the exit wound like some people are claiming, but he never had any reason to doubt it could've happened, like he's been doubting everything that's happened since.

It's not for you to understand, he keeps telling himself. It's for you to wait and patiently serve.

"Take it, take it, cuck. . ."

Enough waiting. Egil gets up and grabs a baseball bat. He almost goes for the niche in the back of the chapel. He hasn't peeked in there since that first day a thousand years ago, when they brought Casper in here. He doesn't understand it and so his first instinct is to go and smash it, but. . .

Abner and the roid-case are making out, woozily shotgunning viscous crack-smoke in a sloppy kiss. Egil crosses the room and swings. Smashes in the back of the juicer's skull so he headbutts Abner and knocks his front teeth down his throat.

"The fuck, bro?" Abner scuttles backward off the couch. Little bald guy jumps up with his hands behind him and runs screaming out of the chapel.

"Thou shalt not. . ." Egil uses the bat on the juicer a few more times to get the point across. Until blood glurts irrhythmically from every god-given hole in his head. Until his skull slumps over on his neck like a bag of broken glass.

Abner sputters through bloody gums, "Bro, if you're jealous. . ." He slips a Buck knife out of his boot and flicks it open.

"You never believed," Egil says. "Get out of his temple." Egil drops the bat and sits on the preacher's stationary bicycle.

Abner's gone or he isn't. Egil doesn't care. His feet find the pegs and clumsily push-pull until they work the tension out the chain. He starts to pedal. His knee screams but he keeps going. The belt behind him snaps taut and the whips start to fall.

The screen lights up. The road rolls at him faster and faster as the whips stripe his back. The gates at the end of the road scroll ever backward, mired in an acid-flashback moire cloud.

He pedals harder. The whips crack. His knee screams. The road unfolds.

He pedals harder.

But he finds no peace, no whispered words of heavenly grace. And somewhere on the road, he forgets himself, and the pain turns to delicious numbness, then ecstatic fire, consuming weakness and evil and purifying his faith, his will.

The pixelated Kelly-green hills in his peripheral vision grow thick with cheering pilgrims, with crosses like barren trees bearing winter fruit of sinners blackened by rot and pecked by crows. The restful dead and the angry unborn genuflect and drip placental blood, respectively, as he passes. Ominous thunderheads gather to entomb the sky, leaving only a single shining shaft of golden light to fall on the threshold of his destination.

Hours pass. Someone pounds on the door but he keeps pedaling. The road rolls on and he stares into the ever-approaching gates of the kingdom of God and he sees through them to the world of white light to come, and he offers himself up for just a glimpse of it, he offers himself—

Somewhere on the morning of the seventh day of riding, he falls off the bicycle. His back is crisscrossed with weeping wounds, elaborate Viking and swastika tattoos shredded and flayed away. He lies on the sticky concrete, staring forlornly into the video feedback on the screen, watching the kingdom of God dwindle further and further away.

His knee howls grand opera, his back wails like a baby on fire, but he hears it.

In his heart, he hears it.

serve me

Egil stirs and climbs up on his good knee, crawls across the chapel to the curtain.

save me

A tiny voice between stampeding heartbeats, louder than bombs in the great silence of his head.

and you will have power

He kneels before it, offering his pain, and feels the fire through the curtain like the door of a furnace. He lifts himself up and reaches for the curtain to pull it aside, to bear witness.

Inside the niche, as before, the tiered shelves lined with jars backlit by fluttering candles that never seem to go out. The shapes in the jars, curled up and unfinished, yet wizened, older than anything alive, stare unblinkingly at him with the pure judgmental fury of angels.

He can almost hear music, faint but growing as he reaches out to touch one of the jars, when he hears the creak of the examination table and feels a heavy, cold hand on his shoulder.

"Come away from there," croaks the preacher. "There is much to be done."

22

It doesn't look like a war from the street, until it is. By then, half of those on the wrong side are already dead.

Silent Radio tried to warn them.

"You know they're coming for you. They will kill you in your homes, if you don't kill them first. All your rage, all your fear, it has a face. Strike at it now and burn it all down. . . .

"You think this will hurt the ones looking down on us from above, but this was always the plan. Both parties were always the left and right hands of the market, perpetuating the boom-bust, binge-purge cycle that they reported like it was weather. But now the party's nearly over.

"They do not need your work, and you cannot afford their products, so *you* are now the product. They have succeeded so totally at stripping knowledge and wealth and health and rights from the American consumer that the system has nearly collapsed under the weight of their greed before the market's final solution can be implemented, and that solution is to divide the market in two and sell guns to both sides, then flee to a private island until the market corrects itself. America has no other cards left to play, so it finally must cannibalize what was always the secret source of its power.

"America is where the impossible almost happens every day. From the beginning, its faith in its own miracle has burned everything they touched, everything but themselves. Their national anthem enshrines the secular miracle, of Fort McHenry surviving the British bombardment because the star-spangled banner survived. America is the world's greatest religion, and all the world believes. Whether they adore the shining city on a hill or curse the Great Satan, they fed it with their prayers, and made of it a god that put a man on the moon and wrote its burning name on the world's face.

But the fire is burning itself out. Over its ashes, they've built a furnace to rekindle it, a hothouse of forced mutation that makes the impossible almost inevitable, to try to monetize and weaponize that dying faith, to change itself as it has always changed the world.

"Pity the fools who feed that fire. Pity yourselves, for you are one of them!"

•

On Christmas Eve, Litchfield's newly anointed Destroying Angels sweep through the surrounding districts, proselytizing and handing out leaflets announcing that HE IS RISEN, and ordering all to GET RIGHT AND REPENT.

The motley Syrian refugees and Afghan and Iraqi detainees hurl rocks and bottles. The zealots fade away without making a single convert.

At 4:01 Xmas morning, rockets rain down on Saladin Road from the nearest superbloque columns. An hour later, the Reverend Litchfield and the Destroying Angels visit the aid station. He heals the dozen or so burn victims who accept Christ, rise from their deathbeds and take up arms. The rest are executed.

Word spreads fast, but few in the polyglot jigsaw of slums, squats, ghettos and waste dumps yet see what's coming.

At 6:01, eighty-two botanicas, strip clubs, bars, grind booths and drug dens on the southern hemisphere of Unamerica explode. Improvised timed devices of every conceivable description kill nearly a thousand and wound three thousand more.

In the Green Man's fiefdom, four bars—the Mousetrap, the Bubble Room, the Nation of Gondwanaland Legion Hall and How Can We Be Karaoke Lounge—are firebombed, along with Listor's cherished vegan McDonalds. Armored personnel carriers roll in with such authority that some mistake the Destroying Angels in their black body armor for the police, until they start rounding up all the drug dealers and crucifying them. A few of Listor's luckier runners escape the pogrom, only to find the Green Man's tower on lockdown. Nobody answers the door, even when the runners are doused with gasoline and set alight.

The black blocks go down harder.

The volatile Yellow District slums jam North African and Haitian refugees together with displaced survivors of every major disaster since Katrina in boxcar high-rises run by a shaky alliance of prison and street gangs. Nearly exterminated by Pantera three years ago, the black district already has its back against the wall, but is all but unprepared for what's coming.

The Crip militia posts snipers on the rooftops and blocks Cleaver and Turner Streets with booby-trapped cargo containers. But they're knocked off-balance by kamikaze drone bombings that splash the battlements with homemade napalm, and a fifth-column movement of black Holy Fire fanatics who shoot their protectors in the back and open the door to the zealot army, new recruits seemingly unimpeded by being grievously burned over most of their bodies.

By noon, it looks like a proper war, but one side is highly coordinated and morbidly fanatical, while nobody else has even had breakfast yet. The surviving southern Yellow Zone gangs make fumbling attempts to align against the enemy but are quickly swept away. Firefights light up half the city and running gun battles choke the streets. The Police man the barricades around the Arcade, but take no action as a phalanx of crosses with wailing sinners are erected all along the ring street, and put to the torch.

It's pretty much over, except for a few pockets of internecine butchery, by 4PM. About a third of Unamerica is lit only by fire.

In every district they tame, the Destroying Angels smash automats and give out food, drink and drugs, but then they kettle the streets. The crowds drawn by the loot are forced to submit to have the "mark of the Beast" burned off their wrists.

Word quickly gets around that if a wild-eyed believer falls into step beside you on the street and starts singing a spiritual, if you don't join in before the chorus, he'll stab you in the neck.

23

You're making love to a beautiful woman when something bites you. Between your skin and hers, a tiny bite that suddenly becomes pain bigger than you, and then another and another.

You pull back the sheets to find huge, pink ants crawling all over her honey-blond skin. They're biting her too, making her scream, but they're coming out of her. You want to help her, but they won't stop biting you and every time they bite, the pain is worse. And worse than the pain is what's inside it.

In every bite, a bit of her life. In every drop of venom, a memory.

That's the good one.

•

You're making love to a beautiful woman and you take her in your arms, and she's big, you like them big, it's nice to have something to hold onto, to lose yourself in flesh, but now she's grown so much bigger than you.

In her arms, you can't even reach her lips and she laughs and holds you to a breast so big you can't see her face around it to suckle her milk.

You drink and you drink but you only grow smaller, shrinking until the breast is the whole world, the curves of it disappear in optical fog, now you're so small you nestle in the chalice of her hands as she lowers you beneath the mound of her belly and pushes you back into the dark—

•

Or take this one:

You're at a luxury car dealer, looking at SUV's. You're drawn to Range Rovers and Escalades from long years of hip-hop conditioning, but there's something sharp about the Audi, and you have to have it. The sales associate nods as if you've ordered a very good wine and goes inside to fetch the key fob, and that's when you notice the dog.

It's inside the SUV, perched on the automated-adjustable Corinthian leather driver's seat with its paws on the glass, pasty gray tongue lolling from panting jaws.

It's an ugly, skinny dog of no recognizable breed, with picket-fence ribs and tattered, flea-encrusted ears, and it's dying in there. It's a warm, sunny day, but inside the hermetically-sealed SUV, it's an oven, the glass burns your hands when you touch it. It's a gorgeous car and its security system is on, and you know if you break the glass, they'll call the cops and the cops will know right away what you really are and they'll treat you accordingly. They'll shoot you down just like they'll shoot the dog.

When you look in its eyes, you are the dog looking at you with eyes clouded by encroaching heat stroke, despairing of help.

So you wait and you watch the dog die and the sales associate returns with the keys and asks, *Who's ready for a test drive?* You try to answer, but you feel like an idiot, because of course there's no dead dog curled up on the heated, memory-foam padded seat and you can't speak, because you can feel the dead dog curled up in your belly.

•

Every time you go to sleep, no matter how hard you drug yourself, the dreams get worse.

•

"So look who's come crawling back."

"Fuck you, Papi."

You like the raft dream, now. The seeing into other people's heads thing is getting worse. Here is the only place you get any relief.

If only you were alone.

"Your city is tearing out its asshole and you're hiding in here because what, it hurts your feelings?"

"Fuck you, Papi."

"You know why it's happening. You took that drug. It broke your brain. Now all the world is leaking in, you can't walk past a sick child without getting a tummy-ache. You know what it did to you?"

You pretend not to hear.

"It made you a Communist!" Your father laughs at this. "But a real bleeding-heart communist, like out of a storybook. You actually feel other people's pain, so you have no choice but to throw your lot in with theirs.

"If you had this drug in Soviet Union, you would be a hero. But this is America, my son. And in America, you can be anything but a Communist."

Your father laughs and laughs. You jump into the ocean and sink, blowing out all your breath, but you can't drown and your ears throb with the booming roar of the ocean laughing at you until it crushes you.

•

It's no better when he wakes up.

He rolls off the futon and puts his feet into fire.

Recoils and rolls into a ball on the cushions, cradling his feet. He can smell his flesh roasting. Hear sizzling fat. Blisters blooming and bursting between his twitching fingers.

These are not my feet.

Don't believe it's happening.

But he thinks as loud as he can, *Keep your feet to yourself. Fuck out of my head, Hatch.*

Brought this on yourself.

Own your shit.

But he's afraid to close his eyes, afraid to blink, and it's a couple twitchy minutes before he can bring himself to touch the floor.

There. Nothing wrong. Just flashbacks. No impossible psychic blood-brother bullshit, just old-fashioned. . .

Guilt?

Get real.

Players don't do guilt. Hatch was his ticket into Listor's inner circle, and he dealt himself out. Smug motherfucker's gone. Los Zeros don't negotiate. They erase.

You got what you wanted.

Enjoy it.

Jaime goes to the sink and washes his face. When he looks in the mirror, he can't find his face.

A luchador mask with a blinking 0 sneers at him, looms behind the speckled, warped glass until he's blackened it with the blowtorch in his hand.

He backs away and sneaks up on it again a couple more times until he's satisfied the man on the other side of the glass is himself.

Fuck off, man. You're gone.

Played yourself.

Stop playing me!

All his life, he's worked to get his emotions under control and just play the Game. If motherfuckers smell fear on you, they'll eat you alive. A lifetime of self-control flushed with one drug. All the walls he's built are leaking, and other people are leaking into him. . .

How long until the flashbacks go away?

Someone pounding on the door. He goes to answer it but flinches away. When he blinks, he sees like x-ray vision through the door and knows it's Tres Ojos.

Think. There's no back door to his place, he didn't get a swimming pool like some motherfuckers, but he's got a window, he could climb down and go in another floor, maybe they don't have the whole building sewn up.

"Jaime! Hey, fool, open up!"

He's fighting his own fear and everyone else's, but he shakes himself and stops cold at the sound of Chud's voice.

He throws the bolt and opens the door a crack with a knife behind his back.

Chud leans into the gap and the overpowering stench of him pushes Jaime back. "Fuck you screaming for?"

"I wasn't screaming," Jaime says, but his voice cracks. His throat raw.

"Whole damn floor's complaining. Sounded like you was getting burned alive in here. . ."

"Shit, fecal-freak, if you was getting it like I was getting it, you'd be screaming, too." Jaime slams the door.

"Know you alone in there. . . !" Chud barks, but he fades away.

Jaime puts on some music and smokes a blunt, but he can't relax. Shit creeps up on him—rigid steel chair—zip-tie restraints cutting into his wrists—stink of his burning flesh. . .

He can't.

He won't.

He's getting out his jacket, his stunglasses and a needle-taser, and then he's down four flights to the lobby of Listor's tower and it's locked down and ankle-deep in lime-green wax from the shattered lava lamps. It's also mobbed up with goons, gunmen, freelancers and cannon-fodder watching the barricaded front doors like they're on an elevator and their floor is coming up next.

Chud lays a paw on his shoulder. "What separated you from that so-good-you're-dying pussy?"

"What's going on?"

"Crazy fucking Xian fanatics tearing up the neighborhood," Chud says. "Some shook freak tried to pop their ayatollah, and somehow, they got the idea we behind it. We just waiting 'em out."

"I need to get out there," Jaime says. "Special mission. Green Man's orders."

Chud smiles like he knows damn well Listor ordered no such fucking thing. "Whyn't you say so, punk? We've been trying to get rid of you since day two."

24

Hatch swims in a purple benthic zone of blood, snot and Axe Body Spray. It's better than it sounds, and way, way better than what follows when they rip off the hood and crack a smelling salt under his nose.

He's zip-tied to an examination chair/birthing stool, a chair with no seat, only a cold steel frame that digs into his skin.

And he's naked. Cold. Shit, he hasn't been cold since that night in the desert when he first came here, what? Six weeks ago?

White light drills his eyes. There's a big adjustable floodlight canopy, like in an operating theater. Because that's what this is.

A maze of trays with gleaming instruments, all lovingly cleaned but hardly sterile or individually packaged. He doubts the doctor will be concerned about staph infection, but maybe that's what the blowtorch is for.

Each item on the trays adds to the panic as he imagines their use on himself.

Okay, this is fucking awful, but you've talked your way out of worse. Nothing is fucked yet. . .

Someone shines a penlight in his eyes, then retreats to call someone else. Red surgical gowns, scarlet masks, telescoping goggles. His head pounds, vision blurry. The beating comes back. His face is hamburger. He remembers who did it.

Lalo. Jesus, what did they do to poor Lalo? He was wired up like those zombie puppet gladiators. . .

It's easy to get hung up on the extravagance of the cruelty, the gold-plated sadism of these Sinaloan hillbillies, but they're so crass and so tiny in their souls that even their insidious cleverness and force of will isn't all that impressive. *What profiteth it a man, to win the world, if he doesn't know what to do with it?*

But they think they're businessmen, so that's how you talk to them. In spite of the operatic costumes and cute Mafioso nicknames, the head of Los Zeros still wants to think of himself as a cop. Anyone willing to do literally anything for money can get into a cartel, but in the federal police, you have to drop nearly 1.5 million dollars just to get *assigned* to a hot narco-state like Chihuahua, so you need backing from a cartel or one of the thirty-five families who own more than half of Mexico outright. Once upon a time, Tres Ojos had both.

Years after getting kicked out of the most corrupt police force in the world, his people still wear cheesy uniforms and spooky wrestling masks, and have numbers instead of names. Hatch knows how to talk to cops, how to let them have their authority games without playing them. And he knows how to work a feud.

Should he be scared? He should be shitting bricks. He should *look* scared, which isn't hard. His heart rate elevated, his breathing quick and shallow, and his face hardly gives anything away, except that he can't protect it for shit in a fight.

A shadowy figure comes over and sits down in front of him. The same white suit, now almost half red. The same blinking mask.

"Do you know who I am?"

"Yes, sir." He carefully uses the honorific as Mexicans do, when they speak of God almighty. "And I assume that you know who *I* am—"

Pistons hit his face. Whip his head back so hard, a zip-tie pops on his arm, leaving deep blue ligature marks across his biceps. Pain blacks him out, whips him back to face the blinking 3.

"Say my name, little man."

"Tres Ojos. . . the warlord of Los Zeros." Sucking blood, he adds, "I've been trying to reach you, actually. . ."

Tres Ojos sits down on a beleaguered, weeping stool and paws a row of shiny knives. He selects one, admiring its keen edge. "That is not my name, *buchon*."

He raises the knife to catch the light on the beveled cutting surface as if reading a secret message. He reaches back to insert the blade into the base of his skull, slices the stitching up to the crown of his pate and peels the luchador mask off a shaven head that seems to swell upon being released from its sheath.

"I am Comandante Jacinto Moxica Vizcaino," he says, tossing away the slashed mask and pivoting on the stool to show Hatch a face like a boxer's fist. Knots of muscle twang under skin pitted with acne-craters and sweat-geysers. Between and just above his hooded eyes and a wide, flaring nose that looks unfinished without a big iron ring through it, the lines etched in his wasteland forehead converge in a snarl of scar tissue and a Tunguska Event-sized divot in the center of his forehead that goes deeper than the bone. The floor of the crater is a convex, colorless, fleshy bulge like a baby's fontanel. Indeed, the nodule of naked brain pulses aggressively when he silently considers Hatch.

"Pleasure to meet you, sir, but this isn't necessary. I've got no secrets. You want to know something, we don't have to have this slumber party and do each other's nails and talk about boys shit. Just ask."

After an eternity, the nightmarish Olmec idol cracks a smile. "I should give you gifts, for you have slain LaToda Madre, my enemy."

Hatch chokes on his spit. "Obregon is dead?"

"Dead inside, which gives me more pleasure. They say he cannot order his business anymore, that he must apologize to his own dinner." He laughs like a giant child, digs a tiny cough drop tin out of his pocket and shakes it in Hatch's face. "This is what you gave him? This new shit that makes people kill themselves. You are a genius."

"I can't take the credit. I'm actually kind of an idiot. I didn't want to hurt anybody. I didn't factor in that giving people a drug that makes them genuinely empathic might be a stupid idea in a cesspool."

"Edify me."

"The drug breaks open the head and connects you to the rest of the world. I thought it would make people stronger, happier, but if they're buried in mean people, it's too much to take."

Tres Ojos laughs, shaking his head. "So he can feel my hatred? I am weakening him just by hating him? Ah, what a gift!" He giggles and punches himself in the crotch. "Can you feel that in your fake balls, Hector? Can you feel me, fucking you to death?"

"Not exactly. Hector isn't going to kill himself. He's strong enough to survive the death of his ego, and if he is, then there're others, too. Once again, he's proven he's stronger than you."

"He is nothing!" Tres Ojos slams a tray, scattering tools. Lackeys in red gowns scurry to recover them.

"Then what does that make you, man? He went into the darkest place inside himself and ripped out what was killing him slowly. If he survived, then he's growing stronger all the time."

Tres Ojos runs out of patience. His hands hover over the knives. "I am nothing but dark places, little man."

"This drug would be a fate worse than death for you, big man. Because you're nothing but ego."

He nods. "I have big ego, yes."

"It's nothing to brag about. Listen to yourself, you're just a machine for acquiring pleasure and power, but you don't even know what pleasure is, anymore. You wouldn't need to kill yourself. Once your ego dissolves, you'd be an empty shell, or worse, you'd watch a new and better you take the controls and get over yourself, and you and La Toda Madre would just fuck each other and get this stupid feud over with."

Tres Ojos stands up, the bulge in the crack in his skull furiously pulsing like a thumb pushing out of his brain. Then he laughs, nervously. "You think to upset me so I kill you quick, no? Hector was ugly fat woman who became pretty little man, but I will still use him like a woman, when all is done. A mouth is a mouth, after all, and what is a mouth but a cunt, when you knock out all the teeth?"

Hatch shakes his head. He's not the only one who's naked, now. "You think this is what you wanted, but what was it, exactly, that you wanted to become? You were a top cop, but that wasn't enough. You went so crooked that the system hated you worse than the cartels. After you betrayed your country, you turned on the only people who could stomach you. When you killed them and took their place, you couldn't even be a decent drug dealer. Your whole reason for existing is to destroy Hector Obregon, so you think he feels the same about you. This little *joto* outsmarted you, outplayed you and struts around your brain in stiletto heels every minute of the day. He was more of a man than you even before he had a dick, but he didn't become a man to show you up. He's moved on. He doesn't need you as much as you need him."

"This is all very edifying," Tres Ojos says, wiping a tear from his eye. "But I don't think anyone else is going to take your drug. The ones who have taken it are all dead or gone mad."

"You may be right, Jacinto my man, but I kind of doubt it. People want to wake up from this nightmare. Not all of them will, but enough of them will, and then this game won't be so fun for you, anymore."

He chuckles indulgently. "I should be afraid of them, your drug people with the big feelings?"

"Absolutely. They'll come for you, and like I said, it'll be worse than death. Your next glass of water, your next snort of coke, could be dosed, and it won't kill you. It'll cure you. But I don't think it'll go that way."

"Oh, no?"

"Oh no. Because once enough of them have taken it, things are going to be different around here. The rules will change, and suddenly everyone else will be connected and you'll be locked out, with nothing but paid stooges for company. Because that's the hard truth you can't face. Nobody likes you, Jacinto. You make nothing anyone wants, you command loyalty by fear. People pay you to leave them alone, and you have to pay people to be around you. It hurts, and the only way you know to mask the pain is to become more of a monster."

Tres Ojos sits back and crosses his arms. "I want to thank you. Most edifying. I cannot get this kind of honesty from a therapist."

"And you didn't even have to torture me." Hatch laughs, astounded at how his voice cracks. How scared was he, and he didn't even feel it until it was over.

Tres Ojos slaps his forehead in a broad, winking gesture. "Oh, I almost forgot! The *torture*!"

Red-robed nurses wheel in another chair with a naked, hooded man bound to it. Hatch doesn't recognize him, is afraid to look, to see Jaime, Solomon Listor, or some other ghost from his past. He is almost grateful when they leave the hood on.

"I want to see how this drug of yours really works," Tres Ojos says, picking up a blowtorch, then handing it to one of his nurses. He takes a pill out of Hatch's tin.

Hatch clamps his mouth shut, but someone behind him traps his head, forces a gloved finger into the hinge of his jaw and wrenches it open so Tres Ojos can toss the pill into it. They massage his throat until he swallows.

"I have been thinking very hard to find something you will not tell me. These new feeling drug people, they are not all dead, but nobody can find them. I want to know where they went."

Hatch vehemently shakes his head. He can feel the pill stuck in his throat slowly dissolving, bitter alkaloid trickle down his esophagus. "I really don't know that. You'd have to ask the Green Man."

Tres Ojos shrugs. "If you don't know, you don't know. But that is beside the point, you see." He snaps his fingers at a lackey, who kneels and begins to burn off the naked man's toes.

"You lecture me about pain and ego, but I don't think you know what pain really is." Tres Ojos settles back on the stool and picks up a bone saw. "You say it makes you feel others' pain, so show me."

Hatch screams as loud, as hard, as high as he can. It isn't fake. The sight of the skin turning to embers and fluttering away from blackening muscle, the smell of sizzling fat, the reflexive wave of hysterical empathy as his imagination puts himself in the other chair, under the flame.

He screams and vomits and screams some more. Tres Ojos eventually waves the nurse off and comes over to study Hatch like a dodgy shipment cut with something. He shakes his head and walks out of the room with the nurses on his tail.

Hatch leans into his chest. Bites his lips. It feels horrible, but he can't keep it in any longer, and he draws in a breath for a hysterical giggle. That shouldn't have worked. But it did. . .

Except the door opens and Tres Ojos steps back in. "My assistant has reminded me that perhaps we are forgetting something." He strolls back to stand over Hatch, looks at the tray of instruments. "For a scientific experiment to be truly *edifying*, there must be a control group."

Hatch panics, breathing hard. "I told you, I'll tell you anything you want to know. You don't have to. . ."

"What did you call it? A slumber party? Yes, let's have one of those. We can talk about boys. . ."

He picks up a pair of pliers and indicates for the nurses to hold down Hatch's left hand.

"And do each other's nails."

25

Tres Ojos steps out of the torture chamber with two hot nurses in red smocks and bends so one of them can stretch a fresh mask over his head and deftly stitch it shut. "That was not particularly edifying," he says. "I think he was faking. Do you think he was faking?"

The other nurse shrugs and nods.

"You," he says, pointing at Jaime Blasco, who sags against the wall with his left hand between his knees. "47. What's your fucking problem? Are you on duty?"

Jaime's brain is juiced with agony. His hand is on fire. Sweat pours down the inside of his mask to drip in his eyes. "Crabs are eating my balls, Comandante Zero-Three."

Tres Ojos laughs. "47, you are an animal. Clean up in there, but leave the *guero* alone. I want him good and high for feeding time."

Tres Ojos walks away with his torturers, leaving an armed guard—73—beside the door. Jaime clings to the wall, rocked by nausea. He keeps his head down, but every step towards that door is a bed of white-hot coals. He reaches for the doorknob with his left hand, recoils and uses his right.

But he makes it.

It was difficult to get in here—half a dozen stupid, suicidal moves was all it took—but it wasn't hard to find. He just aimed at the pain and kept walking into it, warm, warmer, burning, like walking into the sun. He tapped a low-level Zero slinging in Barrio Guevara. Didn't have to fake the shakes and the sweats to pass for a harmless junkie, needled him point-blank and took his mask and jacket and a fistful of Norco derms. Where Jaime left him, without the mask's protection, he'll probably never wake up.

Masked up, he just walked in.

Maybe he'll just walk out. . .

He almost faints when he smells the burning flesh for real, the awful greasy stench so close to food, it makes his mouth water. But the pain is gone, which is a relief, even as it dawns on him that he's probably too late.

Two hooded naked men sit on steel chairs in the center of a room of brushed steel and blood-flecked ceramic tiles. One of them is horribly still, his legs splayed out on gynecologist's stirrups, ending in blackened stumps. The other slumps against the plastic restraints, sucking in the spit-soaked fabric between his lips with frenzied breath.

"Who's there?" Hatch's voice is a querulous rasp through whipsaw breaths. "Jacinto? Hey, I just thought of something else that might be useful. . ."

Jaime rips off the hood and looks at Hatch. Looks him up and down and aside from the beating he got, he's untouched. Then he sees the fingers of the left hand, and the ashtray filled with fingernails, and his own hand throbs in sympathy. "What might be useful?"

"Jaime! Long time no see!" Tears squeeze out his eyes. "Wish you could've stopped by ten minutes ago, when I had fingernails. Look what the fucking freak did to my hand, man!"

Looking at his own fingers, Jaime says, "Sorry I'm late . . ."

"Cut me loose, man. You wouldn't believe what fucking idiots these guys are. . ."

Jaime picks up a pair of pliers. Looking from Hatch to the anonymous footless corpse, he says, "I thought that was you, boss."

"Weird, right? So. . . you could feel it? You actually found your way here, because of that guy?"

Jaime looks at the pliers, then at Hatch's feet. "Yeah, I felt it. . ." Standing there right now, kneeling beside him to cut the zip-ties, he feels nothing at all off Hatch. Nothing but the vague agony of his fingers and the rush of relief as he massages blood into his limbs.

Hatch staggers off the chair, grabs at Jaime for balance, crying out when his mangled fingers brush against fabric, then weaves across the theater to ransack the first aid kit. Slapping derms on his hand and popping pills, he shakes out a rubber glove, fills it with polysporin and snugs it onto his left hand. "Kook was trying to test the empathy factor off the Secret Teacher, so he dosed me and went to town on whoever that is. But you felt it? I mean, I'm sorry, but. . . that's fucking remarkable. Do you know what that means?"

"I felt him," Jaime says. "I didn't feel you."

Hatch sounds less pained, more his annoying, overconfident self as he steps into his soiled white slacks and a t-shirt. Surveying the ruined shirt and coat, he throws on a red surgical robe from a hook on the wall. "Yeah, I wish I had an answer for that, but the important thing right now. . ."

Hatch crosses the room at a brisk clip, headed for the surgical tray. Jaime spots the tin on the tray and grabs it just before Hatch can reach it. Hatch holds out his hand. Jaime shakes a couple pills into his palm. "These aren't Soma."

"Yeah. Brer Rabbit gambit, for the fucking win. I'm actually still in a lot of pain and coming on like gangbusters right now, so if we could maybe get the fuck out of here, I could really use a swim. . ."

"What are these?"

Hatch pockets the tin. "Just garden-variety Ecstasy," he says, eyes twinkling. "What a maroon." Strapping on a surgical mask and cowl from a dispenser, Hatch heads for the door.

"Nothing bad ever happens to you," Jaime says.

He holds up his declawed hand. "This wasn't exactly nothing, man. You saying you wish I got my feet burned off. . .?"

Jaime rips the hood off the corpse. "Look."

Hatch turns, shakes his head at the mangled face. "Aw, shit. Lalo. Well, that sucks."

"Why're you taking Ecstasy?"

"These aren't personal. . . I keep 'em around as party favors. . ."

"What happened to, 'When you get the message, hang up the phone?'"

"You still smoke weed."

"I have to, to drown out everybody else's shit. I can hear people when they're not talking, man. Feel shit I'd rather not fucking feel. It's not getting better, either, it's getting worse. But you don't seem to have any problem with it."

"It gets better, man. But right now isn't the time."

"So I should let you decide when the right time is."

"They're gonna come back any minute—"

"You never took it."

"Come on, man!" Hatch throws open the door and pokes his head out, asks the guard to come in. 73 steps inside, looks around and reaches for his sidearm.

Jaime gasps, "Motherfuck!" and goes for his needler.

Hatch hits 73 edge-on across the back of the neck with a surgical tray. The guard stumbles with his hand on his gun. Jaime puts two needles in him. He jolts and jives across the floor. His gun goes off in its holster.

The sound snaps Jaime's last nerve. Shoving Hatch aside, he opens the door and plunges out into the corridor, walking down the hall towards two Zeros—16 and 29— in bright orange tiger-striped camo fatigues, dragging a naked, insensate woman by her arms and legs.

The stairs at the end of the corridor have cameras and he can just see the boots and tiger-stripes of a couple more guards at the next landing.

"It's no good," he says, veering right just in front of the approaching Zeros, barging into the last door before the stairs. Hatch follows him into the murky depths of the room.

Stinks in here. Like shit, but not the pervasive human variety he's used to. It's spicy, exotic, and alien.

Jaime's never been to one, but he knows a fucking zoo, when he sees one.

It's kind of a tradition with all well-rounded narcos who don't know shit about art. It adds color and sensitivity to keep animals from foreign lands, shows a curiosity for and love of nature, a softer side, and there's no better way to take care of business while adding to your rep, than feeding your enemies to them.

The Zeros have turned the warehouse-sized room into a respectable menagerie, all predators, of course, with an emphasis on big cats. A crocodile pit is the centerpiece, framed by rows of cages with tigers, leopards, jaguars and even one mated pair of stoned-looking lions.

Jaime picks a lock while Hatch finds a stack of steaks in a walk-in freezer. They're encased inside big wheels of blood-flecked ice to force the cats to work a little and not just bolt it down. Hatch throws the steaks across the floor and Jaime lets the tigers out just as the outer door flies open.

Jaime pulls the cage door back and sandwiches himself between it and the bars.

Hatch climbs a ladder up the back of a jaguar cage, the beast inside going berserk leaping up the bars to get at him.

16 is caught flat-footed in the doorway. A huge, hungry male Bengal tiger pounces on him and locks its jaws over his face. 29 turns to run, but the other two tigers go after him and by the sound of his blood-curdling falsetto scream, he doesn't get far.

Gunshots, screams, then quiet.

"Let's go." Jaime runs, not looking back.

The corridor is empty and decorated with buckets of blood and garlands of bowel and bone. No sign of the tigers. Blood pulsing in his ears louder than bombs, Jaime bounds for the stairs.

Two flights and another corridor ending in a door and into thrashing bodies flashing lights and narco-techno from two-story bassbins. An infernal conga line of cocaine-caked masks and bouncing fake tits snakes through the club. Jaime swims through the bodies, entangled in a boiling psychic stew of sublime numbness, empty minds colliding at terminal velocity, when the screams rise up in a wave and blind raving panic strips his senses bare.

A tiger crouches atop the bassbins. Some in the crowd point and scream in drunken rapture. They think it's another lighting effect, a manifestation of their ferocious virility. They scream, "*Mas animo!*" even as it leaps off the speakers and plunges into the dancefloor with paws splayed out to mangle faces and snap limbs in a playful frenzy.

The dance becomes a stampede. Men in masks open fire on anything that moves. In that maze of patterns and shadows, everything looks like a tiger.

Jaime is crushed among the revelers and the mutilated dead and dying, trying to keep the shifting tide of flesh from dragging him under. He climbs the wave and rides it through a foyer choked with bodyguards, dealers, pimps and whores, feeling the tingle of a thousand lasers on his back, cringing in anticipation of the next stupid thing Hatch will do to slam their dicks in a door—

Door security is pushing back a scrimmage line of chanting zealots throwing rocks and Molotov cocktails over a barricade of burning pedicabs strewn across Barrio Guevara. Jaime runs for an overturned garbage dumpster and ducks behind it to strip off his mask.

"Fuck, fuck fuck, that was. . . you are a *maniac*!" Hatch slaps him on the back with his bad hand, making himself scream. He tears off the surgical garb. Balls it up and tosses it in the dumpster. "Where are we going? Do you know where Listor is? He's supposed to be sitting on a bunch of Soma users. All Tres Ojos wanted was to find them. . . That and to bust a nut in La Toda Madre. . . I swear, that guy needs our product more than any motherfucker I've ever seen."

Hatch peeks over the top of the dumpster. The Zeros have finally decided the zealots are worthy of full tactical response. A squad of riflemen open up from the second floor, scattering the handful of surviving rock-throwers.

Gunfire and bullhorn chants echo down the alley around the superbloque, cutting off any easy exit. A team of wildcat paramedics move from corpse to corpse across the alley, slashing and scooping out undamaged vital organs and eyes as efficiently as stealing hubcaps and stuffing them into foil freezer bags. "Catch ya later," one of them smiles at Jaime and waves the melon-baller they use for the eyes.

Jaime scrapes in the gutter and pulls the cover off a manhole. Hatch scuttles into it, dangling his feet into the deeper darkness until he finds the slimy rungs of the ladder.

"Were you afraid to take it," Jaime asks, "or did you know better?"

Hatch freezes, looking up at him. "Fine. I've never tried it. But right here, right now. . . does it really matter?"

Jaime shoots Hatch in the face with the needle-gun. As he twitches and drops out of sight, Jaime drops the cover back over the hole.

"Yeah, asshole," he says. "It matters."

PART THREE

IN WAR, THE MORAL IS TO THE MATERIAL AS THREE
TO ONE.
> NAPOLEON

THAT'S NOT THE WAY THE WORLD REALLY WORKS
ANYMORE. WE'RE AN EMPIRE NOW, AND WHEN WE
ACT, WE CREATE OUR OWN REALITY. AND WHILE
YOU ARE STUDYING THAT REALITY—JUDICIOUSLY,
AS YOU WILL—WE'LL ACT AGAIN, CREATING OTHER
NEW REALITIES, WHICH YOU CAN STUDY TOO,
AND THAT'S HOW THINGS WILL SORT OUT. WE'RE
HISTORY'S ACTORS . . . AND YOU, ALL OF YOU, WILL
BE LEFT TO JUST STUDY WHAT WE DO.
> ANONYMOUS BUSH ADMIN OFFICIAL
> SUMMER 2002
> AS REPORTED BY RON SUSKIND

26

Waking up flat on your back on a scum-encrusted drain-grate amid swirling curds of raw sewage shouldn't feel so fabulous.

He just got his fingernails ripped out by a fucking narco gargoyle, and his only friend in this place just abandoned him down a sewer, but his first coherent thought upon regaining consciousness, even before he ponders where he is or how he got here, is, *Eureka! It's fucking real.*

He can't see his hand in front of his face, but he can sure as fuck feel it. The water pooled around him is a pungent chowder of cigarette butts, syringes, blister packs, condoms and things better left untouched.

Gagging, he retches over his shoulder. The stench is so thick, he can taste it.

He sits up and pats himself down. His head is a numb punching bag and his face tingles where Blasco needled him, but the painkillers, and more importantly, the Ecstasy, are still working.

Crawling out of the current to squat on a narrow catwalk, he peels and applies a couple more opioid derms from the torture chamber. They do wonders for the pain, if not the smell.

Feeling the walls yields all kinds of awful sensations he feels grateful he can't see, before he finds the ladder. He climbs sixteen rungs to the top, but the manhole cover won't budge. Something heavy is on top of it—probably the dumpster, he thinks, remembering how he got here. The near-constant chatter of gunfire convinces him it's not worth pursuing.

He climbs back down and walks away from the sounds of battle as he takes stock of his situation.

What do we know?

1) The drug works. Jaime followed an empathic impression through clear and present danger to rescue you. Not only does this demonstrate a real qualitative change in his cognitive abilities bordering on the paranormal, but its progression since his single exposure to the Secret Teacher suggests a lasting, perhaps permanent alteration. Not only psychogenic telepathy, but psychedelic gene therapy! A new species! *Homo sapiens psilocybus* walks the Earth!

2) Jaime hates your fucking guts.

This last is troubling, but not unexpected. For all his worldly disaffection, Jaime is highly emotional, and seeking a father-figure. Hatch knowingly traded on his need, so he can't be surprised when Jaime turns on him over a point of art like whether Hatch had ever sampled his own product.

But what the hell did the kid expect? What they're doing is hardly an exact science, but Hatch couldn't be the first drunk at his own party. Someone had to stand outside the miracle to protect and guide it.

He would only understand, if he too had spent his life searching the world for the magic bullet of mental evolution, tried and failed and failed again, and even when he succeeded, found in each rare and forbidden drug only the burnt residue of his own exhausted soul after the sense of genuine ascension, of contact with the ultimate Secret Teacher was revealed as just another fairydust hallucination.

Maybe then he would know what it felt like to finally hold The Thing Itself, the key to everything you ever dreamed of in your hand, and be afraid to take it.

No, not afraid. . . cautious. Moses wasn't invited into the Promised Land, either. Anyone who'd take forty years to navigate a couple hundred square miles of desert didn't deserve salvation, anyway.

These circuitous thoughts carry him halfway across the city, always taking the left at any fork in the sewer system, the way you navigate a hedge maze. So slowly that he barely notices, he comes to see the general contours of the sewer from dim green glow strips mounted on the ceiling. He comes across three naked men with headlamps and rags wrapped round their faces mining slabs of deep-fryer fat from a golden glacier completely blocking a tributary tunnel. He tries asking for directions in five languages, even offers them a couple unused derms, but they hiss and fling fistfuls of shit at him until he goes away, jealous to protect their treasure.

He gives up trying to plot his journey against his sketchy mental map of the city, just trying to get away from the war upstairs.

Every manhole he tries is locked or blocked, and the noise from above never quite settles down enough that he feels safer traveling aboveground, anyway. He gets used to the heat, and mercifully, even the smell subsides to a dull brown annoyance. Evolution in action. You can adapt to anything but the stench inside.

The air is sweltering down here, and the miasma only unfolds to reveal subtler layers of pollution beneath the overpowering keynote of human filth. Methane, ammonia, industrial solvents and noxious vapors from burning plastic.

He must be coming down, which is a bummer, but as good a time as any to face facts. All of this is part of a pattern to break him out of his ego, force him to make hard choices.

He's not doing anyone any good, down here. Jaime blew him off. The Green Man has gone underground with the Soma users, who've formed some kind of suicide cult, and a bunch of Christian kooks have declared a jihad on the whole city.

Even if some remarkable breakthroughs have been made, shit has undeniably gone sideways. Whatever the right or the wrong of it, he has set into motion engines of transformation that have their own momentum. He could throw himself into their path without changing the outcome.

Prometheus brought the gift of fire to mankind, but he didn't stick around to teach them to cook. He lit the fuse and fucked off to get his liver eaten out by an eagle, for his trouble.

No, if he can get anywhere, he should find the Orange Zone recycling yard where Jaime brought him in, and get out.

Out.

As soon as he admits it to himself, the idea becomes a panic attack. He squats on the floor and focuses on breathing into the relatively sweet cavity between his knees until it passes.

Yes, he definitely needs to get out.

Maybe this was all a mistake, but it was inevitable, wasn't it? He didn't come looking for this place, and he made the best of it, but it's hardly the right laboratory for his kind of experiment. He created a community of real functioning empaths in the gutter of the American psyche. What other response could they have, but to snuff themselves?

He just needs to find the outermost perimeter of the sewer and work his way around it until he smells fish oil in the runoff, and he'll be in the Asian district.

It'd be better if he had some Secret Teachers or at least more spores, but it's not worth the risk to go back to Listor's. Far better to bug out and start over. Go back to the source. They won't be happy to see him at first, but he'll make it up to them. Shit, maybe just stay there. Why try to save the world, when you can find a corner of it that hasn't yet succumbed to the nightmare?

He's still looking for the outer wall when his tunnel comes out in a great grotto. The ceiling is three stories high, and hills of trash nearly reach it. A few dull orange lights pick out the forms of people working the trash mountains.

His first thought isn't oh shit, sewage-dwellers but, thank fuck, sewage-dwellers! In every corner of the world he's visited, those with the very least are always the most willing to help.

He asks if anyone knows a way to the surface. Nobody answers at first. But then a tall, goony white guy in rubber hip-waders, a shit-caked trenchcoat and a red checked snowplow hat wades over to him, making Pac-Man noises with his mouth, and claps him on the back. "Way you look out your face, I see you a do-man like me. Got fish sewn in the accident. Fuck all the ducks out of order."

"Hell yeah," Hatch says, "that's me all over."

"Pete," the guy says, offering his shit-mittened hand for Hatch to shake. "Vaya con huevos, bruh. To surface, you gotta go *up*."

"Been trying to do that all day, brother, but things upstairs have gotten kind of intense. . ."

"No shinola." Pete bends over and rummages in a sewage-dune of aborted fetuses and surgical tubing and pulls out a pretty serviceable AK-47. "Golden calf, man. Laugh or cry? Laugh *and* cry."

It's always a challenge in a new culture, to distinguish local hipsters from the genuinely mentally ill. Pete's comrades graze on the trash mountain, stowing useful items in big sacks on their backs, animated by none of his good-natured, aphasic mania.

"I'd be much obliged if you could show me the way to the ventilation tunnels, or at least some part of the city that's not tearing itself apart."

"Don't cram my clam, ma'am." Pete leaves him pondering the meaning of this as he moves on to testing a bunch of disposable lighters.

"I've been lost and stuck down here for hours. . ."

"Ain't lost, you found us!" Pete pockets a few lighters that still hold butane, puts his fingers in his mouth and blows a piercing whistle that pricks up every head of the scavenger pack. They leave off digging and gather in a circle around Pete, sit with legs crossed and take out lunchboxes.

Hatch watches them with awed disgust that abruptly turns to envy. With the opening of each uniform black plastic lunchbox, the stench of the sewer is pushed back by a smell like freshly baked bread. Yeasty, wholesome, sweet . . .

Mouth watering. Hatch says, "I don't have anything good to trade unless you guys like Ecstasy, but I am fucking starving, and that smells really good. . ."

Pete looks up from his lunch. "Lunchbox Bunch don't never trade, don't never beg. We self-sufficient. Self-compartmentalized. But you could be one of us. You might-could use Wu's lunchbox." Digging in a Santa-sack propped against his leg, he takes out a black heavy-duty construction worker's lunchbox like everyone else's and hands it to Hatch. "Wu got capped this shift by these bad boys," pointing to a couple pairs of bare feet sticking out of a mound of burnt plastic crates, "but he always packed a number-one lunch, bless his name."

Dubious but mostly ravenous, Hatch blesses departed brother Wu and cracks open the lunchbox to find the whole interior filled with a warm loaf of bread with ingots of vegetable matter and nuts in it. It reminds him of his grandmother's poor-man's bread, with a savory aftertaste of bacon grease. After the first suspicious bite, he finishes the whole thing before Pete can take it away.

Right away, he feels better. His stomach finally fortified against the stench, he finds he can't really perceive it anymore. His nerves settle and his mind stops chasing itself in negative circles or dwelling on his mutilated hand. His confidence restored, he resumes badgering Pete about finding the exit.

"Stick with us," Pete says. "We going out and down, but they's shafts to the Loop and whatever-else upstairs, close to where we going."

Out and down.

The thought of deeper galleries, of levels beneath the city, leaves him baffled. Why the fuck would anyone want to go there? But these intrepid explorers are in their element. Indeed, they seem uneasy in this manmade grotto, exposed, too close to the sun. . .

"What's down there, Pete?"

Pete thinks for a moment how much he can reveal. "Going down to see the Secret Sea. Goony-bird Island. Be kings of the core."

Hatch offers back the empty lunchbox, but Pete tells him to keep it.

The Lunchbox Bunch picks up and rolls out. Hatch walks with Pete, brimming with questions, but Pete hushes him. They slog for what must be hours through dimly lit tunnels that might be looping around and around like impacted bowels. He sees no manholes or ladders, no way out or up, only down.

He's just starting to worry about this when the cramps start. He tries to cover the onslaught of wet, ripping productive farts by splashing, but when a hot jet of acidic diarrhea squirts down his leg, he excuses himself and retreats into a dead-end tunnel to void his bowels in the ankle-deep sludge.

Weakened, dehydrated, but relieved, he catches up to the herd to find them all squatting on a ledge. Grunting, straining and shitting into their Lunchboxes.

Hatch staggers, feeling his empty stomach turn itself inside out. Pete looks at him like he's the one doing something wrong. Stands and puts the top tray back into his Lunchbox, reverently closes the clasps and hangs it on his belt.

"You. . . eat your own shit?"

"Aw naw," Pete says, "that'd be nasty! Lunchbox recycles! Self-contained! Self-compartmentalized! Go for months on one meal. Long way down to Secret Sea, bruh."

The rest of the Lunchbox Bunch stashes their lunchboxes and moves on down the tunnel. Pete hovers over him. "You don't pack your lunch, you go hungry. Don't come crying to Pete."

Hatch follows the Lunchbox Bunch for another hour or so, but at the first junction with a vertical shaft, he quietly ditches them, leaving Wu's lunchbox on a ledge and climbing the ladder for what seems like much longer than an hour. He goads his unraveling mind by singing every song he can remember the words to, then just chants, Out, out, out. . . up, up, up. . .

His feet are sliding off the rungs from exhaustion, so when he finally climbs out onto solid ground, he gratefully sleeps where he falls, though the space around him is blacker than the inside of a dog, and reeking of gasoline and burning rubber.

27

There's an uncomfortable moment on Sendero Luminoso where the police show up and look like they might actually do some law enforcement.

Armored cars and jeeps with machine guns cordon off Colonia Zapata, the pink and purple superbloque operated by the Poison Boys, from Via del Subcommander Marcos to Camino del Carrillo Fuentes, but stay well back from the tower itself, which bristles with snipers and trash-catapults. The wreckage of the Poison Boys' own inadequate street barricades is piled up against the rolldown gates of the storefronts, the gutters clogged with impeccably dressed corpses.

Colonia Zapata's internal defenses have proved harder to crack. Wires strung out from the tower to its neighbors block any drones, all bridges severed or booby-trapped and three armored cars that deployed a berserker squad of Destroying Angels to breach the front entrance lie flattened or fried under a forty-foot shipping container filled with explosive fertilizer that the residents simply cut loose and pushed off the flank of the tower.

His Angels assured him that less than a hundred of the 1200 estimated residents had evacuated when given the chance. The rest had cast their lots with the sodomites. They'd cut off all tunnels and power and communication lines, and the superbloque couldn't possibly have more than a week's worth of food and water. But if they were willing to use the building itself as bombs, they could make the siege more costly than he could afford.

So Litchfield is grateful for the interruption when the police finally arrive.

They roll up in black urban assault vehicles like gigantic half-track mole crickets, bulging with blowback armor and crowd-control artillery, and set up a shield wall opposite the Angels' roadblock and a corridor for Blue Zone paramedics to collect the dead, but they're facing out. It soon becomes clear they're here to contain, not clear, the street.

Egil told Litchfield that they've begun to win converts within the police force itself, but the preacher takes everything they tell him with a grain of salt. They don't mean to lie, but their blind fervor sometimes scares even him.

They want him to come down and raise the dead, but he orders them to let the paramedics take them away. He's tired. When he says he wants to do more minority outreach, they bring him fresh black and brown corpses and say, *reach out to them.*

This thing, he thinks, *it rides me. Not for me to ask where we're going, let alone why.*

His Destroying Angels are children at a birthday party, demanding magic. Most of the men standing around him have already died at least twice. Do they test him when they bring him women and girls with the plea that he must pass on his seed, that he is a new Abraham, and the headwaters of a mighty river-nation of holy blood? The Angel has been silent since Litchfield returned from the dead, but there has been an answer to his prayers, his doubts, his pleas for guidance.

The Fire.

Always the Fire.

So that's what he gives them.

He climbs up onto the back of a garbage truck converted into a siege engine and takes the bullhorn Egil gives him.

"Then Abraham approached him and said, 'Will you destroy the righteous with the wicked? What if there are fifty righteous people in the city? Will you really sweep it away, and not spare the place for the sake of fifty righteous men? Far be it from you to do such a thing. . . to kill the righteous with the wicked. Far be it from you! Will not the judge of all the Earth do right?'

"Though he was but dust and ashes, Abraham did beg the Lord to spare Sodom for the sake of forty, thirty, twenty, yea, even ten righteous men. So have I pleaded with the Lord to spare even this new Sodom. If there reside among you ten righteous men, throw open the doors of this den of abominations, and I vow that the Fire will spare you."

The answer comes in the form of garbage flung from the tower and a burst of sniper fire. Litchfield barely flinches when the bullhorn in his hand explodes into plastic shrapnel, just throws the useless grip aside, climbs down from the truck and orders Egil to proceed with the attack.

He never asked to be a leader, let alone a general. He would touch their heads and hearts and send them into battle, and let any other man shoulder the burden of planning such awful acts. But he has found it all too easy to turn sermons into war-talk, and visions into strategy.

He has only vague recollections of being dead. They come back to him in nightmares when he can sleep, in flashbacks when he closes his eyes. He went to Hell and the devils tortured themselves and he could feel it, somehow it was worse than what he expected. They vicariously tortured him for an eternity until he was empty and could not recollect his earthly sins, and then he went to Heaven, but he didn't stay long, because Heaven was empty.

Egil doesn't hop to it, but the usually eager thug is less than forthright about retrograde progress. "We're still fighting our way to the rooftops on that one," he points to the twelve-story tower across Sendero Luminoso from the Poison Boys, "and that one there," now at the eighteen-story superbloque a hundred yards away across a junkyard no man's land. "Those beaners hate the queers plenty, but they're not cooperating at all."

"Who controls them? I would speak to the ones responsible for impeding His work."

"Yeah," Egil said, deflating with relief, "He wants to speak to you, too."

Egil introduces him to the Devil.

That is what he thinks, the first time he lays eyes upon the man in the skull mask with a blinking 3 on it. In a black paramilitary uniform festooned with fruit salad medals and decorations, the Devil says, "Bless you, father."

"The Lord knows his own," Litchfield snaps. "You control the adjacent buildings to this one?"

"And many others," the Devil says. "We are not easy to step over."

The Devil commands a sizable army, but like everyone else down here, they get most of their weaponry from the Aryans, who have a virtual monopoly on such contraband. This is a man unused to pleading. Litchfield is almost amused by him.

"If you have any fear of the wrath of God, you'll stand down and let us deliver His judgment on these who have rejected His word."

The Devil is not used to ultimatums. "El Señor knows I am a virtuous man, for all my sins. But this one, the man-woman La Toda Madre, is my particular enemy, and I would see him humbled. He killed my family, my comrades. I would have his heart in my hands. I have prayed for salvation, I have made offerings and sacrifices to your god and many others, and the path to my redemption lies through him."

"If you were meant to have him, I warrant that the Lord would've seen fit to deliver him to you. I did not ask for this, but I do it freely, for my body and my soul are not my own. Step aside, sir, and let us send him God's message."

The Devil turns to a subordinate and takes a black silk sack from him. "I heard that the Green Evil, the maker of poisons, tried to strike you down. He allied himself with the monster in the tower, and so set himself against me, but I make a gift of him to you."

Litchfield looks into the sack and his heart skips a beat. How should he feel about this? He lets himself feel the golden fire, though the cold silver congeals spiky crystals in his heart.

"I am unmoved by gifts," he says, "or appeals to my vanity. The Lord shall deal with this one as He will. I shall not spare one who has sinned against Him, but if it is within my power, the Lord shall make you the instrument of his deliverance."

Even through the mask, the Devil's frown as he ponders this deal can be plainly seen. "I could make this crusade of yours very difficult and short, if it amused me, and without this one against whom I set my hands and heart, I would have little else with which to occupy them."

Litchfield cannot abide the stink of this one any longer. Ordering him to have his lackeys surrender the adjacent rooftops, he looks round for Egil when an amplified voice rings out from the inverted black glass stalactite castle suspended over the pink tower.

The voice of La Toda Madre.

"Listen to me.

"We are all as God made us. But we are gifted with the seed to become more.

"God made me as a woman so that, in my journey to becoming a man, I would know struggle. While I cursed him more than once, I have learned that we are each set at the beginning of a painful path. I became lost in my own pain and inflicted pain upon others, but now I see clearly. I cannot ignore any longer the pain of others, now it is too late to live.

"If God made us as we are, and made you to destroy us to earn his love, then I would ask you, what good is God's love? But if all of us must rise and change to discover his true face, then I would ask you if this is your purpose, and I would implore you to look into your hearts and discover what you have never dared to become, and shed your dead skins. . ."

"Fucking smart-ass faggot," Egil growls. "What the fuck does 'implore' mean?"

"My friends, I have found a better way. . ."

Someone shouts in Egil's ear and he relays the message to Litchfield. "They're in position."

"All hatred is hatred of self, for we are all one, hurting itself, trapped in the nightmare of being many. . ."

"Silence his blasphemy," Litchfield says.

La Toda Madre lets out a sound like a sob. Sympathetic vibrations shiver through the buildings, the crowd. "But it is time to wake up—"

Screaming lances of fire from the two towers flanking Colonia Zapata impale the inverted palace, shattering it and severing it from the roof of the cavern. For a moment, cut free of everything, it seems to float like a new moon for this buried world. . . and then it falls.

Litchfield has, of course, witnessed 9/11 and other such grand catastrophes countless times on video, but nothing prepares him for the awesome gravity of it, the sight and sound of such destruction, and the terrible exhilaration of having ordered it.

Obregon's falling glass castle carves into Colonia Zapata like a hatchet into a wedding cake, blasting the individual cargo containers loose and sending shear waves down to the ground floor, so that whole chunks of the building peel away and are flung end over end into the streets. The scream of the tower's collapse, so like an orchestra of horns sounding the final judgment trump, the thought that each colorful brick contains a family, is almost too much to bear.

The howls of those inside come later.

Dust and sand and ashes engulf the street, roiling clouds of yellow smoke. Bystanders stagger past, blind, deaf, coughing up their lungs. Litchfield climbs up onto the truck holding the black sack brought to him by the Devil.

Looking down on the stout masked man pointing at him, snarling. "I wanted him alive—"

"If he is still alive," Litchfield says, "you may have him."

Tres Ojos spits on the pavement. "I will kill you, *buchon*. I will have *your* head."

"Try," Litchfield tells him. "Please try." To the weeping, wailing faces of those peering out of the bloques all down the street, he lifts up the sack and then lets it fall away. Holding the severed head by its ropy white dreadlocks like a new Medusa, he brandishes it so that its scowling green face can look each of them in the eye.

"These are the wages of sin! God is not mocked! His patience with your games and your lies and your miserable little evils is at an end, and I am His messenger! You must pass through the fire to know His love, or burn in Hell forevermore!"

He is as surprised as anyone when the head of Solomon Listor bursts into flame in his hand. He holds it until the crackling flames threaten to spread to his clothing, then flings it down the street. Standing atop the truck, aloof to the building chorus of "This Little Light Of Mine," he sees something coming down out of the dust clouds obscuring the roof of the city.

Remembering the moment of his assassination, the dove that was his soul ascending to heaven, he holds out his hands to accept a blessing.

Suddenly, he is buffeted by thrashing wings, a shrieking beak. Talons rake his face, plunge into his right eye and pluck it out.

He falls into Egil's arms. Gunfire rakes the sky, but the falcon escapes unscathed. He knows now that he will only depart this world one piece at a time. "Damn you, he screams under his breath, "God damn you, God—"

28

Hatch wakes up to someone shouting in his ear about dialectical materialism. Sits up bolt-upright and hits his head against a thick pipe, rolls on the ground with a voice louder than God lecturing him from inside his own head. He was grinding his teeth in his sleep, and accidentally tuned in Silent Radio.

"The free market rules all, but who rules the market? Corporations will try to regulate it to stifle competition, but new innovation will always triumph, the Bright New Idea will always level the playing field, isn't that so? Even North Koreans, who do not recognize the American flag on the bags of relief rice they eat, know the cupidity of that lie.

"Competition gives choice, but competition ends. The free market has no head, and no heart, but it has a plan. The plan was to buy both parties and turn politics into an empty wrestling exhibition everyone knew was rigged. To replace public squares and human rights with private

CODY GOODFELLOW

property and license agreements. To degrade labor and public services and even the military from a sacred patriotic calling to just another job, and to destroy public education to create a generation of *milusos* and *plongeurs*, thugs and welfare queens.

"You know *milusos*—men with nothing, who will do anything for enough money to get by, men who know nothing and thus, will believe anything. Remember that word, for that is what you are. *George Orwell says, a plongeur is a slave, and a wasted slave, doing stupid and largely unnecessary work. He is kept at work, ultimately, because of a vague feeling that he would be dangerous if he had leisure. And educated people, who should be on his side, acquiesce in the process, because they know nothing about him and consequently are afraid of him—*"

"You, the lowest of the low, make America great with your faith in its casino miracles. The harder they squeeze and beat you, the more fiercely do you believe. You give them worship as a cow gives milk.

"And now, they have found a pair of tools to offer you another false choice between knowledge and faith—"

Holy shit, Hatch thinks, I think he's talking about us!

"But do not be fooled again. These are not new ideas. They are as old as slavery. Whatever you choose, America will be reborn like a phoenix, but you are not the bird, you are the kindling."

Silent Radio goes mute as Hatch bites through the receiver. Sounded like a repeat, anyway . . .

He digs the busted receiver piece out of his molars and the sound abruptly vanishes. He sits up and stares pointedly into the darkness. While all around him is blackness, a sputtering lamp illuminates a pool of space several hundred yards away. The tunnel is dry, the floor of corduroy concrete like an urban highway. Fumbling his way across the tunnel, he finds the opposite wall in about twenty paces without hurting himself or stepping in shit. He walks towards the light.

In a few minutes, he closes in on it. Glittery false stars at his feet turn out to be bits of safety glass and plastic brakelight covers. There's nothing special when he gets there, just one working lamp among many that don't. The tunnel stretches beyond it, perhaps bending to the left just before disappearing into blackness. The concrete is scuffed with skidmarks and random splashes of various shades of paint. A dotted white line runs down the center of the tunnel, dividing it into two lanes.

Whatever this is, it's probably not a smart place for pedestrians.

He doesn't see any more shafts like the one he climbed out of, just the endless underground road, and he's putting Silent Radio back in when he hears the roar of engines. It seems to rise and throb down the tunnel over a pulsing core that swiftly resolves into a rising red techno rhythm somewhere north of 150 bpm. The concrete shivers with it.

He aches all over from his myriad untreated injuries and sleeping in the road and his stomach is still in open revolt over the Lunchbox episode, but he starts running. Looks over his shoulder now and again. He hears it getting louder, but he doesn't see any headlights, just the flickering of that one fluorescent lamp, now a couple hundred yards behind him. Then he sees black shapes pour into the light just as it's smashed, snuffing out the last light in the universe.

Except for the lasers.

A brilliant emerald beam spears the length of the tunnel, paralleling the white line. As Hatch watches, it fans out into a wall, then a wave undulating in sync with the throbbing pulse shooting up his legs.

Hatch realizes he's standing still. The dull roar spins out into a mob of motors. Black shapes streaked with deep-sea fish colors, glowstick will-o-wisps. A motorcycle blasts past him, the passenger riding pillion gives a blood-curdling war-whoop and blasts him with a fire extinguisher. He staggers coughing out of the cloud and into the path of another bike that bops its horn and runs over his left foot. Spinning away from the near-collision, he thinks *hug the wall, stupid*, when a third bike passes and throws a weighted nylon cargo net over him.

He trips and goes down hard on his elbows, rolling and trying to find the mouth of the net and get to the wall. A car swerves around him. Lasers everywhere, green blue red particles crawling all over everything and he looks up just in time to see the truck with the laser projector on it.

It's a huge, black Peterbilt semi doing sixty on top of the white centerline. Three big lasers on top of the cab. A bunch of weaker red ones shoot out of the grill to spell out words on his chest. He doesn't stop to read them.

Hatch covers his head and drops flat on his face. The wheels pass close enough to touch. He rolls and rolls and something snatches the net so hard he's whipsawed onto his back and suddenly he's flying along in the truck's wake, dragged by a hook across the unforgiving pavement.

Rolling and screaming trying to protect his exposed skin, he thrashes like a hooked swordfish, thrashes harder when the hook draws him up off the cheese-grater tarmac and onto the flatbed trailer of the truck.

And the middle of a rave.

Maybe fifty of them, all in black with night-vision goggles and blinking LED's embedded in their shaven heads, packed on the dancefloor of a flatbed trailer. They're the whitest people he's ever seen.

At first, he thinks, oh fuck, skinheads, but a lot of Asian and Latino features among the frenetically twitching crowd.

and even a few women. Even so, they remind him of the Nazi zombies from *Shockwaves*, dancing like the German army impaled on divine light at the end of *Raiders*. They shudder in time with the eight-chambered heart attack fulminating out of a stack of bassbins stacked against the cab with a selector hunched behind them, back-to-back with the lasers' cooling tanks.

A ring of them looms over him to detangle the net. The DJ doesn't kill the mix, but throws a filter that gates out all but the deepest sub-bass pulse, so even though it's loud enough to chew your food for you, at least you can scream over it.

The ring of nodding trance-freaks backs up just enough to let him shakily stand. The truck wobbles ever so slightly beneath his feet and seems to accelerate.

The DJ takes up a bullhorn. "*Who the popular boppers who drop all coppers? Who gonna stop the stopping stoppers?*"

The crowd answers, "FINAL TRIBE!"

"*Come alive, you red-eye slags! Oh my bloody god, come the fuck alive!*"

Howls, hollers and air-horns come the fuck alive.

He opens the filter gates and the full force of the shuddering mix hits them like a digital epileptic seizure, a torturous locust-plague rhythm that goes so fast it ties time in knots. Hatch can't escape the recycled second between measures, can't seem to make his way forward on the truck without surrendering to the movement, and before he knows it, he's spastically dancing with an idiotic grin on his face, exhaustion turned to Ecstasy better than the ones he forgot he has in his pocket.

This truck is the world. This tunnel is all of space. This moment, this beat, is eternal.

And it hits him that he's heard of these freaks.

If you only know the history of the UK rave explosion from books, the name blurs into the endless litany of nomad soundsystems and wasteland travelers that toured the British Isles from '89 until the shitbag Tories crushed the burgeoning free festival circuit with a draconian crime bill in '94. Mutoid Waste Company and Planet Dog Collective got the write-ups, but Final Tribe would crack any bell curve distribution of hardcoreness.

Techno-trance purists whose seventy-two-hour psychedelic sundance ritual made Kesey's acid test look like a mistletoe kiss, Final Tribe was widely mistaken for a cult by fellow ravers and a possible terrorist group by the aforementioned Tory shitbags. But terrorist cells and cults live or die by their leaders, and Final Tribe's absolute guru was whoever stood behind the decks at any given time.

They toured England and Scotland with a truck-based soundsystem—maybe even this one under his feet, he realizes—continuously, keeping an uninterrupted mix blasting every minute of every hour, every day, for five years. They fled the UK for Europe, keeping the music alive like an Olympic torch, and eventually crossed glasnost Russia, where they planned to follow the path of the former Bering ice bridge and recolonize the New World with hardcore rave vibes.

But then they *vanished*.

Spotty articles at the time vaguely described a harsh breakup on the Kamchatka Peninsula, while others cited forever-upcoming festival dates in Canada and Washington State as proof they'd crossed over on the sly, and nobody kicked when they failed to show up. But while a few ex-members eventually turned up to repeat vague accounts of getting kicked out by utterly bonkers acid-casualties in the collective's inner circle, conspiracy theories abounded that the US government, or maybe even the Canadians, had seized the soundsystem, and in the wake of so many pear-shaped federal intervention clusterfucks like Waco and Ruby Ridge, the ugly outcome was buried.

But well over a decade later, the outcome is here, driving through lightless tunnels half a mile under Mexico.

He dances until he's sweated out the last dregs of adrenalin from getting run over and the last flakes of sewer slime off his skin, until he finds himself jittering with his head in a bassbin and glowstick bullroarers spinning all around him. A kid hangs by hooks through his ribcage suspended in the sweet acoustic spot before the speakers, thrashing like a fly in a spiderweb.

When Hatch collapses in a grateful heap, the music and countless pale hands drag him upright again. High-fiving and blasting a whistle somebody shoves in his mouth, he climbs the cabinets to speak with the selector.

"Fucking mental, brother," Hatch shouts in his ear. The kid looking at him across the decks probably wasn't even born when kids were yelling that at each other in London. He just nods and goes back to trying to cue a record. "Hey, I wanna join up. . ."

The DJ holds an open hand high and Hatch catches it. "Much love and respect. But it's Dani's initiation. You'll have to wait your turn after we pit stop."

"When's that?"

DJ checks his watch. "About fifty-four hours."

"Can you spin me a tune, then?"

The DJ points at his record crates. Hundreds upon hundreds of blank white-labeled vinyls. "No requests, mate."

"I really need to hear Lord Kitchener," Hatch shouts. "'The Bee's Melody.'"

"No requests!"

"Sez the ted who made me spin Cliff fooking Richard on his blaggy birfday," screams the DJ's closest friend.

"You can't beat a beatsmith," replies the DJ.

"Come on, kid." Hatch takes out the tin of pills. "I've got some top-grade Ecstasy. . ."

The DJ screams, "What the fook is Ecstasy?"

His mate shouts, "Go see the Geezer!"

Hatch finds the handholds bolted all over the cab to climb off the trailer and onto the running-board beneath the driver's side door.

It's another bald guy with goggles, but obviously a lot older than the rest. He smiles at Hatch and grasps his hand, smiles wider when Hatch looks into the truck.

Below the waist, Geezer's legs end in stumps that fit into a rod and lever apparatus to work the pedals. "When I lost me plates and stems," he shouts, "they told me I was gonna die, so I rooked the ol' soundsystem out, and we took back the Loop from them what used to crash cars down here. That was. . . what, seven years ago."

"That's amazing!"

"Final Tribe never stops. Wot you want?"

"I was wondering what keeps you dancing?"

Geezer looks mistrustfully at him. "You mean drugs?"

Hatch nods. "This isn't the place to talk, but I have something. . ."

"Put away those sad little things, boy." Geezer shakes his head sorrowfully. "Let me set you right on drugs. Would you kick down a door to let your sweet in? That's what drugs do. Bloody breaks the door down. This just opens it."

He points at the blinking LED's in his scalp. Hatch looks closer at the web of wires enclosing his skull. "Pretty."

"Pretty godlike, you mean." Takes a phone and shows Hatch an app. "Dial up any mental state you can model, and induce it, mate, like programming the fooking telly. No muss, no fooking fuss."

Hatch nods, intrigued, but these people are probably terrible at recognizing placebo effects. Hatch himself was sucked into the floor, was even capable of intermittent moments of spontaneous dancing, not concentrating on it at all. It takes everything he has not to say something snide, not to let his mouth curl into a smirk.

"Drop you in the pits, they'll get you sorted for one."

With Geezer's distraction, the speedometer has dropped down below forty. The engine lugs uneasily in the upper registers of its sixteen-gear transmission. Kids bang on the roof, screaming, "Highball! Highball!"

"Actually, if you or the tribe could help me find my way to the surface. . ."

"The SURFACE?" Geezer throws out a hand to throttle Hatch's neck.

But Hatch pushes away and for a split-second, he's dancing on diesel fumes, then he's tumbling across the greedy tarmac, then lying facedown in the road.

Final Tribe doesn't stop.

Final Tribe never stops.

29

He can't find the lady of the house. The swimming pool is empty. Nobody comes round to let the dog out at the Audi dealership.

So he goes outside. There's a city in a jungle, or a jungle in a city. People walk around naked, laughing and picking fruit off the trees. A white guy in a flying squirrel onesie and a shit emoji hat chops the top off a weird tropical fruit that looks like a cross between a pineapple and a pancreas, sticks a straw in it and hands it to Jaime. It's the most delicious thing he's ever tasted. He wanders game trail streets, passing more wild animals than people. The people and the animals touch and trade shapes like gossip. He sees the Green Man in the crowd and tries to get to him, but the people around him start bursting into flames and he's trapped among them, screaming until he's inhaling fire, until he—

Opens his eyes.

He looks around, but if he was screaming in his sleep again, nobody seems to care.

Jaime chilling in his new crib. Not a patch on his old one, but so far, they're safe, and in spite of all odds, he's actually risen to *real* power, albeit in the worst possible way, by having everyone above him go missing or dead.

He swigs vodka from a diamond-encrusted bottle. Gold flakes swirl around in it, catching the light as they swirl down his gullet. His next shit will be worth more than the rest of his life.

Los Zeros came in yesterday. Blew open the lobby with a car-bomb while shooters with plastique body armor on dead-man switches came in through the ruined McDonalds. Bombs planted throughout the ten-story bloque brought it down like Jenga.

They're hunkered in a bunker underneath the labs, behind six feet of rubble filling a corridor they collapsed and will have to tunnel out of, if no one finds them first.

Eighteen people up in here. Three of Malverde's gunmen, thirteen Soma cases, Jaime and Dale Agrippa and his stupid three-legged dog. The Soma people are all flat on their backs or curled up on the floor. He resists the urge to kick them in spite of knowing what they're going through. Precisely *because* he knows what they're going through.

Jaime had lit a candle. Poured out a glass of the hideously expensive vodka and set it beside the candle on a shelf on the wall. For the Green Man.

Agrippa told him, "Fuck that guy. This is all his fucking fault, man."

Jaime asked him what he was talking about. Agrippa didn't want to tell, but this was no time to sit on secrets. "Not all of the first test pilots ejected, man. A couple of them were all fired up about something coming, and Sol kept them on ice down here, but he was interested in them because his own damage was braining so hard on that shit, he turned them loose to see what they'd do. One of 'em tried to dose the god-botherin' fuckhead who's now blowing up everybody, so pour one out for all of us, but let him go to hell thirsty."

Jaime said nothing, but he knows whose fault it is.

You gonna witness the end times, Natron Spinks tried to tell him. *By your treachery, you gonna make it happen.*

He'd filed away the whole Spinks episode as pure insanity, but what if it wasn't? What if this was all inevitable, and he'd played his part by throwing Hatch into the sewer? When Hatch insisted he huff that balloon of nitrous, he was testing how Jaime would react in a tense situation with his mind blown. But Hatch had been the treacherous one in the end, and Jaime can't imagine how the situation would be anything but worse, with Hatch down here, too.

The phone rings.

Jaime picks up, though he doesn't recognize the number. "Are you the Smurf?"

Strike One. "Who this?"

"Are you a friend of Nolan Hatch?" The Anglo woman sounds nervous but controlled in a way that instantly puts him on guard. "Are you a real friend of his? Are you real?"

Given Hatch's long and frequent conversations with a brain in a fishtank, he wants to ask her the same question. "That *pindejo* is dead to me, and if you see him, you can tell him from me—"

"Good, you must really know him, then. My name is Jude. . . Our shelter was raided, we're running. . . we need to find each other. . ."

Jaime scratches his head and takes a deep hundred-dollar swig of gold vodka. And then it hits him. It's the crazy nun who runs the women's shelter. Hatch couldn't stop staring but didn't want to talk about her. Jaime knows he's been seeing her because the Green Man had him followed. He'd suspected Hatch laid Soma on her. More guinea pigs. "Sorry, lady, I don't know what you need, but I'm not the one."

She sighs, a sound that closes his eyes and takes him back to the Raft.

And he *feels* her.

He doesn't close his eyes, but they close. Purple dots blossom and envelop his vision. Head-rush when he tries to get up. His blood bubbles and boils. He rises out of himself like steam.

•

You're looking down through narrow second-floor window-slits at torches and flashlights and fireworks among the black tide sweeping Calle Mata Hari. Carrying swords, shields, spears, guns, knives, chains and big twisted crosses of iron rebar, men who patronized these places yesterday have come to burn, rape and pillage to try to buy back their souls.

The clubs, cantinas, massage parlors and boom-booths are all locked down, the power cut. The raiders rip security bars off windows with crowbars and climb in where there's no resistance, toss in Molotov cocktails where someone fights back. Women are dragged kicking and screaming out into the torchlit dark and thrown to the crowd like the food from the vending machines. They're attracted to the flashier clubs and seem to ignore the shelter, but your helpless fury boils over and you scream at them. You condemn them with every weapon you have, but if any of them feels the sting of your words, it only seems to excite the crowd.

They gather in front of the shelter. It's harder to crack. Sheet-metal spot-welded over the barricaded doors keeps them cutting with circular saws while the women inside throw paint, broken glass, furniture, burning clothing, everything. It whips them into a frenzy, but it holds them off long enough for the leader to come.

He's like a skeleton with a stringy white beard, jerked by invisible strings and fire gushing from an empty eyesocket. He paces beneath your window holding a bullhorn, but he doesn't use it. Doesn't even need it. His voice carries over the noise of the mob and the weeping of the women at your back.

"We are not gentlemen, and I beg your forgiveness for what you have witnessed. . . These men are sinners, as are we all, and unused to the service of the Lord. This place and others like it must be cleansed and made ready for Christ's return. These women have earned no mercy.

"But you have set yourselves apart from the license and degradation around you, and for that, I have declared that you shall be spared. . ."

"Lucky us," says the woman next to you. She watches the leader through the scope on a .22 hunting rifle.

"You who come out freely will be made whole and pure and bound over as brides of Christ, or as brides of godly soldiers of the Holy Fire. New women for new men."

The mob catcalls and howls at this. He faces them down. A couple of them literally choke on their words and dry-heave under his wrathful glare.

"If you will not submit to God's will, then I cannot promise you mercy."

A lady with two black eyes and half her hair burned off brings you a microphone, patched into the building's security PA. Your anger spills out your mouth. "Everything a man does to a woman is God's will, until a woman says no."

"I have not come to debate you, woman. . ."

"Nobody does, asshole. Yet here you are."

A few in the crowd laugh. The leader wheels on them like a conductor.

"Tell you what, why don't you and your friends go have a circle jerk and then ask God where He gets His rocks off.

Must suck, with no Mrs. God to knock around when shit doesn't go His way.

"That would explain a lot about the world, wouldn't it? Or maybe God's not just like you. Maybe God isn't a man at all. And maybe men have no answers *because* they have dicks. . ."

"I can take him," the big lady with the rifle says. "Please let me take him."

You want to say yes, you know how this debate is going to go. Already, the leader is signaling to men in the mob to get on with it. A few throw cocktails at the building, the glass and the short-lived alcohol flames dribble harmlessly off the façade.

But you tell her no, because everything hurts, you can feel the pain of women dying all down the street, but somehow the hurt you inflict on others is worse than your own pain.

"We need to go," you say but you're the last one away from the windows just before the tear gas canisters begin pummeling the shutters.

•

"We need to go," Agrippa is saying into his face when he sits up. He can hear the noises on the other side of the rubble. The motherfuckers are tunneling in after them? Seriously?

"Are you still there? Jaime?" The woman he didn't share his name with is still nattering in his ear. He gets up and casts around the bunker but he's looked and looked and there's no other way out, they've only got four guns and eighteen bullets, and none of the Soma cases are going to be any help. They all huddle in a cluster in the corner with their heads pressed together. He doesn't know if he could wake them up, is afraid to get close enough to get sucked into whatever they're sharing.

"Lady, I can't help you! Hatch took off, fucking Green Evil is dead, and we're buried in a bunker. The motherfuckers who killed him are digging us out, so wherever you are, I fucking promise you, we got it worse."

The pile of rubble blocking the door stirs.

"Listen, Jaime? Chill out, okay?" Her voice is soothing, but more, he feels calm like cough syrup spreading warmth through his chest, feels his heart cradled in cool, soothing hands. "We got out of the shelter without anyone's help, we went down into the sewers."

Scraping and thudding from the entrance. Agrippa's dog lurches to its feet and starts barking. The gunmen go to the wall with guns hefted in shaky hands. The Soma cases start screaming. Jaime's heart wants to leap out of his chest, there's nowhere to go, so he goes out, right out of himself and across the black ice of space until he feels the muted glow of others, and he braces himself, knowing every head is a cold black ocean he might drown in, but there's nowhere else to go, nothing else to do, so he reaches out and screams—

"HELP US!"

And something hits him in the face, knocks him clean back into his body.

The rocks fall away from the lintel of the doorway and a face presses into the gap.

A white woman's face.

"What the fuck," says Sister Jude, "are you screaming about?"

30

He climbs a caged ladder up a seemingly endless shaft lined with dusty, narrow windows. He shines a disposable lighter into one after scrubbing away the filth. Nearly falls when he sees someone staring back at him.

He climbs on and on until he emerges in a utility shed and uses a shovel to break down the door. On the outside, a sign that's mostly barcodes says ALPHAVILLE.

He steps out onto grass, falls down and runs his fingers through it, stops just short of kneeling to kiss it.

He looks up at the stars and his heart swells with joy that quickly turns to perplexity, then disgust as he fails to identify a single constellation, and then concludes that the sky is just another ceiling, much better decorated than the one downstairs.

Still, it's good to touch grass and shrubbery and trees. He wanders through them, groping them like a virgin tripper. Emerges on the front lawn of a burnt-down house.

All the houses on this side of the street are in varying stages of destruction and extraction. A few brand-new prefab replacement houses are cut in halves and up on flatbed trailers beside cleared foundations, like fresh dental implants in a dead, decayed mouth.

A chubby guy is out front of a new house across the street, watering his lawn in a pair of bathing trunks and a Teenage Mutant Ninja Turtles t-shirt. The guy looks up and waves at him. "Hey! Welcome to the neighborhood!"

Looking around warily, Hatch crosses the street. "Hi! I'm just passing through, but I sure could use some help. . ."

The guy drops the hose and ambles eagerly down his driveway to shake Hatch's hand. "I'm Gary." Awkward pause as he consciously withholds his last name.

"Good to know you, Gary. I'm Nolan." Right away, he gets the vibe off Gary that he's developmentally disabled, a big, falsely jolly man-child, eager to please but likely to freeze up and narc him out at a moment's notice. But he doesn't eat his own feces out of a lunchbox or play rave-warrior games in a pitch-dark tubeway, so he's going to have to do.

"Well, come on in, anyway. It's great to see someone besides the construction crews and the doctors." He leads Hatch up the driveway into a house that looks like it belongs to his parents.

"You alone here, Gary?"

"Yeah. . . I've been here about a year. Relocated from Ohio State. . ."

"The college? In Columbus?"

"No, Youngstown. The supermax." Gary shakes his head, studying Hatch's moccasins, which are tattered leather held together by sewage. "Would you mind leaving those outside? New carpet."

"No problem, Gary." Hatch has to peel the shredded shoes off. His bare feet aren't any cleaner. "Maybe I should use your bathroom, first."

"Go right ahead." Gary opens the door. "First door on your right. . ."

Hatch goes inside. The house looks large for Gary's needs, but the décor makes sense. Star Trek memorabilia, movie posters, action figures in display cases, a laptop on a beanbag. A mountain of frozen-food boxes spills out of the breakfast nook.

He locks the bathroom door behind him, checks himself out in the mirror. Gary must be truly desperate for company. He would've been well within his rights to spray Hatch down with the garden hose before allowing him in the house. He runs the sink until it's hot while enjoying a truly satisfying bowel movement and looking longingly at the shower, but it probably wouldn't be prudent, until he knows what Gary was sent to a supermax prison for.

He nearly jumps off the toilet when Gary knocks. "Hey, if you feel like changing out of those duds, I got some extra clothes, and a bathrobe. . . They gave me a bunch of stuff. . . It'll be a little baggy on you, but. . ."

"That sounds wonderful, Gary!" Flushing the toilet, he opens the door to receive the bundle of clothing. The socks and underwear are still in plastic. "Thanks for your hospitality."

"Think nothing of it," Gary says through the door. "We're all in this together. . ."

What a lovely philosophy you have, Hatch thinks, as he turns on the shower.

Undressing reminds him he has no fingernails on his left hand, and he gingerly removes the filthy glove to apply more topical antiseptic. A quick search of the medicine cabinet turns up nothing stronger than Advil, but he reminds himself to check upstairs.

He comes out in a luxuriant cloud of steam, dressed in a t-shirt for *Battleship (The Videogame Of The Movie of the Classic Boardgame! CNET 2011)* and a pair of sweatpants.

"How'd that shower treat you, Nolan?" Gary calls from the kitchen.

"Better than I deserve, Gary!" Matching Gary's forced jollity is going to be exhausting. Hatch joins Gary in the kitchen, where he's poring over a library of TV dinner options in his freezer. "I've got a lot of good stuff, if you're not a vegetarian. . ."

"Anything with a lot of pasta would suit me right down to the ground," Hatch says, sitting at a barstool across the counter from Gary. "But really, I'm not picky. Surprise me."

Gary looks at him with that pained expression of a lifelong mark trying to ferret out an insult. A moment later, he unclenches. "Chicken surprise with pasta?"

Hatch affects a delighted laugh. "You're the host with the most, Gary."

Gary pops two shrink-wrapped trays into the microwave. "So, Nolan. Where're you passing through to?"

"Here to there, I guess. Actually had the crazy notion I'd bug out of here in the morning. People to see, things to do, and whatnot."

Gary nods. "What kind of soda you like?"

"Root beer's never done me wrong. . ."

Gary looks in the fridge, fetches Hatch a Virgil's root beer and a Pineapple Fanta for himself. "Those dinners'll be ready in about five minutes. You gotta take the plastic off and stir them, but if you don't leave the plastic on the fruit compote, it tastes like ass." Shrugging as if this is somehow his fault, he takes his soda and leaves the room. "I got some work to do, so if you wanna hang out in there, feel free to fire up a movie, or I gotta lot of comic books. . ."

Hatch tastes the root beer, which is pretty good, if a bit heavy on the licorice flavor. He follows Gary into the living room, where he's sitting on the beanbag. He looks mortified to find Hatch watching him. "Maybe, like I said, you wanna wait in there. . ."

"So what were you in Ohio State for, Gary? Big scholarship screwup?"

"Heh, I wish. . ." He stares at the laptop screen for a while before he says, "Loving not wisely but too well, I guess. That's Shakespeare. I don't just do geek shit, I appreciate the classics. . ."

"I liked *Othello*, too. You ever read *Lolita*, Gary?"

Gary shivers, fights off a surge of panic. "Don't be like them, please? I invited you in my house, but you don't even know me, and I'm not pushing your shit in. . ."

"Gary, it's cool. I'm sorry, I didn't mean anything by it. I'm just making conversation. . . Like, did you know that police who track child pornography have found a disturbing correlation between pedophiles and Star Trek fandom?"

Gary looks sidewise at him the way he must've practiced facing down cons in the chow-line who entertained designs on his fruit compote.

"It's true. Something like two-thirds of pedophiles are self-described Star Trek fans."

"That's a. . . specious statistic. . ."

"I know, it's weird, right? Wesley Crusher aside, there's nothing there that child molesters would even get off on, but the cops think that pedos see an implicit tolerance of their way of loving in the post-racist, post-religious society of the 23rd century. Like, once we all get over our individual hang-ups and bigotry, we'll just come to see pedophilia as just another shade of the rainbow."

Gary looks up at a framed poster of *Star Trek VI: The Undiscovered Country* as if seeing it for the first time. He looks sourly at his meal. "I didn't ask to come here," he says. "They transferred me. Said it was actually cheaper than keeping me in the SHU all the time. It's especially hard in prison. Those guys in there, they get the wrong idea. . ."

"I didn't mean to get the wrong idea, Gary. I'll just go . . ."

"It's alright. Just get the dinners out, would you? Leave the plastic on the dessert compartment, if you don't, you'll be sorry."

Hatch does as Gary told him with the dinners. He comes back to find Gary wearing a shock collar, which is connected to his computer.

He explains that parents of his victims and other concerned citizens can log onto a web site and watch him go about his business in the house, and, for a moderate credit card donation, they can shock him. The site represents itself as being a parents' proto-vigilante group, but Gary's actually the webmaster, and came up with the gimmick as both penance and source of income. He shamefully admits, however, that the collar only shocks him about half the time. "I got real good at faking it. They actually tip more when you foam at the mouth. People can be so cruel. . ."

"So, this is a pretty sweet setup for you. D'you know what happened to all your neighbors, Gary?"

"Heh. . . They're dead. But I'm getting new ones."

"That's horrible."

"I guess. . ."

"How many people were living here, Gary?"

"About a thousand, I think."

"Were they pretty judgmental?"

"You bet they were, and it's not like they were a bunch of angels, either."

"Oh really?"

"They all acted like their shit doesn't stink, but then, like two months ago, out of nowhere, they all went berserk and killed each other. It was crazy, like, like a. . ."

"Kind of a Return Of The Archons situation?"

Gary smiles and nods. "Yeah, kinda, but way nastier. I was the only one left. . ."

"A real-life Omega Man."

"Stop," Gary says, blushing. "You don't know what it was like. It got pretty hairy, when the bad people came."

"Bad people?"

Gary nods, whispers, "Mexicans. I didn't catch the virus, or whatever, because I'm on a strict diet." He nods towards the freezer. "They brought me in for my physical when the Mexicans came in and wrecked everything. . . I was worried about my stuff, but nobody messed with it, which was nice."

"You've got quite a collection. Do you know where the exit is?"

"Why the hell would I want to leave?"

"I don't know . . . All your neighbors are dead? You know, the uh, burnt-out houses everywhere. . . ?"

"You wanna watch a movie? I've got a big library. They let me buy stuff on eBay. . .""

"Gary, have you ever killed anybody?"

Gary blinks. "Not really, no. . ."

"Well, I have, Gary. I killed thirteen people right after dropping out of college, without even trying very hard. Put another thirty-eight in a persistent vegetative state. They'll never walk, say their loved ones' names, or eat solid food again. So maybe I'm not the kind of guy you want for a neighbor."

Gary gets up. "I think this Salisbury steak needs more salt. . ."

Doorbell rings. Gary drops his Salisbury steak.

"Did you call the cops, Gary?"

"Me? No, but like. . . there's cameras everywhere."

Hatch scans the room for somewhere to hide, but it's probably pointless.

Doorbell rings again. "I should answer that," Gary says. Hatch feints left, right, before ducking into the bathroom.

Just the other side of the door, he hears Gary open up and say, "Hi! Welcome to the neighborhood. . ."

"Howdy," says the voice on the other side of the door. "I'm looking for a friend of mine. . . shifty little white fella, calls himself Nolan Hatch, you seen him around?"

Muted clump of boots on tile.

Hatch flattens against the wall, tries to push through it.

There's so many men in the world that nobody needs, no good for themselves or anyone else, and when they go missing, nobody calls the police or makes a fuss, nobody really misses them.

Gary doesn't answer, but Hatch can almost see him with X-ray vision, pointing through the bathroom door.

When they turn up months or years later at the bottom of a river or a lake, it looks like they got drunk and fell off a bridge taking a piss.

Gentle knock on the bathroom door. "You in there, brother Nolan?"

Hatch considers all his options before answering, "Yeah . . . Who's asking?"

"I think you know who this is."

Hatch slowly opens the door and looks into the utterly unremarkable face of the Roadrunner. He's wearing a tan uniform and a dark green jacket with an ID card on the breast. He smiles and says, "Thought I'd find you here. You about ready to go?"

Hatch forces a smile.

Heck, half the time, they thank me, just before they go down—

Gary says, "I gotta clean up this mess. You guys make yourselves at home. . ." He shuffles back to the kitchen, then upstairs and locks himself in a bedroom.

"I'm, um. . . not exactly ready to go, if by go, you mean
. . ."

The Roadrunner chuckles and shakes his head. "I'm
lighting out, thought you could use a ride."

"Oh! Well, that's mighty thoughtful of you. You're. . .
leaving here? You know how to get out?"

"Sure, I like to winter down here, but things are getting
too hot downstairs, and I got to say. . ."

"How did you find me?"

"Well, that's the funny part, I just knew where you were,
and. . . I, before I left, I had to come and thank you."

"For what?"

"That little pill you gave me, it opened up my eyes. I saw
the whole grand design and how I fit in it. . ."

"Awesome!"

"That's the word, amigo. Just like you said, I stepped out
of myself and ever since I came back, I know in my bones,
that I'm doing what God put me here to do. I used to just
sense it, but now. I know. . . Their pain and their emptiness
just calls to me, and I know the peace I'm giving them, it's
a gift."

"That's wonderful," Hatch says. "So. . . we're leaving
soon?"

"Just go on outside, you'll see a truck parked in the
street, with a chunk of a house they totaled out. I made a
place for you to hide in the wall, just pull it shut after you,
in case they inspect it. We'll get on a train out of the landfill
facility and be in Tucson for breakfast."

Hatch thanks him and starts to go look for Gary. The
Roadrunner puts a hand on his shoulder and steers him to
the front door. "I'll be along directly. I just need a minute
with your friend. . ."

Hatch steps outside. The front door locks behind him.
As promised, a semi is parked out front, with a torched
section of prefab house much like Gary's lashed down on

the trailer bed. Hatch circles around it before finding a slit in the clear plastic cover, climbs up on the truck and steps inside a kitchen exactly like Gary's, except all the appliances are ripped out, the walls are blackened with soot and smeared everywhere with bloody slogans and messages. The smell of charred plastic, wood and flesh is so thick he gags, but makes it to the section of wall in the dining room, climbs into the crawlspace and pulls the drywall in after him, using the wall-studs as handles.

The space is cramped, lined with foil and insulation stuff he supposes will mask him from a thermal scan. Bottled water and a couple energy bars are wedged into the insulation.

If he wanted to kill me, he just would have done it there, he tells himself. He's just grateful because my drug has made it easier for him to murder people with a clear conscience.

People like Gary.

He doesn't know how to feel about it, so he doesn't feel anything, but before long, the house begins to hum, and soon it is moving.

Hatch trembles all over with Xmas morning excitement. Though the kitchen is demolished, he has the perverse itch to make somebody breakfast in bed. He holds himself deathly still when the truck hisses to a stop and he hears voices outside. Maybe they have motion detectors, maybe they have parabolic microphones that can detect his hammering heartbeat.

But the truck starts rolling again. He opens the wall and peeks out and is bewitched by the crepuscular blue predawn light pouring into the kitchen through the billowing plastic. He climbs out and goes to the window and marvels at the rolling empty brown landscape, the hills like worn dog's teeth gnawing the hurtfully blue horizon.

He moves from room to room like a househunter, furnishing it with his mind and populating it with his life.

The wind whipping through the bisected house whistles so shrill that it's not until he gets to the family room and the cruel terminator of the house's cleaving that he hears the sirens. Out the back window, instead of a pool, barbecue and rolling green lawn, he sees a fleet of border patrol vans with flashing blue-red lights.

He should go back to his hiding place, but he watches them, and when the trailer jolts and begins to grind to a stop slewed sideways across the two-lane blacktop, he runs back to the kitchen and watches the semi cab speeding away on the razor-straight highway.

He finds himself standing in the empty kitchen with his hands on his head. He shouts, "Hi! Welcome to the neighborhood!" as the agents come through the plastic and force him down on the floor.

He asks if they can't wait just long enough for him to see the sun come up. They put a hood over his head and stuff him in a trunk and then they work him over with a club and a taser. The white light that explodes in his head is nothing like the sun.

31

An hour before sunrise, the King Air prop plane took off from the shadow terminal at McCarran in Las Vegas, exchanged brief cryptic greetings with the tower at Nellis Air Force Base, and then continued on its unfiled flight plan, turning south over the infamous Black Box of top secret real estate at Groom Lake to drop off all civil monitors altogether, before descending to an invisible airstrip on the US-Mexico border to deliver its only passenger.

Lionel Warwick always makes good use of the time reviewing classified dossiers related to his work, all of which bears the government designation TOP SECRET/ COMPARTMENTALIZED: ARCADE ORANGE. This particularly arcane blanket of secrecy covers the foundation and ongoing operations of what the inhabitants have charmingly come to refer to as Unamerica.

But this morning, all of his time is consumed by one fat, hastily compiled file, which, in true governmental cover-your-ass mode, offsets its brief breakdown of internal casualties and ongoing instability with promises that the tactical innovations currently in play could markedly shift the stagnant strategic situation, the mendacity of which almost takes his breath away.

It's more than just a masterpiece of CYA misdirection. For a true believer, it is the Holy Grail, the pony they've been shoveling shit looking for since the beginning. And Warwick, who was appointed nine years ago to run this monstrous thing that should not be, and had his resignation refused twice, is nothing, if not a true believer.

At moments like this, just as a mental exercise, he pauses to reflect upon the morality of what he's doing. The media outdid itself as a red herring factory the last presidential cycle, but Warwick cannot fault them for their role in the climate they helped to create.

No matter if everything they did at ARCADE ORANGE comes to light tomorrow, half the country would at once embrace and actively disbelieve it, simply because the other half of the country angrily denounces it. In such a climate, ordinary people lament that nothing of any substance can be changed, but from Warwick's side of the board, the present internecine divisions create a uniquely fertile environment wherein *everything* can finally be perfected.

And so it must be.

When this project was first created, as a pioneer public-private partnership under the aegis of the Department of Commerce, it was an infinitesimal NAFTA side-hustle. They were already holding border-crossers in detention, so they started using them for market research. They were solid citizens, mostly, now all the drug mules were obsolete. NAFTA insured that drugs didn't come across the river taped to hungry brown bellies; it came up in legions of semis, packaged like every other product in *maquiladoras* owned by the cartels. The labor these people did up north was a concealed but vital pillar of the US economy; the money they sent home was a concealed third leg of the Mexican economy behind drugs and oil, once tourism cratered in the wake of the cartel wars. They were a vital demographic, and the corporate community was very interested in them.

What Warwick saw when he looked at them, was the future.

The project quietly grew and became a permanent installation, they joked, because none of the guinea pigs wanted to leave.

After 9/11, they expanded the research pools by leaps and bounds, expanding and populating the cavern city as it was meant to be filled by its original builders, with toxic human waste wherever they could find it. The prison system, the immigration detention system, the black sites around the world, all became watersheds draining into his secret sea.

Whenever someone in Washington came across the scope of the project, he explained to them the secondary research, the big picture research that could be conducted nowhere else, the reams of data they were getting. He showed them how all the unfulfilled promises of the space program were being redeemed down here.

Warwick has no use for religion, but he firmly believes in a secular apocalypse on the horizon, a Malthusian *Götterdämmerung* that will be the inevitable reckoning between capitalism and democracy, between the haves, and the have-nots.

Such bottlenecks have come before, and humanity has not always recovered gracefully, but at such times, human innovation rises to the occasion, and a new way of thought, of belief, of being, emerges from the crucible to create a new order. He is humbled to be the custodian of that crucible.

•

As the plane touches down, he looks out on the desert and shakes his head at the incongruous span of painfully green, perfect lawn adjacent to his airstrip. He wonders idly what any unlucky wetbacks who might evade the installation's formidable dragnet would make of it, to see water spewed by sprinklers to maintain an oasis in the deadly desert for a fat man's game. A massive resort spa owned and operated by the Juarez cartel, suffered as another piece of camouflage for the city, it would soon be hosting a confidential summit meeting of the western hemisphere's economic authorities with members of the World Bank and assorted financial entities who enjoyed personhood alongside powers denied even to superpower nations. They would wallow in the soaking pools and deliberate most seriously upon the need for a coherent and sustainable economic policy in an uncertain future.

Though it would be a disastrous breach of secrecy, Warwick ponders what how much more useful their retreat might be, if they were to accompany him on his elevator trip a half mile beneath the earth, and get a glimpse of that future.

•

"Walk me through the situation again."

Everybody at the table knows Warwick does his homework. He doesn't expect to be briefed at the briefing. Everything is a test. The brass ring everybody grabs for is anything he doesn't already know. Any time he asks a question, it's a trap.

"How far has the situation deteriorated, and how far are we willing to let it go?"

"Well, a good third of the city is stuck in the Dark Ages," Craig Knott, Chief Operations Officer, says, "and that's probably the good news. . ."

Tom Schnur, Chief of Security, cuts in, "It's not that bad. We've got more eyes in the air than they can shoot down. Local warlords in all the districts are locked down and thumping their chests, but aside from some score-settling, they're preserving the status quo. We have a security cordon around the Arcade itself, and our patrols are preserving order in the Green Zone."

Schnur and Knott are like twins separated at birth, like those two balding, lipless Republican flyover state congressmen you always get confused. As such, they naturally despise each other beyond all reason.

"They don't want to do their fucking jobs," Gould, Senior Corporate Liaison, spits into his oversized coffee mug. "Our vendors are cut off, the infrastructure is trashed, and we're getting fuck-all out of the data feeds."

Teague, the Chief Technical Officer, throws up his hands. "I told you the whole network was a house of cards when I inherited it."

"Looting is golden time," Gould continues. "It's consumer choice on steroids, and we don't even know what they're taking. We're down to eavesdropping on phones."

"We can afford to suspend normal product research protocols," Warwick says, "until this plays out. The whole city is the product, right now."

"We don't have any choice," Uyen Nguyen, informatics, insists. "The lunatics have taken over the asylum." Her eyes dart around the room behind her thick glasses. "If I didn't know better, I'd say the system was compromised from the inside."

"Tell me more about the personalities," Warwick says.

"Orrin Litchfield is the central figure in the evangelical group." Schnur says. "Our informants say he's got an army

of about two thousand and another five to ten thousand
followers. . . It's your basic white trash sample platter. . .
Nazi gangs, militia thugs, redneck jailbirds, Russian and
Balkan Mafiya, Orange Zone mutants. . ."

Gould interrupts, "But the demographics for his church
are all over the place. He's got blacks, Hispanics and even
some Asian and Arab followers. . . And they're all fanatics."

"He's got the whole world in his hands," Warwick
concludes. "And missiles."

Schnur says, "We're pretty sure they were just rockets.
Are we concerned that they may have more? Are we taking
precautions to track and minimize this threat and others
not enumerated? Yes and yes."

"What does their regime look like?"

"Basic Kabul clusterfuck scenario. Lopsided crackdown
on drugs, alcohol and all forms of vice, but the raiders
are consuming as much as they destroy. The inner circle
is running around trying to impose order, but it's total
chaos, down there. All the automats and kiosks and shops
in their areas have been looted, and they're burning people's
barcodes off."

"That shit has to stop," Knott snaps.

"Leave it," Eleanor Myrick, Human Research Director,
says. "The macro dynamics are far more important than
market data." She trumps even corporate on this issue. She's
always the one harping on the other departments about the
spotty data from fecal analysis.

"May I continue?" Schnur snaps. "Thank you. The
cult seems to be playing out as radical Mormonism by
way of the Dark Ages. Litchfield himself is a Lost Boy—a
disinherited stepchild runaway from a Mormon polygamist
sect. It's a charisma cult based around his received visions
and reports of miracles. . ."

"Reports?"

"The usual. . . they say he heals the sick, raises the dead."

"And you don't have documentation of any of this."

"We cut off food and water into there a week ago, and this hasn't settled down, so either he's feeding them loaves and fishes, or they've been preparing for this for years. And Litchfield was nothing, a month ago. A lapsed Mormon, decertified doctor after a brief but notable stint as a Hollywood abortionist."

"How the fuck did he end up here?"

"He just came. Hired on as medical staff, but he broke down and went native and ran a first aid clinic. We tolerated it because he was not interfering with the tests, but he hasn't been in for a physical in about four years. . ."

"We let this former employee start a militant insurrection because why?"

"At his last physical," Myrick says, "he complained of seizures and fatigue, and we ran an MRI."

A graphical cross-section of Orrin Litchfield's brain appears on the screen. The cool gradient colors seem to radiate out from a walnut-sized node of malignant purple on his temporal lobe.

Warwick squints at the graphic. "And the prognosis was . . . ?"

"It should've killed him three years ago," Myrick replies. "We're pretty sure he still has it, because his symptoms are getting worse, but the intensity of this movement that's formed around him indicates maybe he's not just a hoax."

"You think he might be a prophet," Schnur sneers, "and those little dead babies in specimen jars in his church are really angels. . ."

"We've all seen the drone footage of his assassination, and his recovery speaks for itself."

"Nothing about that can't be refuted," Knott argues. "Half the phone feeds show he got shot in the eye with water from a fucking squirt gun. The rest of them are corrupted. . ."

"Because it is believed! Those videos weren't doctored, they were altered by the witnesses' perception. I believe he may be channeling the energy of the zeitgeist. . ."

"Oh, give me a fucking break."

"The power of concentrated human belief is not a joke," Myrick says, "however ineptly we may have tried to mold and wield it in the past. Hearts and minds, gentlemen and ladies, can shape causality, change destiny."

"Belief waves collapse faster than quarks, Eleanor," Knott interjects.

"True, but whether they believe in the miracles because they're real, or the miracles are real because they believe them, something's happening down there we'll be lucky to witness, never mind contain and monetize."

"Then pull the plug," Schnur says. "If the phenomenon can't be transferred from the primary—"

Knott interrupts, "Who's about as stable as a one-legged rocking chair in a minefield—"

"Do you mind?"

"I'm agreeing with you!"

"Don't. If this whole movement rests on Litchfield's shoulders, then it dies with him. Nothing new about what he's doing. You don't turn an 800-pound gorilla loose in the lab to see if it'll accidentally cure cancer."

"We've already let him kill a couple thousand civilians," Warwick says. "The damage is done. Compartmentalize and observe. If it threatens to spill out of its compartment, it would be an excellent opportunity for a wider test of the Insomnia Protocol."

You know that stupid wave maneuver baseball fans do in the stands? A little wave like that goes around the table, everyone leaning back in disgust as the memory of the last Alphaville shock test roils their respective stomachs.

"This isn't another test, it's a fucking insurrection," Knott says. "I thought we all agreed that our budget for these kind of tests. . ."

"What we all agreed was that it was the most significant experiment of its kind since Milgram and the Stanford Prison Experiment. This is what we're fucking here for, isn't it? If you can't take the heat, go back to the lab and blinding rats with shampoo."

"What about the other group?" Warwick asks Schnur. "The Soma people?"

"Extinct, sir, for all intents and purposes. Solomon Listor's gang produced and distributed the drug through a loose alliance with the Poison Boys, but Los Zeros and Litchfield's people have, obviously, wiped them out. . ."

"He sees them as a threat?"

"Maybe as competition. And there's a lot to worry about, there, still. The people who've used it staged some disruptive protests in the Arcade, as we all recall, and the Divine Fire people blame them for Litchfield's assassination—"

"Unsuccessful, staged assassination," says Knott.

"Get over it. But it's more of a pogrom than a holy war. Whatever the drug does to them, they're not fighting back."

"The hell they're not," Myrick says. "We only recognize warfare as such when it's symmetrical. I don't think we have the means to perceive how they're resisting. And more. . . They're changing. This is worth all the resources we can throw at it. Anecdotal data is sketchy, but their brain activity is like a fireworks finale. We don't understand what it's doing to them, but the changes are radical, and I think the genetics results will bear out something more important.

"The changes are permanent, and if we can observe them in situ, they may prove evolutionary."

Gould demands, "This shit is fucking up their genes?"

"It's not fucking them up, it's splicing itself in. Altering the fundamental processes of the brain. By the time we're done, it won't be a question of whether their brains are damaged. It'll be whether or not they're still human."

"That makes this a really hard sell," Gould says, "but it's a product, not a personality, which I can work with, if that makes sense.

"This Divine Fire deal, on the other hand, is developing a very strong brand. It's evangelical Christianity with some muscle in it, and the real live angel makes it a no-brainer. If his people could just soften the edges a bit, they'd have a seeing-is-believing slam dunk, but if they're amenable to feedback, maybe incorporate Hatch's drug into the new religion as a sacrament, if he's willing to massage it into something more like an opiate, tailor the experience. . . at the end of the day, we might have a winner."

"People are still dying down there," Nguyen says, fighting for calm. "Can we please not worry about marketing campaign just yet?"

"None of this pays for itself," Gould says. "Letting the place burn has to generate enough capital to rebuild, and we need to be proactive in selling this, because at the end of the day, nobody's going to want to live in a freefire zone frying on magic mushrooms, unless we can make it sexy."

Warwick flips back through his files. "What about this mystery man who introduced the drug into the system. . ."

"Keller Cockburn, a.k.a. Nolan Hatch, a.k.a. Joaquin Betancourt," Schnur replies. "Age 38, born in Palo Alto, California. He's a burnout. Promoter and small-time dealer at the tail-end of the rave scene in California. He was responsible for a bad batch of synthetic MDMA that fried a few dozen kids. Fled the country and wandered around the hippie trail for a decade before reappearing here with this drug."

"The Stormin' Mormon versus the Shamanarchist," Gould blares. "I like it!"

"Any idea where he came by it? It's organic, yes. . . ?"

"We figure it's a previously unclassified fungus originating in central Mexico," Myrick says. "Prelim gene sequencing puts it squarely in the Psilocybe genus, but the chemistry is closer in effect to DMT. We've isolated three new tryptamines, just on an initial survey. It's potent and unpredictable, but we can engineer it into something to emphasize the lucid dreaming aspect, tone down the empathy stuff, maybe get a handle on some of the blue sky phenomena we've been seeing. . ."

"What kind of phenomena?"

"Clairvoyance, remote viewing, telepathy. . ."

"You're not just making shit up to try to compete with the Jesus-freak people?" Gould asks.

"Yours are burning people alive for their beliefs. Mine set themselves on fire for theirs. I know whose faith I take more seriously."

"It's still gonna be a pretty short war."

Knott barks an ostentatiously fake laugh. "Not like we could shut it down if we wanted, short of invoking a total viral sweep. Tom's security forces are rife with Divine Fire converts—"

"Bullshit!" Schnur shoots back. "Your department has been funneling food and water into their districts. . ."

"My department doesn't have all the guns, Tom. Why don't you ask your head attack dog who he prays to, at night? You're too fucking scared of him to even listen to what's going on, down in Detention. . ."

"We're off-topic," Warwick cuts in. "The burnout. What can you tell me about him that we don't already know?"

"Well," Schnur draws out the word with an uncharacteristic flare of drama, "I have him in custody."

"What?"

"Yeah, he was trying to exit, but we bagged him. He's been under standard depatterning protocols in detention all week."

"Well, finally some good news," Warwick says, signaling the end of the meeting.

32

If they think this is supposed to break him down, they've got another thing coming.

He likes walking in the cloud, mostly. They pump in a fog or something so you can't see your hand in front of your face, and there's a white noise and sound-baffling acoustics so you can't even hear your own voice.

Pretty sure he's running on classic STP-25 and some nasty amphetamines, an ugly, abrasively introspective trip that dredges up every septic memory he's ever buried before seamlessly turning to completely random shit he's never even imagined doing, but still feels guilty about.

He was tied to a chair before, but he got loose. He's been walking for days and hasn't found a wall. Feels like days, anyway. He stops to piss on the floor every so often to make sure he's not walking in circles, but he never gets thirsty or sleepy, he hasn't slept in days, but they're crazy if they think they're going to break him.

Sometimes, he thinks he's still tied to that chair.

He likes the cloud, but he doesn't like to look at it. With nothing to fix on, the eyes start to play tricks, the Ganzfeld effect kicks in, and you start to see things. The tunnel at first, but then your mind starts to fill it with things and people you know and you talk to them until your throat is raw without hearing your own voice.

He likes the cloud way better than the jungle, or the faces.

The jungle comes when he's close to finding the door. Pulsing strobes and loud horrible music and noises and you see things in the ultraviolet undergrowth, but nothing can see you, but then you see a particular intersection of sawtooth leaf and stem and you know it's a mantis and then the jungle is a jumble of mantises, so you have to keep moving or they'll chop off your head, and then you're really fucked.

Though they don't attack him, he far prefers the jungle to the Faces. . .

The first time he really broke his brain open on half a sheet of Santa Cruz Dali blotter acid, after twenty-four hours of ego-death and devastatingly meaningless revelations, he retreated to his bedroom and popped two Xanax, hoping to get to sleep, but his brain kept spastically bombarding him with hallucinations that took the form of an endless slideshow of mugshots of faces he didn't recognize. As they paraded before his eyes, only growing more vivid when he squeezed them shut, he theorized that perhaps his brain was spitting out every face he'd ever seen on the bus or passed on the street from the unexamined dregs of his memories, or perhaps synthesizing them completely as entoptic phenomena, or maybe he'd stimulated a latent capacity for telepathy, and his acid-amplified brain was fumbling to relay the likenesses of everyone in the immediate area, though he wasn't fried enough to actually touch their minds. Later, a crazy Colombian tattoo artist commiserated with him about the Faces, but he had his own theory about them. When your brain is that cracked out, he insisted, you're seeing the dead.

Hatch dialed back his acid intake and pointedly stopped hanging out with that guy after that, but now he begins to suspect maybe he was right, because the faces that float out of the cloud are Unamerican faces, and he sees more than one he recognizes very well—Lalo Beltran Ortiz, Solomon Listor, Nando, the old man who gave him coca leaves, Jaime Blasco—

They come even when he closes his eyes, so maybe if he doesn't have eyes, he won't see Jude's face—

Suddenly, he's back in the jungle. The noise crushes him into the floor and two mantises tower over him, scythe-like arms waving, mandibles clattering. "Good fucking God, how long has he been like this?"

"A week, sir, but we—"

"I don't want to hear it. This is unacceptable. Get him out of this chair, clean him up and get him an optimizer tonic."

One of the mantises creeps away into the pulsing canopy, which is slowly vanishing into the white as the sound fades away in his earballs. He realizes he's still in the chair and he has a tube up one nostril and down the back of his throat and another up his dick. He sits really still until the mantis draws close, then tries to bite it.

"Easy does it, Mr. Cockburn. You've been shamefully mistreated, but it's all behind you now. Yes, here it comes . . ."

The other mantis plugs a bag into the tube dangling from his nose and lifts it, tips it so a deep green, viscous substance that might be melon liqueur or antifreeze races down the tube and into his body. Even thrashing around does nothing to stop it.

But then it hits his brain and things start to fall into place. His name, the form and function of words, the names of things. It's miraculous, only moments before, he was in a state of acute psychosis, but now. . .

"Pretty remarkable, eh?" The man standing over him, not even remotely mantislike, introduces himself as Lionel Warwick. He looks more like a high-ranking career bureaucrat, maybe one who periodically reports to congress, because he wears a tie too nice to have so much vomit on it. He notes about four or five more little clues about the man before observing that he's black.

The guy behind him still looks like a mantis, with a surgical mask and goggles and long, slender rubber hands steepled under his chin, but Hatch likes him, would like more of that green stuff, and then he realizes they know his real name, and then he notices something else when he holds up his hand.

"Holy shit, how'd you do that?" They're stubby and only cover half of the tender pink beds of his fingertips, but he's got fingernails again.

"Oh, that? Just human growth hormone, androgen and biotin, injected into the nail beds. We're not monsters, Mr. Cockburn. We want to help."

"So. . . you know who I am." The masked technician pulls the tube out of his nose, which nearly makes him puke, the sight of it and the maddening violation of his sinuses.

"We don't care. If anything, we empathize. You showed exactly the kind of initiative we prize, here."

He unstraps Keller from the chair and lets him stand up as if he's just had a routine medical exam.

"That shit was amazing. What's in it?" The technician cuts away the soiled paper smock stuck to his backside and slips a new one on him, fastens the Velcro seals. His mind is racing on all eight cylinders, but he still feels light-headed, and staggers back to the chair.

"This and that. I'm not at liberty to say. There are only a handful of controlled substances we outlaw because they're a genuine health hazard, and many more because they threaten the users' conformity and productivity, but which offer a venue to punish and discredit the counter-culture . . . and then there are products like the optimizer tonic, which do their job almost too well, so we can't admit they exist at all."

"So when you guys actually make something that helps people, you just bury it. That figures."

"Not us. Corporations make a lot of noise about competition and the free market, but they hate it like death and taxes. They try to keep innovation to a predictable trickle, but more regulation isn't the answer. We didn't want to get into the business of picking winners and losers, so we offer a forum for unfettered field testing of real innovation."

"I should've just come in the front door, you guys would've offered me a job. As it is, it was only dumb luck I didn't get gassed. . ."

Warwick laughs. "We regret that, but we wouldn't have gassed you. Undesirable demographics are exposed to a universal allergen, and die of systemic anaphylaxis—"

"So you can harvest their organs?"

"Nothing gets past you, does it? Suffice to say, if we'd recognized the value of the new product you were offering on Day One, things would've gone down very differently."

Warwick clears his throat. He's not used to offering a job to clients in his torture cells.

"You may have gathered that we're about much more than testing products here. At its heart, we are working to cope with the future, and identify the minimum at which a society may still function as a viable market.

"We're up against a deadline. Malthus predicted that the human population would exceed even the most rigorously fair distribution of the planet's resources by 2050, and he failed to account for climate change, or for half the world's labor being obsolete. How long can competition continue, when the market can no longer afford to consume products? We're seeing the middle class cannibalize itself to some extraordinary short-term effect, but we're well into the last grinding hours of a Monopoly game, when two players hold all the properties and everyone else is getting bled to death staying in the wrong hotels.

"Our core mission is to tend this hothouse of terminal capitalism and evaluate every weed that crops up as a new staple crop."

"You think my drug is going to save capitalism."

"Or save humanity from capitalism, if you like. We're not ideological stooges, down here."

"You could try raising the top tax rates and offering public services again. . ."

"We've tried all that. The cost of maintaining an educated middle-class is astronomical, it'd be easier to keep them in zoos. Besides, you saw the critical weakness of such societies just recently, I understand, in Alphaville. You may have noticed that they're all dead."

"I heard you killed them all."

"We introduced a prion into the food supply. It interferes with circadian rhythms in rather extraordinary ways, upsetting normal sleep function until the body shuts down, and then it simply never wakes up again. It wiped them out in less than five days."

"A thousand people dead. What did that teach you?"

"Quite a bit, actually, because there never *was* such a prion. You see, we didn't actually introduce anything, only the rumor of it. And within hours, the community broke down into *Lord of the Flies*, people bingeing on stimulants and raiding their neighbors like armed toddlers, because they thought they were going to die if they fell asleep.

"In response to your rather slanted query, we learned quite a bit. Communities with solid communication and common value systems are unified and easy to motivate, but uniquely fragile and susceptible to terminal disinformation. If we knew then what we knew now, we never would've lost control of South America.

"But we also learned something extraordinary about belief itself, when we examined some of the corpses. Can you guess what we found?"

"A new dessert topping?"

"Heh. We found prions in the thalamic regions, where sleep is regulated. Deadly, transmissible prions manufactured out of thin air and a little white lie. Basically, they dreamed them into existence."

"So now, you're hoping to use it to clean up the ghetto downstairs."

"No. Omegaville, for all its chaos and crime, is a more resilient solution to most of the future's problems, but they're also damned difficult to motivate, when it's needed. That's why we've let those Divine Fire maniacs go as far as they have. And you."

"So. . . again, you think the Secret Teacher is some kind of solution to this."

"We think it would be irresponsible not to investigate it." Warwick cracks his knuckles. "But enough about you. I'm sure you have many questions about us, so what would you say to a little tour?"

Keller looks around the white room, sees puddles of piss in the corners and smears of dried spittle and blood where he beat his head into the wall. "Sounds lovely, Lionel."

Warwick helps him stand, but insists he sit in a wheelchair. At first, Keller refuses, but he wobbles and grabs the chair arms, then gratefully accepts.

Warwick pushes him down a blank institutional corridor decorated with rows of framed gold and platinum records, exactly like you'd find outside an old-school, coke-sniffing promotions mogul's office in the Capitol Records tower. Keller doesn't recognize the artists or songs, but he's been away from American radio for a while.

"Ever read those shaggy-dog stories about people with brain trauma becoming virtuoso musicians? We were working on a drug to induce epilepsy. . ."

"Induce it?"

"Long story. Anyway. . . We had a drug that caused crushing seizures, but as a side-effect of these anterior temporal lobe storms, the subjects could suddenly compose and play perfect music. Instant Mozarts. A couple of our guinea pigs wrote stuff so infectious we recorded and sold them. Nineteen gold and five platinum-selling singles came out of these labs, so it's not all doom and gloom."

"What about the songwriters?"

"Stroked out in six months, on average. Was it a perfect drug? No. But we got it to market. Costs about three hundred thousand dollars a bottle, but when a major label artist needs a hit, it's a fair value."

They stop at a door and the technician knocks, then sticks his head in, before opening the door for Warwick to push Keller's chair inside a dark, small room lined with aquariums.

"You talked to Charlene?"

"Charlie Tuna?" Keller shakes his head. "I thought she was just fucking with me."

"She's a pilot subject. But you're already familiar with one of our better ones." Warwick goes to an aquarium and turns on a light illuminating a brain floating in cloudy fluid, attached to a web of sensors.

Warwick knocks on the glass. "Meet Silent Radio."

"Jesus Christ."

Warwick taps on a keyboard. The speakers crackle with the hot, flat monotone of Silent Radio's voice. "El Norte is the land of opportunity, but only for the bold. You must ask yourself what is impossible, and if you cannot do that, what is illegal.

"Here is no different. If you would stay out of trouble, if you would be rich, you must know what is illegal in Unamerica.

"Is it illegal to steal, to kill, to do or sell drugs? Not in the least. Here, this is work for peasants. Here, every day is an exchange of hostages, just to survive. So what is illegal? What is impossible?"

Warwick mutes the speaker. "Jesus Ocampo, alias *El Tabano*. An activist jailed in Mexico City in '68. . . Hundreds massacred in the streets and a week later, the same city hosted the Olympics, which should show anyone who says Mexico never could take care of business.

"He was a gadfly leftwing journalist for decades, but when he tried to dig up the cartels' control of the government, he didn't have the life expectancy of a housefly. He came to the U.S. to hide, but they wouldn't let him alone. He only wanted to keep talking, so this was a solution that made everybody happy.

"What I guess we're trying to show you here, is that Emmanuel Goldstein loves Big Brother. The resistance and the establishment shop at different stores in the same mall. Any revolution they can come up with, with we'll happily sell them."

Warwick backs the chair out of the room and goes down the hall. Two guards flank the next door with cattle prods drawn and held at the ready.

They go inside. A little man with a beard sits cross-legged in a corner of the unfurnished white room, wearing a filthy hospital johnny. He looks up adoringly at Warwick.

"This is Jalaluddin," Warwick says. "Embarrassing story, really. When he was nine, he was a beggar on the streets in Jordan. He was taken into a Christian orphanage and raised in the Gospel. When he was thirteen, he began training to become a terrorist."

"So he didn't like the orphanage."

"No, he was doing what he was supposed to do. The CIA had no reliable HUMINT among the radical Islamic factions, and we knew we'd need some. So we raised our own double agents, built them from the ground up to pray out loud to Allah, but to pledge allegiance to the flag in their hearts. There were stunning successes, and there were grave disappointments, of which Jalaluddin here is the most egregious example.

"We sent him to Afghanistan, but they turned him, and he led a Special Forces unit and a bunch of Pakistani commandos into a massacre at Tora Bora. He did two years at Camp X-Ray, and never gave up enough to fill up an index card. Maimed a guard and killed two other inmates he thought were going to talk. Hardcore fanatic. He has something to show you. . . don't you, Jalaluddin?"

The little man takes the lid off a stainless-steel pot hidden between his legs. The pot is filled with raw, freshly shelled green peas. Instantly, Jalaluddin begins to tremble and a runner of drool leaks out of the thicket of his beard. "Show him."

The words are like a knife cutting the leash on the Taliban prisoner. He takes up one pea and then the next with his eyes practically bugging out on stalks, studying each in turn and discarding it on the floor. He looks like a jeweler trying to find a diamond among piles of shattered safety glass.

"What's he looking for?" Keller asks.

Warwick only smiles and upends the pot on the floor. Jalaluddin whimpers, but follows them, careful not to crush any with his knees as he continues his frantic examination.

Jalaluddin creeps between Keller's feet, picking up peas, studying them and popping them in his mouth. As he pushes Hatch's foot and sweeps the loose peas into a mound that he guards with his hand, Hatch notices a tuneless song leaking out of his clenched teeth. Not a song, a rosary. "Hail Mary, full of grace, blessed art thou among women, and blessed is the fruit of thy womb, Jesus—"

"I'm starting to suspect you were lying to me, Jalaluddin," Warwick says. "You have thirty seconds."

Jalaluddin moves even faster, and, scant seconds before Warwick points and opens his mouth to call time, he leaps up and shouts, "Praise Jesus!" with a pea in his hand.

"Very good, Jalaluddin. Show Mr. Hatch."

Jalaluddin cowers around the pea, but then relents and lets Keller peek into his half-closed fist. It's a pea like all the others. "He can't see it."

"Show him."

"He doesn't believe!"

"Tell him, then."

Jalaluddin turns away, cradling the pea to his lips, praying to it.

"Its wrinkles," Warwick says, "depict a visage of the Virgin Mary."

"Jalaluddin," Warwick murmurs, "go to 7. Artichoke." Jalaluddin blinks and stares resentfully at the pea in his fist, then crushes it.

"Why did you do that, Jalaluddin?" "All graven images are offensive in the sight of God," the prisoner answers, wiping his hands on his smock.

"And what is God's name?"

"There is but one god," Jalaluddin bellows, "and is name is Allah!"

"Go to 3. Asparagus."

All the anger ebbs out of Jalaluddin and he looks around bemusedly. "Why am I here?"

"I'm afraid this man has desecrated your Koran." He points at Keller.

Jalaluddin shakes his head. "There must be some mistake. . . why would I have a Koran?"

"You're not an observant Muslim?"

"That's ridiculous! Religion is an outmoded social construct, and a mechanism for social control—"

"Go to 1. Apple pie."

Jalaluddin tenses up, but the eerily doglike expression returns, and he scoots backwards into a corner as if anticipating a kick in the ribs.

The guards come in. "Very good, Jalaluddin, you've earned a reward." Warwick points his right index finger at the prisoner and says, "bang," with a minimum of drama. Jalaluddin collapses on the ground and soaks his pants. He beats his head against the floor with the intensity of an orgasm.

Warwick pushes Keller out of the room. The guards follow them back to Hatch's cell. "Now, Mr. Cockburn, if I believed for an instant that you really subscribed to all that bullshit you're peddling on our streets, you'd be on the floor with Jalaluddin, sorting peas. It's only because we know you're a liar that we have any use for you. But make no mistake. Those idiots upstairs may talk about the market, and ideals, and perfect societies, but here, we are interested in only two things: Power, and how to keep it."

"You got a hell of a program. Why you need to mess with all this shit is beyond me."

"Treatments like Jalaluddin's are labor-intensive and expensive. Good for making pets, but impossible to mass-produce. Boutique work." He nods at Keller, who understands.

"They make noise about their products and research, but there is only one experiment, and that is the city itself. How much anarchy and crime will an orderly society tolerate? How much authority will they accept, and still call themselves free? How hard will they fend for themselves, with no safety net? For nearly thirty years, this city has been a living laboratory where the hard lessons of the future are being learned. But we are divided by our models of what a city is. For some, it is a prison—citizens are to be contained. For others, it is an insane asylum, or a larger laboratory, or a farm. I suspect the roots of one's allegiance lie too deep in toilet training to be altered without extreme duress, but what do you see, when you look at the city, Mr. Cockburn? Where do your true allegiances lie?"

"It seems to me you all see them pretty much the same, as a bunch of holes you have to stuff with products, and then maybe get some work out of them or just cut them up for parts. I look at a city, and I see a school. You look at how to control them, I look at how to set them free."

"Are you angling for a position on the board, Mr. Cockburn?"

Keller feigns a laugh as he climbs out of the wheelchair. The guards stand ready to zap him. "What do I have to say to get a shower, a decent meal and a seat at the big kids' table?"

"All you have to say is Yes," Warwick says, "but I think you misunderstood my proposal. We would like your help understanding this product of yours, which seems to offer the means to make people more tractable than ever before, but threatens to turn them into something we can't even comprehend. And your explanations of it are, pardon the vulgarity, just so much bullshit, and I don't blame you. You're a salesman, but you clearly don't understand what it is you're selling."

"I don't understand. You want me to. . . ?" The technician comes back and straps Keller into the chair. "That's really not necessary," Keller says. "You want to know where it came from, you want to know anything, I'll tell you. . ."

"We've learned everything we care to, from what you can tell us. We think we can all learn a lot more, if you actually put your money where your mouth is."

Keller realizes what he's talking about. "Oh, come on. Not here. Not like this. . ."

The technician takes out a syringe, squeezes out the air bubbles. "This is six doses of the Soma pills in in a saline solution. You seem to have a pretty remarkable tolerance for psychoactives, so we took the liberty."

"Please don't," Keller begs, pleading like he didn't when Tres Ojos ripped out his fingernails. "Not like *this*. . ."

The technician plunges the needle into Keller's neck and rams home the dose, then leaves.

Warwick steps back and kills the lights. "Remember," he says, "when you get the message, hang up the phone."

He shuts the door.

The blackness comes alive with eyes and teeth.

"Please don't," Keller begs. "I'm sorry. . ."

33

Mornings like this are tiresome, because Tom Schnur simply cannot eat his breakfast of human flesh without authentic Vermont maple syrup, and there's none to be had.

He keeps a bottle in his private compartment of the breakroom fridge, but somebody else obviously shoulder-surfed his combination and stole it.

Tom didn't set out to become a cannibal, but after a motherfucker of a bad practical joke at a party his department threw for his twentieth year of service, he discovered the horrible truth they don't share about cannibalism.

That shit's addictive.

He microwaved a couple of sausage patties from his special stock, procured by a reliable mole in Research & Reclamation, and he's trying not to throw a fit over the missing maple syrup, when he starts to hallucinate.

Shit, I've been dosed, he thinks to himself. He's a veteran of the CIA and remembers the old-timers' stories of the carefree MKULTRA days when anyone in the office was fair game for a dose of LSD in their coffee. And he wonders if he might not have dinged himself, when he dosed Craig Knott.

Because *of course* he dosed Craig Knott.

Right after the morning meeting, the sonofabitch was still trying to throw him under the bus, like he was afraid to crack the whip on his own department. Of course everybody is afraid of Captain Greer, that's the whole point. But every other department's failings seem to end up on his doorstep, and it all came to a head today, so naturally, it was time for fun and games.

Dropped a dose of the freak mushroom into the asshole's coffee, let him handle that shit while padding his monthly budget requests, but he should have known, whatever he's scheming to do to the enemy, the enemy is probably already fixing to do it to him.

He knows he should get back to his office, but he can't find the door, or his feet, or his face—

He goes away.

He comes back.

He rolls on the floor, lashed by intangible waves of joy and anguish. What has he become? In the name of all that he reveres, he has done unspeakable things, but also marvelous things, and the most marvelous thing of all is, he can change—

He feels a shadow fall over him. He turns over and looks up at Knott, standing in the doorway, holding up his jar of maple syrup.

"I'm sorry I took this," Knott says in a strangled, breathless voice. "I'm so sorry—"

"No, Craig, I'm sorry. I'm sorry I always hated you. I just. . ."

Knott offers a hand, helps him to his feet. "I hated in you what I couldn't accept in myself."

"I was trying to poison you, drive you insane. . ."

"I did it too, but you. . ."

"You set me free," Schnur lets out a cracked, dusty laugh. Coughs, tries again. Knott joins in and they both laugh until their sides hurt and they're leaning on each other for support.

Schnur smells Knott's aftershave and the sweat underneath. Knott doesn't use the gym, but he works out in his office. Schnur watches the videos as *he* works out, so he doesn't slack off. He realizes all this, and he bites his lip, then admits, "I talked to God."

Knott sighs and says, "I did too."

"What did he look like?"

"He looked just like you," Knott says, wonderingly. "I was wicked pissed at him for doing it, too. I told him he could look like anyone, so what was he trying to pull. And he said, 'God is a mirror.' That's what he said. . ."

Schnur touches Knott's face for the first time. The peaked, worry-furrowed forehead, the acne-pocked cheeks, the clenched jaws softened by stubble-flecked jowls. How long has he hated this face? This face so like his own that he thought God was a mirror when he appeared, until he rubbed his eyes. "Did he tell you anything else?"

"He said," Knott's breathing turns deep and husky, his essential scent welling up under the acrid tang of his aftershave, "the only sin is regret."

Schnur and Knott kiss, clumsily at first, their mustaches tickling each other, but then deeper as passion overcomes the last gasps of decorum and doubt. Knott sweeps the snack bar and personal junk off the counter and Schnur rips his shirt open, scattering buttons. Knott runs finely callused fingers over the aging but taut muscles of his archenemy's chest, then listens to his heart as Schnur strokes his hair. Breathless at each plateau of this strange exploration, they are just steeling themselves to remove each other's slacks when the door flies open and the cops come in.

"Jesus wept," says Captain Greer, the head of the uniformed security force. Knott and Schnur look into each other's eyes, terrified but unashamed.

Before Greer can point his muzzled shotgun and blow their commingled bowels out their backs, they are already somewhere else.

•

It was not until Virgil Greer first submitted at age seventeen to a background check upon first applying for a position as a correctional officer, that he discovered the perfect symmetry of his career choice.

Born and raised in Huntsville, Texas, the hard core of the Lone Star State's massive correctional network, he was not only a ward and a product of the state, raised in orphanages and foster homes; he was also, in the most very literal sense, a product of the correctional system itself. His mother was serving ten years in Gatesville Women's Unit for attempted murder, while his father was an unidentified guard.

A big, quick-witted boy who naturally ran every institution into which he was enrolled, Virgil topped out at 6'7" and 275 lbs. and went to work as soon as he was able at the trade of a father he never met.

He was as unsparingly harsh on his own race for any infractions and as utterly ruthless with his own staff for any excessive force, for any breach of discipline, as he was with the cons. Maybe that's why, when a riot finally did occur and the prisoners took over half the prison for a long Memorial Day weekend, he was the only one left locked on the wrong side of the gate.

Greer maimed half a dozen Aryan Brothers before he was subdued, and many there wanted to storm the prison gates bearing his head on a broomstick. But cooler heads prevailed, and they did the next best thing, the worst fate they could imagine for a spit-and-polish betrayer of the master race like Virgil Greer.

Greer examines himself in the mirrored chrome of the elevator. His eyes rove over the contours of his face like cartographers mapping a strange new nation, less familiar to him than the mask he wears when he leaves the command center.

They used three bottles of ink and a needle, but they made sure it was clean. They didn't want to risk infecting the captain of the guard. But when the cons surrendered and returned their hostages, Greer's face was as black as this period. They left his lips and the space around his eyes uninked, so he looked like a nightmarish minstrel show comedian.

He returned to the block with a new ferocity and launched a reign of terror that made him a legend. He punished the prisoners unrelentingly, though they were already cowed by the rumors and the sight of his face, which he adamantly refused to submit to laser removal. He seldom needed to, but he took to executing prisoners with little cause and pitting them against each other in gladiator matches to force the state to live up to its unspoken promise, to take out the fucking trash.

They tried to defang him, tried to force him upstairs where, as a warden, he might do less harm. But he refused their weak-ass offerings and solidified his kingdom, surrounded himself with a hardcore cadre of mean motherfuckers and proceeded to outkill Texas's formidable death row for seven straight years.

He was untouchable. He was inviolate. That was when the panic attacks began.

Nightmares. Faces of dead cons whose names he never bothered to learn. He closed his eyes and he was a motherless, crying little boy, abandoned and abused, locked up for life inside a monstrous adult. With the life he'd built, the jailor was himself a jail. The face in the mirror where he searched for escape was a strange black gate. Buried under bullets, bars and stone, yet he was trying to escape, to tunnel under the walls and bring it all down.

Night after night, he drugged himself into a stupor so he wouldn't remember his dreams. He started slipping up: unforced errors that led to escapes, a state investigation. Upon a closed-door review, they transferred him to the only place where his compulsive sadism would never reflect badly on the public face of the state.

In Unamerica, he seemed to thrive on better drugs and the relief of no longer serving the hypocritical myth of correction and rehabilitation, but the attacks only got worse. At any given moment, he might hear a door slam and he would not be the captain of the guard of a secret city, but a scared little boy trapped in a windowless cell.

He became unstable. Asymmetrical. He searched the Bible for answers, interrogated brujos and babalawos, shed chicken blood and ate human hearts from bubbling cauldrons, but still he could feel the walls falling inside.

Then he had a vision.

He was watching the drone captures of the Jesus freak getting shot when he blanked out. In the vision, an old man walked among the street trash with blazing hands, and those upon whom he laid those hands were haloed but not consumed by a white fire that ate away their sins and their failures, and left them pure vessels and swords of tempered steel. It gave him hope in a higher power, but the answers weren't in the Bible.

So when the Jesus freak returned from the dead, Greer went to see him.

"Shall I heal your face?" the old man asked.

"Don't touch my face." Greer put his hands on his chest. "Take away my weakness."

"You serve weak masters," the old man said. "That is why your heart is divided." Greer flinched when the gnarled hand touched his chest. He did not burst into flame as his flesh expected, but he felt the divine white fire kindle in his heart, felt the tortured shadow-self incinerated, smelled charred hair and bone on his breath as he walked away, as the old man reminded him he cannot serve two masters.

Since then, he's suffered no doubt, no weakness. His dreams are rapture and delight, visions of the last days and his instrumental purpose in them, of the walls of this hidden prison turning inside out to enclose all the world, all the liars, cowards and hypocrites consumed in divine white fire. He awakens each morning flushed with new resolve and eager to make his dreams come true.

When the blessing came, he wasted no time. He stalks the corridors of the executive board now with his silent shotgun, cutting down every worker in his path. Teague, he is almost disappointed to discover, is an ally, working to lock down the terminals and automate the outgoing communications. "Should buy us a week," he says.

"We don't need it," Greer says. With Schnur and Knott out, that leaves Corporate, Informatics and Research. Gould is jacking off at his desk, a teledildonic attachment fellating his genitals while he gasps and makes sweet-talk into a VR rig. Greer shoots him in the face and goes down the hall.

Uyen Nguyen refuses to wear a tracker, but her keystroke monitor shows she's steadily typing at her terminal. Her door is locked, and blowing it could trigger panic room protocols, locking down all the modules and alerting Washington of a security breakdown. Likewise with Eleanor Myrick, but her tracker shows she's sitting at her desk.

So as not to offend the boss, Greer straps on his mask, a grinning death's head painted on carbon-fiber and flak-graphite, and knocks on Warwick's door.

"Come in," Warwick says.

Greer steps inside and says, "Hey, boss-nigger."

Warwick shoots him once in the face. Twice in the chest.

Warwick's office is no larger or better-decorated than his inferiors, and the wall of video monitors on the back wall makes it feel even smaller, but he is a slave to every bureaucrat's dream of the Big Desk, which takes up most of a room small enough that when Greer falls, his outstretched arms catch the edge of the desk. He becomes a bulldozer. Drives the desk back into the far wall, knocking over his chair and crushing Warwick's legs. Boss gets off two more shots, but Greer's mask stops one and the other skids off his vest.

Ears ringing, he rips off his mask and grins at Warwick. "It's the judgment you knew was coming."

Gasping with pain, Warwick drops the empty gun, leaning across the desk. "I might've known. . . but you can come out of this ahead."

"Oh, I aim to." The bullets mashed into his vest send a warmth through his chest.

"If I don't report by the end of the day, this place will be on full military lockdown. You'll never get out."

"We don't want get out, sir. We like it here. These are the Last Days, and I can't think of a better place to ride out the tribulations."

"You can't be serious. . . Listen, Virgil. Whatever you think you're getting out of this—"

"I am far past your temptations, sir. I am an instrument of his glorious design, as are you." Greer comes around the desk. "All those nasty little bugs you got stored up down here, all them awful engines of death, what did you think you were making them for, if not for Him?"

"You might get a lot of people killed and you might even bring down this project, but if you think God's done fucking up this world. . ." Warwick's hands search the desk for a button to call for help, for some James Bond shit to turn the tables, but he doesn't have the Lord on his side. "You've got another think coming. . ."

Greer calls in his shadow, a dipshit jailbird Nazi named Egil, who approaches and presents to Warwick the instrument of his deliverance from this vale of tears.

Warwick's train of thought, predictably, derails when he sees the sword.

"He speaks to me in my heart," Greer says into Warwick's ear, not untenderly. "You can't buy that, you can't sell it. Once you hear it, you can only play your part."

"I most certainly have a part to play. You still need me."

"Only from the neck up."

Egil's stroke is swift and true, the bastard sword cleaves clean through the bureaucrat's neck and smashes one of the screens behind him.

Greer stoops and picks up Warwick's head. Frustrating. His close-cropped, kinky silver hair is too short to get a grip, so he holds it by the jaw, thumb clamping down a tongue still twitching as he carries it down the hall to Nguyen's office.

The bitches locked themselves in, but Warwick's retina scan overrides it. He enters the infomaticist's office and puts a round through the big cowled egg chair turned away from the door. The gutted chair spins around empty. A simple robotic arm attached to her laptop taps out a repeating message on the keyboard.

Snail-shells and puppy-dog tails, that's what little boys are made of. . .

"Cunt," he growls. Kicking over the chair, he orders Teague in to crack her laptop, takes Warwick's head like a bowling ball down the hall to Myrick's office.

He holds the head up to the scanner and throws it into the room when the door snaps open. It bounces across the desk with an ominous thud and lands in the lap of the naked veggie sitting in Myrick's chair.

One of the freaks the eggheads use to test products on, the thing is gridded with skin rashes and windows for inserting shit directly into muscle and bowels. It sits rocking and humming tunelessly while its fingers rake a keyboard.

Whatever. Her ID card with tracking chip is on the desk. It'll get him into the biohazard storage, downstairs. He picks it up and his eyes key in on what the freak is doing. His hand drums on the mousepad to OVERRIDE a CONTAMINATION LOCKDOWN.

What the fuck—?

He turns to go to the door just as it slams in his face. Red lights blink on and off in the ceiling. The veggie has stopped typing. He looks right through Greer, smiling crookedly. The monitor on Myrick's desk plays a surveillance cam clip, taken in this room.

A skinny lady in a Level IV cleansuit bustles around the office, painting every surface in the room with swabs from a palette of petri dishes on the desk. Smearing her ID card into a dish marked EXTREME INFECTION RISK—AEROBIC, DERMAL, she sets it on the desk with a magician's flourish and bows out of the office.

"Cunt," Greer snarls, wiping his hands on a moist towelette and pacing round the room. He kicks the door, which doesn't even shake in its frame. Beating himself about the head, he roars, "CUNT," and shoots the lock out of the door.

Alarms and red flashing lights plunge the corridor into gloomy panic. Teague comes down the hall and sees him. "You're contaminated." He turns to run. Greer shoots him in the back. Faithless traitor.

The rest of his men stay well back, but they don't go for their gas masks.

Bitch was fucking with him. He feels fine. He feels free. He feels *right*, like he's exactly where every bit of pain and suffering in his life was meant to bring him, and it is sweet.

He feels hot, feels the fire blazing inside. It will cleanse him, or he will go back to the prophet, who will bless and protect him, for his work is far from done.

He gives over the key to Egil to go clean house in Research, and tries to remember the last item on his shopping list.

34

Nolan Hatch sits in a chair out front of a café in the most beautiful city he's ever seen. Gleaming Venosa spires of crystal trade shimmering spheres of radiant information, their golden nerves singing eerie whalesong harmonies. Winged Gaudi ziggurats and fractal Escher chateaus float overhead, dazzling patterns of migrating birds converge on a river flowing through the sky to commingle with flying fish leaping out of the airborne current.

He reaches for the cup at his elbow, and that is when Keller Cockburn realizes he is not the man in the chair, but someone else looking up at himself from the jade pavement. He is a white, three-legged dog. He stares up at his human self and a low growl emits from his muzzle, along with a string of drool.

"Yes, it must be disconcerting. You finally get to talk to God, and He's just you." Hatch sips the coffee and sets it down. He lights a joint. "But I'm only taking a form from your own subconscious, so ask yourself what it means, later."

Keller lays his muzzle on his paws, contemplates licking himself where only dogs can reach.

"I'm sure you must have a thousand questions. Go on."

Keller thinks a question as hard and clear as he can.

"What's that, boy? Are you trying to talk?"

Keller barks.

"Am I God? A god is any organism that feeds on worship. A sacred tapeworm. I would like very much to be a god. Wouldn't you? Maybe I'm the voice of the collective unconscious, or the avatar of the Gaia spirit, or just the voice of the Secret Teacher, the sentient fungus. Or maybe I'm just a dissociated voice in your head, invested with the illusion of omnipotence necessary to cow your foolish ego. Maybe your whole universe is only a Boltzmann brain in a fishtank, sweating out this cruel, entropic nightmare. If this is so, then you would be a new Prometheus, striving to wake it up. That's easier for you to believe, isn't it, than God?"

Keller frowns and his ears go up, watching the smoke as it curls and spins out of the lit spliff, how motes of light in the fractal waves bloom and evanesce into tiny bubble universes with tiny Hatch, tiny dog, tiny dream-city, but with geometrically progressing variations. He is unable to resist snapping at these tangent realities whenever they form, as any dog is compelled to snap at floating soap bubbles.

"This is your dreamtime," Hatch says. "This is the world you imagine Secret Teacher will bring about. This is the dream you would share with the world. But it is not your dream."

A campesino strolls by, selling bags of oranges. Hatch waves him over and takes one, says a word that curls from his lips like a Maya glyph, that the campesino pinches out of the air and tucks under a cloak of feathers. He turns away and turns into a great bird, flies up to perch on a passing pyramid.

"It's a nice dream, as dreams go. There is no death here. Nobody even eats meat. But there is always a cost." Hatch takes out an orange and cuts it with his thumbnail. The orange emits a piercing scream like a dying rabbit as it gives up its juice into a glass. "The people of the Secret Teacher never share their dreams. Their dreams are a private world, secret and sacred. They need a refuge, for they share every waking thought, every feeling. They live in peace because they have no choice. Any lie, any misdeed, any breach of trust, is plain as a stain on the face as soon as it is conceived. They never hurt each other because each feels the other's pain. To kill is to die."

Keller cocks his head.

"This is what you would share with the world? Even for the Secret Teacher's people, it is a hard road, and they are all the same, with the same little gardens of dream within their high walls.

"You don't want the world to wake up from its dream, but to share your dream, a dream you cannot remember. You do not remember your dreams, because your dreams disown you."

Keller looks up at himself and realizes what everyone he's ever faced must have realized, sooner or later. He is a smug, insufferable prick.

"Would you like to see what you really dream?"

Hatch holds out a wailing wedge of orange. Keller lunges and bites the hand. Eyes rolled back in his head, he watches Hatch laugh.

"Now you're getting it," he says.

Keller blacks out.

He comes to, as he often has when falling out of his own head, on a dancefloor.

The beats, the surging bodies, it feels like home. But where the fuck was he, just now?

Fuck, what a head-trip, he's thinking. He lived a whole life, got old and crazy and went to some kind of hell on a mad mission to raise human consciousness. . .

God damn, he thinks, this shit is good. . . .

He lets the rhythm carry him across the club, a weaponized warehouse space in the industrial hinterlands of Los Angeles. This is a big night, the rollout of their new space, their new drug. He almost didn't make it. The piece of shit red '77 Porsche 924 he bought on a dare last month while thrifting with Jude overheated in traffic on the 10, and he was beginning to think he'd miss it. But he managed to cadge a jug of water off a passing Samaritan and cooled it down enough to make it here. Tristan pressed the new-minted pills into his hand as Jude kicked off her set. The first one hundred entrants to the club were similarly gifted, and the pills were selling healthily in the shadowy margins of the massive dancefloor.

He throws a salute to Jude up in the booth, though he can't see her through the lattice of lasers pulsing above the heads of the crowd. But he thinks she must have seen him, because she savagely wrenches the crossfade to kill the skeletal Richie Hawtin rhythm track and fill the room with The Bees' Melody.

The dancers jolt and twitch to the brutal segue. The mood goes wrong. Sour milk taste in his mouth. He leaps and spins, his head feels like a sunrise, then like fireworks, he's peaking so fucking hard he can't stop dancing but he's hot he needs water, but the dancefloor goes on forever and the people around him are foaming at the mouth. Eyes rolled back in their heads like rabid dogs, like vodun dancers ridden by an unspeakable loa.

His brain is boiling. He stumbles into dead people who can't fall down, can't stop dancing. His arms waving to the

DJ booth, he struggles upstream towards the speakers and mobs of kids are jittering with their heads shoved into the bassbins. A man running in place with his index fingers jammed up to the last knuckle in his ears and blood jetting down his arms like black wings.

How did it all go so wrong?

He staggers to the ladder up to the DJ booth, sour foam streaming from his mouth and his brains must be gushing out his ears like the foam from a shaken beer, but maybe he can make it stop if he can fix the music—

Jude isn't here.

He drags himself upright against the decks and looks out over the dancefloor and everyone is dead but they can't die. He rips the tone-arm off the record with a hideous squawk that cuts their strings. They all fall to the floor in heaps. Feet twitch, hands grasp, but nobody comes when he calls for help over the PA. He can't find his phone, he can't find Jude, he can't remember his name, he can't make his legs stand up, he can't—

He sees them.

Behind the lasers, bodying forth out of the pulsating darkness, he sees a wall of eyes watching, weighing, judging.

The club fades and vanishes but the eyes follow him into the dark, into death—

He sits up in sweltering blackness and a fecund foulness that is hauntingly familiar.

What a weird fucking dream.

In the dream, he made it to the club on the night everything went to shit, instead of missing it and running to Mexico when the shit hit the fan. In the dream, he took the new Ecstasy they'd made and he was with them when all those lovely people's brains were simultaneously destroyed—

"If you didn't like that dream," says a voice in the echo-choked dark, "you're gonna fucking hate this one."

A match is struck, almost in his face.

Solomon Listor stands before him in a white linen suit. At their feet, indigo phalluses of Secret Teacher mushrooms carpet the floor of the low-ceilinged cave.

"This is where you found them," Listor says, but he knows it's not Listor, he's just glad the spirit no longer looks like himself. Just remind yourself you're on a trip. It's nothing but a drug.

"This is where they bury their dead, and where they commune with God. How wondrous that the thing you searched the world to find for so long, was so close, all along?"

His years between the meltdown of the Royal Jelly Krewe to present weren't quite the noble vision quest he'd convinced himself it was. He was stung by what happened in LA, horrified, but he wouldn't go back. The establishment that sought to punish them could never comprehend what they were trying to do, so how could he submit himself to their judgment? He would find his own way to atone for what happened. He had been delivered out of the meltdown for a higher purpose he never dared to spell out consciously, but he let it rule his life.

After bumming around Mexico for a few weeks, trying to get hold of Jude without tipping off the authorities, he'd gone to Europe on a fake passport bought with the last of the collective's cash. From England to Amsterdam to Ibiza, seeking like-minded people for consciousness experimentation, he'd arrived at every node of the utopian drug culture just as the bubble burst. And every time he escaped, he recommitted himself to the quest for the grail that would make the dream real. He sought out visionary shamans. Colombia, Peru, Gabon, Cameroon, Goa, Thailand. Ayahuasca, iboga, datura, salvia, amanita muscaria; *Psilocybe azurescens, semilanceata, stuntzii* and *cubensis* in extremis. In many, if not most, he almost touched a new way of thinking, a way that could transform any human mind it touched for the better. Always the mystic wisdom gifted by the machine elves, the guardians of the gate of horn and ivory, dissolved in his hands when he awoke—half forgotten, the other half lies. The only real wisdom he received came during the iboga ordeal, when he finally saw the lumbering, living tree his extortionist guide told him was Bwiti, the incarnation of iboga itself. He'd seen it, but the god became agitated by the sound of his voice, for he was invisible to Bwiti. "I cannot see you," the hallucination said, "for you do not yet exist."

Following in the McKenna brothers' footsteps, he recklessly combined tryptamine substances in attempts to alter his own DNA, to permanently evolve into a new kind of human. By the time he ran out of drugs, money and friends, he almost didn't listen to the drunken missionary who told him about the lost tribe of Chiricahua Indians who lived in caves in the Sierra Madre Occidental, about how everyone they sent got slipped a magic mushroom that totally brainwashed them out of evangelical Christianity, the one who showed him that God would love him even more, if he would just admit that he was gay.

By the time he heard the story, he was so burned out that he clung to his visions of a psychedelic human revolution like a wet electric blanket, a barrier between himself and any kind of normal life. He'd long thought of sneaking back into America anyway, and if he was far too disillusioned to actually try to Secret Teacher for himself, he was reborn in the prospect of introducing it to the world, and repaying in some small way the dream that he'd helped kill, twelve years ago.

It wasn't healthy to dwell on the past. Forgive yourself and move forward, his mother always told him, or you'll never do anything great.

And was it so awful, what he'd tried to do? Why was this drug trying to give him a hard time about this shit? "I was more than fair with them. I told them what I wanted to do. . ."

"They knew what you were really going to do. Your lies were like shit in their faces, but they never stopped smiling as you told them." Listor walks gingerly around the beds of mushrooms, the carpet of them so thick and broad that it spills out into the moonlight from the low cave entrance. Weird, they were only in little patches in the deepest recesses of the cavern, when Hatch went there to harvest the mushrooms he ground down into the microdots he first brought to Unamerica, less than two months ago. . .

He remembers riding into their canyon, finding the tribe called the Onza people, after a crypto mountain lion nobody had ever caught. He was warned this was lawless country, but had a long memory, so he chose his name carefully. The Hatch clan had deep roots in the Sierra Madre Occidental, one of the few Mormon families to stay on after the Pacheco colony retreated north in the wake of the 1912 revolution. More than once, he was stopped by bandits who would've cut his throat like peeling a banana, if not for the blood tie in the name he gave them. But not even the wildest opium-growing hillbillies in the Sierra Madre had any truck with the Onza people. They're cannibals, he heard; invisible mind-readers, walking ghosts, the inbred cave-dwelling offspring of Geronimo.

Apaches.

The last Chiricahua raiding parties went to ground in the Sierra Madre after Geronimo surrendered in 1883, and never returned. The Onza people's ancestors gave up their warlike ways when they took refuge in the mountain caves, and found the Secret Teacher.

Less than a hundred miles from the border, they had little use for anything the world invented since the Bronze

Age. They kept to themselves and herded their goats, and were quietly happier than anyone on Earth. They wore loincloths in the summer like the Tarahumara and Guarijíos to the south, but had an insatiable penchant for bright nylon soccer shirts, which he brought them in abundance. They never spoke to him, but welcomed him into their caves, fed him boiled vulture stew and filled him with blindingly potent *lechuguilla* until he stopped badgering them about magic mushrooms. When he had stayed with them for several weeks, they agreed to let him take the mushrooms if he would eat them first in the caves. They caught him stealing them from the cave where they buried their dead, but they let him go. "Who are we to stop you?" they said. "This has already happened."

"I did nothing to hurt them," Keller says. "I protected their secret. Nobody knows. . ."

Outside the cavern, the cluster of grass and mud huts at the bottom of the steep *barranca* is a garden of ashes. The little chapel of clay bricks looks like it was bulldozed. Smoke still billows out of a few of the smaller caves around the rim of the canyon, but nothing, living or dead, presents itself.

"Where are they. . . ?" Keller asks.

Listor points back at the cave, at the bumper crop of mushrooms.

"Oh my God." he staggers under the gravity of the evil deed. "Who did it. . . Was it you? Was it the cartels, or that smug government asshole who runs this place. . . ?"

Listor shakes his head until his dreadlocks lift up off his head like white snakes. "The men who came to visit were simply curious about an American who'd go to such lengths to sneak into America, and curious about where you were staying that you would call on a satellite phone to arrange your passage into the United States from such a strange location. No doubt they planned to waylay you as well. . ."

Keller thought of the muckers who ransacked his second cache on the border. The people he'd called were hardly trustworthy, but who would be capable of this. . . ?

"They thought this would be a perfect base of operations for smuggling, and so it will be. Out of respect for the villagers' wishes, they were buried together in the cave, but the cartels have no love for magic mushrooms, and soon, their only habitat will be destroyed to make way for storage of coca and heroin."

"No," Keller says, "this is just a bad fucking trip, that's all it is. "This is some real brown acid Christmas Carol, Wonderful Life-in-reverse bullshit, right here. I didn't do anything to harm these people. I just had a guy pick me up several miles from here. I just had a goddamn bike delivered. . ."

Solomon Listor just shakes his head.

Keller's knees give way under him, his torso folds. He plows his face into the red, rusty dirt. He pounds it with his fists. "I didn't mean to. . . I never meant to hurt anyone. . . but every time I try to do something good. . ."

He looks up at the sky and every single star is an eye looking down on him without judgment, without spite, and that is the worst, that he finally must accept what he has always believed, that no one can judge him, but himself.

"I'm a piece of shit," he says. "I admit it. I'm a selfish piece of shit. You're not the first hallucination to try to tell me that, you know." Listor lets him stew and swallow his pride, until he finally asks, "So what am I supposed to do?"

"Make it right. You have led the new people of the Secret Teacher into the Lower World by selling yourself as a shaman. Only a true shaman can lead them out again."

"I don't know any. . ."

Listor shakes his head, lights another match and throws it at Keller's feet.

"I can't. . . I'm white! I can't be a shaman, we destroyed shamanism. My ancestors burned witches! I can't have a guardian spirit animal, that'd be like marrying a slave."

"Everything that is," the Green Man says, "is alive."

"So what, my spirit animal is a Hamilton Beach Fry Daddy? A turntable? A laptop?"

"White men reject nature. They believe they are their own spirit guardians."

He looks over Keller's shoulder. Keller spins too late to see it.

"Did you never, without benefit of drugs, enjoy a moment, even one, when everything, inside and out, was alright?"

Keller thinks for a moment. "I had a dog once," he says. "Not really, I mean. . . We couldn't have a dog in our apartment, and my mom disliked them. But. I was swimming at Sunset Cliffs and this white German Shepherd came paddling up and grabbed me by my trunks and dragged me out. He thought he was saving me, and I didn't need saving. . . but he made sure I felt saved.

"My mom saw the people who brought him to the beach drive off. They left him in the parking lot. She wouldn't let me keep him, but she thought he'd get gassed at the animal shelter. He was a smart dog and he wanted to be with us, but she told me not to get attached to him. She wouldn't let me name him. Gave him away to some guy who lived across town and needed a dog to watch his yard.

"He came back a week later. Found his way back to a house he'd only lived in for a weekend.

"So she gave him away again. And he came back again.

"She finally gave up. Let me keep him, told me to think of a good name, not the first dumb thing I could think of. She took him to the vet the next day for his shots. When she came back, she didn't have him. She'd said he had mange and had to be put down.

"I called her a liar. I accused her of giving him her made-up disease so all his hair would fall out and not get on the furniture. I wouldn't tell her what his name was, and I never had another pet."

Keller rubs the heel of his hand into his eye.

"Sonofabitch, I can't cry for these people, but I can cry for a stupid dog. . ."

"You tried to do what you thought was good," Listor says, "tried to give them what you thought they needed. It went bad because you never really cared how anyone else felt. You thought it would make you feel good to make others feel good."

"How the hell is anyone supposed to know the difference?"

Listor only says, "Sacrifice," and then he is gone.

The caves are gone. The mountains and the burned village are gone.

Keller is alone with the Eyes.

This is the moment he feared, the flame that he's battered himself against his whole, moth-like life. He waits to become everyone, but one by one, the Eyes wink out, plunging him into blackness for a thousand years.

He's just beginning to rediscover volitional control over his body when a cold fluorescent light falls across him and a lumbering giant in black armor, with a black tattooed face stoops over his shivering carcass and says, "Well, I'll be damned, it's the long lost American." Grabbing Keller by the neck, he drags him out into blinding light and barking dogs. "Didn't I tell you we'd see you get back where you belong?"

35

Of the city's 2,500-strong armed security force, nearly 1800 are heavily deployed throughout the zones not controlled by the Divine Fire, imposing draconian martial law anywhere the lights are still on at all. Fifty-two killed, nearly a hundred more hospitalized fighting the Divine Fire insurrection, before the situation just as mysteriously stabilized.

The rest of them are pulled back to defend the Arcade, which was closed to all civilian traffic the first night of widespread hostilities. Three hundred men and women in masks and body armor stand behind bollards, barricades and crowd-control machinery arrayed around the gaping mouth of the central mall. Many more man the rocket batteries and strategic defense artillery up on the column that is the hub of the city. When the mass of armed men and improvised siege vehicles comes marching on Freedom Circle with burning crosses at their spearpoint, they tense up and await the order to turn the city into a freefire zone. Morale takes a further hit when many of their dead and wounded turn up among the motley zealot army, loudly chanting, "Deus lo volt!"

When the order comes to stand down and make way for the parade, many refuse to obey and are summarily relieved or executed by true believers within the police force. The rest, upon confirming that the order did indeed come straight from Captain Greer, rush to comply.

Nobody down here is paid to ask questions.

The army of Destroying Angels marches into the Arcade and immediately commences looting and burning, hurling offensive clothing and products and interfering employees over the balconies to form a great bonfire mound in front of the gaming complex, while a construction crew salvages material to build a dais in the center of the ice rink for Orrin Litchfield. As the smoke from burning merchandise blurs and mutilates the cavorting holograms overhead, the army begins to admit the wounded, the sick and the lame, to join in ransacking the stores, to plead their case and perhaps be healed by the divine fire and delivered from the Evil Dream.

He has preached until he is blue in the face against it. Told them the vision of the city as a garden of earthly delights was a snare of the Devil and to rebuke it, deny it purchase into their heads and hearts. Only those purified by the divine fire will know salvation. All who refuse that salvation must perish. Lost to God, no sin can be committed against them. Not even the Devil could have invented some of the things his Destroying Angels have done in the Lord's service.

But still he hears them talk about it, still he sees it in their eyes, even as they beg him to heal them and make them whole. Even he cannot resist its insidious creep into his dreams, and so he has not slept. When his will is not enough to keep him alert, he submits to sleep in his chair with a lit cigarette in his hand. Though he never inhales its unholy smoke, he finds the burning of his fingers a fitting retribution to letting himself be beguiled by unclean dreams.

But his flock is not so strong, naturally. The new communion is administered everywhere—two blasts of medical-grade crystal meth for each supplicant, more for every soldier. Anything to keep them awake and out of the clutches of the Evil Dream.

To the exclusion of all else, he has sought to root out the source of it. With the Arcade and police under their control, they now hold all food distribution, though the stores will only last a few weeks, if the earthly powers that feed this place will not continue to supply it. If the rest of the city wants to eat, they will have to submit to his authority.

It was a rash and perhaps reckless stroke to cut the head off the beast, but once the outside world learns of the kind of power he wields, the power of the Seven Seals, he doubts they will try to come down here. They'll do what they always do when confronted with the fruit of their idiotic evil. They'll try to ignore it until it's too late.

His Destroying Angels have searched in vain, and even his other angels have refused to guide him. Sometimes he frets that they've deserted him, that he's outlived his usefulness to the Lord. So he doles out miracles from his throne in the bowels of the blazing Arcade like the last mall Santa Claus, restoring the minds of lobotomized ghosts with visions of Silly Putty, burning away sickness and sending amputees hobbling away on thin air, gobbling with insomniac, infantile joy.

He hazards a pinch of the Satanic white torture that Comandante Moxica has made so abundantly available since they formalized their uneasy alliance. His mind is instantly, preternaturally clear, his command of all the facts in this insane holy war are firmly in his grasp, and even the one who will betray his heretical sect and the infernal dream.

The one sent by divine providence to make clear the way strides in. The mob cuts him a wide swath out of sensible terror, for his notoriety is a lamentable cornerstone of the lore of this godforsaken place, but as he crosses the moat of devoted, bloodied, ash-blackened ice to stand defiantly before him, Litchfield can see the sickness in Captain Greer.

It seethes out of his face, the acrid stink distinct even in the pesthouse lineup assembled for his burning touch. His hands are cramped into claws from touching them, pickled with disinfectant to ward off sickness, and his ruined face burns as if the talon of the sodomite's falcon still gouges it. Without an eye, yet he sees fountains of fire jetting out of his brain superimposed over everything his surviving eye looks upon.

Which makes him laugh, he could never get as much pain as he deserved, at the start of this he only wanted to die, but now he is all that holds this holy ghost awakening together and without him, it will devolve into chaos and mass murder, but if he can only prevail, if he can shut off the goddamn fucking dream and get a good night's sleep, then all will be well, and all manner of things will be well, and unwellness will burn in the white-hot fucking fires of Hell. . .

It takes more than one pinch to restore his concentration now, the diminishing returns of this drug are so palpable, he wonders that anyone enjoys it. But he is alert to one significant detail when Greer stands before him like a man with a list of demands.

"Where is he?" Litchfield rises from his chair. "Where is he, who was sent for?"

"I have him," Greer says. His voice is full of wet sand, setting concrete. Jaundiced, streaming sweat, eyes bloodshot. Glands swollen around his Kevlar collar, listing appreciably to favor one side, suggesting profound internal discomfort. "And all those germs you asked for."

"Bring him," Litchfield growls.

"You will come to no harm in his service, the Lord said unto me." Greer advances on the prophet. Angels with swastika wing tattoos point guns and arc tasers at the captain of the guard, who laughs at them until he coughs up bloody phlegm.

The *comandante* watches from the wings, waiting for a symptom of weakness. They all do, but this one alone could overthrow him. He knows the monstrous cartel leader is torn between his own powerful faith and his ruthless need to destroy everything above him. No doubt he would have turned his militant death cult on Litchfield, if he were not quite certain that the abomination the Mexicans called La Toda Madre were not still alive.

"I see him in the Evil Dream," Moxica said, half mocking and half something else better left unexamined. "He is with the ones behind it. For him, I will serve under you."

For how long, he wonders.

His pride matters not. Strategy matters less. He has learned from the painful lesson of the eye that he cannot heal himself. And whatever he might want, he knows that he needs to live. Just a little longer. Until His kingdom is secure on Earth.

"You have become unclean," Litchfield bellows. "In your flesh is the message of the plague, and in your heart is the defiance of the Adversary, who speaks to us in sleep."

"Had just about enough of your shit, little man," Greer whispers through gritted teeth. His hands hitch up his belt and the menu of tools for harm, dominance and destruction. "I've done everything you asked, and all I ask is you undo what that cu—"

"UNCLEAN!" Litchfield throws out his hand and the fire licks out to crisp the skin off Greer's face before he can finish his blasphemy. His great, heaving lungs draw the fire down into himself and roast him through before he falls to his knees. His sidearm goes off twice, and when he sits down, the jolt is enough that his head and left arm break off like the embers of a torch.

"Who else is unclean?" He slides across the ice towards them, but now the beggars and the blind stagger back in terror, yes, they see now that he's not a fucking magician, he's not bringing them a goddamned thing for Christmas. "Who else will be purified in this holy fire?"

Abner, of all of them, comes forward when the others run away. "Master, maybe. . . Maybe offing the captain of the guards wasn't the best way to keep them in line. . ."

"Are you. . ." Quicker than the words, almost quicker than the thought, the fire leaps from his hands. Abner is spared only because he falls to his knees. Litchfield quenches it in his shame. What is he becoming? He needs to return to his chapel and commune with his angels, ride the penance road and commune with his angels. And then sleep, sleep without dreams sent by the Devil.

"I'm sorry, Master," Abner says, and he is weeping. "I only hope to serve His will through you. . ."

Litchfield turns away and stumbles back to his throne. "Then bring me the fucking hippie."

A litany of conflicting emotions pass across the faces of the security goons who bring the hooded prisoner in a blue paper jumpsuit and force him to his knees before the prophet. Litchfield could give a shit what they think, however. "Get out," he says, "all of you."

Abner and the security guards shuffle away across the ice, but Moxica says, "I will stay and listen, I think." He shrugs and a helix of steeply angled red laser pointers freckle Litchfield's head and chest for just a moment. Snipers in the upper balconies. The mendacity of the masked brown Devil astounds him. He should have healed the monster when he had the chance.

If only he could cure evil, burn it away without destroying the flesh, leaving spotless vessels ready to be filled with his Angels to walk the earth and dispense the Lord's will, so he could sleep—

The little man kneeling on the ice shakes as if he's having a seizure. Litchfield lifts off the hood.

He's laughing. Hands zip-tied together in prayer over his badly bruised face, he falls to the ice and presses his laughter into it. "I'm sorry. I'm trying. Not to. But. Oh God. But I. I didn't know what to. What I was going to. Say, but. . ." Whatever idiocy he's trying to share devolves into hysterical giggles.

"This is the one?"

"That is him," Moxica says, snorting a glass bullet of speed up the slit nostril of his mask. "But he did not have so many fingernails."

The smug young man waggles his fingers. "That's nothing, Jacinto. They have this tonic they pour up your nose. Swear to God, it's gonna put all you tinpot drug-dictators with your crappy cocaine right the fuck out of business. . ."

"This is the one that got away from you."

"I still have three eyes," Moxica chuckles.

Litchfield kicks the laughing man in the face, restrains himself from trampling him. Snipers aren't the only ones watching.

"You shouldn't be so hard on me, boss," the cocky younger man says. "I'm the only one who can still help you."

"Save your temptations, deceiver. We have only one question for you."

"I'm the only one who can still save you from yourself."

Litchfield squeezes the fire in his hand until it burns as brightly as the red volcano in his eye socket. "Where are they? Where are your people?"

"I wish I knew. I'm shut out. They ditched me, and I can't say I blame them."

Litchfield looks at Moxica, who shrugs and takes out a pair of pliers.

The young man is maddeningly calm. "I know what you're going through. You've turned your life inside out trying to make up for some evil you did, trying to save people from themselves and help them be better. I know because I did the same thing. I gave people a drug that changed their minds and connected them to each other, but I got locked out of it.

"I didn't believe in it myself. But I wanted to believe in something so badly, I didn't even understand what belief was. I felt like every accident was a sign of some higher energy pushing me to do its work, to bring about change. And some weird shit has happened, twists to causality that I think happened because I was a believer, not the other way around. I used everybody around me to get closer to what I wanted.

"And that's the trap, when you think God is in control. Everything that happens to everybody around you is some kind of payback for something you did, everyone around you is a puppet in the game between you and God.

"I think you do these miracles and you think God is speaking through you, and all these people around you believe in you because you have the power, but maybe you have the power *because* all these people believe in you."

"You don't know me," Litchfield growls, "and you don't know God."

"But I don't know if you do, either. Where is the message of Christ, in all these burning fucking crosses, man? If God punishes the wicked with plagues and locusts and tornados and whatnot, why would he make your life a trial and tribulation, just to make you into a plague? Why did he make all these people your friends have killed? Did he make them different from you just to test you?"

"He sent his angels to me to make me the instrument of his wrath, and also his mercy. I have fed the hungry, healed the sick, raised the dead."

"Kudos for all that. But how many are hungry tonight, how many are dead?"

"Only the wicked."

"Did you ever wonder if that voice in your head is *really* God?"

"Your blasphemy will not prolong your life any longer. Tell us where the people of the Secret Teacher are hiding."

"I don't know, and I wouldn't tell you if I did. I believe in them. I'm not a part of their thing, but if it's driving you crazy, it's got a lot going for it. See, that's the difference. I'd give my life for them.

"That's how you know. If a voice tells you something and it's exactly what you wanted to hear, it may just be in your head. I may have spent a good chunk of my life taking drugs, but one thing I learned, is never to stop asking myself, *Is this shit really happening?* I've been lied to by some of the best hallucinations in the business. I used to think special things happened to me in my life because I was special, but it was always because I had a duty to *do* something special. . ."

Against his will, Litchfield finds himself nodding. "The angels invested me with His power."

"I believe you. But this doesn't mean it's God. There's a lot of things out there that feed on faith like we eat McNuggets, and they'll tell you anything you need to hear.

They'll make you think they're doing miracles or fulfilling curses, but the power fueling it and *feeding* them, is coming from you, and all these lovely people watching us, right now."

He looks up and sees thousands looking down from the balconies.

"What you think is the power of God, is just the power of belief. That's the ultimate purpose of this place, you know. A big ant farm they can fuck around with to see how human ants react, and they keep it in a constant state of crisis and cognitive upheaval so we'll start to believe crazy shit like magic telepathy mushrooms and go on bloody crusades, because they want to control us. They also want to tinker with belief itself as a weapon. If we all kill each other, they'll chalk it up as a big teaching moment, and order up a fresh batch of ants.

"They're using you just like they're using me, to set up these competing quantum waves of belief, to see which one wins out, but when they're done with us, they spread a crazy rumor like there's a highly infectious virus that kills you in your sleep. They're betting we'll invent our own extinction out of thin air."

"Hija de puta," Moxica snaps.

"Their time is over," Litchfield says, but he looks at Greer. They all do. It's like turning over a stone in a well-tended garden, all manner of despicable vermin scurrying for the nearest shelter. Sometimes he sees through the miracle to the shabby reality and curses his remaining eye for lying to him.

"What if you've got it backwards? What if God's the one sending the dream, and you're an unwitting servant of the Devil?"

"This has gone far enough."

"Let me just ask you this, and you can commence ripping my fingernails out again."

Moxica kicks the false prophet in the ribs so he goes down on all fours on the ice. Quicker than the words can be said, he crouches and chops all four fingers off the young man's hand with a machete. "Grow those back, *buchon*."

The man rears back on his heels, cradling the fingerless hand, gasping, "Wow, oh wow," into the fountain of blood. Then, "Okay. . . handle it. . ." He presses the hand into the ice until the gush of blood becomes a trickle.

"You two *jotos* deserve each other," Moxica says. Bows and makes the sign of the cross as he hastily retreats behind a squad of masked sicarios. "God has other plans for me!"

"I don't. . . think you believe in these angels, any more than I do." His voice, thin and quavering, races faster with the onset of shock. "If you really believe in something, you sacrifice for it. You're hurting yourself because you know you deserve it, and you're killing people to save them, but ask yourself. Would you die to save them? That pussy Abraham was going to knife his only son for God. Would you die for the people who come to you for miracles?

"Your man in the blackface was asking for a miracle, but I think you were more afraid of getting infected, and about what a threat he might pose to your power, than his wrath, or his mercy.

"Is this what God wants, or is it what *you* want?"

"I never wanted anyone to die. . . I pleaded with them to spare just a few. . . but better they all should perish, than stray into the false promise of the Devil's heaven. . ."

"Why should anyone love you? You only wanted to be feared, didn't you? I wanted everybody to love each other, and I got more people killed than Manson."

Litchfield feels sick to his stomach. He feels like he did right before the little freak in the flying squirrel onesie shot him in the face, in the eye that now beams that baleful red fire into his brain. The sickness inside him might be the cocktail of lethal viruses the prison ogre brought under his nose, or the nagging infernal doubt this smooth-talking liberal shitheel has rekindled inside him.

He needs to commune with his angels.

His angels—

He spins around, feeling them scream, feeling the strings that hold every molecule in the universe together strummed like a harp by an idiot.

"It's never too late to turn around," the young man says. Holding the stump of his hand like a lost dog, he says, "If God is real, if God is anything worth worshipping, then God is love." Now, he reaches out with the stump and says, "I love you."

"You say it's never too late." Litchfield folds his hands and considers them for a long moment, then reaches out and takes hold of the young man's head. "How about now? Is it too late now?" The flames erupt from his hands to engulf the sinner's head.

The flames are guttering, purple and green, weaker than when he cremated Greer. The young man rolls away screaming and his screams resound up through the hollow tower of the Arcade, drowned out only by Litchfield's own, as he holds the flaming hands high, and seizes his own head.

He's not screaming because of the fire.

In one shuddering seizure, the world goes away and his world is the cold silver space of a gallon jar. The eternal Christmas of an overfed, isolated brain. He tried to use them to talk to heaven, but he awakened something or trapped something or summoned something, and he worshipped it until it became a god.

Now he shares its life. Nineteen times. And out of that hellish vision, he is cast into the unacceptable heaven of the Dream.

Sunlight on his face, the briny breeze off the rolling slopes of the eternal, endless ocean—

Even his angels have betrayed him.

The ice steams and cracks beneath his feet, fissures radiating out to the edge of the rink, screaming of ruptured Freon coils. Grasping his ears until they melt and crumble through his fingers, then his jaw and the grooves of his occipital bones, he rejoices as his hair and scalp is scoured away by the resurgent flames, his cerebral fluid boils and his only eye shrivel in its socket. Only when the flames have seared the sinews of his neck do his burning hands achieve their purpose, wrenching his head off his neck and lifting it high above his smoldering shoulders.

His body staggers away from the throne, away from the still-smoking pyre of Greer and the altar, offering up the blackened ruin of his head to any god who will accept it.

36

Rockwell Street is deserted, and the pilgrims have all followed the march on the Arcade. Feral children in El Chapo masks stalk stragglers and the wounded with scrap-metal tomahawks. Only a handful of Destroying Angels left to guard the chapel can be seen out front, where they've gotten creative with their flamethrowers.

The party is down in the sewer.

Hordes of refugees huddle in the tunnels, holding children and hastily packed shopping bags, watching and listening and whispering rumors.

You must not sleep, some say. The masters of this place have let loose a bug that kills you in your sleep, or the Lord has done it to punish those who succumb to the temptation of the Dream. But if you eat the flesh of the Secret Teacher, others say, if you believe in the Dream, you will never die at all.

The prophet of the Divine Fire controls the Arcade, some say, and all who would eat must submit to his will. The prophet has gone mad, others say, burning alive those who come for his blessing. The end of the world is coming, is here, is *yesterday*. The Secret Teacher himself has been captured, and the Dream will die in flames, but you must not go to sleep, because. . .

Jaime Blasco doesn't know what to believe. He moves among them without thinking about what's coming next or why he's here helping these people instead of running for his life. Or why he's taking orders.

It's all the witchy woman's fault. *Hatch's ex.* After digging them out, the women led them through the sewers to the bunker complex where the rest of the Secret Teacher's people were hiding. They slept in circles and clusters, clinging to each other like twins in the womb on the floor between hydroponic gardens brimming with contraband homegrown produce. The ones from Jaime's group lay down next to them and dropped off into a trance as one of them tapped out a rhythm, the rhythm of the music always in the background of the Dream.

Weird shit, but weirder still, he feels like he belongs. They are the ones building the Dream and sending it out into the city. Dreaming a better world into being, Sister Jude told them, but she wouldn't let him join them.

The prophet has overthrown the corporate management and is preparing to besiege the remaining two-thirds of the city. His lunatic armies control the food and water supplies. He's in the Arcade right now, judging the sinful and spreading lies, but his shadow is still in his chapel in the Yellow Zone, making those lies come true.

When he closed his eyes, he could see it through all the walls of the city, a node of hateful radiance like a negative sun, throbbing in counterpoint to the blinding fire blazing at the heart of the Arcade.

He can feel the thing getting closer, he's little more than a bloodhound leading them through the branching sewers until they're standing just underneath it. Ida Scarfe shoulders him aside and climbs a ladder up to a locked grate, which she attacks with a hacksaw.

He thinks about Hatch and his heart skips a beat. The scummy bricks beneath his feet crumble and he falls—

You're riding in a van, bound and hooded and fried out of your mind. Praying, but not to God. Praying to everyone you ever wronged, asking forgiveness and making your peace with death, because that's the least you can hope for, wherever you're going.

Jaime feels feathers tickling the back of his neck and his hair stands on end when Hatch says his name.

The van stops and they're dragging you out. Crowds roar and jeer and throw things at you.

Motherfucker, Jaime says, *I don't know if you can hear me, but welcome to the Dream. You late, but wasn't a party til you got here. We need you.*

The voice is so tinny, so weak and remote, it might be his imagination. *I hear you, man—I'm so sorry—*

Fuck all that for now. Just do what you do. Just sell that bullshit. Just keep him on the hook—

Hatch laughs in his head, so loud he thinks the refugees must hear it, because everyone's staring at him.

"What's got up your ass?" Ida Scarfe snarls, tossing the last broken padlock down the ladder to bounce off his forehead. "We got work to do."

She drops down and boosts him up the ladder. He scrambles over the lip into a dank, cloyingly perfumed space.

Only a twinkling strand of Xmas lights nailed to the low ceiling illuminates the room, the gurney and fleet of wheeled crash carts. A minefield of smoldering bodies and a naked, flayed man on the stationary bicycle.

"Sup, beaner," says the man on the bicycle. "God ain't here." He lazily hefts the shotgun on the handlebars and points it at Jaime. "He's gone shopping."

Jaime throws up his hands. "Man, I ain't looking for trouble. Just looking for a safe place to crash."

"You in the wrong fucking goddamn place, then." The man drops the shotgun, cracks a capsule under his nose and sucks deeply. His bare chest is covered in swastikas, runes, crosses, cast-iron calligraphy. His back is naked muscle draped in dangling shreds of flesh. "Anyone falls asleep, they gotta burn." He tips his bushy billy-goat beard at the corpses. "Them angels won't let you rest, but come the Rapture, we all gon' have a big, long sleep. . ."

Jaime gingerly climbs out of the hole, keeping his hands in sight, far from the needler and the arc taser in his pockets. He still sees the man when he closes his eyes, crumbling crust of cherished lies and unforgivable sins around a brutal but childlike hope collapsing in on itself, a dying world in decaying orbit round the black sun concealed behind the curtain at the back of the room.

"Why you gotta do that, man?" He points at the bike.

"Gotta keep 'em fed, I guess. . ." He snorts another capsule. "Go on and look." The man leans forward, his back striped with gaping wounds from the flails attached to the bike. "See what that gets ya." His feet struggle to hit the pedals, legs like wrung-out dishrags. Screen lights up to show a 16-bit simulator of a road and always hovering on the horizon, a chintzy Emerald City princess castle vision of the Pearly Gates. When he hits his stride, grunting with each stroke of the whips, the Xmas lights pulse brighter and something behind the curtain glows. He begins to tunelessly sing, *This little light of mine, I'm gonna let it shine. . ."*

410

Jaime goes over to the curtain, feeling like he's walking into icy, sideways rain, into windblown ashes, into a liquid nitrogen blizzard.

"What the fuck's in these jars?" he asks.

"It ain't mayonnaise," grunts the man on the bike.

He doesn't know what he expected. Maybe some kind of magic telephone hotline to talk to God, or the prophet's beating heart in a white man's voodoo shrine. But the rack of nineteen gallon jars full of cloudy silver liquid leave him frozen, until he realizes he doesn't have control over his body, anymore.

Or his mind.

They were supposed to be some new kind of computer.

Threatened by the impending flattening out of the processor-speed race ten years ago, the deep thinkers of the next tech revolution fetished on notions of parallel, nonlinear and liquid computing, of machines that did more than mimic the mysterious intuitive genius of the human brain. Uneasy with AI, yet they saw the competition clumsily trying to reinvent the wheel. Why try to devise a computer that emulated the intricacies of the human brain, when you could turn the human brain into a computer? Why try to beat nature, when you could just rape it?

The test subjects were human embryos extracted alive from the womb at nearly eight months' gestation and sealed in hermetic containers with a second umbilical interface connected to the spinal cord. With only nutrients and growth-suppressing hormones for food and electrical current and data pouring into the container, the wetware babies were neither alive nor dead. The senior technician working on the project called them Schrodinger's Angels. Brought in because of his previous experience as an abortionist, Dr. Orrin Litchfield wept the first time he heard them sing.

When the project was scrubbed for a dead-end without any deep searching examination of its tragic immorality, Litchfield volunteered to destroy the nineteen prototypes, but he took them with him and went out into the Orange Zone to wait for a sign, to wait for them to speak.

Jaime didn't ask to know any of this, wishes he didn't know it now, as he stands before the racks of translucent jars coated with greasy gray dust. Knurled, ingrown monstrosities, withered limbs like roots curled round tiny bodies dwarfed by hideously overgrown heads that have swollen to fit the shape of the jars. Neither dead nor alive, they quiver in unison in silvery-blue fluid, driving or driven by the pulsing of lights on the computer towers, by the lurching rhythm of the pedaling man on the flagellation bike.

"Hey, you kids," Jaime whispers, though they're far older than he, where every hour is infinity. "Why you wanna go fuck up the Dream?"

Bubbles seethe up the walls of the jars. The full force of their cold contempt, the anger of the unborn, comes thundering down on him, driving him into a fetal curl, crushing him down into the depths of himself.

This is *their* dream, the one they're sharing with the world, the one that folds proteins in the brain, so nobody ever wakes up from it. The dream of the destroying angels.

He fights back with every memory, fights with his whole life, but as he sinks into blessed numbness, he has to admit they're right.

It's better this way. Not to ever have been. What has he ever done, that was not better left undone? What does he know, that's worth knowing? What has he changed, with the life he was given? How much better never to ever have been, than to have so much, and waste it all. . .

Jaime sinks into cold opium bliss, into narcotic nothingness, and as he gives away his life, gives away everything he reaches out for the Dream—

And he is not alone.

The warmth, the light, the music carry him back. The green, food, flowers, laughter, love, life—

And it can be yours, he hears the Dream tell them. All this, everything that could ever be. . .

YES, the angels scream. GIVE US THE DREAM.

At their cold colloidal silver touch, the Dream goes cold, laughing faces pinched by frostbite, dripping icicles like knives from fingers, it's better this way—

You want the Dream, motherfuckers? I'll give you the Dream—

Sun pounding down on broken blue mirrors. The raft, blinding reflections hot enough to singe skin, endlessly rocking.

"Look who's come crawling back," his Papi says. "Tell me, mijo. Who are your friends?"

Jaime looks over his shoulder, at the nineteen knurled, misshapen men and women, unborn bodies with wizened, ancient faces, tilted like flowers to bask in the sun.

"Which one of you ugly fuckers knows how to fish?"

Jaime doesn't answer. Jaime is gone.

He opens his eyes and rolls over. The lights emit a soft, somnolent pulse. The man on the bicycle sleeps with his head on the handlebars. Jaime's limbs ache with cold as if he's slept overnight on ice. Working blood into his tingling limbs, blowing breath he can see on his fingers, he reaches for the thick bundle of cables connecting the nineteen jars to the computers. The dusty bundle gives him a nasty static shock that makes him recoil and half piss his pants. He tries again and gives it a good yank.

Half the cables come out of their sockets, but the computer towers slide out of their bed of dust and topple like dominoes. The rack of jars tilts. Jaime throws himself against it, but his feet slide out from under him, sending him skidding out of the path of the rack and the jars that smash on the sealed concrete floor.

Darkness falls.

Computers stutter and circuits pop and fluid thicker than water drips. The space between breaths stretches into an awful hour.

Wailing and moans and screams well up out of hell. Down in the sewers, they're all going mad.

He hears a rifle cocked and the harsh rasp of Ida Scarfe's voice. "I didn't think you could do it, Smurf, but you did. You made it worse."

37

If offered the choice of how you would like to die, would you turn down the option of passing away gently in your sleep? To pass painlessly from this world to the next while unconscious, without fear, without pain. . . Isn't that the most anyone could ask for, if one has to die at all?

Now try to tell someone that their wish will come true the very next time they lay down their head and close their eyes. . . .

•

The rumors have wormed through the army of the Holy Fire and the cops and the gang warlords and the huddled hundred thousand hostages held or hiding in their midst. The police are standing down not because they're bought off or born again, but because the powers behind the city have released a disease that kills you in your sleep to put down the insurrection. The geeks who cooked up this dubious gift all laughed as they were executed by the Destroying Angels. Ha, ha, joke's on you, there is no antidote!

Or the Lord himself has unleashed the sleeping sickness on them to punish those who would succumb to the Dream.

Nobody wants to sleep anyway, with the city gutted and helpless, and all their worst excesses blessed by the hand of the Almighty. Rival gangs in the remaining two-thirds of the city watch the chaos avidly, poised to strike back when it will hurt most. Chewing kava, khat, tobacco and betel nut; snorting Dexedrine, meth, coke, Adderal, amyl nitrate; skin-popping all of the above and sharing the rumors.

Nobody gives much credence to the rumors until, at the height of their bloody revolution, the Divine Fire in every heart and hand, in every blind eye, withered limb and cold, dead heart flickers and fades out.

Even the most orderly and affluent societies experience a momentary backslide into savagery when the lights go out. Even the best-behaved solid citizen is tempted to knock over some trashcans or smash a window when nobody is looking. For an army of human garbage in the process of establishing a trailer-trash caliphate in a lawless city, fueled by the shared illusion of divine command, of being God's holy warriors in the first battle of Armageddon, how much worse when the light in their hearts, the magic that healed their bodies and minds, the faith that bound them into an army, shuts off like an overloaded power grid?

Chigger is riding the escalator down from the top floor of the Arcade when the lights go out. Like the phosphene afterglow of fireworks, he sees a host of white-hot fires in every head of the motley hordes around him and then a wind out of the space between seems to snuff them all out at once.

At first, he thinks it's a blackout, but the escalator keeps descending and everyone around him can still see. Hands rip away the overflowing shopping bags clutched to his belly. The man behind and above him falls on his back screaming that his miracle-legs are gone, the Devil took away his legs—

Motherfucker took my eyes, Chaz thinks, struggling with someone on the escalator, pulling at the bags of good shit from the top floors and then he shoves and feels the man stumble back over the railing, hears him scream all the way to the ground floor.

All his good shit gone, and blind again, besides. What the fuck kind of God plays games like that? Chaz stumbles through screaming, hurtling knots of bodies, reflexively clawing at his face as if to snatch away a veil.

At the foot of the escalator, he hears shooting and bounces off running men trying to force their way up the descending escalator. Thrown sideways into a plastic potted plant, he falls and crawls and prays.

Wasn't I always your boy, Lord? Didn't I always say to give me a sign if I was doing wrong? And you never said shit, so why you doin' me like this, now?

He crawls until he hits a balcony railing, climbs and clings to it against the battering current of running, screaming madmen. "Lord, I put myself in your hands. Do with me as you will. . ."

Chaz feels his way along the railing until it ends and then he steps out.

For a moment, he feels the stairs underfoot, feels the reassuring vibration of the escalator taking him down out of this madness. . .

And he is walking on faith, he has wings, he is an angel—

And then he is falling, the wind buffeting his face and even the darkness is something to see. He's flying into a twinkling red star that expands into a blinking 3 at the heart of a constellation of Zeros.

Just before all two hundred pounds of him meet God at seventy-two miles per hour, Chaz hears the Lord say, "Hijo de puta," and he takes a split-second of solace in the cosmic realization that God is a Mexican, which explains an awful lot of shit.

•

Across the city, police, fire and rescue units begin to collapse almost immediately upon word of what happened to Greer and the people upstairs who sign their checks. While nearly all the units sympathetic to the Divine Fire were assigned to cover the Arcade, the rest have begun to suspect that nobody is picking up the phone at headquarters when the myriad gangs, tribes and neighborhood watch posses take to the streets to roll the suddenly demoralized Divine Fire back into the Orange Zone. Falling back under heavy lead from all sides, they race through IED-laced streets to the Blue Zone, hoping only to clock out and make for the surface. The few vehicles that make it out of the Yellow Zone blunder into a blue-on-blue crossfire, the motor pool overrun by Divine Fire raiding parties and cops who've gone permanently off-duty that escalates when the main power grid falters and then fails, plunging the overwhelming majority of the underground city into total darkness.

Within an hour, the symmetry of warfare shatters into a fractal mosaic of warring tribes fighting to control resources and territory. Thousands dead in the streets of almost random gunfire until the geography finds a new stable point. Then, raids and massacres resume as the tapestry of battle becomes the War on Sleep.

The terror of terminal sleep has reached a fever pitch. Crews of thugs wired on Fierce hunt for more drugs to help them stay awake and hunt for the Dreamers who made sleep a death-sentence.

Sleepers hear beguiling music in their restless nightmares and come stumbling into the glow of the Dream, of the other city waiting to claim them, a city where trees grow and bend with the weight of fruit and animals and naked, drunken revelers dance in a rain-shower to the pulsing rhythm of the world's heartbeat.

It takes nearly ninety-six hours for the internecine warfare to collapse under its own weight and the last combatants standing to succumb to the irresistible gravity of sleep. Whatever they dream, it must be better than here, because they don't wake up. Whether it's the nefarious folding of rogue proteins in their brains, guided by bad biology or the hands of angels, or their own imaginations rushing to judge them unfit, they submit, one by one, to the cold, silver slumber of the unborn.

38

He wakes up under bowers of trees. A miasma of green jungle smells—overripe fruit, flower perfume, rot.

His hands go to his face and don't find each other.

I have no hands, he thinks. I have no face.

How wonderful. . .

He sits up, tearing away a canopy of vines stretched over his cot on the floor of what appears to be some kind of abandoned field hospital. The trees are growing out of the other patients.

He feels himself and doesn't find a tree. His head and hands are thoroughly bandaged in gauze. He has no fingers on his left hand, which sort of sucks.

He's thirsty. Hungry. He rolls off the cot and looks at the trees. They grow out of the heads or chest cavities of bodies gray with decay but nearly engulfed by roots that bore through the cots and the cracked concrete floor, absorbing the bodies faster than they can rot.

He looks for water. His salivary glands stir painfully at the sight of the gleaming, ripe fruit hanging from the trees, but he can't bring himself to eat it. He stumbles out of the relief station, down a hallway lined with empty boots and out into the street.

Trees line the street, lateral branches spanning the gaps between superbloques so what little light filters through is a deep, mottled green. Ferns and fungi, fly agaric mushrooms and phallic octopus stinkhorns thrust up through cracks in the pavement.

A dog staggers out into the street, gravid belly dragging between bowed legs, collapses whining, and begins give birth. A flock of shrieking green birds explode from its twitching hindquarters and take to the air.

"Thought you was dead," someone says. He looks up and sees Jaime Blasco climbing down out of a tree with a bunch of ripe blue bananas. "Was taking bets on what kind of tree would come out of you."

"Am I dreaming?" Keller asks. "This must be the Dream . . ."

"Keep trying to wake up," Jaime says, handing him a peeled Blue Java banana, which he jams into the slit in his bandages. It hurts to chew, but the mushed fruit is sweeter than ice cream. He crams it into his mouth and wolfs it down, following Jaime down the street.

People pass by, naked, intent as Jivaro tribesman on the game trail. The street ends at Plaza de Pancho Villa, but a spreading banyan tree grows in the center, engulfing the pedestal and the shoes of the missing statue. Children play in the branches and all around, he's never seen so many children in the whole city, figures they must have been hidden, waiting for today.

A group of children stand around two lines of four with their toes on a scrimmage line on the pavement. Two on either side hold their fists up, while all of them stare and rock as if waiting for the snap of a ball, but there's no ball, and they never move, though a crowd cheers and roars.

"What the hell game are they playing?"

"It's the bone game," Jaime says, still walking. "They try to guess which hand the other team is hiding the chicken bone in."

Keller shakes his head. He's heard of it, the Flathead Indians in Montana play it, but he can tell he's not seeing the real game. The children probe the opposition's dreamtime for the location of the bone, soaring over elaborate imaginary defenses with ingenious strategies, the whole game playing out in some kind of shared arena in their minds.

"God damn," Keller says. "How long have I been out?"

"Four days," Jaime tells him, and keeps walking. "We all dreamed about it, everyone who didn't die. Shit was just like this when the lights came on."

"Where are we going?"

"She wants to see you," he says over his shoulder.

"Hey," Keller shouts, stopping in the street.

Jaime turns around.

"Are you pissed at me?"

Jaime shrugs. "None of that really matters, anymore. But you could've been more honest with me."

Keller puts his fingerless hand on Jaime's arm, turns him around. "My real name is Keller Cockburn. I'm wanted for second-degree murder in California. I'm a Libra, and I like sushi and scuba diving."

Jaime shakes his head and walks away. *I know who you are*, he says without saying it. *You did the right thing for all the wrong reasons.*

Keller follows him into thicker crowds. Some are at least partially dressed, while others go proudly or obliviously nude. Nobody carries gadgets or wears goggles. Instead, as they pass each other trading sly glances, he feels the oblique sense of worlds forming, fusing and trading paint with every momentary interaction. He hears no talking but feels the sibilant hum of a chorus.

They pass a suicide booth overgrown with wildflowers and Keller cringes as he spots a tiger crouched on its conical roof, surveying the passersby like any cop.

Behind the booth, watching from a small traffic warden's dais, is someone the crowd does give a wide berth—an imposing figure in white and indigo robes and a silver mask who stretches out a cattle prod to shock a man leering at passing women, smearing them with his filthy id.

"Poison Boys are the cops, now?"

Jaime shrugs. "Not everybody's taken the Teacher yet, and they don't have to. But anyone who can't keep their shit to themselves gets a taste of the empathy taser."

Keller shakes his head wonderingly. "No fucking shit."

"Yeah. Don't hurt bad, but it makes thieves feel robbed, rapists raped, haters hated. . . It's easier than jail. You should try it."

I already have, Keller thinks, catching Jaime's arched eyebrow and nonverbal mental retort. "But anyone who's on it, they can touch minds. . . ? Like telepathy?"

"Yeah. Anyone, just think of them, but watch it, ain't no difference between thinking and speaking."

"I can't think of anyone," he says, but then he does. *Hey Agrippa, did you know Steely Dan was named after a dildo?*

Fuck you, man—

"Wow," he says, running to catch up with Jaime. "How did this happen?"

"I don't know, man. Jude said it was because enough of us took it, it reached some kind of critical mass. Everything changed."

They come around a corner and Freedom Avenue, and the Arcade.

The monolithic column is shaggy with vines and gigantic bromeliads, the yawning mouth of its entrance abuzz with fireflies and parrots, instead of drones and holograms. He stops at the entrance where the police checkpoint stood on his last visit, but now, out of confusion and awe.

How long was I gone? He asks again.

The floor of the Arcade is flooded, and thousands wade or swim in the green waters of a pool engulfing the ice rink and the amusement labyrinth. Children splash each other and the old and the crippled and wounded crawl into the water and float. Perched atop a rock in the center, amid candles, flowers, shells, candy, condoms, burning joints and other offerings, a massive, voluptuous female figure made of melted sex-dolls fused together into a grotesque, faceless apotheosis of the feminine, a silicon fertility goddess. Women whirl and men cavort, imploring the goddess to possess them.

Jaime goes to a glass elevator and pushes a button. They ascend up the wall of the cavernous space, watching divers leap from the balconies five, seven, ten stories up, to splash into the pool.

They get out at the top floor. A shadowy glade encircles the empty dais where the giveaway car usually sits. Three women in white gowns stand on the dais around a canopied bed curtained by morning glories and surrounded by blinking, bleeping medical monitors.

"So," Keller hobbles towards them, stopping when Ida Scarfe steps out of the shadows armed with an axe. He notices how the murky spaces between the trees are filled with faceless lurkers. One of them, wearing a platinum mask and bearing a falcon on his arm, favors him with a tiny nod. "This worked out pretty well for you."

"You think I wanted this?" The tallest of the women crosses the dais to loom above him. "Someone had to step in."

"For someone who didn't want the job, you've changed a lot in four days."

The other women come forward. One is curvy, rosy-cheeked, blinking behind thick glasses, chubby hands clasped over her belly. "This didn't take four days. It took that long for the old world to burn itself out." The other, short and gaunt with pale olive skin and the curious smirk of a sarcophagus. "This world was always imminent in dreamtime, waiting to happen."

Keller feels, rather than hears, their names, their roles in the running of this city. Eleanor Myrick, high priestess of research, and Uyen Nguyen, queen of informatics.

"The population was falling into a hysterical death spiral," Myrick explains. "The quantum wave harnessed by poor Litchfield was doomed to go the way of all patriarchal movements, I'm afraid, and collapse into a new dark age."

"The Secret Teacher changed all that," Nguyen adds.

"The Secret Teacher is just a mushroom, but it was a key to letting the collective mind escape to a higher level of complexity, which in turn has brought a new level of simplicity to society. A just society, and an equal one."

"Two-thirds population was male," Nguyen cuts in. "That was always problem. The Insomnia War let thirty thousand of them take each other out of the equation. Another twenty never woke up. Finally found purpose. Big fertilizer."

"You just laid low and let the bad men kill each other. You didn't push anyone."

"We reached out to those who wanted a better way. We offered them the Dream. The rest, we made sure they knew about the sleeping sickness. They were always free to choose."

"As free as anyone is to be what they are. If they don't want to be turned into trees. . ."

"They had their chance, Keller," Jude says. "Ten thousand years of patriarchy got us here, to the very edge of total ruin. We have a chance to start from scratch. To work with nature, not to ravage it. To share and nurture, instead of dominate and demand. If this isn't what you were trying to do with those pills, what *were* you trying to do?"

"I just don't see how you're going to keep it going. This is kind of a big top-secret installation. They're going to come. . ."

"Not if they want to live," Nguyen says. "They know what we have down here, what we can do."

"The police have surrendered the city. It's ours, now. The army is outside, but they're more afraid of the secret getting out than they are about shutting us down."

"Someone somewhere is still learning too much from all this, to try to stop it."

"Let them watch and learn," Nguyen says. "We shall reach out to them with the Dream until it haunts them all. We will invade and colonize and conquer without spilling a drop of blood, without leaving our beds."

"More made-up plagues?"

"We've had a very real one for quite some time," Myrick says, beaming. "It's not a showstopper like the sleeping sickness, but by the time it's identified, there won't be anyone left to complain." She smiles and adds, "It's a cure for men.

"Magna Mater," she says, gesturing to the pool far below. "She is a retrovirus that suppresses production of COUP-TFII protein that regulates production of the Wolffian duct that becomes male reproductive organs. Testes never form. Mankind goes extinct. Womankind reigns supreme."

"That sounds divine," Keller says, waving his fingerless hand. "You ladies have it all figured out. I'll just show myself out. . ."

He turns and runs into Ida Scarfe.

"You can't leave," Jude says. "You started this thing. You have a responsibility to watch over it, and help it grow."

"I don't even know what the fuck this is," he says, as kindly as he can manage. "I didn't choose it. . ."

"Does anyone get to choose what their child becomes?"

"I wanted to give people a dream that could inspire them to be better people. I thought I'd have to trick them into it, but I never wanted to force it on anyone. You haven't made the Dream real, you've just made reality unreal. How long can it last? You're making the same mistakes Litchfield did . . ."

"Don't say that," her eyes darken and a chill seeps into the marrow of his bones. "Don't run away again."

"Moses didn't get into the promised land."

"Have you ever even looked at a map of the Sinai? Anyone could cross it on foot in six days. It took him forty years, so maybe he didn't deserve to get into the promised land. But you. . ."

"Maybe he kept leading them in circles because they weren't ready. Maybe he knew they'd be better people when they were going, than when they got there."

"That's not for you to judge."

"Nothing is, I guess. Listen, Jude, if I stayed, it might be beautiful for a while, but sooner or later, we'd get into the same old arguments, and I don't want to have them with someone who can turn people into trees."

"It won't be like it was," Jude says. "Nothing will ever be the same again."

"That's what fucking scares me, darlin'. You're trying to reinvent a golden age that never was. You're going to love being feared more than you feared being loved, and your god is going to start demanding sacrifices. And I don't want to be in charge of that, do you?"

"We are only the custodians," Jude says. Myrick and Nguyen draw back the curtain of morning glories. Lying in the center of the bed in the clenched posture of a mummy, wrapped in sensors and tubes and pumps, the body of Orrin Litchfield lies on the bed. His charred head is reattached to his body, but the transplant looks less than successful. The head, slathered in skin grafts and herbal poultices, twitches uneasily in sleep.

"What the fuck are you keeping him for?"

"Poor Orrin has a brain tumor. It developed while he was working on the wetware project, his unfortunate angels. Uyen surmises that it was a vestigial organ for communicating with the embryo computers, which enabled him to influence the minds and change the bodies of his followers. But when the angels were disconnected, something happened. The only proper scientific term for it is a miracle."

Nguyen waves an ultrasound wand over Litchfield's skull. On the monitor screen attached to the headboard, a granular blur of organic forms swirls past until she settles it on his forehead, and a convex nodule of smooth tissue erupting from the bifurcated cloud of whorled gray matter of the anterior cortex of the fallen prophet's brain. She adjusts the gain a bit and bisects the sheath of the tumor to show an embryo like a frog nested inside the womb.

"It's a girl," Nguyen grins.

Keller thinks of the goddess of wisdom, sprung from the skull like incarnate thought from the brow of her profligate, tyrannical father. *I can't wait to hear somebody try to explain this in church someday*, he thinks.

"I gotta go," he says.

Scarfe raises the axe, but Jude pushes her aside with a mental nudge. She follows Keller to the elevator.

"You want to be the king, is that it? You'd feel better with a leader who pees standing up."

"You know it isn't. I'd be gone twice as fast if you tried to put me in charge. Jaime is twice the shaman I'll ever be." He looks at Jaime, who shrugs.

"I know what it is. You don't know how to stick to something and build it. You only know how to disrupt, and leave everyone else to clean up the mess." Her eyes well up with tears. "You can't leave me to do this alone."

Keller pulls her close so only she can hear. "I took the drug, Jude. I was afraid to, but they forced me, and what I saw was exactly what I was afraid of. I've lived my whole life thinking you could trick people into waking up, but I can't wake up from my own dream. I searched the world looking for magic and when I finally found it, I destroyed it. The universe used me to nudge itself closer to waking up, but I can't go back to sleep. You're right, I don't know how to stay and build. If I did, I never would have come here."

He kisses her on the forehead. "Sainthood agrees with you," he says. "You've never looked so beautiful." He knows how much this pisses her off, but he takes her hand in his. "I'm happy for you, really. I hope this works."

He pulls away and stumbles towards the elevator, he's going to need a shit-ton of painkillers.

He looks over the railing, down into the Arcade. The people in the water are singing and some of them are lifted up out of the water, soaring and swooping up to the vaulted ceiling, looking at him with impassive eyes. He wipes away a tear and waves at them.

"There's nowhere to go," she calls out after him. "The exits are sealed! The army is waiting up there to shoot you! Just go sleep it off, you'll thank me later!"

Jaime braces him at the door, slips a tin into his good hand. "We don't need them anymore. Find someone who does." Keller shakes the tin and smiles, then beams when Jaime touches his chest.

A glow—not a fire—kindles in his heart and races down arteries, capillaries and veins, a pulse of well-being that leaves him standing taller and flexing battered muscles, even as Jaime shivers and clutches his left hand.

"Your face won't look the same when them bandages come off," Jaime says. "You're welcome."

Keller laughs, steps back into the elevator. Jaime reaches in and passes a card on a lanyard over the buttons, then presses a series of buttons on the ten-key above the Arcade's directory.

The elevator goes up.

Surging on magnetic rails, ascending through half a mile of basalt and sedimentary rock, it stops and opens before Keller can swallow a painkiller.

He steps out in a low, plain room opening on a long, plain corridor. An abandoned security station beside a parked golf cart. He gets in the golf cart and drives down the long corridor, passing junctions blocked by rolldown steel barricades and slaloming round empty armored personnel carriers. He sees no people, but here and there, a helmet, a glove, a gun.

The tunnel is a mile long. At the end, he comes out of a hangar backed against a rocky hill on a private airstrip. A helicopter and a King Air prop plane wait on the tarmac, but he drives around them more by accident than design, looking up into the sky.

It's a deeper blue than it ought to be, with the sun just behind the horizon. The air is cold and crisp and clean. He turns north, wondering where he'll go and what he'll call himself. He wonders if he'll go back to Unamerica, if he'll read about them on the news, or if he'll share the Dream when he sleeps, if he'll be able to go there whenever he closes his eyes.

He can see military choppers circling and landing about a mile to the west, so he just drives north on a freshly paved road. A helicopter passes overhead and he clenches his teeth, waiting for its guns or missiles or whatever the fuck, but it turns back and leaves him alone. *Damn right, you can't fuck with me, I'm an American citizen.* If they haven't killed him already, maybe they won't. Maybe, so long as he keeps their secrets, they'll keep his. Maybe they only let him out as a mule for their genocidal war on penises. Maybe he's Patient Zero, the Prometheus of Planet XX.

Suddenly, there's a loud brown sound and he's so sick that he throws up on the road. His bowels spasm and contort and swell inside him like a basket of angry snakes. The golf cart continues on down the road while he thrashes in the seat, trying to throw himself out.

Nobody around. Microwaves? Maybe. . . He feels like his insides were stirred up with a stick. He must be hallucinating, or else he's driving across a putting green. Maybe he's still thrashing in his hospital cot. He's a fool to think she'd let him leave, but the only thing worse than doing it without him would be doing it with him. She knows better, but the others—

He swerves off the road at a cluster of luxury cottages and a glimpse of blue between them. That's what he needs, a swim to clear his head. He climbs out of the golf cart and two men in white with towels on their arms approach him. Whatever this place is, they're a step behind figuring out if the faceless staggering maniac is cleared to use the pool. He looks between them and pushes past. He sees something break the surface and flail towards the side before it goes under again. A white flank like the foam come to life. It's all like something out of a dream.

He steps off the edge and falls into the pool. The towel boys jump in after him. He kicks and claws across the pool to throw himself into the patch of bubbles where he saw the dog swimming. His legs are useless, the pain in his belly so bad, he can't even remember having legs, but he throws his arms around the German Shepherd pup just as they grab him by the sodden paper pajamas and drag him out of the pool.

He lies on the side as they go through his pockets, finding only the tin, which is only full of water.

"What the fuck is that?" someone standing over him asks.

He tries to tell them he's Joaquin Betancourt, US citizen, and he needs an ambulance, but he giggles and coughs up blood.

"Fucking nut," says another voice, sitting beside him and checking his vitals. "Must've busted out of the detention center down the road. Looks like he caught a dose of the perimeter measures. I don't think he's gonna make it."

"Well, get him the fuck out of here. It's time to slop the hogs. . ."

They lift Keller onto a stretcher and roll him out of the soaking pool area as a long line of old men in bathrobes and towels comes plodding out of the sauna and slip like arthritic wildebeests into the pool.

Keller holds his dog close and whispers its name in its ear until he falls asleep.

His visions are awesome.

39

From *Google News*

INTERNATIONAL FINANCE CONFERENCE
DEADLOCK CONTINUES INTO SECOND WEEK

What was expected to be a routine policy summit between regional economic leaders and World Bank officials at an undisclosed location in the southwestern United States, has become a flashpoint of controversy this holiday week when World Bank officials issued a manifesto which the organization itself has disavowed as the work of ultrasocialist radicals.

"We were wrong for so long. . . but NO LONGER," begins the manifesto penned by WTO Chairman Hugo Montalbano, which itemizes a decades-long policy of systematic economic and political dirty tricks to maintain American and European hegemony over the hemisphere. Wrought with sincere agony over the plight of disenfranchised countries like Haiti and indigenous peoples from Alaska to Patagonia, the document describes a mystical "awakening" in terms more appropriate for a drug-fueled religious conversion, and demands that the world accept the message of the Secret Teachers, as the group now calls itself, turn away from exploitative capitalism and into the utopian future of the Dream, a consciousness evolution which will make anarchic socialism not only necessary, but inevitable.

Medical authorities have been unable to get access to the conference attendees, who have barricaded themselves inside the spa facility where the conference was held and refused to leave the soaking pool until their demands are taken seriously, but sources close to the conference claim that the event has many speculating that a narcotic "spiking" of the conference may have occurred, leading to the explosive policy declaration.

The World Trade Organization has suspended the conference attendees and suppressed the text of the document, and expressed regret that its tireless efforts to promote a better, more prosperous world have been spotlighted under such sordid circumstances. . .

UNAMERICA

ACKNOWLEDGEMENTS

From conception to completion, this book has taken my entire adult life, and almost everyone in my life has helped shape it. I am forever indebted to all of them, from friends who shared the experiences that gave birth to the idea—Steve Cordova, Adam Barnes, Cory Evans, Rob Winfield and Leena Sheet, among others—to friends who nurtured its difficult delivery—above all, Alicia Graves for her love and trust and shelter and red-lining me when my protagonist became too unlikable even for this book; John Skipp for his wisdom and mentorship; Michael Kazepis for his fierce faith in my work and fanatical commitment to getting it right; Tiffany Scandal, J. David Osborne and Alicia (again) for proofreading; Matthew Revert for his incomparable cover design, and Gwen Callahan for restoring my shoulder after I blew it out completing the first draft. Special thanks to Axel Guell, whose horrifying story of coming to America informs the biography of Jaime Blasco.

Thanks and pre-emptive apologies to the authors who inspired Unamerica and enhanced my limited understanding of the wrenching social issues I exploited for it—off the top of my head, Mike Davis, Greil Marcus, Terrence McKenna, Daniel Pinchbeck, Mircea Eliade, Michael Harner, Charles Bowden, Bruce Sterling, Cory Doctorow, Hakim Bey, Guy DeBord, Jon Krakauer, Naomi Klein, Robert Perkinson, Luis Alberto Urrea, Anabel Hernandez, Sam Quinones, John Shirley, William Gibson, Neal Stephenson, J.G. Ballard and Philip K. Dick. And thanks, as always, to the music that got me through—Amon Tobin, Two Fingers, Run The Jewels, The Bug, John Carpenter, Ennio Morricone, Secret Chiefs 3, Future Sound Of London, Oneohtrix Point Never, Bostich and the Nortec Collective, Mexican Institute Of Sound, Shpongle, The Orb, Ott, Liquid Stranger, Plaid, Massive Attack, Portishead, Pentaphobe, Test Dept., Skinny Puppy and the indomitable Spiral Tribe.

CODY GOODFELLOW has written eight novels. His first two collections, Silent Weapons For Quiet Wars and All-Monster Action, received the Wonderland Book Award. As an actor, he has appeared in numerous short films, TV shows, music videos and commercials. He "lives" in Portland.

Thank you for picking up this title. We are small presses based in Portland, Oregon and El Paso, Texas, dedicated to the publication of weird, brilliant literature. If you enjoyed this book, do please tell your friends about it. For more information about us, see kingshotpress.com and brokenriverbooks.com.

Available from Broken River Books

Available from King Shot Press

Leverage by Eric Nelson
Strategies Against Nature by Cody Goodfellow
Killer & Victim by Chris Lambert
Marigold by Troy James Weaver
Noctuidae by Scott Nicolay
I Miss The World by Violet LeVoit
All-Monster Action by Cody Goodfellow
Nasty (ed. Tiffany Scandal)
Drift by Chris Campanioni
The Deadheart Shelters by Forrest Armstrong
Blood and Water by J David Osborne
The Yeezus Book
Scarstruck by Violet LeVoit
Nasty Vol. 2 (ed. Tiffany Scandal)
Unamerica by Cody Goodfellow
Killer Unconquered by Chris Lambert
Matthew Revert: A Design Retrospective

CPSIA information can be obtained
at www.ICGtesting.com
Printed in the USA
LVHW031600110919
630728LV00003B/489